OXFORD WORLD'S CLASSICS

NEWS FROM NOWHERE

WILLIAM MORRIS was born in Walthamstow, Essex, in March 1834. His father was a wealthy businessman in the City of London, and Morris was brought up in a comfortable middle-class Anglican household. He attended Marlborough College, and later studied at Exeter College, Oxford. After a brief period articled to G. E. Street, a prominent architect, Morris embarked on a career combining decorative art and creative writing. He founded what became Morris & Co., a firm whose work (including stained glass, embroidery, and painted furniture) established a landmark in English domestic architecture. Morris registered the first two of his well-known wallpaper designs in 1864. He published the narrative poem *The Life and Death of Jason* in 1867, but achieved his first great literary success with *The Earthly Paradise* published between 1868 and 1870. Morris would later decline approaches to take up the positions of Professor of Poetry at Oxford and Poet Laureate. An interest in Icelandic language and literature resulted in several publications, including a translation, with Eiríkr Magnússon, of *The Story of Grettir the Strong* in 1869. Morris was also a founder member of the Society for the Protection of Ancient Buildings, established in 1877. His developing political interests found new expression in the early 1880s when he became a socialist. Morris helped found the Socialist League in 1884, and between 1883 and 1890 he addressed over 1,000 meetings and contributed nearly 500 pieces to socialist periodicals. In 1890, Morris published his best known work, the utopian novel *News From Nowhere*. In later years, he established the Kelmscott Press, and wrote a number of prose romances, including *The Well at the World's End*. In 1859, Morris had married Jane Burden, and they had two daughters to whom he was deeply devoted. Morris died in Hammersmith, London, in October 1896.

DAVID LEOPOLD is a Senior Research Fellow at Mansfield College, Oxford.

OXFORD WORLD'S CLASSICS

For over 100 years Oxford World's Classics have brought readers closer to the world's great literature. Now with over 700 titles—from the 4,000-year-old myths of Mesopotamia to the twentieth century's greatest novels—the series makes available lesser-known as well as celebrated writing.

The pocket-sized hardbacks of the early years contained introductions by Virginia Woolf, T. S. Eliot, Graham Greene, and other literary figures which enriched the experience of reading. Today the series is recognized for its fine scholarship and reliability in texts that span world literature, drama and poetry, religion, philosophy and politics. Each edition includes perceptive commentary and essential background information to meet the changing needs of readers.

OXFORD WORLD'S CLASSICS

WILLIAM MORRIS

News From Nowhere

OR

An Epoch of Rest

Being Some Chapters From a Utopian Romance

Edited with an Introduction and Notes by
DAVID LEOPOLD

UNIVERSITY PRESS

Published in the United States
by Oxford University Press Inc., New York

First published as a World's Classics paperback 2003
Reissued 2009

British Library Cataloguing in Publication Data
Data available

Library of Congress Cataloging in Publication Data
Morris, William, 1834–1896
News from nowhere, or, An epoch of rest: being some chapters from a utopian
romance / William Morris; edited with an introduction and notes by David Leopold.
p. cm.—(Oxford world's classics)
Includes bibliographical references.
1. Utopias. I. Title: News from nowhere. II. Title: Epoch of rest. III. Leopold, David.
IV. Title. V. Oxford world's classics (Oxford University Press)
HX811.M67 2003
321′.07—dc21
2002030310

ISBN 978–0–19–953919–2

1

Typeset in Ehrhardt
by RefineCatch Limited, Bungay, Suffolk
Printed in Great Britain by
Clays Ltd, St Ives plc

CONTENTS

ACKNOWLEDGEMENTS

I would like to thank those friends, colleagues, and complete strangers, who responded to my requests for information or materials. They include Victor Adams, Pamela S. Anderson, Michael Freeman, David Rumsey, and Anne Wheeldon. I have also learnt much from previous editors of *News From Nowhere*, including Krishan Kumar, Michael Liberman, and James Redmond. My Introduction to the present volume was much improved by the criticism of two good and clever friends: Mark Griffith and Matthew Kempshall. Lucinda Rumsey helped in many ways, proving an indefatigable source of support and good sense throughout. I would also like to record my appreciation to the Warden and Fellows of Merton College, Oxford, who helped me find the time to complete this work. I am especially grateful to John Carey, who, by not sharing it, reminded me of my affection for *News From Nowhere*. Finally, I would like to thank Judith Luna of OUP for providing me with an excuse to walk the Thames Path.

D.L.

INTRODUCTION

Political Origins

William Morris (1834–96) might be described as the greatest ever English designer, a poet ranked by contemporaries alongside Tennyson and Browning, and an internationally renowned figure in the history of modern socialism. However, this brief inventory elides some very different skills—as if furniture and pattern making were pretty much the same thing—and neglects many of his other attainments. Morris also played a significant role, for example, in the development of modern architecture, in the rediscovery of the art of stained glass, in the revival of tapestry, in the history of typography, in the creation of the private press movement, and in the translation and interpretation of Old Norse literature. Visitors to the exhibition held at the Victoria and Albert Museum on the centenary of Morris's death found it hard to imagine that this was all the work of one man. Indeed, it can come as some relief to happen upon a creative field (painting, for example) with which Morris struggled and upon which he had little influence.

Assessments of the place of *News From Nowhere* (1890) within this extraordinary body of work have typically reflected the commentator's attitude towards Morris's socialism. Consider the contrasting responses of J. W. Mackail, Morris's first serious biographer, and A. L. Morton, the Communist historian. Mackail's biography (first published in 1899) remains important, not only because of his unique access to Morris's friends and family (he was the son-in-law of Edward and Georgiana Burne-Jones) but also because he reproduced much material which was subsequently lost. However, Mackail viewed Morris's socialist commitment with disapproval—as George Bernard Shaw wryly, but not inaccurately, observed: 'From [Mackail's] point of view Morris took to Socialism as Poe took to drink'[1]—and his account of this dimension of Morris's life and work is limited and problematic. Mackail's discussion of *News From Nowhere* occupies no more than a page of his two-volume study, and is mainly concerned to convey surprise at the popularity of 'this

[1] *The Observer*, 6 Nov. 1949, p. 7.

slightly constructed and essentially insular romance', especially in continental Europe.[2] (Although its critical reception was somewhat muted, Morris's novel was a popular success; in the form of a thick trimmed pamphlet with paper covers, it sold some 8,000 copies in the first year, and by 1898 there were French, German, and Italian editions in circulation.) Writing some fifty years after Mackail, Morton offered a very different account. He belonged to a distinctive tradition of British Communist authors (including Robin Page Arnot and E. P. Thompson) who entered the lists for Morris's reputation. In his parallel history of 'two islands' (the Island of Utopia and the Island of Britain), Morton identified the utopian novel as a literary form peculiarly suited to Morris's 'genius', and portrayed *News From Nowhere* as 'the crown and climax of his whole work'.[3]

Morris had become a socialist in the early 1880s, making a notorious declaration of revolutionary faith to an outraged middle-class audience in Oxford in November 1883. The seeds of that conversion are many and complex. His visits to Iceland, a growing disenchantment with Liberal and Radical politics, and the foundation of the Society for the Protection of Ancient Buildings (the 'Anti-Scrape'), were all contributory factors. However, in his own account of how he became a socialist, Morris chose to emphasize a continuity in his views before and after this conversion.

'The leading passion of my life', Morris asserted, 'has been and is hatred of modern civilisation.' This hatred had grown out of an enthusiasm for history and a 'deep love of the earth and life on it', and was fuelled, at a formative stage, by the writings of Carlyle and Ruskin. However, before his conversion, this hostility had taken a pessimistic form. Morris recalled a characteristic despair about the direction of historical change: 'Think of it! Was it all to end in a counting-house on the top of a cinder-heap, with Podsnap's drawing room in the offing, and a Whig committee dealing out champagne to the rich and margarine to the poor in such convenient proportions as would make all men contented together, though the pleasure of the eyes was gone from the world, and the place of Homer was to be taken by [T. H.] Huxley'.[4]

[2] J. W. Mackail, *The Life of William Morris*, ii (London, 1901), 243.

[3] A. L. Morton, *The English Utopia* (London, 1952), 161.

[4] 'How I Became a Socialist', in *Collected Works of William Morris*, ed. May Morris, xxiii (London, 1915), 280.

What shocked Morris out of this pessimism was that 'amidst all this filth of civilisation' he began to discern the 'seeds' of a 'great change' beginning to germinate. In the emerging socialist movement, Morris identified both hope for the future and the means of realizing that hope. From this point on, his involvement in the 'practical' movement for socialism was intense and sustained. Between 1883 (when he first 'studied socialism from the scientific point of view') and 1890 (when the serial publication of *News From Nowhere* began), Morris addressed over 1,000 meetings, and published nearly 500 signed articles in *Justice* and *Commonweal* (two leading socialist periodicals of the day).[5] He joked that he might be described as a 'professional agitator' except that he was not paid except 'by general loss of reputation'.[6] Morris's socialism was certainly regretted by many of his contemporaries (his family doctor, for example, would later diagnose 'enthusiasm for spreading the principles of socialism' as the primary cause of Morris's death).[7] Morris himself, however, always insisted that socialism had saved him from the twin fates which customarily consumed those members of his class who possessed 'artistic perceptions': he had neither wasted his time and energy on futile schemes 'to make art grow when it no longer has any root' nor had he crystallized into 'a mere railer against "progress"'.[8]

In summary accounts of his socialist principles, Morris repeatedly emphasized the importance of equality and community. The economic arrangements of a socialist society would be governed by 'equality of condition', ensuring that the balance of amenity and burden in the life of one person was roughly comparable with that in the life of any other. Morris once described his first, and most fundamental, 'vision' of the society of the future as being of a day 'when the words poor and rich, though they will still be found in our dictionaries, will have lost their old meaning; which will have to be

[5] The quotation is from a letter to John Lincoln Mahon, 20 May 1884, in *The Collected Letters of William Morris*, ed. Norman Kelvin, ii/1. *1881–1884* (Princeton, 1987), 282. The estimates of Morris's socialist activities are from Nicholas Salmon, 'Introduction', in *Political Writings: Contributions to Justice and Commonweal 1883–1890*, ed. Nicholas Salmon (Bristol, 1994), pp. vii and xlvi.

[6] Letter to William Bell Scott, 8 Sept. 1886, in *Collected Letters of William Morris*, ed. Kelvin, ii/2. *1885–1888* (Princeton, 1987), 575.

[7] Mackail, *Life of William Morris*, ii. 336.

[8] 'How I Became a Socialist', 281.

explained with care by great men of the analytical kind, spending much time and many words over the job, and not succeeding in the end in making people do more than pretend to understand them'.[9] An egalitarian society, he insisted, was impossible as long as private property had not been replaced by common ownership. Only in a socialist commonwealth would people participate in the everyday business of life not as 'individuals', concerned solely with their own self-regarding interests, but with a genuine, and not merely instrumental, concern for the needs of others. In characterizing the community that would result from this change, Morris offered analogies with friendship and family ties, but maintained that these future bonds of mutuality would extend to 'that great corporation—humanity'.[10] This non-instrumental commitment to others would eventually find expression in the realization of a principle of distributive justice—'To *every one* according to his needs, *from* everyone according to his capacities'[11]—which would break the connection between individual contribution and individual benefits.

These broad and familiar commitments to equality and community are reflected in the narrative of *News From Nowhere*, in which a visitor from the late nineteenth century (William Guest) describes his encounter with a future socialist society. Morris's utopian novel was also the product of a more specific historical context, and of other social and political views that he held. Morris's optimism about the long-term future of socialism never seriously waned, but in the late 1880s his political spirits were marked by a certain despondency. Increasing difficulties within the Socialist League and the growing popularity of alternative forms of socialism contributed to these low spirits. The Socialist League had been formed by Morris together with Eleanor Marx, E. Belfort Bax, and others, in 1884 (as a breakaway group from the Social Democratic Federation led by H. M. Hyndman). Despite much initial optimism, the organization had suffered a series of setbacks, including a number of internal disputes and a failure to connect with the larger industrial struggles of the day. Morris found himself besieged on two distinct

[9] 'The Society of the Future', in *William Morris: Artist, Writer, Socialist*, ed. May Morris (Oxford, 1936), ii. 455–6.

[10] 'True and False Society', in *Collected Works of William Morris*, ed. May Morris, xxiii. 215.

[11] 'Equality', in *William Morris: Artist, Writer, Socialist*, ed. May Morris, ii. 201.

ideological fronts. Inside the Socialist League, the growing influence of the anarchists would eventually force Morris to reconsider his position within the organization (see below). At the same time, outside the Socialist League, Morris was confronted by the wider popularity of what he called 'state socialism'. This took a variety of forms, but, for Morris, appears to have had two main characteristics, each with a corresponding weakness. First, as its name might suggest, state socialism was preoccupied with state direction, or even ownership; treating what Morris saw as a temporary means as if it were an end in itself. Secondly, state socialism was preoccupied with narrowly economic benefits; as if extending a dull level of utilitarian comfort from the middle to the working classes were the extent of socialist ambition.

News From Nowhere can be seen as both a response to, and a comfort amidst, these frustrations. This opportunity to explore his long-term hopes gave Morris solace and renewed his energies (his daughter May would later describe the book as partly written 'to keep up his courage in a time of the quarrelling of comrades').[12] In addition, Morris used his utopian novel to intervene directly in those disputes, providing a perspective from which the inadequacies of both state socialism and anarchism might become more readily apparent to his contemporaries.

Looking Backward

The sources of, and influences on, *News From Nowhere* are many. However, its most immediate impetus was provided by the unprecedented success of Edward Bellamy's *Looking Backward* (1888). In Bellamy's utopian novel, Julian West wakes from a lengthy cataleptic sleep to find himself in Boston, Massachusetts, in the year 2000. West discovers a transformed world in which poverty and corruption have been eradicated, and finds personal happiness with the great-granddaughter of his long-deceased fiancée. The novel is now rather less well known than the rejoinder that it provoked from Morris. At the time, however, it enjoyed an extraordinary degree of popularity. In Bellamy's native America, *Looking Backward* became the second best-selling novel of the century (after *Uncle Tom's*

[12] May Morris, 'Later Years', ibid. i, 503.

Cabin), and led to the creation of the so-called 'Nationalist' movement propagating his ideas. By 1891, Dutch, Italian, French, German, and Portuguese translations had appeared, and worldwide sales may have topped a million copies. As late as 1935, three distinguished American intellectuals (John Dewey, Charles Beard, and Edward Weeks), when asked to list the most influential books of the past fifty years, ranked *Looking Backward* in second place after Marx's *Capital*.

Morris first read Bellamy's novel in May 1889, having agreed to lecture on it to the Hammersmith Branch of the Socialist League. Although no record of this talk has survived, Morris's initial reaction appears to have been one of unqualified hostility. In a contemporaneous letter, he announced that 'I wouldn't care to live in such a cockney paradise as [Bellamy] imagines'. (Morris often used the word 'cockney' idiosyncratically to denote the vulgar and materialistic.)[13] The following month, Morris contributed a significant review of *Looking Backward* to *Commonweal*. It contains some brief reflections on the character of utopian literature, a more considered reaction to Bellamy, and an outline of his own contrasting vision of future society. The last two elements are related. In criticizing certain aspects of Bellamy's account of future society, Morris began to frame the central threads of his own utopia. Barely six months after this review, *News From Nowhere* started to appear in serialized form, it would seem as a reaction against the limitations of Bellamy's vision of the future.

Morris may not have found the book congenial but he regarded its popularity as symptomatic of a widespread interest in, and misunderstanding of, the nature of socialism. 'The success of Mr Bellamy's utopian book,' he observed, 'deadly dull as it is, is a straw to show which way the wind blows.'[14] It was the 'serious essay' on socialism and not the 'slight envelope of romance' which had attracted readers in both America and Britain. Indeed, Morris's judgement on the literary merits of the novel was disparaging. It might have been cast in the form of a romance, but, as Bellamy had himself conceded, this was merely 'a sugar coating to the pill'. Moreover, Morris continued, the 'device of making a man wake up

[13] Letter to John Bruce Glasier, 13 May 1889, in *Collected Letters of William Morris*, ed. Kelvin, iii. *1889–1892* (Princeton, 1996), 59.

[14] 'Where Are We Now?', in *Political Writings*, ed. Salmon, 493.

in a new world' had not only 'grown so common' but had also been developed with greater 'care and art' elsewhere.[15] The 'serious essay' contained in *Looking Backward* was not without value—Morris welcomed its forceful criticism of the 'present monopolist system', for example—but he remained ambivalent about the popularity of the book. Morris's main objection to Bellamy's work was that it reflected, and encouraged, a widespread misunderstanding of the nature of socialism. He identified Bellamy as another enthusiast for the state socialism which he had already criticized in other forms. (*Looking Backward* was always associated, in Morris's mind, with the growth of Fabianism in Britain.)

In an earlier article, Morris had noted two related errors into which certain 'practical' socialists were apt to fall. The first of these was to become absorbed in the economic part of socialism, and to neglect its other aspects. The second was to read 'the present into the future' by imagining that, although socialism would transform the economic foundations of society, 'in other areas of life, people's ways of life and habits of thought will be pretty much as they are now'.[16] Morris now found these same mistakes reproduced in *Looking Backward*.

In his review, Morris characterized the 'temperament' exemplified by Bellamy as the 'unmixed modern one'. It makes its 'owner', if a socialist, 'perfectly satisfied with modern civilization, if only the injustice, misery, and waste of class society could be got rid of'. Morris insisted that this 'half change', although attractive to the 'industrious *professional* middle-class', was neither possible nor desirable.[17] It was not possible because of the foundational role of economic concerns. Equality could only be established by a change of ownership and control, and this, in turn, would inevitably have an impact on other areas of life. It was not desirable, in his view, because its 'economic machinery' was only one of the problems with modern civilization.

Morris makes a series of criticisms of the 'half change' advanced in *Looking Backward*. He identifies five distinct concerns—work, technology, centralization, cities, and art—which demonstrate the

[15] 'Looking Backward', in *William Morris: Artist, Writer, Socialist*, ed. May Morris, ii. 502.

[16] 'On Some "Practical" Socialists', in *Political Writings*, ed. Salmon, 336–7.

[17] 'Looking Backward', 502–3.

'curiously limited' nature of Bellamy's ideas of life. In each of these instances, Morris's review contains an alternative vision of future society, providing the framework which, in due course, he would attempt to elaborate and make palpable in *News From Nowhere*.

Throughout *Looking Backward*, Bellamy treats work as a necessary evil, as something which can only be made more tolerable by reducing the amount of it (through the application of machinery to production). Morris is keen to challenge this view, insisting, in the first place, that Bellamy misidentifies the end of socialist action. The appropriate goal, Morris suggests, is not to reduce labour to a minimum, but rather to reduce the 'pain' of labour to a minimum. This, as will become apparent, is a rather guarded formulation of his own desideratum, for Morris elsewhere maintains that certain kinds of work are 'not far removed from a blessing'.[18]

Morris acknowledges that nature 'does not give us our livelihood gratis', but that 'we must win it by toil of some sort or degree'. However, he suggests that nature provides compensation for this necessity by ensuring that 'it is of the nature of man, when he is not diseased, to take pleasure in his work under certain conditions'. In a striking, if rather cautiously expressed, analogy between labour and sexual intercourse, Morris suggests that nature tends to make acts necessary for the continuation of the species 'not only endurable, but even pleasurable'.[19] In *News From Nowhere*, this analogy is echoed, in slightly more direct language, when Hammond (the knowledgeable antiquarian living in the British Museum, who tries to help Guest understand something of the essential character and historical evolution of the new society) observes, of the request to be paid for the pleasure of creation in work, that 'the next thing we shall hear of will be a bill sent in for the begetting of children' (p. 79).

The pleasure of work is a frequent subject of Morris's lectures. His own experience of that pleasure—expressed most immediately in the remarkable breadth and scale of his creative output—underpins his reflections, and lends them an additional interest. Work is worth doing, Morris claims, when there is an expectation of pleasure in both the activity and the product of labour. The pleasure deriving from the activity of labour appears to revolve around

[18] 'Useful Work *versus* Useless Toil', in *Collected Works of William Morris*, ed. May Morris, xxiii. 99.

[19] Ibid. 98.

self-realization, that is, the satisfaction of developing and deploying our essential human powers (including the 'energies' of 'mind and soul as well as body'). Morris suggests that there are both individual and collective dimensions to this process; a worker's hands are guided not only by 'his own thoughts' but also by the 'memory and imagination' of others. The pleasure deriving from the product of labour depends on that product possessing, in the first place, some 'obvious usefulness' to the community. An understanding that others will benefit from our endeavours, Morris suggests, can help 'in sweetening tasks otherwise irksome'. In addition, the product of this attractive labour should itself be beautiful. Morris sees no necessary conflict between these two characteristics, indeed, he suggests that in the best examples of what is sometimes called 'popular art', it would be hard to distinguish the 'mere utilitarian' element of a worker's product from its 'ornamental' qualities.[20]

The possibility of attractive labour depends on the satisfaction of a variety of additional conditions. Not least, such work must take place in congenial surroundings, involve a variety of tasks, and take up only a small part of the day. The need for 'pleasant surroundings' is often mentioned in Morris's work, and he considered the possibility of transforming factories into centres of beauty, intellectual activity, sociability, and leisure, in some detail. To sceptics, he would observe that factories already supported handsome gardens and extensive libraries, albeit that they were usually many 'miles away' from the smokestacks and 'kept up for *one member of the factory only*'.[21] Morris also emphasized the need for 'variety of work', advocating, in particular, the benefits of an individual pursuing both active tasks requiring 'bodily energy' and sedentary pursuits 'in which the mind had more to do'. He was correspondingly scathing about the contemporary division of labour, asserting that 'for a man to be the whole of his life hopelessly engaged in one repulsive and never-ending task, is an arrangement fit enough for the hell imagined by theologians, but scarcely fit for any other form of society'.[22] Finally, Morris maintained that, in order for labour to be attractive, the day's work must be short. He appears to have had few

[20] Ibid. 100 and 112.

[21] 'A Factory As It Might Be', in *William Morris: Artist, Writer, Socialist*, ed. May Morris, ii. 132.

[22] 'Useful Work *versus* Useless Toil', 112 and 118.

doubts about the ease with which this reduction might be accomplished, once speculating that a community with no idlers and little waste might only require a four-hour working day in order to provide for the necessities of life. Work and rest, on Morris's account, are interdependent, and—although some commentators have doubted whether, on the evidence of his prodigious output, he can be considered an authority on inactivity—his enthusiasm for the rewards of labour did not blind him to the pleasures of relaxation.

Morris never imagined that all work could be made attractive, and he repeatedly acknowledged that some labour might be intrinsically burdensome or repugnant. In such cases, he recommended that society use machinery to reduce that burden, share what remained more equitably, and consider carefully how far such work might be necessary ('let us see if the heavens will fall on us if we leave it undone').[23]

Many of these ideas are reflected in *News From Nowhere*. Guest is struck by the widespread enthusiasm for work in the new society, even for such necessary labour as road-mending and hay-making. As Hammond explains: 'All work which would be irksome to do by hand is done by immensely improved machinery' and that which remains 'is an exercise of the mind and body more or less pleasant to be done; so that instead of avoiding work everybody seeks it' (p. 84). Morris also used the novel to suggest his solution to the problem of incentives, that is, the provision of an egalitarian alternative to 'the fear of starvation' which motivated workers in contemporary society. He maintained that the real incentive to useful and happy labour was always pleasure in the work itself. At one point, Hammond describes this pleasure as the reward of creation: 'The wages which God gets' (p. 79).

As well as disagreeing with Bellamy's objective (the reduction of labour to a minimum) Morris is also sceptical about the efficacy of the means suggested in *Looking Backward* (the use of ever-improved machinery). Morris viewed fashionable talk of 'labour saving' machinery as a misnomer, since its present effect was rather to 'reduce the skilled labourer to the ranks of the unskilled', intensify the workload of those who 'serve the machines', and increase the general 'precariousness' of employment.[24] More generally, there are few signs in Morris's writings of Bellamy's unqualified enthusiasm

[23] Ibid. 119.
[24] Ibid. 117.

for technology, apparent, for example, in the lengthy and somewhat awed descriptions in *Looking Backward* of the complex network of pneumatic tubes (facilitating the ordering and delivery of manufactured goods) and the omnipresent telephone system (broadcasting music and sermons into every home).

This is not, however, to endorse the surprisingly resilient 'Luddite' account of Morris as opposed to 'machinery' of any description. Morris always maintained that where it was needed, and especially in order to release people 'from the more mechanical and repulsive part of necessary labour', machinery should be 'used freely'. Indeed, in this context, he believed that machinery would become both more widespread and more ingenious once the condition for its adoption depended upon whether it would benefit the community rather than whether it would pay the individual manufacturer. Morris's considered objection was to a system which allowed 'machines to be our masters and not our servants'; it was this enslavement to 'monsters which we have created', and not machinery itself, which disfigured modern life.[25] At one point, he distinguished between machinery of the 'old' type, that is 'the improved tool, which is auxiliary to man, and only works as long as his hand is thinking', and the 'modern' machine, 'which is as it were alive, and to which the man is auxiliary'.[26] It was, however, Morris's conviction that, in certain applications, the use of 'hand-work' might make labour more pleasurable. It was his hope and belief that, 'conscious of a wish to keep life simple', the society of the future would forgo the further conquest of nature if that were necessary in order to achieve a 'more human and less mechanical' organization of life.[27] Morris acknowledged that the cost of such a decision might be a loss of luxury and refinement, but maintained that this would be a price worth paying.

In *News From Nowhere*, the adoption of handicraft techniques is portrayed as a product, not of economic backwardness, but of reflective choice. As Henry Morsom (the Wallingford man with an interest in the fate of the 'arts of life' during the period of transition to the new society) explains to Guest, the 'new handwork' emerged not as

[25] 'How We Live and How We Might Live', in *Collected Works of William Morris*, ed. May Morris, xxiii. 24.

[26] 'The Aims of Art', in *Collected Works of William Morris*, ed May Morris, xxiii. 87.

[27] 'The Society of the Future', 466.

the result of 'what used to be called material necessity' but rather from growing dissatisfaction with 'a mechanical life' (pp. 153–4). Moreover, this handicraft production is underpinned by a variety of advanced technological developments, such as the 'force-barges' (p. 140) whose method of propulsion can also work vehicles on land, and the smokeless furnaces (p. 40) operating in the banded-workshop making pottery and glass. The secondary role given to these technological features in the narrative of *News From Nowhere* reflects both Morris's unwillingness to venture into the kind of speculation which would quickly date (such as Bellamy's vacuum tubes and musical telephone), and his conviction that machinery should be the servant and not the master of humankind.

Morris's acknowledgement of a due place for technology was reflected not only in *News From Nowhere* but also in his own creative work. 'The Firm' (Morris & Co.), for example, was never exclusively craft-based, and the workshops at Merton Abbey used machinery for dull and repetitive tasks. Even the Kelmscott Press, often portrayed as the archetypal embodiment of Morris's personal longing for a pre-industrial age, utilized the most advanced of contemporary technology. In addition to mechanically cut types, mass-produced inks, and electrotyped ornaments, Morris and Emery Walker used photography, both to enlarge examples of early printing (in order to clarify the shape of letters) and to transfer Morris's own designs onto wood blocks.

Looking Backward was also marked by the belief that the organization of life and labour could only be dealt with 'by a huge national centralization, working by a kind of magic for which no one feels himself responsible'.[28] This was a view that Morris—who once described himself as having 'an Englishman's wholesome horror of government interference and centralization'—did not share.[29] Whilst accepting that state direction and ownership would play a central role in the early, and transitional, stages of a future society (in which distributive principles had not yet broken with the connection between individual contribution and individual benefit), Morris resisted their application to a fully developed socialist commonwealth. Echoing an enduring, if scarcely transparent, socialist

[28] 'Looking Backward', 506.

[29] Letter to John Glasse, 23 May 1887, in *Collected Letters of William Morris*, ii/2, ed. Kelvin, 658.

formulation (used by Saint-Simon and later adopted by Marx), Morris envisaged 'the government of persons' being eventually replaced by an 'administration of things' in which all individuals shared.[30] This would only be brought about, he suggested, by a massive decentralization, in which the unit of administration was 'small enough for every citizen to feel himself responsible for its details, and be interested in them'. Rather than 'shuffle off the business of life on to the shoulders of an abstraction called the State', individuals should 'deal with it in conscious association with each other'.[31]

Morris always insisted that a self-governing community of this kind was not to be confused with anarchism, and he repeatedly denied being, or ever having been, an anarchist. Indeed, *News From Nowhere* was consciously directed against the rising anarchist influence within the Socialist League (in whose journal, *Commonweal*, the novel was first serialized), influence which would eventually force Morris's resignation. Morris associated anarchism with a radical individualism and a rejection of all authority that he found hard to take seriously. In *News From Nowhere*, the suggestion that 'every man should be quite independent of every other, and that thus the tyranny of society should be abolished' would cause Hammond and Guest to 'burst out laughing very heartily' (p. 77). Morris maintained that authority would be necessary in any conceivable community, not only to prevent coercion but also in order to pursue 'collective action' which 'without being in itself immoral or oppressive' might 'give pain to some of its Members'.[32] Morris's own vision was of a commonwealth in which authority was collective and decentralized rather than non-existent.

A further aspect of Bellamy's 'curiously limited' perspective, with which Morris took issue, is that 'he has no idea of life beyond existence in a great city'; his vision of the future is simply of Boston 'beautified'. Indeed, the single mention of villages in *Looking Backward* suggests that they fall outside the compass of Bellamy's egalitarian scheme, and function as 'mere servants' of the great centres of civilization. Morris rejects this exclusively urban vision and suggests that 'our experience ought to have taught us that such aggregations

30 'How Shall We Live Then?', *International Review of Social History*, 16 (1971), 233.

31 'Looking Backward', 507.

32 'Correspondence', in *Political Writings*, ed. Salmon, 416.

of population afford us the worst possible form of dwelling-place, whatever the second-worst might be'.[33]

Nevertheless, despite such formulations, Morris's own vision of the future was of cities transformed and not eradicated. The ideal city—which was neither medieval nor contemporary (neither a fortress nor a monstrosity of haphazard growth) but of a type which has not yet existed—formed a recurring theme in his later lectures. Morris once described his goal as making 'the town a part of the country and the country a part of the town'. The aim was not one of uniformity, but rather of weakening the starkness of the contrast. This was to be achieved by introducing the best features of each into the other. 'I want the town to be impregnated with the beauty of the country', Morris insisted, 'and the country with the intelligence and vivid life of the town.'[34]

Mesmerized by the creation of 'elbow room' and the introduction of nature in a variety of cultivated forms—the 'wide sunny meadows' of Hammersmith (p. 20); the 'whispering trees' of the orchard in Trafalgar Square (p. 36); and the 'beautiful rose-gardens' laid out on the side of Endell Street (p. 42);—readers of *News From Nowhere* often overlook the fact that London remains a great city. The brick and mortar sprawl may have disappeared, but there are numerous reminders of its size and density: there are 'crowds' in Piccadilly (p. 29); Hampstead is described as a well-built 'town' (p. 59); building continues in Long Acre even though the houses already stand 'thick' (p. 42); and the numbers of people milling about in the early evening are sufficient to slow the return of Guest and Dick (the great-grandson of Hammond who accompanies and guides the visitor on his travels) to Hammersmith (p. 119). Moreover, despite its transformation, the urban topography remains broadly familiar. Not least, the 'Anti-Scrape' (Society for the Protection of Ancient Buildings) has cast a lengthy shadow and many recognizable landmarks have been retained; not only buildings, such as Westminster Abbey, which Morris cherished, but also those, like St Paul's, whose importance he questioned and which he could not love.

What *have* disappeared are the manufacturing districts, along with the hunt for profit which first crowded people into houses 'for whose

[33] 'Looking Backward', 505.

[34] 'Town and Country', in Mackail, *Life of William Morris*, ii. 305.

wretchedness there is no name', which failed to 'take the most ordinary precautions against wrapping a whole district in a cloud of sulphurous smoke', and which turned 'beautiful rivers into filthy sewers'.[35] These environmental concerns are apparent throughout *News From Nowhere*. There are signs of mixed usage (Guest passes a large banded workshop making pottery and glass near the National Gallery) but the pollution, noise, and squalor of the factory districts is a distant memory, only half-recalled by a solemn annual feast in the areas east of the City. In the worst cases, Morris's novel gives flesh to an earlier suggestion that he had ventured, namely to break up the manufacturing districts and let 'nature heal the horrible scars that man's heedless greed and stupid terror have made'.[36] Silvertown, in London, is given over to pleasant meadowland, and the whole of Manchester has, seemingly, disappeared.

The last of Bellamy's 'curiously limited' ideas of life, considered by Morris, concerns his conception of art. This might initially appear an unlikely target for criticism, since art plays such a marginal role in *Looking Backward* (classical music is relayed via the telephone, and paintings and sculptures appear on public buildings). In part, however, this is Morris's objection. He insists that art, 'using that word in its widest and due signification', is not 'a mere adjunct of life which free and happy men can do without' but rather 'the necessary expression and indispensable instrument of human happiness'.[37] Morris resisted the contemporary restriction of 'art' to painting, sculpture, music, and literature. He maintained that art should rather include anything 'that is made by man and has form'.[38] All of the 'externals of our life'—a house, a cup, a steam engine, the arrangements of a field—can be either 'beautiful' or 'ugly'; 'elevating' or 'degrading'; a 'torment' or a 'pleasure'; a 'burden' or a 'solace'.[39] Throughout *News From Nowhere*, Morris takes time to describe a wide variety of material objects in some detail (the leather belt around Dick's waist, the chair that Hammond sits on, the lines of the carriage that transports Guest, the plates in the dining-hall in

35 'How We Live and How We Might Live', 22.

36 'The Society of the Future', 461.

37 'Looking Backward', 507.

38 'The Socialist Ideal', in *Collected Works of William Morris*, ed. May Morris, xxiii. 255.

39 'Art under Plutocracy', in *Collected Works of William Morris*, ed. May Morris, xxiii. 165.

Bloomsbury, and so on) in an attempt to capture the texture of everyday life in the society of the future.

Morris held that good art in this expansive sense can only be the expression of pleasure in the activity of production. This link between art and work was central both to his social and political thought and to his own creative practice. Art, he asserted, must be 'either in its abundance or its barrenness, in its sincerity or its hollowness, the expression of the society amongst which it exists'.[40] In this context, readers are sometimes surprised by his judgement of the past.

Morris was famously attracted to the art of the Middle Ages, in which he found beauty, thought, humour, and hope, lavished on everything from cathedrals to porridge-pots. (The Renaissance, for all its admitted brilliance, marked for him a transition into a more intellectual and elitist art.) However, that enthusiasm was not unalloyed. Morris acknowledged that the pleasure in productive activity which underpinned these medieval achievements was often accompanied by violence, superstition, ignorance, and tyranny, in other areas of life. Moreover, he insisted that his purpose in turning to the art of the past lay in showing 'where lies the hope for the future, and not in mere empty regret for the days which can never come again'.[41]

Morris's verdict on the contemporary world is wholly unforgiving: modern civilization is incompatible with art. As other ages are known to historians as the age of 'chivalry' or of 'faith', he suggests that his own should be known as the 'age of makeshift'.[42] His contemporaries had, Morris feared, become contented with 'makeshifts', that is with inferior substitutes for material items which could be genuinely useful or beautiful. Art increasingly survives only in a 'sham' form, the product of dilettanti working for the amusement of the rich.

Only socialism, Morris argued, could sweep away this 'sham' art and renew beauty and usefulness in everyday life. In *News From Nowhere*, he imagines the forms that this might take, both indulging and qualifying his medieval enthusiasms. The public buildings in

[40] 'Aims of Art', 84.

[41] 'Art and Labour', in *The Unpublished Lectures of William Morris*, ed. Eugene D. Lemire (Detroit, 1969) 96.

[42] 'Makeshift', in *William Morris: Artist, Writer, Socialist*, ed. May Morris, ii. 469.

Hammersmith embrace the best of the Gothic without 'copying' it (p. 21), whilst the dresses of the women who welcome the visitor to the Guest House remind him of fourteenth-century garments without being an 'imitation' (p. 13). Art in the society of the future, he suggests, will surpass and not simply imitate the past.

The Utopian Tradition

As well as providing a vehicle for Morris's distinctive account of the contours of a future socialist society, *News From Nowhere* is also a contribution to a tradition of utopian literature. 'Utopia' and its cognates are not the least slippery of terms. The neologism was coined by Thomas More as the name of the fictional island in his book of the same name (first published in 1516). More added a Latin ending (*ia*) to a combination of a Greek adverb for 'not' (*ou*) and a noun for 'place' (*topos*), thereby creating a word for 'nowhere' which also suggested a 'happy' or 'fortunate' (*eu*) place (this latter association was made explicit in the poem which formed part of the prefatory materials to *Utopia*). Both book and neologism proved a great success, spreading quickly and spawning many imitations.

The definition of 'utopia' is much contested, but two influential alternatives might usefully be outlined here. The narrower, and perhaps more traditional, approach treats utopia as a subset of descriptions of ideal societies, specifically fictional narratives in which, typically, a visitor encounters a superior civilization. The broader, and more fashionable, approach extends the characterization of utopia beyond the association with a particular literary form to include *any* envisaging of ideal (or even improved) social arrangements. On both accounts, *News From Nowhere* clearly warrants the label.

That Morris's novel is located unambiguously within the utopian tradition is widely, but not universally, accepted. A minority of commentators, possessed of a typological bent and keen to distinguish different types of ideal society, have categorized *News From Nowhere* as an 'arcadia', a portrait of an undemanding pastoral life. There seems little reason to deny the possibility of identifying arcadian threads in Morris's novel, for example, in his assumption that essential human needs are temperate. However, the suggestion that it might be better classified as an arcadia rather than a utopia is unconvincing. This alternative typology is overly restrictive, narrowing the meaning of 'utopia' to a point where a classical literary portrayal of an ideal world is no longer included in that tradition. In addition, even if the alternative typology were accepted, the proposed classification of this particular novel is an implausible one. As has been shown above, despite his enthusiasm for overcoming the rupture between town and country, Morris's society of the future is no rural idyll. London, for example, is transfigured rather than destroyed. Moreover, the moderate abundance of that society is built, not on the generosity of nature, but on the success of humankind in wresting a living from nature through attractive labour and due use of machinery.

Morris's contribution to the tradition that More named is a knowing one. Morris was familiar with a wide range of utopian literature. He had serious and interesting things to say about *Utopia* itself (he wrote an introduction to More's work for the Kelmscott Press); he refers to Thomas Campanella, author of *La Città del Sole* (1623), perhaps the second most important of Renaissance utopias, as a 'prophetic' voice contesting the triumph of early commercialism; and he is known to have enjoyed Samuel Butler's *Erewhon* (1872), a book which he read to his friend Edward Burne-Jones.

It is possible to detect echoes of all these classic utopias in *News From Nowhere*. The last words of *Utopia*, in which More differentiates between the 'wish for' and the 'expectation of' change along utopian lines, is recalled by the final sentence of Morris's novel. The exchange between the two figures of 'Hospitaler' and 'Genoese' in Campanella's poetical dialogue may be reflected in the overly didactic conversation between Hammond and Guest in Chapter XI of *News From Nowhere* (although the coincidence in the initials of the two pairs of protagonists is perhaps just that). Finally, not only are Butler's therapeutic approach to crime and his denunciation of contemporary education paralleled in Morris's novel, but also 'Erewhon' (a 'household word' in the Morris family, according to his daughter May) is, of course, an anagram of 'Nowhere'.

The only utopian thinker to be mentioned explicitly in *News From Nowhere* is Charles Fourier. The most obvious affinities between Fourier and Morris include their pejorative use of the word 'civilization' and their accounts of attractive labour. It was the latter which Morris himself associated with the French author. Of the generation of utopian socialists whose work pre-dated that of Marx, it was

Fourier whom Morris singled out for praise 'since his doctrine of the necessity and possibility of making labour attractive is one which socialism can by no means do without'.[43] Morris was less enthusiastic about the communal experimentation of Fourier and his followers. In part, it was the regimented and inegalitarian character of Fourier's utopian designs which appears to have repelled Morris, but he also propounded a more general objection to the creation of what modern 'utopists' (that is, those who study utopianism) call intentional communities. These 'experiments in association' were, to Morris's mind, antisocial, in that they embodied an exclusive attempt to escape from society which was, in turn, left to take care of itself. In this respect, Morris saw communal experiments as a reheated form of 'monasticism' which would inevitably fail, rather than as a serious vehicle for modern socialism. Despite this considered response, it is far from certain that Morris's knowledge of Fourier was obtained first hand. There are certainly no barriers of language here. It was in French that Morris had first read Karl Marx's *Capital*, for example, and, less happily, communicated with the 'Froggy Weaver' (one Louis Bazin) whose brocading skills and mechanical Jacquard loom he had brought from Lyons in 1877. However, there is nothing in Morris's account of Fourier, either in *News From Nowhere* or elsewhere, that he could not have picked up from secondary sources with which he was familiar, from Victor Considérant's *Destinée sociale*, or J. S. Mill's posthumously published 'Chapters on Socialism', for example.

Morris offers a distinctive as well as a knowing contribution to the utopian tradition, breaking with many of the expectations that readers might have of this literary form. *News From Nowhere* provides no comprehensive and static portrait of perfection. As its subtitle suggests, this being only 'some chapters' from a utopian romance, we should not expect the kind of complete or systematic overview of social and political life found in other utopias. Perhaps the most noticeable omission concerns the relative paucity of information that Morris provides about the economic relations of his society of the future. As has been suggested above, this neglect was deliberate, a reflection of his reaction against predominantly economic accounts of the nature of socialism. In addition, Morris's

[43] 'The Hopes of Civilisation', in *Collected Works of William Morris*, ed. May Morris, xxiii. 73.

society of the future is a dynamic creation. Not only does it have a history (see below), but it also possesses a future whose outline is contested and unpredictable. Old Hammond is sanguine about the likelihood of the work-famine which many of the younger generation fear, whilst Henry Morsom's confidence in the future is grounded in self-assurance and not knowledge (he laughingly admits that he has no idea what will come next but still maintains that 'we will meet it when it comes') (p. 155). In short, *News From Nowhere* was written in accordance with a principle that Morris articulated elsewhere, namely that 'socialism denies the finality of human progress'.[44] Lastly, the society of the future may be radically transformed, but it is not a model of limitless perfection. Not least, Morris portrays a world in which a variety of familiar human failings remain. There are, for example, individuals who harm others (the 'death by violence' reported by Walter Allen), people whose wants and preferences are frustrated (the disappointed suitors surrounding Ellen), and characters who remain obtuse and irritating (the curmudgeonly 'old grumbler' of Runnymede).

Perhaps the two most distinctive formal features of Morris's utopia are its location and its origin. As already noted, utopian narratives typically involve a visitor who encounters a superior civilization. However, towards the end of the nineteenth century, the predominant destination of utopian journeys shifted from a geographical to a chronological location, from *terra incognita* to *tempora incognita*. The conceit of a known geography visited at a time in the distant future is certainly central to *News From Nowhere*. It helps to sustain the autobiographical layer of the book, which is signalled in a dozen smaller clues—in Guest's first name, his age, the flash of temper at the League meeting, and so on—but which is perhaps most obvious in the two journeys that structure its narrative: the drive (from Hammersmith to Bloomsbury) through the great city in which Morris spent the bulk of his life and with which he had a complex and ambiguous relationship; and the Thames voyage from the site of Morris's London home (Kelmscott House), along the river that he knew well, to the Oxfordshire retreat which he loved so deeply (Kelmscott Manor). In addition, the use of such a familiar topography (documented in some of the Explanatory Notes to this

[44] William Morris and E. Belfort Bax, 'Socialism from the Root Up', in *Political Writings*, ed. Salmon, 622.

edition) helps to sustain the tension between the ideal and the real which is central to the novel, and which culminates in Guest's return to the unhappy past to which he belongs.

News From Nowhere, moreover, has a historical as well as a geographical location. Morris provides a lengthy and detailed account of 'how the change came', which draws on both his understanding of past events (such as the Paris Commune), and his own political experiences (of 'Bloody Sunday' and the strike wave of 1888–9, for example). Morris's utopia is not chanced upon but fought for, emerging out of a difficult and uneven advance through demonstrations, general strike, and civil war. Morris portrays this revolutionary struggle between classes as an educational prerequisite as well as an instrumental necessity. Revolution provided both the only means by which the old society could be overthrown, and the schooling without which the new society would fail. As Hammond is keen to explain, it was 'the very conflict itself' which helped develop the required habits of self-reliance and the 'due talent for administration' (p. 111). The actual chronology of these revolutionary events is a little less clear, an opacity which is compounded by Morris's adjustment of most of his dates between the serialization in *Commonweal* and publication in book form. (The central disagreement here depends on whether a reference by Hammond to a time two hundred years earlier is thought to pinpoint the beginning of social conflict at the end of the nineteenth century or the triumph of the revolution in 1952.) But differences over chronology do not alter Morris's fundamental view of revolution as a protracted and difficult process, nor the wider historical context in which his utopia is located. *News From Nowhere* portrays a situation long after the revolution and largely passes over the transitional period which divides the present from the 'ideal'. As Jane Morris remarked at the time of its serialization, the novel embodied her husband's attempt to picture 'what he considers likely to take place later on, when socialism shall have taken deeper roots'.[45]

This consideration of Morris's novel as part of a utopian tradition provides another vantage point from which to view the impact of *Looking Backward*. As has been shown, Bellamy's mechanical and soulless account of state socialism provoked the composition, and

[45] Jane Morris to Wilfrid Scawen Blunt, 11 Feb. 1890, in Peter Faulkner (ed.), *Jane Morris to Wilfrid Scawen Blunt* (Exeter, 1986), 41–2.

shaped the content, of Morris's own utopian novel. However, *Looking Backward* also shares several formal features with *News From Nowhere*. Not least, Bellamy operated within the more recent convention of a utopian journey to *tempora incognita*, sketching the social order of Boston in the closing year of the twentieth century. In addition, *Looking Backward* offered an account of transition, whereby state socialism emerged as the evolutionary result of growing centralization and monopolization in the capitalist economy. Morris viewed Bellamy's belief that socialism would emerge without any social breakdown or even disturbance, as a reflection of 'the author's satisfaction with the best part of modern life', insisting that the present development of trusts and monopolies in America provided a rather uncertain 'sheet-anchor' for socialism, since it was likely to be followed by a period of commercial 'break-ups and re-formations'. In place of Bellamy's 'economic semi-fatalism' (which he viewed as 'deadening and disparaging'), Morris preferred to place his trust in the conscious striving to realize the 'free and equal life' whose attainment was now possible.[46]

Introducing a lecture on the society of the future (first delivered in 1887), Morris acknowledged the unconventional nature of his hopes: 'I daresay', he remarked, 'you will find some of my visions strange enough'.[47] Modern readers are typically struck by the prescience of his ecological sensibilities (*News From Nowhere* has been plausibly described as an early 'Ecotopia'), but often remain sceptical about other aspects of his account of the future. For all that they might be amused by Guest's misjudged invocations of an extinct commercial morality (his attempt to offer a gratutity to Dick, for example), few now share Morris's confidence in the easy operation of a successful economic life built on mutuality. Other readers are likely to seize on his apparent endorsement of a sexual division of labour in which housekeeping remains the province of women (albeit that the complexity and value of that occupation is seemingly recognized and respected) as evidence not only of the unevenness of Morris's egalitarianism, but perhaps also of his own failure to avoid reading the present into the future. In response to earlier objections to her father's account of everyday life in the society of the future, May Morris suggested that some readers might prefer 'to skip all the

[46] 'Looking Backward', 503–4.
[47] 'Society of the Future', 455.

explanations of old Hammond and read the tale as a romance, full of the joy of life, full of fun, with sly digs at the author's self, and gibes at some of the falsities of modern life'.[48] Her suggestion is perhaps a useful reminder of the 'romance' element of the book. The drama and pathos in *News From Nowhere* undoubtedly rests on Morris's account of Guest's developing relationship with those who accompany him on his travels, with Dick, Clara (Dick's wife), and especially Ellen (the granddaughter of the 'old grumbler'). However, the attractions of this narrative should not detract from the intellectual seriousness and political intent that pervade the entire novel, not excluding this sub-plot of romance. (In his introduction to *Utopia*, Morris had himself warned against treating More's work as 'nothing more serious than a charming literary exercise, spiced with the interest given to it by the allusions to the history of the time and by our knowledge of the career of its author'.)[49] In addition, such a reading risks neglecting the open-ended and heuristic character of Morris's speculation about the future. Clear and honest disagreement about how we might live, especially from those engaged 'in a common adventure for the present', was something that he welcomed.[50] Morris reserved his disdain for the 'smug satisfaction in existing society' displayed by those who were usually 'at once well-to-do and thoughtless'.[51]

Morris identified two related dangers facing readers of socialist utopias. The risk to those who found a particular portrayal of socialism 'pleasing and satisfactory' was that it could 'warp their efforts [to bring about a free and equal society] in futile directions'. Conversely, the risk to those who found a particular portrayal of socialism 'displeasing and unsatisfactory' was that it could incline them to reject socialism altogether. Morris went on to suggest that both of these putative dangers result from an assumption that the vision in question consists of 'conclusive statements of facts and rules of action'. This assumption, however, should in his view be rejected, since utopian descriptions are bound to contain 'errors and fallacies'.[52]

[48] May Morris, 'Later Years', 505.

[49] 'More's Utopia: Foreword by William Morris', in *William Morris: Artist, Writer, Socialist*, ed. May Morris, ii. 289.

[50] 'How Shall We Live Then?', 222.

[51] 'The End and the Means', in *William Morris: Artist, Writer, Socialist*, ed. May Morris, ii. 421–2.

[52] 'Looking Backward', 502.

Elsewhere, Morris offers some account of those necessary mistakes. Attempts to describe the society of the future, he suggests, will necessarily reflect present preoccupations (they will always be *our* picture of the future), they are bound to underestimate some element 'whose force we have not duly appreciated', and they can present, at best, only 'the skeleton of the full life which will go on in those times to come'.[53] As a result, he maintains, we should avoid thinking of utopias as blueprints, that is, as social and political patterns requiring only to be implemented.

Instead, Morris recommends that the 'only safe way of reading a utopia is to consider it as the expression of the temperament of its author'. In particular, utopias are best understood as a speculative expression of the author's real desires and hopes for the society of the future. Morris does not mean to suggest that an individual's description of the society of the future is wholly 'personal to himself'.[54] Utopia involves the revelation of aspirations whose scope can be more or less universal. In presenting his own speculations on 'how we might live', Morris sought to distance himself from the 'egoistical' appearance of his subject matter by drawing a distinction between 'the voice', which 'is mine', and the hopes for the future, which 'are not only mine' but shared by 'many others'.[55]

Since descriptions of future societies are necessarily 'incomplete and even vague', Morris acknowledges that they fall short of the degree of certainty that is required by claims to knowledge. However, it does not follow—as those socialists who 'plume' themselves on their practicality are apt to imagine—that these hopes for the future are of no value. Morris identifies several important functions that utopian speculations can still fulfil: they can offer solace amidst the often 'dull and discouraging' work of progress; they can lend necessary direction to those pragmatic short-term measures 'which we are likely to attain'; they can motivate those 'wise' activists who need to 'see and feel' that any sacrifice is merited; and they can provide a critical vantage-point from which to view 'the conditions of life which surround us all to-day'.[56] These last two results, in particular, are recalled in the closing pages of *News From Nowhere*.

[53] William Morris and E. Belfort Bax, 'Socialism from the Root Up', 611.

[54] 'Looking Backward', 502 and 506.

[55] 'How Shall We Live Then?', 223.

[56] 'The End and the Means', 420–1.

With the conclusion of the journey up the Thames to Kelmscott, the reader is robbed of a conventional romantic ending. Recognizing that he belongs completely to the sorrows of the past, Guest is forced to part from his dream. His separation from Ellen, the young woman with whom he has risked falling in love—and whose beauty, energy, and intelligence are clearly emblematic of the new society—provides not only the emotional climax of the novel but also the occasion for a statement on the purpose of utopia. It is Ellen's last 'mournful look' which suggests the lessons of this visit to the future (p. 181). Guest is to return to his own unhappy time with a fresh insight into its privations, and a renewed enthusiasm for the work of building something better. The reader is, of course, expected to share in that experience, and in this way, *News From Nowhere* is intended to form part of the struggle to realize, as well as an opportunity to rehearse, Morris's hopes for the future. As Guest reflects, 'if others can see it as I have seen it' then this picture of the society of the future might be a premonition of something that could be, rather than an unrealizable longing, might be a 'vision rather than a dream' (p. 182).

NOTE ON THE TEXT

News From Nowhere appeared in four editions during Morris's lifetime. It was originally written and serialized in thirty-nine instalments in the journal *Commonweal* between 11 January 1890 and 4 October 1890. This serial edition was then published, without revisions, as a book by Roberts Brothers of Boston, Massachusetts, in 1890. H. Buxton Forman later recalled that Morris 'told me with an amused air that he had not been consulted about it', and, on this basis, this edition is often described as an unauthorized one.[1] Almost immediately on finishing the serial, Morris began to 'touch up N from N. for its book form' (see letter to John Bruce Glasier dated 7 October 1890).[2] This revised edition was published in the spring of 1891 by Reeves & Turner, in three different forms (including a popular edition in the form of a 'thick trimmed pamphlet in a paper wrapper'). There were several major changes between the serialized version and this revised edition of the text. They include: the addition of several pages to Chapter VII ('Trafalgar Square'); the addition of three paragraphs at the beginning of Chapter XIV ('How Matters are Managed'); the insertion of several pages in Chapter XVII ('How the Change Came'); the addition of a new Chapter XXVI ('The Obstinate Refusers'); the division (and renumbering) of the original Chapter XXVI ('The Upper Waters') into two (Chapter XXVII 'The Upper Waters' and Chapter XXVIII 'The Little River'); and alterations to the dating of the revolutionary change. These changes are detailed further in the Explanatory Notes to the present volume. Finally, a Kelmscott Press version of *News From Nowhere* appeared in an octavo volume, printed in Golden Type with black and red ornaments, in 1893. It was based on the revised 1891 edition but included shoulder notes and 'a few slight corrections'. It also introduced a number of new errors (the Press was marked by careless proof-reading throughout its history). Moreover, many of Morris's changes arose out of typological issues—improving the word-spacing of particular lines and coping with the

[1] H. Buxton Forman, *The Books of William Morris* (London, 1897), 149.

[2] In *The Collected Letters of William Morris*, ed. Norman Kelvin, iii. *1889–1892* (Princeton, 1996), 218.

absence of an italic version of Golden Type—rather than from any concern with his subject matter. The present volume is based on the third of these texts, that is, the first revised edition published by Reeves and Turner in 1891. Morris's spelling and punctuation have been retained with the exception of typographical errors which have been silently amended.

SELECT BIBLIOGRAPHY

Works by Morris

The Collected Works of William Morris, ed. May Morris, 24 vols. (London, 1910–15).

William Morris: Artist, Writer, Socialist, ed. May Morris, vol. i. *The Art of William Morris; Morris as a Writer*, vol. ii. *Morris as a Socialist*, with an account of *William Morris as I Knew Him*, by Bernard Shaw (Oxford, 1936).

The Unpublished Lectures of William Morris, ed. Eugene D. Lemire (Detroit, 1969).

The Collected Letters of William Morris, 4 vols., ed. Norman Kelvin (Princeton, 1984–96).

Political Writings: Contributions to 'Justice' and 'Commonweal' 1883–1890, ed. and introd. Nicholas Salmon (Bristol, 1994).

Journalism: Contributions to 'Commonweal' 1885–1890, ed. Nicholas Salmon (Bristol, 1996).

Biography

J. W. Mackail, *The Life of William Morris*, 2 vols. (London 1899).

E. P. Thompson, *William Morris: Romantic to Revolutionary*, 2nd edn. (London, 1977).

Jan Marsh, *Jane and May Morris: A Biographical Story 1839–1938* (London, 1986).

Fiona McCarthy, *William Morris: A Life for Our Time* (London, 1994).

General Studies

Peter Faulkner, *Against the Age: An Introduction to William Morris* (London, 1980).

Peter Stansky, *William Morris* (Oxford, 1983).

Paul Thompson, *The Work of William Morris* (Oxford 1991).

Linda Parry (ed.), *William Morris* (London, 1996).

Peter Faulkner and Peter Preston (eds.), *William Morris: Centenary Essays* (Exeter, 1999).

Morris as an Artist

Aymer Vallance, *William Morris: his Art, his Writing, and his Public Life* (London, 1898).

Charles A. Sewter, *The Stained Glass of William Morris and his Circle*, 2 vols. (New Haven, 1974–5).

Linda Parry, *William Morris Textiles* (London, 1983).

Peter Stansky, *Redesigning the World: William Morris, the 1880s and the Arts and Crafts Movement* (Princeton, 1985).

William S. Peterson, *The Kelmscott Press: A History of William Morris's Typographical Adventure* (Oxford, 1991).

Charles Harvey and Jon Press, *William Morris: Design and Enterprise in Victorian Britain* (Manchester, 1991).

Morris's Political Thought

R. Page Arnot, *William Morris: A Vindication* (London, 1934).

Margaret R. Grennan, *William Morris, Medievalist and Revolutionary* (New York, 1945).

R. Page Arnot, *William Morris: The Man and the Myth* (London, 1964).

E. P. Thompson, *William Morris: Romantic to Revolutionary*, 2nd edn. (London, 1977).

John Goode, 'William Morris and the Dream of Revolution', in John Lucas (ed.), *Literature and Politics in the Nineteenth Century* (London, 1971), 221–79.

Paul Meier, *William Morris: The Marxist Dreamer*, 2 vols., trans. Frank Gubb, with a preface by Robin Page Arnot (Brighton, 1978).

Perry Anderson, *Arguments within English Marxism* (London, 1980), ch. 6.

Ruth Kinna, *William Morris and the Art of Socialism* (Cardiff, 2000).

Studies of News from Nowhere

Patrick Brantlinger, '*News From Nowhere*: Morris's Socialist Anti-Novel', *Victorian Studies*, 19 (1975), 35–49.

Patrick Parrinder, '*News From Nowhere*, *The Time Machine* and the Break-Up of Classical Realism', *Science Fiction Studies*, 3 (1976), 265–74.

Michael Liberman, 'Textual Changes in William Morris's *News From Nowhere*', *Nineteenth-Century Literature*, 41 (1986), 349–56.

Paddy O'Sullivan, 'The Ending of the Journey: William Morris, *News From Nowhere* and Ecology', in Stephen Coleman and Paddy O'Sullivan (eds.), *William Morris and News From Nowhere: A Vision for our Time* (Bideford, 1990), 169–81.

Krishan Kumar, '*News From Nowhere*: The Renewal of Utopia', *History of Political Thought*, 14 (1993), 133–43.

Ruth Levitas, '"Who Holds the Hose?" Domestic Labour in the Work of Bellamy, Gilman, and Morris', *Utopian Studies*, 6 (1995), 65–84.

On Utopianism

A. L. Morton, *The English Utopia* (London, 1952), ch. 6.

Frank E. and Fritzie P. Manuel, *Utopian Thought in the Western World* (Oxford: Basil Blackwell, 1979).

J. C. Davis, *Utopia and the Ideal Society* (Cambridge, 1981).

Ruth Levitas, *The Concept of Utopia* (Hemel Hempstead, 1990).

Lyman Tower Sargent, 'The Three Faces of Utopianism Revisited', *Utopian Studies*, 5 (1994), 1–37.

John Carey (ed.), *The Faber Book of Utopias* (London, 1999).

Roland Schaer, Gregory Claeys, and Lyman Tower Sargent, *Utopia: The Search for the Ideal Society in the Western World* (New York, 2001).

On Edward Bellamy and Looking Backward

Edward Bellamy, *Looking Backward: 2000–1887* (Boston, 1888).

Arthur Lipow, *Authoritarian Socialism in America: Edward Bellamy and the Nationalist Movement* (Berkeley and Los Angeles, 1982).

Sylvia E. Bowman, *Edward Bellamy* (Boston, 1986).

Krishan Kumar, *Utopia and Anti-Utopia* (Oxford, 1987), ch. 5.

Daphne Patai (ed.), *Looking Backward, 1988–1888: Essays on Edward Bellamy* (Amherst, 1988).

Other Sources

Journal of the William Morris Society, published by the William Morris Society, Kelmscott House, 26 Upper Mall, Hammersmith, London W6 9TA.

Gary Aho, *William Morris: A Reference Guide* (Boston, 1985).

David and Sheila Latham, *An Annotated Critical Bibliography of William Morris* (London, 1991).

Nicholas Salmon with Derek Baker, *The William Morris Chronology* (Bristol, 1996).

Further Reading in Oxford World's Classics

Three Early Modern Utopias, ed. Susan Bruce.

Jerome K. Jerome, *Three Men in a Boat/Three Men on the Bummel*, ed. Geoffrey Harvey.

Karl Marx, *Capital—An Abridged Edition*, ed. David McLellan.

A CHRONOLOGY OF WILLIAM MORRIS

1834 (24 Mar.) born at Elm House, Walthamstow, Essex, to William Morris (Senior) and Emma Morris (née Shelton).

1840 Family (Morris had three surviving brothers and four sisters) moves to Woodford Hall, Essex.

1847 Father dies (aged 50) leaving an estate valued at £60,000.

1848 Attends Marlborough College ('I think I may fairly say I learned next to nothing there'); family moves to Water House, Walthamstow.

1851 Leaves Marlborough College to study privately with the Revd Dr F. B. Guy in Walthamstow.

1853 Attends Exeter College, Oxford; makes friends with Edward Burne-Jones; (Aug.) travels to Belgium and northern France visiting Gothic churches.

1855 Comes into his inheritance (thirteen shares in Devon Great Consolidated Copper Mining, paying some £700 p.a.); (July–Aug.) travels to France, visits the Louvre and the Exposition Universelle in Paris.

1856 Edits *The Oxford and Cambridge Magazine* (contributing 'The Story of the Unknown Church' and a poem 'Winter Weather'); is articled to G. E. Street, the Oxford architect.

1857 Leaves Street in order to paint; experiments with sculpture, stained-glass design, and embroidery; works on the Oxford Union frescos with Rossetti, Burne-Jones, and others.

1858 Publishes *The Defence of Guenevere & Other Poems* (a review in the *Spectator*: 'To our taste, the style is as bad as bad can be'); (Aug.–Sept.) visits France.

1859 (Apr.) marries Jane Burden—none of Morris's family attend the wedding; work begins on the Red House (designed by Philip Webb).

1860 (June) moves into the Red House (Burne-Jones describes Morris as making it 'the beautifullest place on earth').

1861 (Jan.) birth of daughter Jane Alice ('Jenny'); (Apr.) 'The Firm' opens (Morris, Marshall, Faulkner & Co., reconstituted as Morris & Co. in 1875) with premises in Red Lion Square, London.

1862 (Mar.) birth of daughter, Mary ('May'); The Firm exhibits stained glass, embroidery, and painted furniture at the International Exhibition held at the South Kensington Museum (now the V & A).

1864 Registers his first two wallpaper designs (*Trellis* and *Daisy*).

1865 The Morris Firm and family move to Queen Square, Bloomsbury, London (the Red House was sold and Morris never went back there).

1866 (June) Morris and Jane tour northern France; The Firm's commissions include the Green Dining Room at the South Kensington Museum.

1867 Publishes *The Life and Death of Jason* (Henry James describes it as 'a book of real value' and compares Morris with Chaucer).

1868 Publishes first volume of *The Earthly Paradise*; begins studying Icelandic with the help of Eiríkr Magnússon.

1869 (May) publishes his and Magnússon's translation of *The Story of Grettir the Strong*; (July–Sept.) travels with Jane to Bad Ems; (Nov.) publishes second volume of *The Earthly Paradise*.

1870 Publishes final volume of *The Earthly Paradise*; completes an illuminated manuscript, *A Book of Verse*, for Georgiana Burne-Jones.

1871 Publishes translation with Magnússon of *The Story of Frithiof the Bold*; (June) rents Kelmscott Manor, Oxfordshire ('a heaven on earth'); (July–Sept.) visits Iceland, returning 'with the complexion of a trading skipper and much thinner'.

1872 Completes an illuminated manuscript, *The Rubaiyat of Omar Khayyam*, for Georgiana Burne-Jones; publishes *Love is Enough*.

1873 (Jan.) the family moves from Queen Square to Horrington House, Turnham Green Road, London; (Apr.) visits Florence and Siena (with Burne-Jones); (July–Sept.) visits Iceland (Burne-Jones: 'Morris has come back more enslaved with a passion for ice and snow and raw fish than ever—I fear I shall never drag him to Italy again').

1874 Takes family on visit to Belgium.

1875 Publishes *Three Northern Love Stories and Other Tales*; (July) makes first of many visits to Leek, Staffordshire, to learn the art of dyeing; publishes *The Aeneids of Virgil: Done into English Verse*.

1876 Publishes *The Tale of Sigurd the Volsung and the Fall of the Niblings*; becomes treasurer of the Eastern Question Association.

1877 Declines approach regarding the post of Professor of Poetry at the

University of Oxford; helps found the Society for the Protection of Ancient Buildings (the 'Anti-Scrape'); Morris & Co. open a shop on Oxford Street; publishes translation of the *Odyssey*.

1878 Teaches himself the technique of hand-knotting carpets; (Apr.–May) travels in Italy with family (suffers from gout); rents Kelmscott House in Upper Mall, Hammersmith, on a long lease.

1879 Weaves *Acanthus & Vine* (spending 516 hours on the tapestry).

1880 (10–16 Aug.) travels with friends and family in the 'Ark' from Kelmscott House to Kelmscott Manor along the Thames.

1881 (July) signs the lease on Merton Abbey Works in Surrey (and starts manufacturing prints, wallpapers, and stained glass); (8–15 Aug.) makes second trip with friends and family in the 'Ark' from Kelmscott House to Kelmscott Manor along the Thames.

1882 Publishes a collection of lectures *Hopes and Fears for Art*; joins (and becomes treasurer of) Icelandic Famine Relief Committee; (Apr.) Crom Price records that Morris 'was full of Karl Marx which he had begun to read in French'.

1883 (January) joins the Democratic Federation (later Social Democratic Federation) led by H. M. Hyndman; made Honorary Fellow of Exeter College; (May) registers the pattern for *Strawberry Thief*.

1884 Begins writing for *Justice*, contributing articles and some of his *Chants for Socialists*; (Dec.) leaves Social Democratic Federation (along with Eleanor Marx and others) to found the Socialist League.

1885 Becomes editor of *Commonweal* (until 1890); lectures frequently on socialism; (Sept.) is charged, and acquitted, of assaulting a policeman; publishes *Chants for Socialists* and the first seven instalments of *The Pilgrims of Hope*.

1886 Publishes *Socialism from the Root Up* (written with E. Belfort Bax); publishes the first seven instalments of *A Dream of John Ball*.

1887 Publishes two-volume translation of *The Odyssey of Homer* (Oscar Wilde calls it 'the most perfect and the most satisfying' of the English translations); his play *The Tables Turned; or, Nupkins Awakened* is performed (Morris taking the part of the Archbishop of Canterbury); (13 Nov.) present at 'Bloody Sunday' demonstration; (18 Dec.) speaks at the funeral of Alfred Linnell.

1888 Publishes *The House of the Wolfings*, and a second collection of lectures, *Signs of Change* ('all of the simply Socialist lectures written for *viva voce* delivery').

1889 (May) reads Edward Bellamy's *Looking Backward*; (July) attends the International Socialist Congress in Paris, as a delegate of the Socialist League; publishes *The Roots of the Mountains*.

1890 (Jan.–Oct.) *News From Nowhere* appears in serial form in *Commonweal*; (May) resigns editorship of *Commonweal* after anarchists gain control of the Council of the Socialist League; (Nov.) Hammersmith Branch leaves the Socialist League to form the Hammersmith Socialist Society; becomes a more active book and manuscript buyer; begins preparations for the Kelmscott Press; agrees arrangements for 6-volume Saga Library in collaboration with Eiríkr Magnússon.

1891 (Jan.) prints first trial page at the Kelmscott Press; *The Story of the Glittering Plain* (one of his 'own little stories') is the first book published (May); revised version of *News From Nowhere* appears in book form; health begins to decline ('I am ashamed to say that I am not as well as I should like and am even such a fool as to be rather anxious'); (Aug.) travels (with Jenny) in northern France visiting churches.

1892 (Oct.) declines approach concerning poet laureateship ('I am a sincere republican, and therefore could not accept a post which would give me even the appearance of serving a court for complaisance sake').

1893 Publishes *Socialism: Its Growth and Outcome* with E. Belfort Bax.

1894 Publishes *The Wood Beyond the World*; Emma Morris (his mother) dies (aged 89).

1895 Publishes *The Tale of Beowulf*; purchases the thirteenth-century Huntingfield Psalter (the most important manuscript in his collection); (Dec.) speaks at the funeral of Sergius Stepniak.

1896 Health continues to decline ('I don't seem to mend a bit; am weak and belly-achy'); (Jan.) speaks for the last time in public ('on checking the abuses of public advertising') at the 'Anti-Scrape'; publishes *The Well at the World's End* in two volumes; (May) Kelmscott Press edition of Chaucer is completed; (July) doctors recommend sea voyage to Norway (Morris suffers hallucinations and seasickness); (3 October) dies peacefully 11.15 a.m. at Kelmscott House; (6 October) interred in the churchyard at Kelmscott.

FACING PAGE

Engraved frontispiece from a design by C. M. Gere for the 1893 Kelmscott Press edition

THIS IS THE PICTURE OF THE OLD
HOUSE BY THE THAMES TO WHICH
THE PEOPLE OF THIS STORY WENT
HEREAFTER FOLLOWS THE BOOK IT-
SELF WHICH IS CALLED NEWS FROM
NOWHERE OR AN EPOCH OF REST &
IS WRITTEN BY WILLIAM MORRIS

CHAPTER I

DISCUSSION AND BED

Up at the League, says a friend,* there had been one night a brisk conversational discussion, as to what would happen on the Morrow of the Revolution, finally shading off into a vigorous statement by various friends of their views on the future of the fully-developed new society.

Says our friend: Considering the subject, the discussion was good-tempered; for those present being used to public meetings and after-lecture debates, if they did not listen to each other's opinions (which could scarcely be expected of them), at all events did not always attempt to speak all together, as is the custom of people in ordinary polite society when conversing on a subject which interests them. For the rest, there were six persons present, and consequently six sections of the party were represented, four of which had strong but divergent Anarchist opinions.* One of the sections, says our friend, a man whom he knows very well indeed, sat almost silent at the beginning of the discussion, but at last got drawn into it, and finished by roaring out very loud, and damning all the rest for fools; after which befell a period of noise, and then a lull, during which the aforesaid section, having said good-night very amicably, took his way home by himself to a western suburb, using the means of travelling which civilisation has forced upon us like a habit. As he sat in that vapour-bath of hurried and discontented humanity, a carriage of the underground railway,* he, like others, stewed discontentedly, while in self-reproachful mood he turned over the many excellent and conclusive arguments which, though they lay at his fingers' ends, he had forgotten in the just past discussion. But this frame of mind he was so used to, that it didn't last him long, and after a brief discomfort, caused by disgust with himself for having lost his temper (which he was also well used to),* he found himself musing on the subject-matter of discussion, but still discontentedly and unhappily. 'If I could but see a day of it,' he said to himself; 'if I could but see it!'

As he formed the words, the train stopped at his station, five minutes' walk from his own house, which stood on the banks of the Thames, a little way above an ugly suspension bridge.* He went out of the station, still discontented and unhappy, muttering 'If I could but see it! if I could but see it!' but had not gone many steps towards the river before (says our friend who tells the story) all that discontent and trouble seemed to slip off him.

It was a beautiful night of early winter, the air just sharp enough to be refreshing after the hot room and the stinking railway carriage. The wind, which had lately turned a point or two north of west, had blown the sky clear of all cloud save a light fleck or two which went swiftly down the heavens. There was a young moon halfway up the sky, and as the home-farer caught sight of it, tangled in the branches of a tall old elm, he could scarce bring to his mind the shabby London suburb where he was, and he felt as if he were in a pleasant country place—pleasanter, indeed, than the deep country was as he had known it.

He came right down to the river-side, and lingered a little, looking over the low wall to note the moonlit river, near upon high water, go swirling and glittering up to Chiswick Eyot:* as for the ugly bridge below, he did not notice it or think of it, except when for a moment (says our friend) it struck him that he missed the row of lights down stream. Then he turned to his house door and let himself in;* and even as he shut the door to, disappeared all remembrance of that brilliant logic and foresight which had so illuminated the recent discussion; and of the discussion itself there remained no trace, save a vague hope, that was now become a pleasure, for days of peace and rest, and cleanness and smiling goodwill.

In this mood he tumbled into bed, and fell asleep after his wont, in two minutes' time; but (contrary to his wont) woke up again not long after in that curiously wide-awake condition which sometimes surprises even good sleepers; a condition under which we feel all our wits preternaturally sharpened, while all the miserable muddles we have ever got into, all the disgraces and losses of our lives, will insist on thrusting themselves forward for the consideration of those sharpened wits.

In this state he lay (says our friend) till he had almost begun to enjoy it: till the tale of his stupidities amused him, and the entanglements before him, which he saw so clearly, began to shape themselves into an amusing story for him.

He heard one o'clock strike, then two and then three; after which he fell asleep again. Our friend says that from that sleep he awoke once more, and afterwards went through such surprising adventures that he thinks that they should be told to our comrades, and indeed the public in general, and therefore proposes to tell them now. But, says he, I think it would be better if I told them in the first person, as if it were myself who had gone through them; which, indeed, will be the easier and more natural to me, since I understand the feelings and desires of the comrade of whom I am telling better than any one else in the world does.

CHAPTER II

A MORNING BATH

Well, I awoke, and found that I had kicked my bed-clothes off; and no wonder, for it was hot and the sun shining brightly. I jumped up and washed and hurried on my clothes, but in a hazy and half-awake condition, as if I had slept for a long, long while, and could not shake off the weight of slumber. In fact, I rather took it for granted that I was at home in my own room than saw that it was so.*

When I was dressed, I felt the place so hot that I made haste to get out of the room and out of the house; and my first feeling was a delicious relief caused by the fresh air and pleasant breeze; my second, as I began to gather my wits together, mere measureless wonder: for it was winter when I went to bed the last night, and now, by witness of the riverside trees, it was summer, a beautiful bright morning seemingly of early June. However, there was still the Thames sparkling under the sun, and near high water, as last night I had seen it gleaming under the moon.

I had by no means shaken off the feeling of oppression, and wherever I might have been should scarce have been quite conscious of the place; so it was no wonder that I felt rather puzzled in despite of the familiar face of the Thames. Withal I felt dizzy and queer; and remembering that people often got a boat and had a swim in mid-stream, I thought I would do no less. It seems very early, quoth I to myself, but I daresay I shall find someone at Biffin's* to take me. However, I didn't get as far as Biffin's, or even turn to my left thitherward, because just then I began to see that there was a landing-stage right before me in front of my house: in fact, on the place where my next-door neighbour had rigged one up, though somehow it didn't look like that either. Down I went on to it, and sure enough among the empty boats moored to it lay a man on his sculls in a solid-looking tub of a boat clearly meant for bathers. He nodded to me, and bade me good-morning as if he expected me, so I jumped in without any words, and he paddled away quietly as I peeled for my swim. As we went, I looked down on the water, and couldn't help saying—

'How clear the water is this morning!'

'Is it?' said he; 'I didn't notice it. You know the flood-tide always thickens it a bit.'

'H'm,' said I, 'I have seen it pretty muddy even at half-ebb.'

He said nothing in answer, but seemed rather astonished; and as he now lay just stemming the tide,* and I had my clothes off, I jumped in without more ado. Of course when I had my head above water again I turned towards the tide, and my eyes naturally sought for the bridge, and so utterly astonished was I by what I saw, that I forgot to strike out, and went spluttering under water again, and when I came up made straight for the boat; for I felt I that I must ask some questions of my waterman, so bewildering had been the half-sight I had seen from the face of the river with the water hardly out of my eyes; though by this time I was quit of the slumbrous and dizzy feeling, and was wide-awake and clear-headed.

As I got in up the steps which he had lowered, and he held out his hand to help me, we went drifting speedily up towards Chiswick; but now he caught up the sculls and brought her head round again, and said—

'A short swim, neighbour; but perhaps you find the water cold this morning, after your journey. Shall I put you ashore at once, or would you like to go down to Putney* before breakfast?'

He spoke in a way so unlike what I should have expected from a Hammersmith waterman, that I stared at him, as I answered, 'Please to hold her a little; I want to look about me a bit.'

'All right,' he said; 'it's no less pretty in its way here than it is off Barn Elms;* it's jolly everywhere this time in the morning. I'm glad you got up early; it's barely five o'clock yet.'

If I was astonished with my sight of the river banks, I was no less astonished at my waterman, now that I had time to look at him and see him with my head and eyes clear.

He was a handsome young fellow, with a peculiarly pleasant and friendly look about his eyes,—an expression which was quite new to me then, though I soon became familiar with it. For the rest, he was dark-haired and berry-brown of skin, well-knit and strong, and obviously used to exercising his muscles, but with nothing rough or coarse about him, and clean as might be. His dress was not like any modern work-a-day clothes I had seen, but would have served very well as a costume for a picture of fourteenth-century life: it was of dark blue cloth, simple enough, but of fine web, and without a stain on it. He had a brown leather belt round his waist, and I noticed that its clasp was of damascened* steel beautifully wrought. In short, he seemed to be like some specially manly and refined young gentleman, playing waterman for a spree, and I concluded that this was the case.

I felt that I must make some conversation; so I pointed to the Surrey bank,* where I noticed some light plank stages running down the foreshore, with windlasses at the landward end of them, and said, 'What are they doing with those things here? If we were on the Tay,* I should have said that they were for drawing the salmon nets; but here—'

'Well,' said he, smiling, 'of course that is what they *are* for. Where there are salmon, there are likely to be salmon-nets, Tay or Thames; but of course they are not always in use; we don't want salmon *every* day of the season.'

I was going to say, 'But is this the Thames?' but held my peace in my wonder, and turned my bewildered eyes eastward to look at the bridge again, and thence to the shores of the London river; and surely there was enough to astonish me. For though there was a bridge across the stream and houses on its banks, how all was changed from last night! The soap-works with their smoke-vomiting chimneys were gone; the engineer's works gone; the lead-works gone; and no sound of riveting and hammering came down the west wind from Thorneycroft's.* Then the bridge! I had perhaps dreamed of such a bridge, but never seen such an one out of an illuminated manuscript; for not even the Ponte Vecchio* at Florence came anywhere near it. It was of stone arches, splendidly solid, and as graceful as they were strong; high enough also to let ordinary river traffic through easily. Over the parapet showed quaint and fanciful little buildings, which I supposed to be booths or shops, beset with painted and gilded vanes and spirelets. The stone was a little weathered, but showed no marks of the grimy sootiness which I was used to on every London building more than a year old. In short, to me a wonder of a bridge.

The sculler noted my eager astonished look, and said, as if in answer to my thoughts—

'Yes, it *is* a pretty bridge, isn't it? Even the up-stream bridges, which are so much smaller, are scarcely daintier, and the down-stream ones are scarcely more dignified and stately.'

I found myself saying, almost against my will, 'How old is it?'

'Oh, not very old,' he said; 'it was built or at least opened, in 2003.* There used to be a rather plain timber bridge before then.'

The date shut my mouth as if a key had been turned in a padlock fixed to my lips; for I saw that something inexplicable had happened, and that if I said much, I should be mixed up in a game of cross questions and crooked answers. So I tried to look unconcerned, and to glance in a matter-of-course way at the banks of the river, though this is what I saw up to the bridge and a little beyond; say as far as the site of the soap-works. Both shores had a line of very pretty houses, low and not large, standing back a little way from the river; they were mostly built of red brick and roofed with tiles, and looked, above all, comfortable, and as if they were, so to say, alive, and sympathetic with the life of the dwellers in them. There was a continuous garden in front of them, going down to the water's edge, in which the flowers were now blooming luxuriantly, and sending delicious waves of summer scent over the eddying stream. Behind the houses, I could see great trees rising, mostly planes, and looking down the water there were the reaches towards Putney almost as if they were a lake with a forest shore, so thick were the big trees; and I said aloud, but as if to myself—

'Well, I'm glad that they have not built over Barn Elms.'

I blushed for my fatuity as the words slipped out of my mouth, and my companion looked at me with a half smile which I thought I understood; so to hide my confusion I said, 'Please take me ashore now: I want to get my breakfast.'

He nodded, and brought her head round with a sharp stroke, and in a trice we were at the landing-stage again. He jumped out and I followed him; and of course I was not surprised to see him wait, as if for the inevitable after-piece* that follows the doing of a service to a fellow-citizen. So I put my hand in my waistcoat-pocket, and said, 'How much?' though still with the uncomfortable feeling that perhaps I was offering money to a gentleman.

He looked puzzled, and said, 'How much? I don't quite understand what you are asking about. Do you mean the tide? If so, it is close on the turn now.'

I blushed, and said, stammering, 'Please don't take it amiss if I ask you; I mean no offence: but what ought I to pay you? You see I am a stranger, and don't know your customs—or your coins.'

And therewith I took a handful of money out of my pocket, as one does in a foreign country. And by the way, I saw that the silver had oxidised, and was like a blackleaded stove in colour.

He still seemed puzzled, but not at all offended; and he looked at the coins with some curiosity. I thought, Well after all, he *is* a waterman, and is considering what he may venture to take. He seems such a nice fellow that I'm sure I don't grudge him a little over-payment. I wonder, by the way, whether I couldn't hire him as a guide for a day or two, since he is so intelligent.

Therewith my new friend said thoughtfully:

'I think I know what you mean. You think that I have done you a service; so you feel yourself bound to give me something which I am not to give to a neighbour, unless he has done something special for me. I have heard of this kind of thing; but pardon me for saying, that it seems to us a troublesome and roundabout custom; and we don't know how to manage it. And you see this ferrying and giving people casts* about the water is my *business*, which I would do for anybody; so to take gifts in connection with it would look very queer. Besides, if one person gave me something, then another might, and another, and so on; and I hope you won't think me rude if I say that I shouldn't know where to stow away so many mementos of friendship.'

And he laughed loud and merrily, as if the idea of being paid for his work was a very funny joke. I confess I began to be afraid that the man was mad, though he looked sane enough; and I was rather glad to think that I was a good swimmer, since we were so close to a deep swift stream. However, he went on by no means like a madman:

'As to your coins, they are curious, but not very old; they seem to be all of the reign of Victoria;* you might give them to some scantily-furnished museum. Ours has enough of such coins, besides a fair number of earlier ones, many of which are beautiful, whereas these nineteenth century ones are so beastly ugly, ain't they? We have a piece of Edward III., with the king in a ship, and little leopards and fleurs-de-lys all along the gunwale, so delicately worked.* You see,' he said, with something of a smirk, 'I am fond of working in gold and fine metals; this buckle here is an early piece of mine.'

No doubt I looked a little shy of him under the influence of that doubt as to his sanity. So he broke off short, and said in a kind voice:

'But I see that I am boring you, and I ask your pardon. For, not to mince matters, I can tell that you *are* a stranger, and must come from a place very unlike England. But also it is clear that it won't do to overdose you with information about this place, and that you had best suck it in little by little. Further, I should take it as very kind in you if you would allow me to be the showman of our new world to you, since you have stumbled on me first. Though indeed it will be a mere kindness on your part, for almost anybody would make as good a guide, and many much better.'

There certainly seemed no flavour in him of Colney Hatch;* and besides I thought I could easily shake him off if it turned out that he really was mad; so I said:

'It is a very kind offer, but it is difficult for me to accept it, unless—' I was going to say, Unless you will let me pay you properly; but fearing to stir up Colney Hatch again, I changed the sentence into, 'I fear I shall be taking you away from your work—or your amusement.'

'O,' he said, 'don't trouble about that, because it will give me an opportunity of doing a good turn to a friend of mine, who wants to take my work here. He is a weaver from Yorkshire, who has rather overdone himself between his weaving and his mathematics, both indoor work, you see; and being a great friend of mine, he naturally came to me to get him some outdoor work. If you think you can put up with me, pray take me as your guide.'

He added presently: 'It is true that I have promised to go up-stream to some special friends of mine, for the hay-harvest; but they won't be ready for us for more than a week: and besides, you might go with me, you know, and see some very nice people, besides making notes of our ways in Oxfordshire. You could hardly do better if you want to see the country.'

I felt myself obliged to thank him, whatever might come of it; and he added eagerly:

'Well, then, that's settled. I will give my friend a call; he is living in the Guest House like you, and if he isn't up yet, he ought to be this fine summer morning.'

Therewith he took a little silver bugle-horn from his girdle and blew two or three sharp but agreeable notes on it; and presently from the house which stood on the site of my old dwelling (of which more hereafter) another young man came sauntering towards us. He was not so well-looking or so strongly made as my sculler friend, being sandy-haired, rather pale, and not stout-built; but his face was not wanting in that happy and friendly expression which I had noticed in his friend. As he came up smiling towards us, I saw with pleasure that I must give up the Colney Hatch theory as to the waterman, for no two madmen ever behaved as they did before a sane man. His dress also was of the same cut as the first man's, though somewhat gayer, the surcoat being light green with a golden spray embroidered on the breast, and his belt being of filigree silver-work.

He gave me good-day very civilly, and greeting his friend joyously, said:

'Well, Dick, what is it this morning? Am I to have my work, or rather your work? I dreamed last night that we were off up the river fishing.'

'All right, Bob,' said my sculler; 'you will drop into my place, and if you find it too much, there is George Brightling on the lookout for a stroke of work, and he lives close handy to you. But see, here is a stranger who is willing to amuse me to-day by taking me as his guide about our country-side, and you may imagine I don't want to lose the opportunity; so you had better take to the boat at once. But in any case I shouldn't have kept you out of it for long, since I am due in the hayfields in a few days.'

The newcomer rubbed his hands with glee, but turning to me, said in a friendly voice:

'Neighbour, both you and friend Dick are lucky, and will have a good time to-day, as indeed I shall too. But you had better both come in with me at once and get something to eat, lest you should forget your dinner in your amusement. I suppose you came into the Guest House after I had gone to bed last night?'

I nodded, not caring to enter into a long explanation which would have led to nothing, and which in truth by this time I should have begun to doubt myself. And we all three turned toward the door of the Guest House.

CHAPTER III
THE GUEST HOUSE AND BREAKFAST THEREIN

I lingered a little behind the others to have a stare at this house, which, as I have told you, stood on the site of my old dwelling.

It was a longish building with its gable ends turned away from the road, and long traceried windows coming rather low down set in the wall that faced us. It was very handsomely built of red brick with a lead roof; and high up above the windows there ran a frieze of figure subjects in baked clay, very well executed, and designed with a force and directness which I had never noticed in modern work before. The subjects I recognised at once, and indeed was very particularly familiar with them.*

However, all this I took in in a minute; for we were presently within doors, and standing in a hall with a floor of marble mosaic and an open timber roof. There were no windows on the side opposite to the river, but arches below leading into chambers, one of which showed a glimpse of a garden beyond, and above them a long space of wall gaily painted (in fresco, I thought) with similar subjects to those of the frieze outside; everything about the place was handsome and generously solid as to material; and though it was not very large (somewhat smaller than Crosby Hall* perhaps), one felt in it that exhilarating sense of space and freedom which satisfactory architecture always gives to an unanxious man who is in the habit of using his eyes.

In this pleasant place, which of course I knew to be the hall of the Guest House, three young women were flitting to and fro. As they were the first of the sex I had seen on this eventful morning, I naturally looked at them very attentively, and found them at least as good as the gardens, the architecture, and the male men. As to their dress, which of course I took note of, I should say that they were decently veiled with drapery, and not bundled up with millinery; that they were clothed like women, not upholstered like arm-chairs, as most women of our time are. In short, their dress was somewhat between that of the ancient classical costume and the simpler forms of the fourteenth century garments, though it was clearly not an imitation of either: the materials were light and gay to suit the season. As to the women themselves, it was pleasant indeed to see them, they were so kind and happy-looking in expression of face, so shapely and well-knit of body, and thoroughly healthy-looking and strong. All were at least comely, and one of them very handsome and regular of feature. They came up to us at once merrily and without the least affectation of shyness, and all three shook hands with me as if I were a friend newly come back from a long journey: though I could not help noticing that they looked askance at my garments; for I had on my clothes of last night, and at the best was never a dressy person.

A word or two from Robert the weaver, and they bustled about on our behoof, and presently came and took us by the hands and led us to a table in the pleasantest corner of the hall, where our breakfast was spread for us; and, as we sat down, one of them hurried out by the chambers aforesaid, and came back again in a little while with a great bunch of roses, very different in size and quality to what Hammersmith had been wont to grow, but very like the produce of an old country garden. She hurried back thence into the buttery, and came back once more with a delicately made glass, into which she put the flowers and set them down in the midst of our table. One of the others, who had run off also, then came back with a big cabbage-leaf filled with strawberries, some of them barely ripe, and said as she set them on the table, 'There, now; I thought of that before I got up this morning; but looking at the stranger here getting into your boat, Dick, put it out of my head; so that I was not before *all* the blackbirds: however, there are a few about as good as you will get them anywhere in Hammersmith this morning.'

Robert patted her on the head in a friendly manner; and we fell to on our breakfast, which was simple enough, but most delicately cooked, and set on the table with much daintiness. The bread was particularly good, and was of several different kinds, from the big, rather close, dark-coloured, sweet-tasting farmhouse loaf, which was most to my liking, to the thin pipe-stems of wheaten crust, such as I have eaten in Turin.*

As I was putting the first mouthfuls into my mouth, my eye caught a carved and gilded inscription on the panelling, behind what we should have called the High Table in an Oxford college hall,* and a familiar name in it forced me to read it through. Thus it ran:

> *'Guests and neighbours, on the site of this Guest-hall once stood the lecture-room of the Hammersmith Socialists.* Drink a glass to the memory! May 1962.'*

It is difficult to tell you how I felt as I read these words, and I suppose my face showed how much I was moved, for both my friends looked curiously at me, and there was silence between us for a little while.

Presently the weaver, who was scarcely so well mannered a man as the ferryman, said to me rather awkwardly:

'Guest, we don't know what to call you: is there any indiscretion in asking you your name?'

'Well,' said I, 'I have some doubts about it myself; so suppose you call me Guest, which is a family name, you know, and add William* to it if you please.'

Dick nodded kindly to me; but a shade of anxiousness passed over the weaver's face, and he said—

'I hope you don't mind my asking, but would you tell me where you come from? I am curious about such things for good reasons, literary reasons.'

Dick was clearly kicking him underneath the table; but he was not much abashed, and awaited my answer somewhat eagerly. As for me, I was just going to blurt out 'Hammersmith,' when I bethought me what an entanglement of cross purposes that would lead us into; so I took time to invent a lie with circumstance, guarded by a little truth, and said:

'You see, I have been such a long time away from Europe that things seem strange to me now; but I was born and bred on the edge of Epping Forest; Walthamstow and Woodford,* to wit.'

'A pretty place, too,' broke in Dick; 'a very jolly place, now that the trees have had time to grow again since the great clearing of houses in 1955.'

Quoth the irrepressible weaver: 'Dear neighbour, since you knew the Forest some time ago, could you tell me what truth there is in the rumour that in the nineteenth century the trees were all pollards?'

This was catching me on my archaeological natural-history side, and I fell into the trap without any thought of where and when I was; so I began on it, while one of the girls, the handsome one, who had been scattering little twigs of lavender and other sweet-smelling herbs about the floor, came near to listen, and stood behind me with her hand on my shoulder, in which she held some of the plant that I used to call balm:* Its strong sweet smell brought back to my mind my very early days in the kitchen-garden at Woodford, and the large blue plums which grew on the wall beyond the sweet-herb patch,—a connection of memories which all boys will see at once.

I started off: 'When I was a boy, and for long after, except for a piece about Queen Elizabeth's Lodge,* and for the part about High Beech,* the Forest was almost wholly made up of pollard hornbeams mixed with holly thickets. But when the Corporation of London* took it over about twenty-five years ago, the topping and lopping, which was a part of the old commoners' rights, came to an end, and the trees were let to grow. But I have not seen the place now for many years, except once, when we Leaguers went a-pleasuring to High Beech. I was very much shocked then to see how it was built-over and altered; and the other day we heard that the philistines were going to landscape-garden it. But what you were saying about the building being stopped and the trees growing is only too good news;—only you know—'

At that point I suddenly remembered Dick's date, and stopped short rather confused. The eager weaver didn't notice my confusion, but said hastily, as if he were almost aware of his breach of good manners, 'But, I say, how old are you?'

Dick and the pretty girl both burst out laughing, as if Robert's conduct were excusable on the grounds of eccentricity; and Dick said amidst his laughter:

'Hold hard, Bob; this questioning of guests won't do. Why, much learning is spoiling you. You remind me of the radical cobblers in the silly old novels, who, according to the authors, were prepared to trample down all good manners in the pursuit of utilitarian knowledge.* The fact is, I begin to think that you have so muddled your head with mathematics, and with grubbing into those idiotic old books about political economy (he he!), that you scarcely know how to behave. Really, it is about time for you to take to some open-air work, so that you may clear away the cobwebs from your brain.'

The weaver only laughed good-humouredly; and the girl went up to him and patted his cheek and said laughingly, 'Poor fellow! he was born so.'

As for me, I was a little puzzled, but I laughed also, partly for company's sake, and partly with pleasure at their unanxious happiness and good temper; and before Robert could make the excuse to me which he was getting ready, I said:

'But, neighbours' (I had caught up that word), 'I don't in the least mind answering questions, when I can do so: ask me as many as you please; it's fun for me. I will tell you all about Epping Forest when I was a boy, if you please; and as to my age, I'm not a fine lady, you know, so why shouldn't I tell you? I'm hard on fifty-six.'*

In spite of the recent lecture on good manners, the weaver could not help giving a long 'whew' of astonishment, and the others were so amused by his *naïveté* that the merriment flitted all over their faces, though for courtesy's sake they forbore actual laughter; while I looked from one to the other in a puzzled manner, and at last said:

'Tell me, please, what is amiss: you know I want to learn from you. And please laugh; only tell me.'

Well, they *did* laugh, and I joined them again, for the above-stated reasons. But at last the pretty woman said coaxingly—

'Well, well, he *is* rude, poor fellow! but you see I may as well tell you what he is thinking about: he means that you look rather old for your age. But surely there need be no wonder in that, since you have been travelling; and clearly from all you have been saying, in unsocial countries. It has often been said, and no doubt truly, that one ages very quickly if one lives amongst unhappy people. Also they say that southern England is a good place for keeping good looks.' She blushed and said: 'How old am I, do you think?'

'Well,' quoth I, 'I have always been told that a woman is as old as she looks, so without offence or flattery, I should say that you were twenty.'

She laughed merrily, and said, 'I am well served out for fishing for compliments, since I have to tell you the truth, to wit, that I am forty-two.'

I stared at her, and drew musical laughter from her again; but I might well stare, for there was not a careful line on her face; her skin was as smooth as ivory, her cheeks full and round, her lips as red as the roses she had brought in; her beautiful arms, which she had bared for her work, firm and well-knit from shoulder to wrist. She blushed a little under my gaze, though it was clear that she had taken me for a man of eighty; so to pass it off I said—

'Well, you see, the old saw is proved right again, and I ought not to have let you tempt me into asking you a rude question.'

She laughed again, and said: 'Well, lads, old and young, I must get to my work now. We shall be rather busy here presently; and I want to clear it off soon, for I began to read a pretty old book yesterday, and I want to get on with it this morning: so good-bye for the present.'

She waved a hand to us, and stepped lightly down the hall, taking (as Scott says)* at least part of the sun from our table as she went.

When she was gone, Dick said: 'Now, guest, won't you ask a question or two of our friend here? It is only fair that you should have your turn.'

'I shall be very glad to answer them,' said the weaver.

'If I ask you any questions, sir,' said I, 'they will not be very severe; but since I hear that you are a weaver, I should like to ask you something about that craft, as I am—or was—interested in it.'

'Oh,' said he, 'I shall not be of much use to you there, I'm afraid. I only do the most mechanical kind of weaving, and am in fact but a poor craftsman, unlike Dick here. Then besides the weaving, I do a little with machine printing and composing, though I am little use at the finer kinds of printing; and moreover machine printing is beginning to die out, along with the waning of the plague of book-making; so I have had to turn to other things that I have a taste for, and have taken to mathematics; and also I am writing a sort of antiquarian book about the peaceable and private history, so to say, of the end of the nineteenth century,—more for the sake of giving a picture of the country before the fighting began than for anything else. That was why I asked you those questions about Epping Forest. You have rather puzzled me, I confess, though your information was so interesting. But later on, I hope, we may have some more talk together, when our friend Dick isn't here. I know he thinks me rather a grinder,* and despises me for not being very deft with my hands: that's the way nowadays. From what I have read of the nineteenth century literature (and I have read a good deal), it is clear to me that this is a kind of revenge for the stupidity of that day, which despised everybody who *could* use his hands. But, Dick, old fellow, *Ne quid nimis!** Don't overdo it!'

'Come now,' said Dick, 'am I likely to? Am I not the most tolerant man in the world? Am I not quite contented so long as you don't make me learn mathematics, or go into your new science of æsthetics, and let me do a little practical æsthetics with my gold and steel, and the blowpipe and the nice little hammer? But, hillo! here come another questioner for you, my poor guest. I say, Bob, you must help me defend him now.'

'Here, Boffin,' he cried out, after a pause; 'here we are, if you must have it!'

I looked over my shoulder, and saw something flash and gleam in the sunlight that lay across the hall; so I turned round, and at my ease saw a splendid figure slowly sauntering over the pavement; a man whose surcoat was embroidered most copiously as well as elegantly, so that the sun flashed back from him as if he had been clad in golden armour. The man himself was tall, dark-haired, and exceedingly handsome, and though his face was no less kindly in expression than that of the others, he moved with that somewhat haughty mien which great beauty is apt to give to both men and women. He came and sat down at our table with a smiling face, stretching out his long legs and hanging his arm over the chair in the slowly graceful way which tall and well-built people may use without affectation. He was a man in the prime of life, but looked as happy as a child who has just got a new toy. He bowed gracefully to me and said—

'I see clearly that you are the guest, of whom Annie has just told me, who have come from some distant country that does not know of us, or our ways of life. So I daresay you would not mind answering me a few questions; for you see—'

Here Dick broke in: 'No, please, Boffin! let it alone for the present. Of course you want the guest to be happy and comfortable; and how can that be if he has to trouble himself with answering all sorts of questions while he is still confused with the new customs and people about him? No, no: I am going to take him where he can ask questions himself, and have them answered; that is, to my great-grandfather in Bloomsbury: and I am sure you can't have anything to say against that. So instead of bothering, you had much better go out to James Allen's* and get a carriage for me, as I shall drive him up myself; and please tell Jim to let me have the old grey, for I can drive a wherry* much better than a carriage. Jump up, old fellow, and don't be disappointed; our guest will keep himself for you and your stories.'

I stared at Dick; for I wondered at his speaking to such a dignified-looking personage so familiarly, not to say curtly; for I thought that this Mr. Boffin, in spite of his well-known name out of Dickens,* must be at the least a senator of these strange people. However, he got up and said, 'All right, old oar-wearer, whatever you like; this is not one of my busy days; and though' (with a condescending bow to me) 'my pleasure of a talk with this learned guest is put off, I admit that he ought to see your worthy kinsman as soon as possible. Besides, perhaps he will be the better able to answer *my* questions after his own have been answered.'

And therewith he turned and swung himself out of the hall.

When he was well gone, I said: 'Is it wrong to ask what Mr. Boffin is? whose name, by the way, reminds me of many pleasant hours passed in reading Dickens.'

Dick laughed. 'Yes, yes,' said he, 'as it does us. I see you take the allusion. Of course his real name is not Boffin, but Henry Johnson; we only call him Boffin as a joke, partly because he is a dustman, and partly because he will dress so showily, and get as much gold on him as a baron of the Middle Ages. As why should he not if he likes? only we are his special friends, you know, so of course we jest with him.'

I held my tongue for some time after that; but Dick went on:

'He is a capital fellow, and you can't help liking him; but he has a weakness: he will spend his time in writing reactionary novels, and is very proud of getting the local colour right, as he calls it; and as he thinks you come from some forgotten corner of the earth, where people are unhappy, and consequently interesting to a story-teller, he thinks he might get some information out of you. O, he will be quite straightforward with you, for that matter. Only for your own comfort beware of him!'

'Well, Dick,' said the weaver, doggedly, 'I think his novels are very good.'

'Of course you do,' said Dick; 'birds of a feather flock together; mathematics and antiquarian novels stand on much the same footing. But here he comes again.'

And in effect the Golden Dustman hailed us from the hall-door; so we all got up and went into the porch, before which, with a strong grey horse in the shafts, stood a carriage ready for us which I could not help noticing. It was light and handy, but had none of that sickening vulgarity which I had known as inseparable from the carriages of our time, especially the 'elegant' ones, but was as graceful and pleasant in line as a Wessex wagon.* We got in, Dick and I. The girls, who had come into the porch to see us off, waved their hands to us; the weaver nodded kindly; the dustman bowed as gracefully as a troubadour; Dick shook the reins, and we were off.

CHAPTER IV
A MARKET BY THE WAY

We turned away from the river at once, and were soon in the main road that runs through Hammersmith. But I should have had no guess as to where I was, if I had not started from the waterside; for King Street* was gone, and the highway ran through wide sunny meadows and garden-like tillage. The Creek,* which we crossed at once, had been rescued from its culvert, and as we went over its pretty bridge we saw its waters, yet swollen by the tide, covered with gay boats of different sizes. There were houses about, some on the road, some amongst the fields with pleasant lanes leading down to them, and each surrounded by a teeming garden. They were all pretty in design, and as solid as might be, but countryfied in appearance, like yeomen's dwellings; some of them of red brick like those by the river, but more of timber and plaster, which were by the necessity of their construction so like mediæval houses of the same materials that I fairly felt as if I were alive in the fourteenth century; a sensation helped out by the costume of the people that we met or passed, in whose dress there was nothing 'modern.' Almost everybody was gaily dressed, but especially the women, who were so well-looking, or even so handsome, that I could scarcely refrain my tongue from calling my companion's attention to the fact. Some faces I saw that were thoughtful, and in these I noticed great nobility of expression, but none that had a glimmer of unhappiness, and the greater part (we came upon a good many people) were frankly and openly joyous.

I thought I knew the Broadway* by the lie of the roads that still met there. On the north side of the road was a range of buildings and courts, low, but very handsomely built and ornamented, and in that way forming a great contrast to the unpretentiousness of the houses round about; while above this lower building rose the steep lead-covered roof and the buttresses and higher part of the wall of a great hall, of a splendid and exuberant style of architecture, of which one can say little more than that it seemed to me to embrace the best qualities of the Gothic of northern Europe with those of the Saracenic and Byzantine,* though there was no copying of any one of these styles. On the other, the south side, of the road was an octagonal building with a high roof, not unlike the Baptistry at Florence* in outline, except that it was surrounded by a lean-to that clearly made an arcade or cloisters to it: it also was most delicately ornamented.

This whole mass of architecture which we had come upon so suddenly from amidst the pleasant fields was not only exquisitely beautiful in itself, but it bore upon it the expression of such generosity and abundance of life that I was exhilarated to a pitch that I had never yet reached. I fairly chuckled for pleasure. My friend seemed to understand it, and sat looking on me with a pleased and affectionate interest. We had pulled up amongst a crowd of carts, wherein sat handsome healthy-looking people, men, women, and children very gaily dressed, and which were clearly market carts, as they were full of very tempting-looking country produce.

I said, 'I need not ask if this is a market, for I see clearly that it is; but what market is it that it is so splendid? And what is the glorious hall there, and what is the building on the south side?'

'O,' said he, 'it is just our Hammersmith market; and I am glad you like it so much, for we are really proud of it. Of course the hall inside is our winter Mote-House;* for in summer we mostly meet in the fields down by the river opposite Barn Elms. The building on our right hand is our theatre: I hope you like it.'

'I should be a fool if I didn't,' said I.

He blushed a little as he said: 'I am glad of that, too, because I had a hand in it; I made the great doors, which are of damascened bronze. We will look at them later in the day, perhaps: but we ought to be getting on now. As to the market, this is not one of our busy days; so we shall do better with it another time, because you will see more people.'

I thanked him, and said: 'Are these the regular country people? What very pretty girls there are amongst them.'

As I spoke, my eye caught the face of a beautiful woman, tall, dark-haired, and white-skinned, dressed in a pretty light-green dress in honour of the season and the hot day, who smiled kindly on me, and more kindly still, I thought on Dick; so I stopped a minute, but presently went on:

'I ask because I do not see any of the country-looking people I should have expected to see at a market—I mean selling things there.'

'I don't understand,' said he, 'what kind of people you would expect to see; nor quite what you mean by "country" people. These are the neighbours, and that like they run in the Thames valley. There are parts of these islands which are rougher and rainier than we are here, and there people are rougher in their dress; and they themselves are tougher and more hard-bitten than we are to look at. But some people like their looks better than ours; they say they have more character in them—that's the word. Well, it's a matter of taste.—Anyhow, the cross between us and them* generally turns out well,' added he, thoughtfully.

I heard him, though my eyes were turned away from him, for that pretty girl was just disappearing through the gate with her big basket of early peas, and I felt that disappointed kind of feeling which overtakes one when one has seen an interesting or lovely face in the streets which one is never likely to see again; and I was silent a little. At last I said: 'What I mean is, that I haven't seen any poor people about—not one.'

He knit his brows, looked puzzled, and said: 'No, naturally; if anybody is poorly, he is likely to be within doors, or at best crawling about the garden: but I don't know of any one sick at present. Why should you expect to see poorly people on the road?'

'No, no,' I said; 'I don't mean sick people. I mean poor people, you know; rough people.'

'No,' said he, smiling merrily, 'I really do not know. The fact is, you must come along quick to my great-grandfather, who will understand you better than I do. Come on, Greylocks!' Therewith he shook the reins, and we jogged along merrily eastward.

CHAPTER V
CHILDREN ON THE ROAD

Past the Broadway there were fewer houses on either side. We presently crossed a pretty little brook that ran across a piece of land dotted over with trees, and awhile after came to another market and town-hall, as we should call it. Although there was nothing familiar to me in its surroundings, I knew pretty well where we were, and was not surprised when my guide said briefly, 'Kensington Market.'*

Just after this we came into a short street of houses; or rather, one long house on either side of the way, built of timber and plaster, and with a pretty arcade over the footway before it.

Quoth Dick: 'This is Kensington proper. People are apt to gather here rather thick, for they like the romance of the wood; and naturalists haunt it, too; for it is a wild spot even here, what there is of it; for it does not go far to the south: it goes from here northward and west right over Paddington and a little way down Notting Hill: thence it runs north-east to Primrose Hill, and so on; rather a narrow strip of it gets through Kingsland to Stoke-Newington and Clapton, where it spreads out along the heights above the Lea marshes;* on the other side of which, as you know, is Epping Forest holding out a hand to it. This part we are just coming to is called Kensington Gardens; though why "gardens" I don't know.'*

I rather longed to say, 'Well, *I* know'; but there were so many things about me which I did *not* know, in spite of his assumptions, that I thought it better to hold my tongue.

The road plunged at once into a beautiful wood spreading out on either side, but obviously much further on the north side, where even the oaks and sweet chestnuts were of a good growth; while the quicker-growing trees (amongst which I thought the planes and sycamores too numerous) were very big and fine-grown.

It was exceedingly pleasant in the dappled shadow, for the day was growing as hot as need be, and the coolness and shade soothed my excited mind into a condition of dreamy pleasure, so that I felt as if I should like to go on for ever through that balmy freshness. My companion seemed to share in my feelings, and let the horse go slower and slower as he sat inhaling the green forest scents, chief amongst which was the smell of the trodden bracken near the wayside.

Romantic as this Kensington wood was, however, it was not lonely. We came on many groups both coming and going, or wandering in the edges of the wood. Amongst these were many children from six or eight years old up to sixteen or seventeen. They seemed to me to be especially fine specimens of their race, and were clearly enjoying themselves to the utmost; some of them were hanging about little tents pitched on the greensward, and by some of these fires were burning, with pots hanging over them gipsy fashion. Dick explained to me that there were scattered houses in the forest, and indeed we caught a glimpse of one or two. He said they were mostly quite small, such as used to be called cottages when there were slaves in the land, but they were pleasant enough and fitting for the wood.

'They must be pretty well stocked with children,' said I, pointing to the many youngsters about the way.

'O,' said he, 'these children do not all come from the near houses, the woodland houses, but from the countryside generally. They often make up parties, and come to play in the woods for weeks together in summer-time, living in tents, as you see. We rather encourage them to it; they learn to do things for themselves, and get to notice the wild creatures; and, you see, the less they stew inside houses the better for them. Indeed, I must tell you that many grown people will go to live in the forests through the summer; though they for the most part go to the bigger ones, like Windsor, or the Forest of the Dean,* or the northern wastes. Apart from the other pleasures of it, it gives them a little rough work, which I am sorry to say is getting somewhat scarce for these last fifty years.'

He broke off, and then said, 'I tell you all this, because I see that if I talk I must be answering questions, which you are thinking, even if you are not speaking them out; but my kinsman will tell you more about it.'

I saw that I was likely to get out of my depth again, and so merely for the sake of tiding over an awkwardness and to say something, I said—

'Well, the youngsters here will be all the fresher for school when the summer gets over and they have to go back again.'

'School?' he said; 'yes, what do you mean by that word? I don't see how it can have anything to do with children. We talk, indeed, of a school of herring, and a school of painting, and in the former sense we might talk of a school of children—but otherwise,' said he, laughing, 'I must own myself beaten.'

Hang it! thought I, I can't open my mouth without digging up some new complexity. I wouldn't try to set my friend right in his etymology; and I thought I had best say nothing about the boy-farms which I had been used to call schools, as I saw pretty clearly that they had disappeared; and so I said after a little fumbling, 'I was using the word in the sense of a system of education'*

'Education?' said he, meditatively, 'I know enough Latin to know that the word must come from *educere*, to lead out; and I have heard it used; but I have never met anybody who could give me a clear explanation of what it means.'

You may imagine how my new friends fell in my esteem when I heard this frank avowal; and I said, rather contemptuously, 'Well, education means a system of teaching young people.'

'Why not old people also?' said he with a twinkle in his eye. 'But,' he went on, 'I can assure you our children learn, whether they go through a "system of teaching" or not. Why you will not find one of these children about here, boy or girl, who cannot swim; and every one of them has been used to tumbling about the little forest ponies—there's one of them now! They all of them know how to cook; the bigger lads can mow; many can thatch and do odd jobs at carpentering; or they know how to keep shop. I can tell you they know plenty of things.'

'Yes, but their mental education, the teaching of their minds,' said I, kindly translating my phrase.

'Guest,' said he, 'perhaps you have not learned to do these things I have been speaking about; and if that's the case, don't you run away with the idea that it doesn't take some skill to do them, and doesn't give plenty of work for one's mind: you would change your opinion if you saw a Dorsetshire lad thatching, for instance. But, however, I understand you to be speaking of book-learning; and as to that, it is a simple affair. Most children, seeing books lying about, manage to read by the time they are four years old; though I am told it has not always been so. As to writing, we do not encourage them to scrawl too early (though scrawl a little they will), because it gets them into a habit of ugly writing; and what's the use of a lot of ugly writing being done, when rough printing can be done so easily. You understand that handsome writing we like, and many people will write their books out when they make them, or get them written; I mean books of which only a few copies are needed—poems, and such like, you know.* However, I am wandering from my lambs;* but you must excuse me, for I am interested in this matter of writing, being myself a fair-writer.'

'Well,' said I, 'about the children; when they know how to read and write, don't they learn something else—languages, for instance?'

'Of course,' he said; 'sometimes even before they can read, they can talk French, which is the nearest language talked on the other side of the water; and they soon get to know German also, which is talked by a huge number of communes and colleges on the mainland. These are the principal languages we speak in these islands, along with English or Welsh, or Irish, which is another form of Welsh; and children pick them up very quickly, because their elders all know them; and besides our guests from over sea often bring their children with them, and the little ones get together, and rub their speech into one another.'

'And the older languages?' said I.

'O, yes,' said he, 'they mostly learn Latin and Greek along with the modern ones, when they do anything more than merely pick up the latter.'

'And history?' said I; 'how do you teach history?'

'Well,' said he, 'when a person can read, of course he reads what he likes to; and he can easily get someone to tell him what are the best books to read on such or such a subject, or to explain what he doesn't understand in the books when he is reading them.'

'Well,' said I, 'what else do they learn? I suppose they don't all learn history?'

'No, no,' said he; 'some don't care about it; in fact, I don't think many do. I have heard my great-grandfather say that it is mostly in periods of turmoil and strife and confusion that people care much about history; and you know,' said my friend, with an amiable smile, 'we are not like that now. No; many people study facts about the make of things and the matters of cause and effect, so that knowledge increases on us, if that be good; and some, as you heard about friend Bob yonder, will spend time over mathematics. 'Tis no use forcing people's tastes.'

Said I: 'But you don't mean that children learn all these things?'

Said he: 'That depends on what you mean by children; and also you must remember how much they differ. As a rule, they don't do much reading, except for a few story-books, till they are about fifteen years old; we don't encourage early bookishness: though you will find some children who *will* take to books very early; which perhaps is not good for them; but it's no use thwarting them; and very often it doesn't last long with them, and they find their level before they are twenty years old. You see, children are mostly given to imitating their elders, and when they see most people about them engaged in genuinely amusing work, like house-building and street-paving, and gardening, and the like, that is what they want to be doing; so I don't think we need fear having too many book-learned men.'

What could I say? I sat and held my peace, for fear of fresh entanglements. Besides, I was using my eyes with all my might, wondering as the old horse jogged on, when I should come into London proper, and what it would be like now.

But my companion couldn't let his subject quite drop, and went on meditatively:

'After all, I don't know that it does them much harm, even if they do grow up book-students. Such people as that, 'tis a great pleasure seeing them so happy over work which is not much sought for. And besides, these students are generally such pleasant people; so kind and sweet-tempered; so humble, and at the same time so anxious to teach everybody all that they know. Really, I like those that I have met prodigiously.'

This seemed to me such *very* queer talk that I was on the point of asking him another question; when just as we came to the top of a rising ground, down a long glade of the wood on my right I caught sight of a stately building whose outline was familiar to me, and I cried out, 'Westminster Abbey!'*

'Yes,' said Dick, 'Westminster Abbey—what there is left of it.'

'Why, what have you done with it?' quoth I in terror.

'What have *we* done with it?' said he; 'nothing much, save clean it. But you know the whole outside was spoiled centuries ago: as to the inside, that remains in its beauty after the great clearance, which took place over a hundred years ago, of the beastly monuments to fools and knaves,* which once blocked it up, as great-grandfather says.'

We went on a little further, and I looked to the right again, and said, in a rather doubtful tone of voice, 'Why, there are the Houses of Parliament! Do you still use them?'*

He burst out laughing, and was some time before he could control himself; then he clapped me on the back and said:

'I take you, neighbour; you may well wonder at our keeping them standing, and I know something about that, and my old kinsman has given me books to read about the strange game that they played there. Use them! Well, yes, they are used for a sort of subsidiary market, and a storage place for manure, and they are handy for that, being on the water-side. I believe it was intended to pull them down quite at the beginning of our days; but there was, I am told, a queer antiquarian society, which had done some service in past times, and which straightway set up its pipe* against their destruction, as it has done with many other buildings, which most people looked upon as worthless, and public nuisances; and it was so energetic, and had such good reasons to give, that it generally gained its point; and I must say that when all is said I am glad of it: because you know at the worst these silly old buildings serve as a kind of foil to the beautiful ones which we build now. You will see several others in these parts; the place my great-grandfather lives in, for instance, and a big building called St. Paul's.* And you see, in this matter we need not grudge a few poorish buildings standing, because we can always build elsewhere; nor need we be anxious as to the breeding of pleasant work in such matters, for there is always room for more and more work in a new building, even without making it pretentious. For instance, elbow-room *within* doors is to me so delightful that if I were driven to it I would almost sacrifice out-door space to it. Then, of course, there is the ornament, which, as we must all allow, may easily be overdone in mere living houses, but can hardly be in mote-halls and markets, and so forth. I must tell you, though, that my great-grandfather sometimes tells me I am a little cracked on this subject of fine building; and indeed I *do* think that the energies of mankind are chiefly of use to them for such work; for in that direction I can see no end to the work, while in many others a limit does seem possible.'

CHAPTER VI

A LITTLE SHOPPING

As he spoke, we came suddenly out of the woodland into a short street of handsomely built houses, which my companion named to me at once as Piccadilly:* the lower part of these I should have called shops, if it had not been that, as far as I could see, the people were ignorant of the arts of buying and selling. Wares were displayed in their finely designed fronts, as if to tempt people in, and people stood and looked at them, or went in and came out with parcels under their arms, just like the real thing. On each side of the street ran an elegant arcade to protect foot-passengers, as in some of the old Italian cities. About half-way down, a huge building of the kind I was now prepared to expect told me that this also was a centre of some kind, and had its special public buildings.

Said Dick: 'Here, you see, is another market on a different plan from most others: the upper stories of these houses are used for guest-houses; for people from all over the country are apt to drift up hither from time to time, as folk are very thick upon the ground, which you will see evidence of presently, and there are people who are fond of crowds, though I can't say that I am.'

I couldn't help smiling to see how long a tradition would last. Here was the ghost of London still asserting itself as a centre,—an intellectual centre, for aught I knew. However, I said nothing, except that I asked him to drive very slowly, as the things in the booths looked exceedingly pretty.

'Yes,' said he, 'this is a very good market for pretty things, and is mostly kept for the handsomer goods, as the Houses-of-Parliament market, where they set out cabbages and turnips and such like things, along with beer and the rougher kind of wine, is so near.'

Then he looked at me curiously, and said, 'Perhaps you would like to do a little shopping, as 'tis called.'

I looked at what I could see of my rough blue duds,* which I had plenty of opportunity of contrasting with the gay attire of the citizens we had come across; and I thought that if, as seemed likely, I should presently be shown about as a curiosity for the amusement of this most unbusinesslike people, I should like to look a little less like a discharged ship's purser. But in spite of all that had happened, my hand went down to my pocket again, where to my dismay it met nothing metallic except two rusty old keys, and I remembered that amidst our talk in the guest-hall at Hammersmith I had taken the cash out of my pocket to show to the pretty Annie, and had left it lying there. My face fell fifty per cent., and Dick, beholding me, said rather sharply—

'Hilloa, Guest! what's the matter now? Is it a wasp?'

'No,' said I, 'but I've left it behind.'

'Well,' said he, 'whatever you have left behind, you can get in this market again, so don't trouble yourself about it.'

I had come to my senses by this time, and remembering the astounding customs of this country, had no mind for another lecture on social economy and the Edwardian coinage; so I said only—

'My clothes—Couldn't I? You see—What do you think could be done about them?'

He didn't seem in the least inclined to laugh, but said quite gravely:

'O don't get new clothes yet. You see, my great-grandfather is an antiquarian, and he will want to see you just as you are. And, you know, I mustn't preach to you, but surely it wouldn't be right for you to take away people's pleasure of studying your attire, by just going and making yourself like everybody else. You feel that, don't you?' said he, earnestly.

I did *not* feel it my duty to set myself up for a scarecrow amidst this beauty-loving people, but I saw I had got across some ineradicable prejudice, and that it wouldn't do to quarrel with my new friend. So I merely said 'O certainly, certainly.'

'Well,' said he, pleasantly, 'you may as well see what the inside of these booths is like: think of something you want.'

Said I: 'Could I get some tobacco and a pipe?'

'Of course,' said he; 'what was I thinking of, not asking you before? Well, Bob is always telling me that we non-smokers are a selfish lot, and I'm afraid he is right. But come along; here is a place just handy.'

Therewith he drew rein and jumped down, and I followed. A very handsome woman, splendidly clad in figured silk, was slowly passing by, looking into the windows as she went. To her quoth Dick: 'Maiden, would you kindly hold our horse while we go in for a little while?' She nodded to us with a kind smile, and fell to patting the horse with her pretty hand.

'What a beautiful creature!' said I to Dick as we entered.

'What, old Greylocks?' said he, with a sly grin.

'No, no,' said I; 'Goldylocks,—the lady.'

'Well, so she is,' said he. ''Tis a good job there are so many of them that every Jack may have his Jill: else I fear that we should get fighting for them. Indeed,' said he, becoming very grave, 'I don't say that it does not happen even now, sometimes. For you know love is not a very reasonable thing, and perversity and self-will are commoner than some of our moralists think.' He added, in a still more sombre tone: 'Yes, only a month ago there was a mishap down by us, that in the end cost the lives of two men and a woman, and, as it were, put out the sunlight for us for a while. Don't ask me about it just now; I may tell you about it later on.'

By this time we were within the shop or booth, which had a counter, and shelves on the walls, all very neat, though without any pretence of showiness, but otherwise not very different to what I had been used to. Within were a couple of children—a brown-skinned boy of about twelve, who sat reading a book, and a pretty little girl of about a year older, who was sitting also reading behind the counter; they were obviously brother and sister.

'Good morning, little neighbours,' said Dick. 'My friend here wants tobacco and a pipe; can you help him?'

'O yes, certainly,' said the girl with a sort of demure alertness which was somewhat amusing. The boy looked up, and fell to staring at my outlandish attire, but presently reddened and turned his head, as if he knew that he was not behaving prettily.

'Dear neighbour,' said the girl, with the most solemn countenance of a child playing at keeping shop, 'what tobacco is it you would like?'

'Latakia,'* quoth I, feeling as if I were assisting at a child's game, and wondering whether I should get anything but make-believe.

But the girl took a dainty little basket from a shelf beside her, went to a jar, and took out a lot of tobacco and put the filled basket down on the counter before me, where I could both smell and see that it was excellent Latakia.

'But you haven't weighed it,' said I, 'and—and how much am I to take?'

'Why,' she said, 'I advise you to cram your bag, because you may be going where you can't get Latakia. Where is your bag?'

I fumbled about, and at last pulled out my piece of cotton print which does duty with me for a tobacco pouch. But the girl looked at it with some disdain, and said—

'Dear neighbour, I can give you something much better than that cotton rag.' And she tripped up the shop and came back presently, and as she passed the boy whispered something in his ear, and he nodded and got up and went out. The girl held up in her finger and thumb a red morocco bag, gaily embroidered, and said, 'There, I have chosen one for you, and you are to have it: it is pretty, and will hold a lot.'

Therewith she fell to cramming it with the tobacco, and laid it down by me and said, 'Now for the pipe: that also you must let me choose for you; there are three pretty ones just come in.'

She disappeared again, and came back with a big-bowled pipe in her hand, carved out of some hard wood very elaborately, and mounted in gold sprinkled with little gems. It was, in short, as pretty and gay a toy as I had ever seen; something like the best kind of Japanese work, but better.

'Dear me!' said I, when I set my eyes on it, 'this is altogether too grand for me, or for anybody but the Emperor of the World. Besides, I shall lose it: I always lose my pipes.'

The child seemed rather dashed, and said, 'Don't you like it, neighbour?'

'O yes,' I said, 'of course I like it.'

'Well, then, take it,' said she, 'and don't trouble about losing it. What will it matter if you do? Somebody is sure to find it, and he will use it, and you can get another.'

I took it out of her hand to look at it, and while I did so, forgot my caution, and said, 'But however am I to pay for such a thing as this?'

Dick laid his hand on my shoulder as I spoke, and turning I met his eyes with a comical expression in them, which warned me against another exhibition of extinct commercial morality; so I reddened and held my tongue, while the girl simply looked at me with the deepest gravity, as if I were a foreigner blundering in my speech, for she clearly didn't understand me a bit.

'Thank you so very much,' I said at last, effusively, as I put the pipe in my pocket, not without a qualm of doubt as to whether I shouldn't find myself before a magistrate presently.

'O, you are so very welcome,' said the little lass, with an affectation of grown-up manners at their best which was very quaint. 'It is such a pleasure to serve dear old gentlemen like you; especially when one can see at once that you have come from far over sea.'

'Yes, my dear,' quoth I, 'I have been a great traveller.'

As I told this lie from pure politeness, in came the lad again, with a tray in his hands, on which I saw a long flask and two beautiful glasses. 'Neighbours,' said the girl (who did all the talking, her brother being very shy, clearly), 'please to drink a glass to us before you go, since we do not have guests like this every day.'

Therewith the boy put the tray on the counter and solemnly poured out a straw-coloured wine into the long bowls. Nothing loth, I drank, for I was thirsty with the hot day; and thinks I, I am yet in the world, and the grapes of the Rhine have not yet lost their flavour; for if ever I drank good Steinberg,* I drank it that morning; and I made a mental note to ask Dick how they managed to make fine wine when there were no longer labourers compelled to drink rot-gut instead of the fine wine which they themselves made.

'Don't you drink a glass to us, dear little neighbours?' said I.

'I don't drink wine,' said the lass; 'I like lemonade better: but I wish your health!'

'And I like ginger-beer better,' said the little lad.

Well, well, thought I, neither have children's tastes changed much. And therewith we gave them good day and went out of the booth.

To my disappointment, like a change in a dream, a tall old man was holding our horse instead of the beautiful woman. He explained to us that the maiden could not wait and that he had taken her place; and he winked at us and laughed when he saw how our faces fell, so that we had nothing for it but to laugh also.

'Where are you going?' said he to Dick.

'To Bloomsbury,' said Dick.

'If you two don't want to be alone, I'll come with you,' said the old man.

'All right,' said Dick, 'tell me when you want to get down and I'll stop for you. Let's get on.'

So we got under way again; and I asked if children generally waited on people in the markets. 'Often enough,' said he, 'when it isn't a matter of dealing with heavy weights, but by no means always. The children like to amuse themselves with it, and it is good for them, because they handle a lot of diverse wares and get to learn about them, how they are made, and where they come from, and so on. Besides, it is such very easy work that anybody can do it. It is said that in the early days of our epoch there were a good many people who were hereditarily afflicted with a disease called Idleness, because they were the direct descendants of those who in the bad times used to force other people to work for them—the people, you know, who are called slave-holders or employers of labour in the history books. Well, these Idleness-stricken people used to serve booths *all* their time, because they were fit for so little. Indeed, I believe that at one time they were actually *compelled* to do some such work, because they, especially the women, got so ugly and produced such ugly children if their disease was not treated sharply, that the neighbours couldn't stand it. However, I am happy to say that all that is gone by now; the disease is either extinct, or exists in such a mild form that a short course of aperient medicine carries it off. It is sometimes called the Blue-devils now, or the Mulleygrubs.* Queer names, ain't they?'

'Yes,' said I, pondering much. But the old man broke in:

'Yes, all that is true, neighbour; and I have seen some of those poor women grown old. But my father used to know some of them when they were young; and he said that they were as little like young women as might be: they had hands like bunches of skewers, and wretched little arms like sticks; and waists like hour-glasses, and thin lips and peaked noses and pale cheeks; and they were always pretending to be offended at anything you said or did to them. No wonder they bore ugly children, for no one except men like them could be in love with them—poor things!'

He stopped, and seemed to be musing on his past life, and then said:

'And do you know, neighbours, that once on a time people were still anxious about that disease of Idleness: at one time we gave ourselves a great deal of trouble in trying to cure people of it. Have you not read any of the medical books on the subject?'

'No,' said I; for the old man was speaking to me.

'Well,' said he, 'it was thought at the time that it was the survival of the old mediæval disease of leprosy: it seems it was very catching, for many of the people afflicted by it were much secluded, and were waited upon by a special class of diseased persons queerly dressed up, so that they might be known. They wore amongst other garments, breeches made of worsted velvet, that stuff that used to be called plush some years ago.'

All this seemed very interesting to me, and I should like to have made the old man talk more. But Dick got rather restive under so much ancient history: besides, I suspect he wanted to keep me as fresh as he could for his great-grandfather. So he burst out laughing at last, and said: 'Excuse me, neighbours, but I can't help it. Fancy people not liking to work!—it's too ridiculous. Why, even you like to work, old fellow—sometimes,' said he, affectionately patting the old horse with the whip. 'What a queer disease! it may well be called Mulleygrubs!'

And he laughed out again most boisterously; rather too much so, I thought, for his usual good manners; and I laughed with him for company's sake, but from the teeth outward only; for *I* saw nothing funny in people not liking to work, as you may well imagine.

CHAPTER VII

TRAFALGAR SQUARE

And now again I was busy looking about me, for we were quite clear of Piccadilly Market, and were in a region of elegantly-built much ornamented houses, which I should have called villas if they had been ugly and pretentious, which was very far from being the case. Each house stood in a garden carefully cultivated, and running over with flowers. The blackbirds were singing their best amidst the garden-trees, which, except for a bay here and there, and occasional groups of limes, seemed to be all fruit-trees: there were a great many cherry-trees, now all laden with fruit, and several times as we passed by a garden we were offered baskets of fine fruit by children and young girls. Amidst all these gardens and houses it was of course impossible to trace the sites of the old streets: but it seemed to me that the main roadways were the same as of old.

We came presently into a large open space, sloping somewhat toward the south, the sunny site of which had been taken advantage of for planting an orchard, mainly, as I could see, of apricot-trees, in the midst of which was a pretty gay little structure of wood, painted and gilded, that looked like a refreshment-stall. From the southern side of the said orchard ran a long road, chequered over with the shadow of tall old pear trees, at the end of which showed the high tower of the Parliament House, or Dung Market.

A strange sensation came over me; I shut my eyes to keep out the sight of the sun glittering on this fair abode of gardens, and for a moment there passed before them a phantasmagoria of another day. A great space surrounded by tall ugly houses, with an ugly church at the corner and a nondescript ugly cupolaed building at my back;* the roadway thronged with a sweltering and excited crowd, dominated by omnibuses crowded with spectators. In the midst a paved befountained square, populated only by a few men dressed in blue, and a good many singularly ugly bronze images (one on top of a tall column). The said square guarded up to the edge of the roadway by a four-fold line of big men clad in blue, and across the southern roadway the helmets of a band of horse-soldiers, dead white in the greyness of the chilly November afternoon—*

I opened my eyes to the sunlight again and looked round me, and cried out among the whispering trees and odorous blossoms, 'Trafalgar Square!'*

'Yes,' said Dick, who had drawn rein again, 'so it is. I don't wonder at your finding the name ridiculous: but after all, it was nobody's business to alter it, since the name of a dead folly doesn't bite. Yet sometimes I think we might have given it a name which would have commemorated the great battle which was fought on the spot itself in 1952,—*that* was important enough, if the historians don't lie.'

'Which they generally do, or at least did,' said the old man. 'For instance what can you make of this, neighbours? I have read a muddled account in a book—O a stupid book!—called James' Social Democratic History,* of a fight which took place here in or about the year 1887 (I am bad at dates). Some people, says this story, were going to hold a ward-mote* here, or some such thing, and the Government of London, or the Council, or the Commission, or what not other barbarous half-hatched body of fools, fell upon these citizens (as they were then called) with the armed hand. That seems too ridiculous to be true; but according to this version of the story, nothing much came of it, which certainly *is* too ridiculous to be true.'

'Well,' quoth I, 'but after all your Mr. James is right so far, and it *is* true; except that there was no fighting, merely unarmed and peaceable people attacked by ruffians armed with bludgeons.'

'And they put up with that?' said Dick, with the first unpleasant expression I had seen on his good-tempered face.

Said I reddening: 'We *had* to put up with it; we couldn't help it.'

The old man looked at me keenly, and said: 'You seem to know a great deal about it, neighbour! And is it really true that nothing came of it?'

'This came of it,' said I, 'that a good many people were sent to prison because of it.'

'What, of the bludgeoners?' said the old man. 'Poor devils!'

'No, no,' said I, 'of the bludgeoned.'

Said the old man rather severely: 'Friend, I expect that you have been reading some rotten collection of lies, and have been taken in by it too easily.'

'I assure you,' said I, 'what I have been saying is true.'

'Well, well, I am sure you think so, neighbour,' said the old man, 'but I don't see why you should be so cocksure.'

As I couldn't explain why, I held my tongue. Meanwhile Dick, who had been sitting with knit brows, cogitating, spoke at last, and said gently and rather sadly:

'How strange to think that there have been men like ourselves, and living in this beautiful and happy country, who I suppose had feelings and affections like ourselves, who could yet do such dreadful things.'

'Yes,' said I, in a didactic tone; 'yet after all, even those days were a great improvement on the days that had gone before them. Have you not read of the Mediæval period, and the ferocity of its criminal laws; and how in those days men fairly seemed to have enjoyed tormenting their fellow-men?—nay, for the matter of that, they made their God a tormentor and a jailer rather than anything else.'

'Yes,' said Dick, 'there are good books on that period also, some of which I have read. But as to the great improvement of the nineteenth century, I don't see it. After all, the Mediæval folk acted after their conscience, as your remark about their God (which is true) shows, and they were ready to bear what they inflicted on others; whereas the nineteenth century ones were hypocrites, and pretended to be humane, and yet went on tormenting those whom they dared to treat so by shutting them up in prison, for no reason at all, except that they were what they themselves, the prison-masters, had forced them to be. O, it's horrible to think of!'

'But perhaps,' said I, 'they did not know what the prisons were like.'*

Dick seemed roused, and even angry. 'More shame for them,' said he, 'when you and I know it all these years afterwards. Look you, neighbour, they couldn't fail to know what a disgrace a prison is to the Commonwealth at the best, and that their prisons were a good step on towards being at the worst.'

Quoth I: 'But have you no prisons at all now?'

As soon as the words were out of my mouth, I felt that I had made a mistake, for Dick flushed red and frowned, and the old man looked surprised and pained; and presently Dick said angrily, yet as if restraining himself somewhat—

'Man alive! how can you ask such a question? Have I not told you that we know what a prison means by the undoubted evidence of really trustworthy books, helped out by our own imaginations? And haven't you specially called me to notice that the people about the roads and streets look happy? and how could they look happy if they knew that their neighbours were shut up in prison, while they bore such things quietly? And if there were people in prison, you couldn't hide it from folk, like you may an occasional man-slaying; because that isn't done of set purpose, with a lot of people backing up the slayer in cold blood, as this prison business is. Prisons, indeed! O no, no, no!'

He stopped, and began to cool down, and said in a kind voice: 'But forgive me! I needn't be so hot about it, since there are *not* any prisons: I'm afraid you will think the worse of me for losing my temper. Of course, you, coming from the outlands, cannot be expected to know about these things. And now I'm afraid I have made you feel uncomfortable.'

In a way he had; but he was so generous in his heat, that I liked him the better for it, and I said: 'No, really 'tis all my fault for being so stupid. Let me change the subject, and ask you what the stately building is on our left just showing at the end of that grove of plane trees?'

'Ah,' he said, 'that is an old building built before the middle of the twentieth century,* and as you see, in a queer fantastic style not over beautiful; but there are some fine things inside it, too, mostly pictures, some very old. It is called the National Gallery; I have sometimes puzzled as to what the name means: anyhow, nowadays wherever there is a place where pictures are kept as curiosities permanently it is called a National Gallery, perhaps after this one. Of course there are a good many of them up and down the country.'

I didn't try to enlighten him, feeling the task too heavy; but I pulled out my magnificent pipe and fell a-smoking, and the old horse jogged on again. As we went, I said:

'This pipe is a very elaborate toy, and you seem so reasonable in this country, and your architecture is so good, that I rather wonder at your turning out such trivialities.'

It struck me as I spoke that this was rather ungrateful of me, after having received such a fine present; but Dick didn't seem to notice my bad manners, but said:

'Well, I don't know; it *is* a pretty thing, and since nobody need make such things unless they like, I don't see why they shouldn't make them, *if* they like. Of course, if carvers were scarce they would all be busy on the architecture, as you call it, and then these "toys" (a good word) would not be made; but since there are plenty of people who can carve—in fact, almost everybody, and as work is somewhat scarce, or we are afraid it may be, folk do not discourage this kind of petty work.'

He mused a little, and seemed somewhat perturbed; but presently his face cleared, and he said: 'After all, you must admit that the pipe is a very pretty thing, with the little people under the trees all cut so clean and sweet;—too elaborate for a pipe, perhaps, but—well, it is very pretty.'

'Too valuable for its use, perhaps,' said I.

'What's that?' said he; 'I don't understand.'

I was just going in a helpless way to try to make him understand, when we came by the gates of a big rambling building, in which work of some sort seemed going on. 'What building is that?' said I, eagerly; for it was a pleasure amidst all these strange things to see something a little like what I was used to: 'it seems to be a factory.'

'Yes,' he said, 'I think I know what you mean, and that's what it is; but we don't call them factories now, but Banded-workshops; that is, places where people collect who want to work together.'

'I suppose,' said I, 'power of some sort is used there?'

'No, no,' said he. 'Why should people collect together to use power, when they can have it at the places where they live, or hard by, any two or three of them, or any one, for the matter of that? No; folk collect in these Banded-workshops to do hand-work in which working together is necessary or convenient; such work is often very pleasant. In there, for instance, they make pottery and glass,—there, you can see the tops of the furnaces. Well, of course it's handy to have fair-sized ovens and kilns and glass-pots, and a good lot of things to use them for: though of course there are a good many such places, as it would be ridiculous if a man had a liking for pot-making or glass-blowing that he should have to live in one place or be obliged to forego the work he liked.'

'I see no smoke coming from the furnaces,' said I.

'Smoke?' said Dick; 'why should you see smoke?'

I held my tongue, and he went on: 'It's a nice place inside, though as plain as you see outside. As to the crafts, throwing the clay must be jolly work: the glass-blowing is rather a sweltering job; but some folk like it very much indeed; and I don't much wonder: there is such a sense of power, when you have got deft in it, in dealing with the hot metal. It makes a lot of pleasant work,' said he, smiling, 'for however much care you take of such goods, break they will, one day or another, so there is always plenty to do.'

I held my tongue and pondered.*

We came just here on a gang of men road-mending, which delayed us a little; but I was not sorry for it; for all I had seen hitherto seemed a mere part of a summer holiday; and I wanted to see how this folk would set to on a piece of real necessary work. They had been resting, and had only just begun work again as we came up; so that the rattle of the picks was what woke me from my musing. There were about a dozen of them, strong young men, looking much like a boating party at Oxford would have looked* in the days I remembered, and not more troubled with their work: their outer raiment lay on the road-side in an orderly pile under the guardianship of a six-year-old boy, who had his arm thrown over the neck of a big mastiff, who was as happily lazy as if the summer-day had been made for him alone. As I eyed the pile of clothes, I could see the gleam of gold and silk embroidery on it, and judged that some of these workmen had tastes akin to those of the Golden Dustman of Hammersmith. Beside them lay a good big basket that had hints about it of cold pie and wine: a half dozen of young women stood by watching the work or the workers, both of which were worth watching, for the latter smote great strokes and were very deft in their labour, and as handsome clean-built fellows as you might find a dozen of in a summer day. They were laughing and talking merrily with each other and the women, but presently their foreman looked up and saw our way stopped. So he stayed his pick and sang out, 'Spell ho,* mates! here are neighbours want to get past.' Whereon the others stopped also, and drawing around us, helped the old horse by easing our wheels over the half undone road, and then, like men with a pleasant task on hand, hurried back to their work, only stopping to give us a smiling good-day; so that the sound of the picks broke out again before Greylocks had taken to his jog-trot. Dick looked back over his shoulder at them and said:

'They are in luck to-day: it's right down good sport trying how much pick-work one can get into an hour; and I can see those neighbours know their business well. It is not a mere matter of strength getting on quickly with such work; is it, guest?'

'I should think not,' said I, 'but to tell you the truth, I have never tried my hand at it.'

'Really?' said he gravely, 'that seems a pity; it is good work for hardening the muscles, and I like it; though I admit it is pleasanter the second week than the first. Not that I am a good hand at it: the fellows used to chaff me at one job where I was working, I remember, and sing out to me, "Well rowed, stroke!" "Put your back into it, bow!" '

'Not much of a joke,' quoth I.

'Well,' said Dick, 'everything seems like a joke when we have a pleasant spell of work on, and good fellows merry about us; we feel so happy, you know.' Again I pondered silently.

CHAPTER VIII

AN OLD FRIEND

We now turned into a pleasant lane where the branches of great plane-trees nearly met overhead, but behind them lay low houses standing rather close together.

'This is Long Acre,'* quoth Dick; 'so there must once have been a cornfield here. How curious it is that places change so, and yet keep their old names! Just look how thick the houses stand! and they are still going on building, look you!'

'Yes,' said the old man, 'but I think the cornfields must have been built over before the middle of the nineteenth century. I have heard that about here was one of the thickest parts of the town. But I must get down here, neighbours; I have got to call on a friend who lives in the gardens behind this Long Acre. Good-bye and good luck, Guest!'

And he jumped down and strode away vigorously, like a young man.

'How old should you say that neighbour will be?' said I to Dick as we lost sight of him; for I saw that he was old, and yet he looked dry and sturdy like a piece of old oak; a type of old man I was not used to seeing.

'O, about ninety, I should say,' said Dick.

'How long-lived your people must be!' said I.

'Yes,' said Dick, 'certainly we have beaten the threescore-and-ten of the old Jewish proverb-book.* But then you see that was written of Syria, a hot dry country, where people live faster than in our temperate climate. However, I don't think it matters much, so long as a man is healthy and happy while he *is* alive. But now, Guest, we are so near to my old kinsman's dwelling-place that I think you had better keep all future questions for him.'

I nodded a yes; and therewith we turned to the left, and went down a gentle slope through some beautiful rose-gardens, laid out on what I took to be the side of Endell Street.* We passed on, and Dick drew rein an instant as we came across a long straightish road with houses scantily scattered up and down it. He waved his hand right and left, and said, 'Holborn that side, Oxford Road that. This was once a very important part of the crowded city outside the ancient walls of the Roman and Mediæval burg: many of the feudal nobles of the Middle Ages, we are told, had big houses on either side of Holborn. I daresay you remember that the Bishop of Ely's house is mentioned in Shakespeare's play of King Richard III.;* and there are some remains of that still left. However, this road is not of the same importance, now that the ancient city is gone, walls and all.'

He drove on again, while I smiled faintly to think how the

nineteenth century, of which such big words have been said, counted for nothing in the memory of this man, who read Shakespeare and had not forgotten the Middle Ages.

We crossed the road into a short narrow lane between the gardens, and came out again into a wide road, on one side of which was a great and long building, turning its gables away from the highway, which I saw at once was another public group. Opposite to it was a wide space of greenery, without any wall or fence of any kind. I looked through the trees and saw beyond them a pillared portico quite familiar to me—no less old a friend, in fact, than the British Museum.* It rather took my breath away, amidst all the strange things I had seen; but I held my tongue and let Dick speak. Said he:

'Yonder is the British Museum, where my great-grandfather mostly lives; so I won't say much about it. The building on the left is the Museum Market, and I think we had better turn in there for a minute or two; for Greylocks will be wanting his rest and his oats; and I suppose you will stay with my kinsman the greater part of the day; and to say the truth, there may be some one there whom I particularly want to see, and perhaps have a long talk with.'

He blushed and sighed, not altogether with pleasure, I thought; so of course I said nothing, and he turned the horse under an archway which brought us into a very large paved quadrangle, with a big sycamore tree in each corner and a plashing fountain in the midst. Near the fountain were a few market stalls, with awnings over them of gay striped linen cloth, about which some people, mostly women and children, were moving quietly, looking at the goods exposed there. The ground floor of the building round the quadrangle was occupied by a wide arcade or cloister, whose fanciful but strong architecture I could not enough admire. Here also a few people were sauntering or sitting reading on the benches.

Dick said to me apologetically: 'Here, as elsewhere there is little doing to-day; on a Friday you would see it thronged, and gay with people, and in the afternoon there is generally music about the fountain. However, I daresay we shall have a pretty good gathering at our mid-day meal.'

We drove through the quadrangle and by an archway, into a large handsome stable on the other side, where we speedily stalled the old nag and made him happy with horse-meat, and then turned and walked back again through the market, Dick looking rather thoughtful, as it seemed to me.

I noticed that people couldn't help looking at me rather hard; and considering my clothes and theirs, I didn't wonder; but whenever they caught my eye they made me a very friendly sign of greeting.

We walked straight into the forecourt of the Museum, where, except that the railings were gone, and the whispering boughs of the trees were all about, nothing seemed changed; the very pigeons were wheeling about the building and clinging to the ornaments of the pediment as I had seen them of old.

Dick seemed grown a little absent, but he could not forbear giving me an architectural note, and said:

'It is rather an ugly old building, isn't it? Many people have wanted to pull it down and rebuild it: and perhaps if work does really get scarce we may yet do so. But, as my great-grandfather will tell you, it would not be quite a straightforward job; for there are wonderful collections in there of all kinds of antiquities, besides an enormous library with many exceedingly beautiful books in it, and many most useful ones as genuine records, texts of ancient works and the like; and the worry and anxiety, and even risk, there would be in moving all this has saved the buildings themselves. Besides, as we said before, it is not a bad thing to have some record of what our forefathers thought a handsome building. For there is plenty of labour and material in it.'

'I see there is,' said I, 'and I quite agree with you. But now hadn't we better make haste to see your great-grandfather?'

In fact, I could not help seeing that he was rather dallying with the time. He said, 'Yes, we will go into the house in a minute. My kinsmen is too old to do much work in the Museum, where he was a custodian of the books for many years; but he still lives here a good deal; indeed I think,' said he, smiling, 'that he looks upon himself as a part of the books, or the books a part of him, I don't know which.'

He hesitated a little longer, then flushing up, took my hand, and saying, 'Come along, then!' led me toward the door of one of the old official dwellings.

CHAPTER IX
CONCERNING LOVE

'Your kinsman doesn't much care for beautiful buildings, then,' said I, as we entered the rather dreary classical house; which indeed was as bare as need be, except for some big pots of the June flowers which stood about here and there; though it was very clean and nicely whitewashed.

'O, I don't know,' said Dick, rather absently. 'He is getting old, certainly, for he is over a hundred and five, and no doubt he doesn't care about moving. But of course he could live in a prettier house if he liked: he is not obliged to live in any one place any more than any one else. This way, Guest.'

And he led the way upstairs, and opening a door we went into a fair-sized room of the old type, as plain as the rest of the house, with a few necessary pieces of furniture, and those very simple and even rude, but solid and with a good deal of carving about them, well designed but rather crudely executed. At the furthest corner of the room, at a desk near the window, sat a little old man in a roomy oak chair, well becushioned. He was dressed in a sort of Norfolk jacket* of blue serge worn threadbare, with breeches of the same, and grey worsted stockings. He jumped up from his chair, and cried out in a voice of considerable volume for such an old man, 'Welcome, Dick, my lad; Clara is here, and will be more than glad to see you; so keep your heart up.'

'Clara here?' quoth Dick; 'if I had known, I would not have brought—At least, I mean I would—'

He was stuttering and confused, clearly because he was anxious to say nothing to make me feel one too many. But the old man, who had not seen me at first, helped him out by coming forward and saying to me in a kind tone:

'Pray pardon me, for I did not notice that Dick, who is big enough to hide anybody, you know, had brought a friend with him. A most hearty welcome to you! All the more, as I almost hope that you are going to amuse an old man by giving him news from over sea, for I can see that you are come from over the water and far off countries.'

He looked at me thoughtfully, almost anxiously, as he said in a changed voice, 'Might I ask you where you come from, as you are so clearly a stranger?'

I said in an absent way: 'I used to live in England, and now I am come back again; and I slept last night at the Hammersmith Guest House.'

He bowed gravely, but seemed, I thought, a little disappointed with my answer. As for me, I was now looking at him harder than good manners allowed of, perhaps; for in truth his face, dried-apple-like as it was seemed strangely familiar to me; as if I had seen it before—in a looking-glass it might be, said I to myself.*

'Well,' said the old man, 'wherever you come from, you are come among friends. And I see my kinsman Richard Hammond has an air about him as if he had brought you here for me to do something for you. Is that so, Dick?'

Dick, who was getting still more absent-minded and kept looking uneasily at the door, managed to say, 'Well, yes, kinsman: our guest finds things much altered, and cannot understand it; nor can I; so I thought I would bring him to you, since you know more of all that has happened within the last two hundred years than anybody else does.—What's that?'

And he turned toward the door again. We heard footsteps outside; the door opened, and in came a very beautiful young woman, who stopped short on seeing Dick, and flushed as red as a rose, but faced him nevertheless. Dick looked at her hard, and half reached out his hand toward her, and his whole face quivered with emotion.

The old man did not leave them long in this shy discomfort, but said, smiling with an old man's mirth: 'Dick, my lad, and you, my dear Clara, I rather think that we two oldsters are in your way; for I think you will have plenty to say to each other. You had better go into Nelson's room up above; I know he has gone out; and he has just been covering the walls all over with mediæval books, so it will be pretty enough even for you two and your renewed pleasure.'

The girl reached out her hand to Dick, and taking his led him out of the room, looking straight before her; but it was easy to see that her blushes came from happiness, not anger; as, indeed, love is far more self-conscious than wrath.

When the door had shut on them the old man turned to me, still smiling, and said:

'Frankly, my dear guest, you will do me a great service if you are come to set my old tongue wagging. My love of talk still abides with me, or rather grows on me; and though it is pleasant enough to see these youngsters moving about and playing together so seriously, as if the whole world depended on their kisses (as indeed it does somewhat), yet I don't think my tales of the past interest them much. The last harvest, the last baby, the last knot of carving in the market-place is history enough for them. It was different, I think, when I was a lad, when we were not so assured of peace and continuous plenty as we are now—Well, well! Without putting you to the question, let me ask you this: Am I to consider you as an enquirer who knows a little of our modern ways of life, or as one who comes from some place where the very foundations of life are different from ours,—do you know anything or nothing about us?

He looked at me keenly and with growing wonder in his eyes as he spoke; and I answered in a low voice:

'I know only so much of your modern life as I could gather from using my eyes on the way here from Hammersmith, and from asking some questions of Richard Hammond, most of which he could hardly understand.'

The old man smiled at this. 'Then,' said he, 'I am to speak to you as—'

'As if I were a being from another planet,' said I.

The old man, whose name, by the bye, like his kinsman's, was Hammond, smiled and nodded, and wheeling his seat round to me, bade me sit in a heavy oak chair, and said, as he saw my eyes fix on its curious carving:

'Yes, I am much tied to the past, *my* past, you understand. These very pieces of furniture belong to a time before my early days; it was my father who got them made; if they had been done within the last fifty years they would have been much cleverer in execution; but I don't think I should have liked them the better. We were almost beginning again in those days: and they were brisk, hot-headed times. But you hear how garrulous I am: ask me questions, ask me questions about anything, dear guest; since I *must* talk, make my talk profitable to you.'

I was silent for a minute, and then I said, somewhat nervously: 'Excuse me if I am rude; but I am so much interested in Richard, since he has been so kind to me, a perfect stranger, that I should like to ask a question about him.'

'Well,' said old Hammond, 'if he were not "kind," as you call it, to a perfect stranger he would be thought a strange person, and people would be apt to shun him. But ask on, ask on! don't be shy of asking.'

Said I: 'That beautiful girl, is he going to be married to her?'

'Well,' said he, 'yes, he is. He has been married to her once already, and now I should say it is pretty clear that he will be married to her again.'

'Indeed,' quoth I, wondering what that meant.

'Here is the whole tale,' said old Hammond; 'a short one enough; and now I hope a happy one: they lived together two years the first time; were both very young; and then she got it into her head that she was in love with somebody else. So she left poor Dick; I say *poor* Dick, because he had not found any one else. But it did not last long, only about a year. Then she came to me, as she was in the habit of bringing her troubles to the old carle, and asked me how Dick was, and whether he was happy, and all the rest of it. So I saw how the land lay, and said that he was very unhappy, and not at all well; which last at any rate was a lie. There, you can guess the rest. Clara came to have a long talk with me to-day, but Dick will serve her turn much better. Indeed, if he hadn't chanced in upon me to-day I should have had to have sent for him to-morrow.'

'Dear me,' said I. 'Have they any children?'

'Yes,' said he, 'two; they are staying with one of my daughters at present, where, indeed, Clara has mostly been. I wouldn't lose sight of her, as I felt sure they would come together again: and Dick, who is the best of good fellows, really took the matter to heart. You see, he had no other love to run to, as she had. So I managed it all; as I have done with such-like matters before.'

'Ah,' said I, 'no doubt you wanted to keep them out of the Divorce Court: but I suppose it often has to settle such matters.'

'Then you suppose nonsense,' said he. 'I know that there used to be such lunatic affairs as divorce-courts: but just consider; all the cases that came into them were matters of property quarrels: and I think, dear guest,' said he, smiling, 'that though you do come from another planet, you can see from the mere outside look of our world that quarrels about private property could not go on amongst us in our days.'

Indeed, my drive from Hammersmith to Bloomsbury, and all the quiet happy life I had seen so many hints of, even apart from my shopping, would have been enough to tell me that 'the sacred rights of property,' as we used to think of them, were now no more. So I sat silent while the old man took up the thread of the discourse again, and said:

'Well, then, property quarrels being no longer possible, what remains in these matters that a court of law could deal with? Fancy a court for enforcing a contract of passion or sentiment! If such a thing were needed as a *reductio ad absurdum* of the enforcement of contract, such a folly would do that for us.'

He was silent again a little, and then said: 'You must understand once for all that we have changed these matters; or rather, that our way of looking at them has changed, as we have changed within the last two hundred years. We do not deceive ourselves, indeed, or believe that we can get rid of all the trouble that besets the dealings between the sexes. We know that we must face the unhappiness that comes of man and woman confusing the relations between natural passion, and sentiment, and the friendship which, when things go well, softens the awakening from passing illusions: but we are not so mad as to pile up degradation on that unhappiness by engaging in sordid squabbles about livelihood and position, and the power of tyrannising over the children who have been the results of love or lust.'

Again he paused awhile, and again went on: 'Calf love, mistaken for a heroism that shall be life-long, yet early waning into disappointment; the inexplicable desire that comes on a man of riper years to be the all-in-all to some one woman, whose ordinary human kindness and human beauty he has idealised into superhuman perfection, and made the one object of his desire; or lastly the reasonable longing of a strong and thoughtful man to become the most intimate friend of some beautiful and wise woman, the very type of the beauty and glory of the world which we love so well,—as we exult in all the pleasure and exaltation of spirit which goes with these things, so we set ourselves to bear the sorrow which not unseldom goes with them also; remembering those lines of the ancient poet (I quote roughly from memory one of the many translations of the nineteenth century):

'For this the gods have fashioned man's grief and evil day
That still for man hereafter might be the tale and the lay.'*

Well, well, 'tis little likely anyhow that all tales shall be lacking, or all sorrow cured.'

He was silent for some time, and I would not interrupt him. At last he began again: 'But you must know that we of these generations are strong and healthy of body, and live easily; we pass our lives in reasonable strife with nature, exercising not one side of ourselves only, but all sides, taking the keenest pleasure in all the life of the world. So it is a point of honour with us not to be self-centred; not to suppose that the world must cease because one man is sorry; therefore we should think it foolish, or if you will, criminal, to exaggerate these matters of sentiment and sensibility: we are no more inclined to eke out our sentimental sorrows than to cherish our bodily pains; and we recognise that there are other pleasures besides love-making. You must remember, also, that we are long-lived, and that therefore beauty both in man and woman is not so fleeting as it was in the days when we were burdened so heavily by self-inflicted diseases. So we shake off these griefs in a way which perhaps the sentimentalists of other times would think contemptible and unheroic, but which we think necessary and manlike. As on the other hand, therefore, we have ceased to be commercial in our love-matters, so also we have ceased to be *artificially* foolish. The folly which comes by nature, the unwisdom of the immature man, or the older man caught in a trap, we must put up with that, nor are we much ashamed of it; but to be conventionally sensitive or sentimental—my friend, I am old and perhaps disappointed, but at least I think we have cast off *some* of the follies of the older world.'

He paused, as if for some words of mine; but I held my peace: then he went on: 'At least, if we suffer from the tyranny and fickleness of nature or our own want of experience, we neither grimace about it, nor lie. If there must be sundering betwixt those who meant never to sunder, so it must be: but there need be no pretext of unity when the reality of it is gone: nor do we drive those who well know that they are incapable of it to profess an undying sentiment which they cannot really feel: thus it is that as that monstrosity of venal lust is no longer possible, so also it is no longer needed. Don't misunderstand me. You did not seem shocked when I told you that there were no law-courts to enforce contracts of sentiment or passion; but so curiously are men made, that perhaps you will be shocked when I tell you that there is no code of public opinion which takes the place of such courts, and which might be as tyrannical and unreasonable as they were. I do not say that people don't judge their neighbours' conduct, sometimes, doubtless, unfairly. But I do say that there is no unvarying conventional set of rules by which people are judged; no bed of Procrustes* to stretch or cramp their minds and lives; no hypocritical excommunication which people are *forced* to pronounce, either by unconsidered habit, or by the unexpressed threat of the lesser interdict if they are lax in their hypocrisy. Are you shocked now?'

'N-o—no,' said I, with some hesitation. 'It is all so different.'

'At any rate,' said he, 'one thing I think I can answer for: whatever sentiment there is, it is real—and general; it is not confined to people very specially refined. I am also pretty sure, as I hinted to you just now, that there is not by a great way as much suffering involved in these matters either to men or to women as there used to be. But excuse me for being so prolix on this question! You know you asked to be treated like a being from another planet.'

'Indeed I thank you very much,' said I. 'Now may I ask you about the position of women in your society?'

He laughed very heartily for a man of his years, and said: 'It is not without reason that I have got a reputation as a careful student of history. I believe I really do understand "the Emancipation of Women movement" of the nineteenth century. I doubt if any other man now alive does.'

'Well?' said I, a little bit nettled by his merriment.

'Well,' said he, 'of course you will see that all that is a dead controversy now. The men have no longer any opportunity of tyrannising over the women, or the women over the men; both of which things took place in those old times. The women do what they can do best, and what they like best, and the men are neither jealous of it or injured by it. This is such a commonplace that I am almost ashamed to state it.'

I said, 'O; and legislation? do they take any part in that?'

Hammond smiled and said: 'I think you may wait for an answer to that question till we get on to the subject of legislation. There may be novelties to you in that subject also.'

'Very well,' I said; 'but about this woman question? I saw at the Guest House that the women were waiting on the men: that seems a little like reaction, doesn't it?'

'Does it?' said the old man; 'perhaps you think housekeeping an unimportant occupation, not deserving of respect. I believe that was the opinion of the "advanced" women of the nineteenth century, and their male backers. If it is yours, I recommend to your notice an old Norwegian folk-lore tale called How the Man minded the House, or some such title,* the result of which minding was that, after various tribulations, the man and the family cow balanced each other at the end of a rope, the man hanging half-way up the chimney, the cow dangling from the roof, which, after the fashion of the country, was of turf and sloping down low to the ground. Hard on the cow, *I* think. Of course no such mishap could happen to such a superior person as yourself,' he added, chuckling.

I sat somewhat uneasy under this dry gibe.* Indeed, his manner of treating this latter part of the question seemed to me a little disrespectful.

'Come, now, my friend,' quoth he, 'don't you know that it is a great pleasure to a clever woman to manage a house skilfully, and to do it so that all the house-mates about her look pleased, and are grateful to her? And then, you know, everybody likes to be ordered about by a pretty woman: why, it is one of the pleasantest forms of flirtation. You are not so old that you cannot remember that. Why, I remember it well.'

And the old fellow chuckled again, and at last fairly burst out laughing.

'Excuse me,' said he, after a while; 'I am not laughing at anything you could be thinking of, but at that silly nineteenth-century fashion, current amongst rich so-called cultivated people, of ignoring all the steps by which their daily dinner was reached, as matters too low for their lofty intelligence. Useless idiots! Come, now, I am a "literary man," as we queer animals used to be called, yet I am a pretty good cook myself.'

'So am I,' said I.*

'Well, then,' said he, 'I really think you can understand me better than you would seem to do, judging by your words and your silence.'

Said I: 'Perhaps that is so; but people putting in practice commonly this sense of interest in the ordinary occupations of life rather startles me. I will ask you a question or two presently about that. But I want to return to the position of women amongst you. You have studied the "emancipation of women" business of the nineteenth century: don't you remember that some of the "superior" women wanted to emancipate the more intelligent part of their sex from the bearing of children?'

The old man grew quite serious again. Said he: 'I *do* remember about that strange piece of baseless folly, the result, like all other follies of the period, of the hideous class tyranny which then obtained. What do we think of it now? you would say. My friend, that is a question easy to answer. How could it possibly be but that maternity should be highly honoured amongst us? Surely it is a matter of course that the natural and necessary pains which the mother must go through form a bond of union between man and woman, an extra stimulus to love and affection between them, and that this is universally recognised. For the rest, remember that all the *artificial* burdens of motherhood are now done away with. A mother has no longer any mere sordid anxieties for the future of her children. They may indeed turn out better or worse; they may disappoint her highest hopes; such anxieties as these are a part of the mingled pleasure and pain which goes to make up the life of mankind. But at least she is spared the fear (it was most commonly the certainty) that artificial disabilities would make her children something less than men and women: she knows that they will live and act according to the measure of their own faculties. In times past, it is clear that the "Society" of the day helped its Judaic god, and the "Man of Science" of the time, in visiting the sins of the fathers upon the children.* How to reverse this process, how to take the sting out of heredity, has for long been one of the most constant cares of the thoughtful men amongst us. So that, you see, the ordinarily healthy woman (and almost all our women are both healthy and at least comely), respected as a child-bearer and rearer of children, desired as a woman, loved as a companion, unanxious for the future of her children, has far more instinct for maternity than the poor drudge and mother of drudges of past days could ever have had; or than her sister of the upper classes, brought up in affected ignorance of natural facts, reared in an atmosphere of mingled prudery and prurience.'

'You speak warmly,' I said, 'but I can see that you are right.'

'Yes,' he said, 'and I will point out to you a token of all the benefits which we have gained by our freedom. What did you think of the looks of the people whom you have come across to-day?'

Said I: 'I could hardly have believed that there could be so many good-looking people in any civilised country.'

He crowed a little, like the old bird he was. 'What! are we still civilised?' said he. 'Well, as to our looks, the English and Jutish* blood, which on the whole is predominant here, used not to produce much beauty. But I think we have improved it. I know a man who has a large collection of portraits printed from photographs of the nineteenth century, and going over those and comparing them with the everyday faces in these times, puts the improvement in our good looks beyond a doubt. Now, there are some people who think it not too fantastic to connect this increase of beauty directly with our freedom and good sense in the matters we have been speaking of: they believe that a child born from the natural and healthy love between a man and a woman, even if that be transient, is likely to turn out better in all ways, and especially in bodily beauty, than the birth of the respectable commercial marriage bed, or of the dull despair of the drudge of that system. They say, Pleasure begets pleasure. What do you think?'

'I am much of that mind,' said I.

CHAPTER X

QUESTIONS AND ANSWERS

'Well,' said the old man, shifting in his chair, 'you must get on with your questions, guest; I have been some time answering this first one.'

Said I: 'I want an extra word or two about your ideas of education; although I gathered from Dick that you let your children run wild and didn't teach them anything; and in short, that you have so refined your education, that now you have none.'

'Then you gathered left-handed,'* quoth he. 'But of course I understand your point of view about education, which is that of times past, when "the struggle for life," as men used to phrase it (*i.e.*, the struggle for a slave's rations on one side, and for a bouncing share* of the slaveholders' privilege on the other), pinched "education" for most people into a niggardly dole of not very accurate information;

something to be swallowed by the beginner in the art of living whether he liked it or not, and was hungry for it or not: and which had been chewed and digested over and over again by people who didn't care about it in order to serve it out to other people who didn't care about it.'

I stopped the old man's rising wrath by a laugh, and said: 'Well, *you* were not taught that way, at any rate, so you may let your anger run off you a little.'

'True, true,' said he, smiling. 'I thank you for correcting my ill-temper: I always fancy myself as living in any period of which we may be speaking. But, however, to put it in a cooler way: you expected to see children thrust into schools when they had reached an age conventionally supposed to be the due age, whatever their varying faculties and dispositions might be, and when there, with like disregard to facts to be subjected to a certain conventional course of "learning." My friend, can't you see that such a proceeding means ignoring the fact of *growth*, bodily and mental? No one could come out of such a mill uninjured; and those only would avoid being crushed by it who would have the spirit of rebellion strong in them. Fortunately most children have had that at all times, or I do not know that we should ever have reached our present position. Now you see what it all comes to. In the old times all this was the result of *poverty*. In the nineteenth century, society was so miserably poor, owing to the systematised robbery on which it was founded, that real education was impossible for anybody. The whole theory of their so-called education was that it was necessary to shove a little information into a child, even if it were by means of torture, and accompanied by twaddle which it was well known was of no use, or else he would lack information lifelong: the hurry of poverty forbade anything else. All that is past; we are no longer hurried, and the information lies ready to each one's hand when his own inclinations impel him to seek it. In this as in other matters we have become wealthy: we can afford to give ourselves time to grow.'

'Yes,' said I, 'but suppose the child, youth, man, never wants the information, never grows in the direction you might hope him to do: suppose, for instance, he objects to learning arithmetic or mathematics; you can't force him when he *is* grown; can't you force him while he is growing, and oughtn't you to do so?'

'Well,' said he, 'were you forced to learn arithmetic and mathematics?'

'A little,' said I.

'And how old are you now?'

'Say fifty-six,' said I.

'And how much arithmetic and mathematics do you know now?' quoth the old man, smiling rather mockingly.

Said I: 'None whatever, I am sorry to say.'

Hammond laughed quietly, but made no other comment on my admission, and I dropped the subject of education, perceiving him to be hopeless on that side.

I thought a little, and said: 'You were speaking just now of households: that sounded to me a little like the customs of past times; I should have thought you would have lived more in public.'

'Phalangsteries,* eh?' said he. 'Well, we live as we like, and we like to live as a rule with certain house-mates that we have got used to. Remember, again, that poverty is extinct, and that the Fourierist phalangsteries and all their kind, as was but natural at the time, implied nothing but a refuge from mere destitution. Such a way of life as that, could only have been conceived of by people surrounded by the worst form of poverty. But you must understand therewith, that though separate households are the rule amongst us, and though they differ in their habits more or less, yet no door is shut to any good-tempered person who is content to live as the other house-mates do: only of course it would be unreasonable for one man to drop into a household and bid the folk of it to alter their habits to please him, since he can go elsewhere and live as he pleases. However, I need not say much about all this, as you are going up the river with Dick, and will find out for yourself by experience how these matters are managed.'

After a pause, I said: 'Your big towns, now; how about them? London, which—which I have read about as the modern Babylon of civilisation, seems to have disappeared.'

'Well, well,' said old Hammond, 'perhaps after all it is more like ancient Babylon* now than the "modern Babylon" of the nineteenth century was. But let that pass. After all, there is a good deal of population in places between here and Hammersmith; nor have you seen the most populous part of the town yet.'

'Tell me, then,' said I, 'how is it towards the east?'

Said he: 'Time was when if you mounted a good horse and rode straight away from my door here at a round trot for an hour and a half, you would still be in the thick of London, and the greater part of that would be "slums," as they were called; that is to say, places of torture for innocent men and women; or worse, stews for rearing and breeding men and women in such degradation that that torture should seem to them mere ordinary and natural life.'

'I know, I know,' I said, rather impatiently. 'That was what was; tell me something of what is. Is any of that left?'

'Not an inch,' said he; 'but some memory of it abides with us, and I am glad of it. Once a year, on May-day,* we hold a solemn feast in those easterly communes of London to commemorate The Clearing of Misery, as it is called. On that day we have music and dancing, and merry games and happy feasting on the site of some of the worst of the old slums, the traditional memory of which we have kept. On that occasion the custom is for the prettiest girls to sing some of the old revolutionary songs, and those which were the groans of the discontent, once so hopeless, on the very spots where those terrible crimes of class-murder were committed day by day for so many years. To a man like me, who have studied the past so diligently, it is a curious and touching sight to see some beautiful girl, daintily clad, and crowned with flowers from the neighbouring meadows, standing amongst the happy people, on some mound where of old time stood the wretched apology for a house, a den in which men and women lived packed amongst the filth like pilchards in a cask; lived in such a way that they could only have endured it, as I said just now, by being degraded out of humanity—to hear the terrible words of threatening and lamentation coming from her sweet and beautiful lips, and she unconscious of their real meaning: to hear her, for instance, singing Hood's Song of the Shirt,* and to think that all the time she does not understand what it is all about—a tragedy grown inconceivable to her and her listeners. Think of that, if you can, and of how glorious life is grown!'

'Indeed,' said I, 'it is difficult for me to think of it.'

And I sat watching how his eyes glittered, and how the fresh life seemed to glow in his face, and I wondered how at his age he should think of the happiness of the world, or indeed anything but his coming dinner.

'Tell me in detail,' said I, 'what lies east of Bloomsbury now?'

Said he: 'There are but few houses between this and the outer part of the old city; but in the city we have a thickly-dwelling population. Our forefathers, in the first clearing of the slums, were not in a hurry to pull down the houses in what was called at the end of the nineteenth century the business quarter of town, and what later got to be known as the Swindling Kens.* You see, these houses, though they stood hideously thick on the ground, were roomy and fairly solid in building, and clean, because they were not used for living in, but as mere gambling booths; so the poor people from the cleared slums took them for lodgings and dwelt there, till the folk of those days had time to think of something better for them; so the buildings were pulled down so gradually that people got used to living thicker on the ground there than in most places; therefore it remains the most populous part of London, or perhaps of all these islands. But it is very pleasant there, partly because of the splendour of the architecture, which goes further than what you will see elsewhere. However, this crowding, if it may be called so, does not go further than a street called Aldgate,* a name that perhaps you may have heard of. Beyond that the houses are scattered wide about the meadows there, which are very beautiful, especially when you get on to the lovely river Lea (where old Isaak Walton* used to fish, you know) about the places called Stratford and Old Ford,* names which of course you will not have heard of, though the Romans were busy there once upon a time.'

Not heard of them! thought I to myself. How strange! that I who had seen the very last remnant of the pleasantness of the meadows by the Lea destroyed, should have heard them spoken of with pleasantness come back to them in full measure.

Hammond went on: 'When you get down to the Thames side you come on the Docks, which are works of the nineteenth century, and are still in use, although not so thronged as they once were, since we discourage centralisation all we can, and we have long ago dropped the pretension to be the market of the world. About these Docks are a good few houses, which, however, are not inhabited by many people permanently; I mean, those who use them come and go a good deal, the place being too low and marshy for pleasant dwelling. Past the Docks eastward and landward it is all flat pasture, once marsh, except for a few gardens, and there are very few permanent dwellings there: scarcely anything but a few sheds, and cots for the men who come to look after the great herds of cattle pasturing there. But however, what with the beasts and the men, and the scattered red-tiled roofs and the big hayricks, it does not make a bad holiday to get a quiet pony and ride about there on a sunny afternoon of autumn, and look over the river and the craft passing up and down, and on to Shooters' Hill* and the Kentish uplands, and then turn round to the wide green sea of the Essex marsh-land, with the great domed line of the sky, and the sun shining down in one flood of peaceful light over the long distance. There is a place called Canning's Town, and further out, Silvertown,* where the pleasant meadows are at their pleasantest: doubtless they were once slums, and wretched enough.'

The names grated on my ear, but I could not explain why to him. So I said: 'And south of the river, what is it like?'

He said: 'You would find it much the same as the land about Hammersmith. North, again, the land runs up high, and there is an agreeable and well-built town called Hampstead,* which fitly ends London on that side. It looks down on the north-western end of the forest you passed through.'

I smiled. 'So much for what was once London,' said I. 'Now tell me about the other towns of the country.'

He said: 'As to the big murky places which were once, as we know, the centres of manufacture, they have, like the brick and mortar desert of London, disappeared; only, since they were the centres of nothing but "manufacture," and served no purpose but that of the gambling market, they have left less signs of their existence than London. Of course, the great change in the use of mechanical force made this an easy matter, and some approach to their break-up as centres would probably have taken place, even if we had not changed our habits so much: but they being such as they were, no sacrifice would have seemed too great a price to pay for getting rid of the "manufacturing districts," as they used to be called. For the rest, whatever coal or mineral we need is brought to grass and sent whither it is needed with as little as possible of dirt, confusion, and the distressing of quiet people's lives. One is tempted to believe from what one has read of the condition of those districts in the nineteenth century, that those who had them under their power worried, befouled, and degraded men out of malice prepense:* but it was not so; like the mis-education of which we were talking just now, it came of their dreadful poverty. They were obliged to put up with everything, and even pretend that they liked it; whereas we can now deal with things reasonably, and refuse to be saddled with what we do not want.'

I confess I was not sorry to cut short with a question his glorifications of the age he lived in. Said I: 'How about the smaller towns? I suppose you have swept those away entirely?'

'No, no,' said he, 'it hasn't gone that way. On the contrary, there has been but little clearance, though much rebuilding, in the smaller towns. Their suburbs, indeed, when they had any, have melted away into the general country, and space and elbow-room has been got in their centres: but there are the towns still with their streets and squares and market-places; so that it is by means of these smaller towns that we of to-day can get some kind of idea of what the towns of the older world were like;—I mean to say at their best.'

'Take Oxford,* for instance,' said I.

'Yes,' said he, 'I suppose Oxford was beautiful even in the nineteenth century. At present it has the great interest of still preserving a great mass of pre-commercial building, and is a very beautiful place, yet there are many towns which have become scarcely less beautiful.'

Said I: 'In passing, may I ask if it is still a place of learning?'

'Still?' said he, smiling. 'Well, it has reverted to some of its best traditions; so you may imagine how far it is from its nineteenth-century position. It is real learning, knowledge cultivated for its own sake—the Art of Knowledge, in short—which is followed there, not the Commercial learning of the past. Though perhaps you do not know that in the nineteenth century Oxford and its less interesting sister Cambridge* became definitely commercial. They (and especially Oxford) were the breeding places of a peculiar class of parasites, who called themselves cultivated people; they were indeed cynical enough, as the so-called educated classes of the day generally were; but they affected an exaggeration of cynicism in order that they might be thought knowing and worldly-wise. The rich middle classes (they had no relation with the working classes) treated them with the kind of contemptuous toleration with which a mediæval baron treated his jester; though it must be said that they were by no means so pleasant as the old jesters were, being, in fact, *the* bores of society. They were laughed at, despised—and paid. Which last was what they aimed at.'

Dear me! thought I, how apt history is to reverse contemporary judgements. Surely only the worst of them were as bad as that. But I must admit that they were mostly prigs, and that they *were* commercial. I said aloud, though more to myself than to Hammond, 'Well, how could they be better than the age that made them?'

'True,' he said, 'but their pretensions were higher.'

'Were they?' said I, smiling.

'You drive me from corner to corner,' said he, smiling in turn. 'Let me say at least that they were a poor sequence to the aspirations of Oxford of "the barbarous Middle Ages."'

'Yes, that will do,' said I.

'Also,' said Hammond, 'what I have been saying of them is true in the main. But ask on!'

I said: 'We have heard about London and the manufacturing districts and the ordinary towns: how about the villages?'

Said Hammond: 'You must know that toward the end of the nineteenth century the villages were almost destroyed, unless where they became mere adjuncts to the manufacturing districts, or formed a sort of minor manufacturing district themselves. Houses were allowed to fall into decay and actual ruin; trees were cut down for the sake of the few shillings which the poor sticks would fetch; the building became inexpressibly mean and hideous. Labour was scarce; but wages fell nevertheless. All the small country arts of life which once added to the little pleasures of country people were lost. The country produce which passed through the hands of the husbandman never got so far as their mouths. Incredible shabbiness and niggardly pinching reigned over the fields and acres which, in spite of the rude and careless husbandry of the times, were so kind and bountiful. Had you any inkling of all this?'

'I have heard that it was so,' said I; 'but what followed?'

'The change,' said Hammond, 'which in these matters took place very early in our epoch, was most strangely rapid. People flocked into the country villages, and, so to say, flung themselves upon the freed land like a wild beast upon his prey; and in a very little time the villages of England were more populous than they had been since the fourteenth century, and were still growing fast. Of course, this invasion of the country was awkward to deal with, and would have created much misery, if the folk had still been under the bondage of class monopoly. But as it was, things soon righted themselves. People found out what they were fit for, and gave up attempting to push themselves into occupations in which they must needs fail. The town invaded the country; but the invaders, like the warlike invaders of early days, yielded to the influence of their surroundings, and became country people; and in their turn, as they became more numerous than the townsmen, influenced them also; so that the difference between town and country grew less and less; and it was indeed this world of the country vivified by the thought and briskness of town-bred folk which has produced that happy and leisurely but eager life of which you have had a first taste. Again I say, many blunders were made, but we have had time to set them right. Much was left for the men of my earlier life to deal with. The crude ideas of the first half of the twentieth century,* when men were still oppressed by the fear of poverty, and did not look enough to the present pleasure of ordinary daily life, spoilt a great deal of what the commercial age had left us of external beauty: and I admit that it was but slowly that men recovered from the injuries that they inflicted on themselves even after they became free. But slowly as the recovery came, it *did* come; and the more you see of us, the clearer it will be to you that we are happy. That we live amidst beauty without any fear of becoming effeminate; that we have plenty to do, and on the whole enjoy doing it. What more can we ask of life?'

He paused, as if he were seeking for words with which to express his thought. Then he said:

'This is how we stand. England was once a country of clearings amongst the woods and wastes, with a few towns interspersed, which were fortresses for the feudal army, markets for the folk, gathering places for the craftsmen. It then became a country of huge and foul workshops and fouler gambling-dens, surrounded by an ill-kept, poverty-stricken farm, pillaged by the masters of the workshops. It is now a garden, where nothing is wasted and nothing is spoilt, with the necessary dwellings, sheds, and workshops scattered up and down the country, all trim and neat and pretty. For, indeed, we should be too much ashamed of ourselves if we allowed the making of goods, even on a large scale, to carry with it the appearance, even, of desolation and misery. Why my friend, those housewives we were talking of just now would teach us better than that.'

Said I: 'This side of your change is certainly for the better. But though I shall soon see some of these villages, tell me in a word or two what they are like, just to prepare me.'

'Perhaps,' said he, 'you have seen a tolerable picture of these villages as they were before the end of the nineteenth century. Such things exist.'

'I have seen several of such pictures,' said I.

'Well,' said Hammond, 'our villages are something like the best of such places, with the church or mote-house of the neighbours for their chief building. Only note that there are no tokens of poverty about them: no tumble-down picturesque; which, to tell you the truth, the artist usually availed himself of to veil his incapacity for drawing architecture. Such things do not please us, even when they indicate no misery. Like the mediævals, we like everything trim and clean, and orderly and bright; as people always do when they have any sense of architectural power; because then they know that they can have what they want, and they won't stand any nonsense from Nature in their dealings with her.'

'Besides the villages, are there any scattered country houses?' said I.

'Yes, plenty,' said Hammond; 'in fact, except in the wastes and forests and amongst the sand-hills (like Hindhead in Surrey),* it is not easy to be out of sight of a house; and where the houses are thinly scattered they run large, and are more like the old colleges than ordinary houses as they used to be. That is done for the sake of society, for a good many people can dwell in such houses, as the country dwellers are not necessarily husbandmen; though they almost all help in such work at times. The life that goes on in these big dwellings in the country is very pleasant, especially as some of the most studious men of our time live in them, and altogether there is a great variety of mind and mood to be found in them which brightens and quickens the society there.'

'I am rather surprised,' said I, 'by all this, for it seems to me that after all the country must be tolerably populous.'

'Certainly,' said he; 'the population is pretty much the same as it was at the end of the nineteenth century; we have spread it, that is all. Of course, also, we have helped to populate other countries—where we were wanted and were called for.'

Said I: 'One thing, it seems to me, does not go with your word of "garden" for the country. You have spoken of wastes and forests, and I myself have seen the beginning of your Middlesex and Essex forest.* Why do you keep such things in a garden? and isn't it very wasteful to do so?'

'My friend,' he said, 'we like these pieces of wild nature, and can afford them, so we have them; let alone that as to the forests, we need a great deal of timber, and suppose that our sons and our sons' sons will do the like. As to the land being a garden, I have heard that they used to have shrubberies and rockeries in gardens once; and though I might not like the artificial ones, I assure you that some of the natural rockeries of our garden are worth seeing. Go north this summer and look at the Cumberland and Westmoreland ones,*—where, by the way, you will see some sheep-feeding, so that they are not so wasteful as you think; not so wasteful as forcing-grounds for fruit out of season, *I* think. Go and have a look at the sheep-walks high up the slopes between Ingleborough and Pen-y-gwent,* and tell me if you think we *waste* the land there by not covering it with factories for making things that nobody wants, which was the chief business of the nineteenth century.'

'I will try to go there,' said I.

'It won't take much trying,' said he.

CHAPTER XI

CONCERNING GOVERNMENT

'Now,' said I, 'I have come to the point of asking questions which I suppose will be dry for you to answer and difficult for you to explain; but I have foreseen for some time past that I must ask them, will I 'nill I. What kind of a government have you? Has republicanism finally triumphed? or have you come to a mere dictatorship, which some persons in the nineteenth century used to prophesy as the ultimate outcome of democracy? Indeed, this last question does not seem so very unreasonable, since you have turned your Parliament House into a dung-market. Or where do you house your present Parliament?'

The old man answered my smile with a hearty laugh, and said:

'Well, well, dung is not the worst kind of corruption; fertility may come of that, whereas mere dearth came from the other kind, of which those walls once held the great supporters. Now, dear guest, let me tell you that our present parliament would be hard to house in one place, because the whole people is our parliament.'

'I don't understand,' said I.

'No, I suppose not,' said he. 'I must now shock you by telling you that we have no longer anything which you, a native of another planet, would call a government.'

'I am not so much shocked as you might think,' said I, 'as I know something about governments. But tell me, how do you manage, and how have you come to this state of things?'

Said he: 'It is true that we have to make some arrangements about our affairs, concerning which you can ask presently; and it is also true that everybody does not always agree with the details of these arrangements; but, further, it is true that a man no more needs an elaborate system of government, with its army, navy, and police, to force him to give way to the will of the majority of his *equals*, than he wants a similar machinery to make him understand that his head and a stone wall cannot occupy the same space at the same moment. Do you want further explanation?'

'Well, yes, I do,' quoth I.

Old Hammond settled himself in his chair with a look of enjoyment which rather alarmed me, and made me dread a scientific disquisition:* so I sighed and abided. He said:

'I suppose you know pretty well what the process of government was in the bad old times?'

'I am supposed to know,' said I.

(Hammond) What was the government of those days? Was it really the Parliament or any part of it?

(I) No.

(H.) Was not the Parliament on the one side a kind of watch-committee sitting to see that the interests of the Upper Classes took no hurt; and on the other side a sort of blind to delude the people into supposing that they had some share in the management of their own affairs?

(I) History seems to show us this.

(H.) To what extent did the people manage their own affairs?

(I) I judge from what I have heard that sometimes they forced the Parliament to make a law to legalise some alteration which had already taken place.

(H.) Anything else?

(I) I think not. As I am informed, if the people made any attempt to deal with the *cause* of their grievances, the law stepped in and said, this is sedition, revolt, or what not, and slew or tortured the ringleaders of such attempts.

(H.) If Parliament was not the government then, nor the people either, what was the government?

(I) Can you tell me?

(H.) I think we shall not be far wrong if we say that government was the Law-Courts, backed up by the executive, which handled the brute force that the deluded people allowed them to use for their own purposes; I mean the army, navy, and police.

(I) Reasonable men must needs think you are right.

(H.) Now as to those Law-Courts. Were they places of fair dealing according to the ideas of the day? Had a poor man a good chance of defending his property and person in them?

(I) It is a commonplace that even rich men looked upon a law-suit as a dire misfortune, even if they gained the case; and as for a poor one—why, it was considered a miracle of justice and beneficence if a poor man who had once got into the clutches of the law escaped prison or utter ruin.

(H.) It seems, then, my son, that the government by law-courts and police, which was the real government of the nineteenth century, was not a great success even to the people of that day, living under a class system which proclaimed inequality and poverty as the law of God and the bond which held the world together.

(I) So it seems, indeed.

(H.) And now that all this is changed, and the 'rights of property,' which mean the clenching the fist on a piece of goods and crying out to the neighbours, You shan't have this!—now that all this has disappeared so utterly that it is no longer possible even to jest upon its absurdity, is such a Government possible?

(I) It is impossible.

(H.) Yes, happily. But for what other purpose than the protection of the rich from the poor, the strong from the weak, did this Government exist?

(I) I have heard that it was said that their office was to defend their own citizens against attack from other countries.

(H.) It was said; but was anyone expected to believe this? For instance, did the English Government defend the English citizen against the French?

(I) So it was said.

(H.) Then if the French had invaded England and conquered it, they would not have allowed the English workmen to live well?

(I, laughing) As far as I can make out, the English masters of the English workmen saw to that: they took from their workmen as much of their livelihood as they dared, because they wanted it for themselves.

(H.) But if the French had conquered, would they not have taken more still from the English workmen?

(I) I do not think so; for in that case the English workmen would have died of starvation; and then the French conquest would have ruined the French, just as if the English horses and cattle had died of under-feeding. So that after all, the English *workmen* would have been no worse off for the conquest: their French masters could have got no more from them than their English masters did.

(H.) This is true; and we may admit that the pretensions of the government to defend the poor (*i.e.*, the useful) people against other countries come to nothing. But that is but natural; for we have seen already that it was the function of government to protect the rich against the poor. But did not the government defend its rich men against other nations?

(I) I do not remember to have heard that the rich needed defence; because it is said that even when two nations were at war, the rich men of each nation gambled with each other pretty much as usual, and even sold each other weapons wherewith to kill their own countrymen.

(H.) In short, it comes to this, that whereas the so-called government of protection of property by means of the law-courts meant destruction of wealth, this defence of the citizens of one country against those of another country by means of war or the threat of war meant pretty much the same thing.

(I) I cannot deny it.

(H.) Therefore the government really existed for the destruction of wealth?

(I) So it seems. And yet—

(H.) Yet what?

(I) There were many rich people in those times.

(H.) You see the consequences of that fact?

(I) I think I do. But tell me out what they were.

(H.) If the government habitually destroyed wealth, the country must have been poor?

(I) Yes, certainly.

(H.) Yet amidst this poverty the persons for the sake of whom the government existed insisted on being rich whatever might happen?

(I) So it was.

(H.) What *must* happen if in a poor country some people insist on being rich at the expense of the others?

(I) Unutterable poverty for the others. All this misery, then, was caused by the destructive government of which we have been speaking?

(H.) Nay, it would be incorrect to say so. The government itself was but the necessary result of the careless, aimless tyranny of the times; it was but the machinery of tyranny. Now tyranny has come to an end, and we no longer need such machinery; we could not possibly use it since we are free. Therefore in your sense of the word we have no government. Do you understand this now?

(I) Yes, I do. But I will ask you some more questions as to how you as free men manage your affairs.

(H.) With all my heart. Ask away.

CHAPTER XII

CONCERNING THE ARRANGEMENT OF LIFE

'Well,' I said, 'about those "arrangements" which you spoke of as taking the place of government, could you give me any account of them?'

'Neighbour,' he said, 'although we have simplified our lives a great deal from what they were, and have got rid of many conventionalities and many sham wants, which used to give our forefathers much trouble, yet our life is too complex for me to tell you in detail by means of words how it is arranged; you must find that out by living amongst us. It is true that I can better tell you what we don't do, than what we do do.'

'Well?' said I.

'This is the way to put it,' said he: 'We have been living for a hundred and fifty years, at least, more or less in our present manner, and a tradition or habit of life has been growing on us; and that habit has become a habit of acting on the whole for the best. It is easy for us to live without robbing each other. It would be possible for us to contend with and rob each other, but it would be harder for us than refraining from strife and robbery. That is in short the foundation of our life and our happiness.'

'Whereas in the old days,' said I, 'it was very hard to live without strife and robbery. That's what you mean, isn't it, by giving me the negative side of your good conditions?'

'Yes,' he said, 'it was so hard, that those who habitually acted fairly to their neighbours were celebrated as saints and heroes, and were looked up to with the greatest reverence.'

'While they were alive?' said I.

'No,' said he, 'after they were dead.'

'But as to these days,' I said; 'you don't mean to tell me that no one ever transgresses this habit of good fellowship?'

'Certainly not,' said Hammond, 'but when the transgressions occur, everybody, transgressors and all, know them for what they are; the errors of friends, not the habitual actions of persons driven into enmity against society.'

'I see,' said I; 'you mean that you have no "criminal" classes.'

'How could we have them,' said he, 'since there is no rich class to breed enemies against the state by means of the injustice of the state?'

Said I: 'I thought that I understood from something that fell from you a little while ago that you had abolished civil law. Is that so, literally?'

'It abolished itself, my friend,' said he. 'As I said before, the civil law-courts were upheld for the defence of private property; for nobody ever pretended that it was possible to make people act fairly to each other by means of brute force. Well, private property being abolished, all the laws and all the legal "crimes" which it had manufactured of course came to an end. Thou shalt not steal,* had to be translated into, Thou shalt work in order to live happily. Is there any need to enforce that commandment by violence?'

'Well,' said I, 'that is understood, and I agree with it; but how about the crimes of violence? would not their occurrence (and you admit that they occur) make criminal law necessary?'

Said he: 'In your sense of the word, we have no criminal law either. Let us look at the matter closer, and see whence crimes of violence spring. By far the greater part of these in past days were the result of the laws of private property, which forbade the satisfaction of their natural desires to all but a privileged few, and of the general visible coercion which came of those laws. All *that* cause of violent crime is gone. Again, many violent acts came from the artificial perversion of the sexual passions, which caused overweening jealousy and the like miseries. Now, when you look carefully into these, you will find that what lay at the bottom of them was mostly the idea (a law-made idea) of the woman being the property of the man, whether he were husband, father, brother, or what not. *That* idea has of course vanished with private property, as well as certain follies about the "ruin" of women for following their natural desires in an illegal way, which of course was a convention caused by the laws of private property.'

'Another cognate cause of crimes of violence was the family tyranny, which was the subject of so many novels and stories of the past and which once more was the result of private property. Of course that is all ended, since families are held together by no bond of coercion, legal or social, but by mutual liking and affection, and everybody is free to come or go as he or she pleases. Furthermore, our standards of honour and public estimation are very different from the old ones; success in besting our neighbours is a road to renown now closed, let us hope for ever. Each man is free to exercise his special faculty to the utmost, and every one encourages him in so doing. So that we have got rid of the scowling envy, coupled by the poets with hatred, and surely with good reason; heaps of unhappiness and ill-blood were caused by it, which with irritable and passionate men—*i.e.*, energetic and active men—often led to violence.'

I laughed, and said: 'So that you now withdraw your admission, and say that there is no violence amongst you?'

'No,' said he, 'I withdraw nothing; as I told you, such things will happen. Hot blood will err sometimes. A man may strike another, and the stricken strike back again, and the result be a homicide, to put it at the worst. But what then? Shall we the neighbours make it worse still? Shall we think so poorly of each other as to suppose that the slain man calls on us to revenge him, when we *know* that if he had been maimed, he would, when in cold blood and able to weigh all the circumstances, have forgiven his maimer? Or will the death of the slayer bring the slain man to life again and cure the unhappiness his loss has caused?'

'Yes,' I said, 'but consider, must not the safety of society be safeguarded by some punishment?'

'There, neighbour!' said the old man, with some exultation. 'You have hit the mark. That *punishment* of which men used to talk so wisely and act so foolishly, what was it but the expression of their fear? And they had need to fear, since *they—i.e.*, the rulers of society—were dwelling like an armed band in a hostile country. But we who live amongst our friends need neither fear nor punish. Surely if we, in dread of an occasional rare homicide, an occasional rough blow, were solemnly and legally to commit homicide and violence, we could only be a society of ferocious cowards. Don't you think so, neighbour?'

'Yes, I do, when I come to think of it from that side,' said I.

'Yet you must understand,' said the old man, 'that when any violence is committed, we expect the transgressor to make any atonement possible to him, and he himself expects it. But again, think if the destruction or serious injury of a man momentarily overcome by wrath or folly can be any atonement to the commonwealth? Surely it can only be an additional injury to it.'

Said I: 'But suppose the man has a habit of violence,—kills a man a year, for instance?'

'Such a thing is unknown,' said he. 'In a society where there is no punishment to evade, no law to triumph over, remorse will certainly follow transgression.'

'And lesser outbreaks of violence,' said I, 'how do you deal with them? for hitherto we have been talking of great tragedies, I suppose?'

Said Hammond: 'If the ill-doer is not sick or mad (in which case he must be restrained till his sickness or madness is cured) it is clear that grief and humiliation must follow the ill-deed; and society in general will make that pretty clear to the ill-doer if he should chance to be dull to it; and again, some kind of atonement will follow,—at the least, an open acknowledgement of the grief and humiliation. Is it so hard to say, I ask your pardon, neighbour?—Well, sometimes it is hard—and let it be.'

'You think that enough?' said I.

'Yes,' said he, 'and moreover it is all that we *can* do. If in addition we torture the man, we turn his grief into anger, and the humiliation he would otherwise feel for *his* wrong-doing is swallowed up by a hope of revenge for *our* wrong-doing to him. He has paid the legal penalty, and can "go and sin again" with comfort. Shall we commit such a folly, then? Remember Jesus had got the legal penalty remitted before he said "Go and sin no more."* Let alone that in a society of equals you will not find any one to play the part of torturer or jailer, though many to act as nurse or doctor.'

'So,' said I, 'you consider crime a mere spasmodic disease, which requires no body of criminal law to deal with it?'

'Pretty much so,' said he; 'and since, as I have told you, we are a healthy people generally, so we are not likely to be much troubled with *this* disease.'

'Well, you have no civil law, and no criminal law. But have you no laws of the market, so to say—no regulation for the exchange of wares? for you must exchange, even if you have no property.'

Said he: 'We have no obvious individual exchange, as you saw this morning when you went a-shopping; but of course there are regulations of the markets, varying according to the circumstances and guided by general custom. But as these are matters of general assent, which nobody dreams of objecting to, so also we have made no provision for enforcing them: therefore I don't call them laws. In law, whether it be criminal or civil, execution always follows judgment, and someone must suffer. When you see the judge on his bench, you see through him, as clearly as if he were made of glass, the policeman to emprison, and the soldier to slay some actual living person. Such follies would make an agreeable market, wouldn't they?'

'Certainly,' said I, 'that means turning the market into a mere battle-field, in which many people must suffer as much as in the battle-field of bullet and bayonet. And from what I have seen I should suppose that your marketing, great and little, is carried on in a way that makes it a pleasant occupation.'

'You are right, neighbour,' said he. 'Although there are so many, indeed by far the greater number amongst us, who would be unhappy if they were not engaged in actually making things, and things which turn out beautiful under their hands,—there are many, like the housekeepers I was speaking of, whose delight is in administration and organisation, to use long-tailed words; I mean people who like keeping things together, avoiding waste, seeing that nothing sticks fast uselessly. Such people are thoroughly happy in their business, all the more as they are dealing with actual facts, and not merely passing counters round to see what share they shall have in the privileged taxation of useful people, which was the business of the commercial folk in past days. Well, what are you going to ask me next?'

CHAPTER XIII

CONCERNING POLITICS

Said I: 'How do you manage with politics?'

Said Hammond, smiling: 'I am glad that it is of *me* that you ask that question; I do believe that anybody else would make you explain yourself, or try to do so, till you were sickened of asking questions. Indeed, I believe I am the only man in England who would know what you mean; and since I know, I will answer your question briefly by saying that we are very well off as to politics,—because we have none. If ever you make a book out of this conversation, put this in a chapter by itself, after the model of old Horrebow's Snakes in Iceland.'*

'I will,' said I.

CHAPTER XIV

HOW MATTERS ARE MANAGED

Said I: 'How about your relations with foreign nations?'*

'I will not affect not to know what you mean,' said he, 'but I will tell you at once that the whole system of rival and contending nations which played so great a part in the "government" of the world of civilisation has disappeared along with the inequality betwixt man and man in society.'

'Does not that make the world duller?' said I.

'Why?' said the old man.

'The obliteration of national variety,' said I.

'Nonsense,' he said, somewhat snappishly. 'Cross the water and see. You will find plenty of variety: the landscape, the building, the diet, the amusements, all various. The men and women varying in looks as well as in habits of thought; the costume far more various than in the commercial period. How should it add to the variety or dispel the dulness, to coerce certain families or tribes, often heterogeneous and jarring with one another, into certain artificial and mechanical groups, and call them nations, and stimulate their patriotism—*i.e.*, their foolish and envious prejudices?'

'Well—I don't know how,' said I.

'That's right,' said Hammond cheerily; 'you can easily understand that now we are freed from this folly it is obvious to us that by means of this very diversity the different strains of blood in the world can be serviceable and pleasant to each other, without in the least wanting to rob each other: we are all bent on the same enterprise, making the most of our lives. And I must tell you whatever quarrels or misunderstandings arise, they very seldom take place between people of different race; and consequently since there is less unreason in them, they are the more readily appeased.'

'Good,' said I, 'but as to those matters of politics; as to general differences of opinion in one and the same community. Do you assert that there are none?'

'No, not at all,' said he, somewhat snappishly; 'but I do say that differences of opinion about real solid things need not, and with us do not, crystallise people into parties permanently hostile to one another, with different theories as to the build of the universe and the progress of time. Isn't that what politics used to mean?'

'H'm, well,' said I, 'I am not so sure of that.'

Said he: 'I take you, neighbour; they only *pretended* to this serious difference of opinion; for if it had existed they could not have dealt together in the ordinary business of life; couldn't have eaten together, bought and sold together, gambled together, cheated other people together, but must have fought whenever they met: which would not have suited them at all. The game of the masters of politics was to cajole or force the public to pay the expense of a luxurious life and exciting amusement for a few cliques of ambitious persons: and the *pretence* of serious difference of opinion, belied by every action of their lives, was quite good enough for that. What has all that got to do with us?'

Said I: 'Why, nothing, I should hope. But I fear— In short, I have been told that political strife was a necessary result of human nature.'

'Human nature!' cried the old boy, impetuously; 'what human nature? The human nature of paupers, of slaves, of slave-holders, or the human nature of wealthy freemen? Which? Come, tell me that!'

'Well,' said I, 'I suppose there would be a difference according to circumstances in people's action about these matters.'

'I should think so, indeed,' said he. 'At all events, experience shows that it is so. Amongst us, our differences concern matters of business, and passing events as to them, and could not divide men permanently. As a rule, the immediate outcome shows which opinion on a given subject is the right one; it is a matter of fact, not of speculation. For instance, it is clearly not easy to knock up a political party on the question as to whether haymaking in such and such a country-side shall begin this week or next, when all men agree that it must at latest begin the week after next, and when any man can go down into the fields himself and see whether the seeds are ripe enough for the cutting.'

Said I: 'And you settle these differences, great and small, by the will of the majority, I suppose?'

'Certainly,' said he; 'how else could we settle them? You see in matters which are merely personal which do not affect the welfare of the community—how a man shall dress, what he shall eat and drink, what he shall write and read, and so forth—there can be no difference of opinion, and everybody does as he pleases. But when the matter is of common interest to the whole community, and the doing or not doing something affects everybody, the majority must have their way; unless the minority were to take up arms and show by force that they were the effective or real majority; which, however, in a society of men who are free and equal is little likely to happen; because in such a community the apparent majority *is* the real majority, and the others, as I have hinted before, know that too well to obstruct from mere pigheadedness; especially as they have had plenty of opportunity of putting forward their side of the question.'

'How is that managed?' said I.

'Well,' said he, 'let us take one of our units of management, a commune, or a ward, or a parish (for we have all three names, indicating little real distinction between them now, though time was there was a good deal). In such a district, as you would call it, some neighbours think that something ought to be done or undone: a new town-hall built; a clearance of inconvenient houses; or say a stone bridge substituted for some ugly old iron one,—there you have undoing and doing in one. Well, at the next ordinary meeting of the neighbours, or Mote, as we call it, according to the ancient tongue of the times before bureaucracy, a neighbour proposes the change, and of course, if everybody agrees, there is an end of discussion, except about details. Equally, if no one backs the proposer,—"seconds him," it used to be called—the matter drops for the time being; a thing not likely to happen amongst reasonable men, however, as the proposer is sure to have talked it over with others before the Mote. But supposing the affair proposed and seconded, if a few of the neighbours disagree to it, if they think that the beastly iron bridge will serve a little longer and they don't want to be bothered with building a new one just then, they don't count heads that time, but put off the formal discussion to the next Mote; and meantime arguments *pro* and *con* are flying about, and some get printed, so that everybody knows what is going on; and when the Mote comes together again there is a regular discussion and at last a vote by show of hands. If the division is a close one, the question is again put off for further discussion; if the division is a wide one, the minority are asked if they will yield to the more general opinion, which they often, nay, most commonly do. If they refuse, the question is debated a third time, when, if the minority has not perceptibly grown, they always give way; though I believe there is some half-forgotten rule by which they might still carry it on further; but I say, what always happens is that they are convinced, not perhaps that their view is the wrong one, but they cannot persuade or force the community to adopt it.'

'Very good,' said I; 'but what happens if the divisions are still narrow?'

Said he: 'As a matter of principle and according to the rule of such cases, the question must then lapse, and the majority, if so narrow, has to submit to sitting down under the *status quo*. But I must tell you that in point of fact the minority very seldom enforces this rule, but generally yields in a friendly manner.'

'But do you know,' said I, 'that there is something in all this very like democracy; and I thought that democracy was considered to be in a moribund condition many, many years ago.'

The old boy's eyes twinkled. 'I grant you that our methods have that drawback. But what is to be done? We can't get *anyone* amongst us to complain of his not always having his own way in the teeth of the community, when it is clear that *everybody* cannot have that indulgence. What *is* to be done?'

'Well,' said I, 'I don't know.'

Said he: 'The only alternatives to our method that I can conceive of are these. First, that we should choose out, or breed, a class of superior persons capable of judging on all matters without consulting the neighbours; that, in short, we should get for ourselves what used to be called an aristocracy of intellect; or, secondly, that for the purpose of safe-guarding the freedom of the individual will, we should revert to a system of private property again, and have slaves and slave-holders once more. What do you think of those two expedients?'

'Well,' said I, 'there is a third possibility—to wit, that every man should be quite independent of every other, and that thus the tyranny of society should be abolished.'

He looked hard at me for a second or two, and then burst out laughing very heartily; and I confess that I joined him. When he recovered himself he nodded at me, and said: 'Yes, yes, I quite agree with you—and so we all do.'

'Yes,' I said, 'and besides, it does not press hardly on the minority: for, take this matter of the bridge, no man is obliged to work on it if he doesn't agree to its building. At least, I suppose not.'

He smiled, and said: 'Shrewdly put; and yet from the point of view of the native of another planet. If the man of the minority does find his feelings hurt, doubtless he may relieve them by refusing to help in building the bridge. But, dear neighbour, that is not a very effective salve for the wound caused by the "tyranny of a majority" in our society; because all work that is done is either beneficial or hurtful to every member of society. The man is benefited by the bridge-building if it turns out a good thing, and hurt by it if it turns out a bad one, whether he puts a hand to it or not; and meanwhile he is benefiting the bridge-builders by his work, whatever that may be. In fact, I see no help for him except the pleasure of saying "I told you so" if the bridge-building turns out to be a mistake and hurts him; if it benefits him he must suffer in silence. A terrible tyranny our Communism, is it not? Folk used often to be warned against this very unhappiness in times past, when for every well-fed, contented person you saw a thousand miserable starvelings. Whereas for us, we grow fat and well-liking on the tyranny; a tyranny, to say the truth, not to be made visible by any microscope I know. Don't be afraid, my friend; we are not going to seek for troubles by calling our peace and plenty and happiness by ill names whose very meaning we have forgotten!'

He sat musing for a little, and then started and said: 'Are there any more questions, dear guest? The morning is waning fast amidst my garrulity.'

CHAPTER XV

ON THE LACK OF INCENTIVE TO LABOUR IN A COMMUNIST SOCIETY

'Yes,' said I. 'I was expecting Dick and Clara to make their appearance any moment: but is there time to ask just one or two questions before they come?'

'Try it, dear neighbour—try it,' said old Hammond. 'For the more you ask me the better I am pleased; and at any rate if they do come and find me in the middle of an answer, they must sit quiet and pretend to listen till I come to an end. It won't hurt them; they will find it quite amusing enough to sit side by side, conscious of their proximity to each other.'

I smiled, as I was bound to, and said: 'Good; I will go on talking without noticing them when they come in. Now, this is what I want to ask you about—to wit, how you get people to work when there is no reward of labour, and especially how you get them to work strenuously?'

'No reward of labour?' said Hammond, gravely. 'The reward of labour is *life*. Is that not enough?'

'But no reward for especially good work,' quoth I.

'Plenty of reward,' said he—the reward of creation. The wages which God gets, as people might have said time agone. If you are going to ask to be paid for the pleasure of creation, which is what excellence in work means, the next thing we shall hear of will be a bill sent in for the begetting of children.'

'Well, but,' said I, 'the man of the nineteenth century would say there is a natural desire towards the procreation of children, and a natural desire not to work.'

'Yes, yes,' said he, 'I know the ancient platitude,—wholly untrue; indeed, to us quite meaningless. Fourier,* whom all men laughed at, understood the matter better.'

'Why is it meaningless to you?' said I.

He said: 'Because it implies that all work is suffering, and we are so far from thinking that, that, as you may have noticed, whereas we are not short of wealth, there is a kind of fear growing up amongst us that we shall one day be short of work. It is a pleasure which we are afraid of losing, not a pain.'

'Yes,' said I, 'I have noticed that, and I was going to ask you about that also. But in the meantime, what do you positively mean to assert about the pleasurableness of work amongst you?'

'This, that *all* work is now pleasurable; either because of the hope of gain in honour and wealth with which the work is done, which causes pleasurable excitement, even when the actual work is not pleasant; or else because it has grown into a pleasurable *habit*, as in the case with what you may call mechanical work; and lastly (and most of our work is of this kind) because there is conscious sensuous pleasure in the work itself; it is done, that is, by artists.'

'I see,' said I. 'Can you now tell me how you have come to this happy condition? For, to speak plainly, this change from the conditions of the older world seems to me far greater and more important than all the other changes you have told me about as to crime, politics, property, marriage.'

'You are right there,' said he. 'Indeed, you may say rather that it is this change which makes all the others possible. What is the object of Revolution? Surely to make people happy. Revolution having brought its foredoomed change about, how can you prevent the counter-revolution from setting in except by making people happy? What! shall we expect peace and stability from unhappiness? The gathering of grapes from thorns and figs from thistles* is a reasonable expectation compared with that! And happiness without happy daily work is impossible.'

'Most obviously true,' said I: for I thought the old boy was preaching a little. 'But answer my question, as to how you gained this happiness.'

'Briefly,' said he, 'by the absence of artificial coercion, and the freedom for every man to do what he can do best, joined to the knowledge of what productions of labour we really wanted. I must admit that this knowledge we reached slowly and painfully.'

'Go on,' said I, 'give me more detail; explain more fully. For this subject interests me intensely.'

'Yes, I will,' said he; 'but in order to do so I must weary you by talking a little about the past. Contrast is necessary for this explanation. Do you mind?'

'No, no,' said I.

Said he, settling himself in his chair again for a long talk: 'It is clear from all that we hear and read, that in the last age of civilisation men had got into a vicious circle in the matter of production of wares. They had reached a wonderful facility of production, and in order to make the most of that facility they had gradually created (or allowed to grow, rather) a most elaborate system of buying and selling, which has been called the World-Market; and that World-Market, once set a-going, forced them to go on making more and more of these wares, whether they needed them or not. So that while (of course) they could not free themselves from the toil of making real necessaries, they created in a never-ending series sham or artificial necessaries, which became, under the iron rule of the aforesaid World-Market, of equal importance to them with the real necessaries which supported life. By all this they burdened themselves with a prodigious mass of work merely for the sake of keeping their wretched system going.'

'Yes—and then?' said I.

'Why, then, since they had forced themselves to stagger along under this horrible burden of unnecessary production, it became impossible for them to look upon labour and its results from any other point of view than one—to wit, the ceaseless endeavour to expend the least possible amount of labour on any article made, and yet at the same time to make as many articles as possible. To this "cheapening of production," as it was called, everything was sacrificed: the happiness of the workman at his work, nay, his most elementary comfort and bare health, his food, his clothes, his dwelling, his leisure, his amusement, his education—his life, in short—did not weigh a grain of sand in the balance against this dire necessity of "cheap production" of things, a great part of which were not worth producing at all. Nay, we are told, and we must believe it, so overwhelming is the evidence, though many of our people scarcely *can* believe it, that even rich and powerful men, the masters of the poor devils aforesaid, submitted to live amidst sights and sounds and smells which it is in the very nature of man to abhor and flee from, in order that their riches might bolster up this supreme folly. The whole community, in fact, was cast into the jaws of this ravening monster, "the cheap production" forced on it by the World-Market.'

'Dear me!' said I. 'But what happened? Did not their cleverness and facility in production master this chaos of misery at last? Couldn't they catch up with the World-Market, and then set to work to devise means for relieving themselves from this fearful task of extra labour?'

He smiled bitterly. 'Did they even try to?' said he. 'I am not sure. You know that according to the old saw the beetle gets used to living in dung; and these people, whether they found the dung sweet or not, certainly lived in it.'

His estimate of the life of the nineteenth century made me catch my breath a little; and I said feebly, 'But the labour-saving machines?'

'Heyday!' quoth he. 'What's that you are saying? the labour-saving machines? Yes, they were made to "save labour" (or, to speak more plainly, the lives of men) on one piece of work in order that it might be expended—I will say wasted—on another, probably useless, piece of work. Friend, all their devices for cheapening labour simply resulted in increasing the burden of labour. The appetite of the World-Market grew with what it fed on: the countries within the ring of "civilisation" (that is, organised misery) were glutted with the abortions of the market,* and force and fraud were used unsparingly to "open up" countries *outside* that pale. This process of "opening up" is a strange one to those who have read the professions of the men of that period and do not understand their practice; and perhaps shows us at its worst the great vice of the nineteenth century, the use of hypocrisy and cant to evade the responsibility of vicarious ferocity. When the civilised World-Market coveted a country not yet in its clutches, some transparent pretext was found—the suppression of a slavery different from and not so cruel as that of commerce; the pushing of a religion no longer believed in by its promoters; the "rescue" of some desperado or homicidal madman whose misdeeds had got him into trouble amongst the natives of the "barbarous" country—any stick, in short, which would beat the dog at all. Then some bold, unprincipled, ignorant adventurer was found (no difficult task in the days of competition), and he was bribed to "create a market" by breaking up whatever traditional society there might be in the doomed country, and by destroying whatever leisure or pleasure he found there. He forced wares on the natives which they did not want, and took their natural products in "exchange," as this form of robbery was called, and thereby he "created new wants," to supply which (that is, to be allowed to live by their new masters) the hapless, helpless people had to sell themselves into the slavery of hopeless toil so that they might have something wherewith to purchase the nullities of "civilisation." Ah,' said the old man, pointing to the Museum, 'I have read books and papers in there, telling strange stories indeed of the dealings of civilisation (or organised misery) with "non-civilisation"; from the time when the British Government deliberately sent blankets infected with small-pox as choice gifts to inconvenient tribes of Red-skins,* to the time when Africa was infested by a man named Stanley,* who—'

'Excuse me,' said I, 'but as you know, time presses; and I want to keep our question on the straightest line possible; and I want at once to ask this about these wares made for the World-Market—how about their quality; these people who were so clever about making goods, I suppose they made them well?'

'Quality!' said the old man crustily, for he was rather peevish at being cut short in his story; 'how could they possibly attend to such trifles as the quality of the wares they sold? The best of them were of a lowish average, the worst were transparent make-shifts for the things asked for, which nobody would have put up with if they could have got anything else. It was a current jest of the time that the wares were made to sell and not to use; a jest which you, as coming from another planet, may understand, but which our folk could not.'

Said I: 'What! did they make nothing well?'

'Why, yes,' said he, 'there was one class of goods which they did make thoroughly well, and that was the class of machines which were used for making things. These were usually quite perfect pieces of workmanship, admirably adapted to the end in view. So that it may be fairly said that the great achievement of the nineteenth century was the making of machines which were wonders of invention, skill, and patience, and which were used for the production of measureless quantities of worthless make-shifts. In truth, the owners of the machines did not consider anything which they made as wares, but simply as means for the enrichment of themselves. Of course, the only admitted test of utility in wares was the finding of buyers for them—wise men or fools, as it might chance.'

'And people put up with this?' said I.

'For a time,' said he.

'And then?'

'And then the overturn,' said the old man, smiling, 'and the nineteenth century saw itself as a man who has lost his clothes whilst bathing, and has to walk naked through the town.'

'You are very bitter about that unlucky nineteenth century,' said I.

'Naturally,' said he, 'since I know so much about it.'

He was silent a little, and then said: 'There are traditions—nay, real histories—in our family about it: my grandfather was one of its victims. If you know something about it, you will understand what he suffered when I tell you that he was in those days a genuine artist, a man of genius, and a revolutionist.'*

'I think I do understand,' said I: 'but now, as it seems, you have reversed all this?'

'Pretty much so,' said he. 'The wares which we make are made because they are needed: men make for their neighbours' use as if they were making for themselves, not for a vague market of which they know nothing, and over which they have no control: as there is no buying and selling, it would be mere insanity to make goods on the chance of their being wanted; for there is no longer any one who can be *compelled* to buy them. So that whatever is made is good, and thoroughly fit for its purpose. Nothing *can* be made except for genuine use; therefore no inferior goods are made. Moreover, as aforesaid, we have now found out what we want, so we make no more than we want; and as we are not driven to make a vast quantity of useless things, we have time and resources enough to consider our pleasure in making them. All work which would be irksome to do by hand is done by immensely improved machinery; and in all work which it is a pleasure to do by hand machinery is done without. There is no difficulty in finding work which suits the special turn of mind of everybody; so that no man is sacrificed to the wants of an other. From time to time, when we have found out that some piece of work was too disagreeable or troublesome, we have given it up and done altogether without the thing produced by it. Now, surely you can see that under these circumstances all the work that we do is an exercise of the mind and body more or less pleasant to be done: so that instead of avoiding work everybody seeks it: and, since people have got defter in doing the work generation after generation, it has become so easy to do, that it seems as if there were less done, though probably more is produced. I suppose this explains that fear, which I hinted at just now, of a possible scarcity in work, which perhaps you have already noticed, and which is a feeling on the increase, and has been for a score of years.'

'But do you think,' said I, 'that there is any fear of a work-famine amongst you?'

'No, I do not,' said he, 'and I will tell why; it is each man's business to make his own work pleasanter and pleasanter, which of course tends towards raising the standard of excellence, as no man enjoys turning out work which is not a credit to him, and also to greater deliberation in turning it out; and there is such a vast number of things which can be treated as works of art, that this alone gives employment to a host of deft people. Again, if art be inexhaustible, so is science also; and though it is no longer the only innocent occupation which is thought worth an intelligent man spending his time upon, as it once was, yet there are, and I suppose will be, many people who are excited by its conquest of difficulties, and care for it more than anything else. Again, as more and more of pleasure is imported into work, I think we shall take up kinds of work which produce desirable wares, but which we gave up because we could not carry them on pleasantly. Moreover, I think that it is only in parts of Europe which are more advanced than the rest of the world that you will hear this talk of the fear of a work-famine. Those lands which were once the colonies of Great Britain, for instance, and especially

America—that part of it, above all, which was once the United States—are now and will be for a long while a great resource to us. For these lands, and, I say, especially the northern parts of America, suffered so terribly from the full force of the last days of civilisation, and became such horrible places to live in, that they are now very backward in all that makes life pleasant. Indeed, one may say that for nearly a hundred years the people of the northern parts of America have been engaged in gradually making a dwelling-place out of a stinking dust-heap; and there is still a great deal to do, especially as the country is so big.'

'Well,' said I, 'I am exceedingly glad to think that you have such a prospect of happiness before you. But I should like to ask a few more questions, and then I have done for to-day.'

CHAPTER XVI

DINNER IN THE HALL OF THE BLOOMSBURY MARKET

As I spoke, I heard footsteps near the door; the latch yielded, and in came our two lovers, looking so handsome that one had no feeling of shame in looking on at their little-concealed love-making; for indeed it seemed as if all the world must be in love with them. As for old Hammond, he looked on them like an artist who has just painted a picture nearly as well as he thought he could when he began it, and was perfectly happy. He said:

'Sit down, sit down, young folk, and don't make a noise. Our guest here has still some questions to ask me.'

'Well, I should suppose so,' said Dick; 'you have only been three hours and a half together; and it isn't to be hoped that the history of two centuries could be told in three hours and a half: let alone that, for all I know, you may have been wandering into the realms of geography and craftsmanship.'

'As to noise, my dear kinsman,' said Clara, 'you will very soon be disturbed by the noise of the dinner-bell, which I should think will be very pleasant music to our guest, who breakfasted early, it seems, and probably had a tiring day yesterday.'

I said: 'Well, since you have spoken the word, I begin to feel that it is so; but I have been feeding myself with wonder this long time past: really, it's quite true,' quoth I, as I saw her smile, O so prettily!

But just then from some tower high up in the air came the sound of silvery chimes playing a sweet clear tune, that sounded to my unaccustomed ears like the song of the first blackbird in the spring, and called a rush of memories to my mind, some of bad times, some of good, but all sweetened now into mere pleasure.

'No more questions now before dinner,' said Clara; and she took my hand as an affectionate child would, and led me out of the room and down stairs into the forecourt of the Museum, leaving the two Hammonds to follow as they pleased.

We went into the market-place which I had been in before, a thinnish stream of elegantly[1] dressed people going in along with us. We turned into the cloister and came to a richly moulded and carved doorway, where a very pretty dark-haired young girl gave us each a beautiful bunch of summer flowers, and we entered a hall much bigger than that of the Hammersmith Guest House, more elaborate in its architecture and perhaps more beautiful. I found it difficult to keep my eyes off the wall-pictures (for I thought it bad manners to stare at Clara all the time, though she was quite worth it). I saw at a glance that their subjects were taken from queer old-world myths and imaginations which in yesterday's world only about half a dozen people in the country knew anything about; and when the two Hammonds sat down opposite to us, I said to the old man, pointing to the frieze:

'How strange to see such subjects here!'

'Why?' said he. 'I don't see why you should be surprised; everybody knows the tales; and they are graceful and pleasant subjects, not too tragic for a place where people mostly eat and drink and amuse themselves, and yet full of incident.'

I smiled, and said: 'Well I scarcely expected to find record of the Seven Swans and the King of the Golden Mountain and Faithful Henry, and such curious pleasant imaginations as Jacob Grimm* got together from the childhood of the world, barely lingering even in

[1] 'Elegant,' I mean, as a Persian pattern is elegant; not like a rich 'elegant' lady out for a morning call. I should rather call that *genteel*.

his time: I should have thought you would have forgotten such childishness by this time.'

The old man smiled, and said nothing; but Dick turned rather red, and broke out:

'What *do* you mean, Guest? I think them very beautiful, I mean not only the pictures, but the stories; and when we were children we used to imagine them going on in every wood-end, by the bight* of every stream: every house in the fields was the Fairyland King's House to us. Don't you remember, Clara?'

'Yes,' she said; and it seemed to me as if a slight cloud came over her fair face. I was going to speak to her on the subject, when the pretty waitresses came to us smiling, and chattering sweetly like reed warblers by the river-side, and fell to giving us our dinner. As to this, as at our breakfast, everything was cooked and served with a daintiness which showed that those who had prepared it were interested in it; but there was no excess either of quantity or of gourmandise; everything was simple, though so excellent of its kind; and it was made clear to us that this was no feast, only an ordinary meal. The glass, crockery, and plate were very beautiful to my eyes, used to the study of mediæval art; but a nineteenth-century club-haunter* would, I daresay, have found them rough and lacking in finish; the crockery being lead-glazed pot-ware, though beautifully ornamented; the only porcelain being here and there a piece of old oriental ware. The glass, again, though elegant and quaint, and very varied in form, was somewhat bubbled and hornier in texture than the commercial articles of the nineteenth century. The furniture and general fittings of the hall were much of a piece with the table-gear, beautiful in form and highly ornamented, but without the commercial 'finish' of the joiners and cabinet-makers of our time. Withal, there was a total absence of what the nineteenth century calls 'comfort'—that is, stuffy inconvenience; so that, even apart from the delightful excitement of the day, I had never eaten my dinner so pleasantly before.

When we had done eating, and were sitting a little while, with a bottle of very good Bordeaux wine before us, Clara came back to the question of the subject-matter of the pictures, as though it had troubled her.

She looked up at them, and said: 'How is it that though we are interested with our life for the most part, yet when people take to writing poems or painting pictures they seldom deal with our modern life, or if they do, take good care to make their poems or pictures unlike that life? Are we not good enough to paint ourselves? How is it that we find the dreadful times of the past so interesting to us—in pictures and poetry?'

Old Hammond smiled. 'It always was so, and I suppose always will be,' said he, 'however it may be explained. It is true that in the nineteenth century, when there was so little art and so much talk about it, there was a theory that art and imaginative literature ought to deal with contemporary life; but they never did so; for, if there was any pretence of it, the author always took care (as Clara hinted just now) to disguise, or exaggerate, or idealise, and in some way or another make it strange; so that, for all the verisimilitude there was, he might just as well have dealt with the times of the Pharaohs.'

'Well,' said Dick, 'surely it is but natural to like these things strange; just as when we were children, as I said just now, we used to pretend to be so-and-so in such-and-such a place. That's what these pictures and poems do; and why shouldn't they?'

'Thou hast hit it, Dick,' quoth old Hammond; 'it is the child-like part of us that produces works of imagination. When we are children time passes so slow with us that we seem to have time for everything.'

He sighed, and then smiled and said: 'At least let us rejoice that we have got back our childhood again. I drink to the days that are!'

'Second childhood,' said I in a low voice, and then blushed at my double rudeness, and hoped that he hadn't heard. But he had, and turned to me smiling, and said: 'Yes why not? And for my part, I hope it may last long; and that the world's next period of wise and unhappy manhood, if that should happen, will speedily lead us to a third childhood: if indeed this age be not our third. Meantime, my friend, you must know that we are too happy, both individually and collectively, to trouble ourselves about what is to come hereafter.'

'Well, for my part,' said Clara, 'I wish we were interesting enough to be written or painted about.'

Dick answered her with some lover's speech, impossible to be written down, and then we sat quiet a little.

CHAPTER XVII
HOW THE CHANGE CAME

Dick broke the silence at last, saying: 'Guest, forgive us for a little after-dinner dulness. What would you like to do? Shall we have out Greylocks and trot back to Hammersmith? or will you come with us and hear some Welsh folk sing in a hall close by here? or would you like presently to come with me into the City and see some really fine building? or—what shall it be?'

'Well,' said I 'as I am a stranger, I must let you choose for me.'

In point of fact, I did not by any means want to be 'amused' just then; and also I rather felt as if the old man, with his knowledge of past times, and even a kind of inverted sympathy for them caused by his active hatred of them, was as it were a blanket for me against the cold of this very new world, where I was, so to say, stripped bare of every habitual thought and way of acting; and I did not want to leave him too soon. He came to my rescue at once, and said—

'Wait a bit, Dick; there is some one else to be consulted besides you and the guest here, and that is I. I am not going to lose the pleasure of his company just now, especially as I know he has something else to ask me. So go to your Welshmen, by all means; but first of all bring us another bottle of wine to this nook, and then be off as soon as you like; and come again and fetch our friend to go westward, but not too soon.'

Dick nodded smilingly, and the old man and I were soon alone in the great hall, the afternoon sun gleaming on the red wine in our tall quaint-shaped glasses. Then said Hammond:

'Does anything especially puzzle you about our way of living, now you have heard a good deal and seen a little of it?'

Said I; 'I think what puzzles me most is how it all came about.'

'It well may,' said he, 'so great as the change is. It would be difficult indeed to tell you the whole story, perhaps impossible: knowledge, discontent, treachery, disappointment, ruin, misery, despair—those who worked for the change because they could see further than other people went through all these phases of suffering; and doubtless all the time the most of men looked on, not knowing what was doing, thinking it all a matter of course, like the rising and setting of the sun—and indeed it was so.'

'Tell me one thing, if you can,' said I. 'Did the change, the "revolution" it used to be called, come peacefully?'

'Peacefully?' said he; 'what peace was there amongst those poor confused wretches of the nineteenth century? It was war from beginning to end: bitter war, till hope and pleasure put an end to it.'

'Do you mean actual fighting with weapons?' said I, 'or the strikes and lock-outs and starvation of which we have heard?'

'Both, both,' he said. 'As a matter of fact, the history of the terrible period of transition from commercial slavery to freedom may thus be summarised. When the hope of realising a communal condition of life for all men arose, quite late in the nineteenth century, the power of the middle classes, the then tyrants of society, was so enormous and crushing, that to almost all men, even those who had, you may say despite themselves, despite their reason and judgement, conceived such hopes, it seemed a dream. So much was this the case that some of those more enlightened men who were then called Socialists, although they well knew, and even stated in public, that the only reasonable condition of Society was that of pure Communism (such as you now see around you), yet shrunk from what seemed to them the barren task of preaching the realisation of a happy dream. Looking back now, we can see that the great motive-power of the change was a longing for freedom and equality, akin if you please to the unreasonable passion of the lover; a sickness of heart that rejected with loathing the aimless solitary life of the well-to-do educated man of that time: phrases, my dear friend, which have lost their meaning to us of the present day; so far removed we are from the dreadful facts which they represent.'

'Well, these men, though conscious of this feeling, had no faith in it, as a means of bringing about the change. Nor was that wonderful: for looking around them they saw the huge mass of the oppressed classes too much burdened with the misery of their lives, and too much overwhelmed by the selfishness of misery, to be able to form a conception of any escape from it except by the ordinary way prescribed by the system of slavery under which they lived; which was nothing more than a remote chance of climbing out of the oppressed into the oppressing class.'

'Therefore, though they knew that the only reasonable aim for those who would better the world was a condition of equality; in their impatience and despair they managed to convince themselves that if they could by hook or by crook get the machinery of production and the management of property so altered that the "lower classes" (so the horrible word ran) might have their slavery somewhat ameliorated, they would be ready to fit into this machinery, and would use it for bettering their condition still more and still more, until at last the result would be a practical equality (they were very fond of using the word "practical"), because "the rich" would be forced to pay so much for keeping "the poor" in a tolerable condition that the condition of riches would become no longer valuable and would gradually die out. Do you follow me?'

'Partly,' said I. 'Go on.'

Said old Hammond: 'Well, since you follow me, you will see that as a theory this was not altogether unreasonable; but "practically," it turned out a failure.'

'How so?' said I.

'Well, don't you see,' said he, 'because it involved the making of a machinery by those who didn't know what they wanted the machines to do. So far as the masses of the oppressed class furthered this scheme of improvement, they did it to get themselves improved slave-rations—as many of them as could. And if those classes had really been incapable of being touched by that instinct which produced the passion for freedom and equality aforesaid, what would have happened, I think, would have been this: that a certain part of the working classes would have been so far improved in condition that they would have approached the condition of the middling rich men; but below them would have been a great class of most miserable slaves, whose slavery would have been far more hopeless than the older class-slavery had been.'

'What stood in the way of this?' said I.

'Why, of course,' said he, 'just that instinct for freedom aforesaid. It is true that the slave-class could not conceive the happiness of a free life. Yet they grew to understand (and very speedily too) that they were oppressed by their masters, and they assumed, you see how justly, that they could do without them, though perhaps they scarce knew how; so that it came to this, that though they could not look forward to the happiness or peace of the freeman, they did at least look forward to the war which a vague hope told them would bring that peace about.'

'Could you tell me rather more closely what actually took place?' said I; for I thought *him* rather vague here.

'Yes,' he said, 'I can. That machinery of life for the use of people who didn't know what they wanted of it, and which was known at the time as State Socialism, was partly put in motion, though in a very piecemeal way. But it did not work smoothly; it was, of course, resisted at every turn by the capitalists; and no wonder, for it tended more and more to upset the commercial system I have told you of, without providing anything really effective in its place. The result was growing confusion, great suffering amongst the working classes, and, as a consequence, great discontent. For a long time matters went on like this. The power of the upper classes had lessened, as their command over wealth lessened, and they could not carry things wholly by the high hand as they had been used to in earlier days. So far the State Socialists were justified by the result. On the other hand, the working classes were ill-organised, and growing poorer in reality, in spite of the gains (also real in the long run) which they had forced from the masters. Thus matters hung in the balance; the masters could not reduce their slaves to complete subjection, though they put down some feeble and partial riots easily enough. The workers forced their masters to grant them ameliorations, real or imaginary, of their condition, but could not force freedom from them. At last came a great crash.* To explain this you must understand that very great progress had been made amongst the workers, though as before said but little in the direction of improved livelihood.'

I played the innocent and said: 'In what direction could they improve, if not in livelihood?'

Said he: 'In the power to bring about a state of things in which livelihood would be full, and easy to gain. They had at last learned how to combine after a long period of mistakes and disasters. The workmen had now a regular organisation in the struggle against their masters, a struggle which for more than half a century had been accepted as an inevitable part of the conditions of the modern system of labour and production. This combination had now taken the form of a federation of all or almost all the recognised wage-paid employments, and it was by its means that those betterments of the condition of the workmen had been forced from the masters: and though they were not seldom mixed up with the rioting that happened, especially in the earlier days of their organisation, it by no means formed an essential part of their tactics; indeed at the time I am now speaking of they had got to be so strong that most commonly the mere threat of a "strike" was enough to gain any minor point: because they had given up the foolish tactics of the ancient trades unions of calling out of work a part only of the workers of such and such an industry, and supporting them while out of work on the labour of those that remained in. By this time they had a biggish fund of money for the support of strikes, and could stop a certain industry altogether for a time if they so determined.'

Said I: 'Was there not a serious danger of such moneys being misused—of jobbery* in fact?'

Old Hammond wriggled uneasily on his seat, and said:

'Though all this happened so long ago, I still feel the pain of mere shame when I have to tell you that it was more than a danger: that such rascality often happened; indeed more than once the whole combination seemed dropping to pieces because of it: but at the time of which I am telling, things looked so threatening, and to the workmen at least the necessity of their dealing with the fast-gathering trouble which the labour-struggle had brought about, was so clear, that the conditions of the times had begot a deep seriousness amongst all reasonable people; a determination which put aside all non-essentials, and which to thinking men was ominous of the swiftly-approaching change; such an element was too dangerous for mere traitors and self-seekers, and one by one they were thrust out and mostly joined the declared reactionaries.'

'How about those ameliorations,' said I; 'what were they? or rather of what nature?'

Said he: 'Some of them, and these of the most practical importance to the men's livelihood, were yielded by the masters by direct compulsion on the part of the men; the new conditions of labour so gained were indeed only customary, enforced by no law: but, once established, the masters durst not attempt to withdraw them in face of the growing power of the combined workers. Some again were steps on the path of "State Socialism"; the most important of which can be speedily summed up. At the end of the nineteenth century the cry arose for compelling the masters to employ their men a less number of hours in the day: this cry gathered volume quickly, and the masters had to yield to it. But it was, of course, clear that unless this meant a higher price for work per hour, it would be a mere nullity, and that the masters, unless forced, would reduce it to that. Therefore after a long struggle another law was passed fixing a minimum price for labour in the most important industries; which again had to be supplemented by a law fixing the maximum price on the chief wares then considered necessary for a workman's life.'

'You were getting perilously near to the late Roman poor-rates,' said I, smiling, 'and the doling out of bread to the proletariat.'

'So many said at the time,' said the old man drily; 'and it has long been a commonplace that that slough awaits State Socialism in the end, if it gets to the end, which as you know it did not with us. However it went further than this minimum and maximum business, which by the by we can now see was necessary. The government now found it imperative on them to meet the outcry of the master class at the approaching destruction of commerce (as desirable, had they known it, as the extinction of the cholera, which has since happily taken place). And they were forced to meet it by a measure hostile to the masters, the establishment of government factories for the production of necessary wares, and markets for their sale. These measures taken altogether did do something: they were in fact of the nature of regulations made by the commander of a beleaguered city. But of course to the privileged classes it seemed as if the end of the world were come when such laws were enacted.

'Nor was that altogether without a warrant: the spread of communistic theories, and the partial practice of State Socialism had at first disturbed, and at last almost paralysed the marvellous system of commerce under which the old world had lived so feverishly, and had produced for some few a life of gambler's pleasure, and for many, or most, a life of mere misery: over and over again came "bad times" as they were called, and indeed they were bad enough for the wage-slaves. The year 1952 was one of the worst of these times; the workmen suffered dreadfully: the partial, inefficient government factories, which were terribly jobbed, all but broke down, and a vast part of the population had for the time being to be fed on undisguised "charity" as it was called.

'The Combined Workers watched the situation with mingled hope and anxiety. They had already formulated their general demands; but now by a solemn and universal vote of the whole of their federated societies, they insisted on the first step being taken toward carrying out their demands: this step would have led directly to handing over the management of the whole natural resources of the country, together with the machinery for using them into the power of the Combined Workers, and the reduction of the privileged classes into the position of pensioners obviously dependent on the pleasure of the workers. The "Resolution," as it was called, which was widely published in the newspapers of the day, was in fact a declaration of war, and was so accepted by the master class. They began henceforward to prepare for a firm stand against the "brutal and ferocious communism of the day," as they phrased it. And as they were in many ways still very powerful, or seemed so to be, they still hoped by means of brute force to regain some of what they had lost, and perhaps in the end the whole of it. It was said amongst them on all hands that it had been a great mistake of the various governments not to have resisted sooner; and the liberals and radicals (the name as perhaps you may know of the more democratically inclined part of the ruling classes) were much blamed for having led the world to this pass by their mis-timed pedantry and foolish sentimentality: and one Gladstone, or Gledstein* (probably, judging by this name, of Scandinavian descent), a notable politician of the nineteenth century, was especially singled out for reprobation in this respect. I need scarcely point out to you the absurdity of all this. But terrible tragedy lay hidden behind this grinning through a horse-collar of the reactionary party. "The insatiable greed of the lower classes must be repressed"—"The people must be taught a lesson"— these were the sacramental phrases current amongst the reactionists, and ominous enough they were.'

The old man stopped to look keenly at my attentive and wondering face; and then said:

'I know, dear guest, that I have been using words and phrases which few people amongst us could understand without long and laborious explanation; and not even then perhaps. But since you have not yet gone to sleep, and since I am speaking to you as to a being from another planet, I may venture to ask you if you have followed me thus far?'

'O yes,' said I, 'I quite understand: pray go on; a great deal of what you have been saying was commonplace with us—when—when —'

'Yes,' said he gravely, 'when you were dwelling in the other planet. Well, now for the crash aforesaid.

'On some comparatively trifling occasion a great meeting was summoned by the workmen leaders to meet in Trafalgar Square (about the right to meet in which place there had for years and years been bickering). The civic bourgeois guard (called the police) attacked the said meeting with bludgeons, according to their custom; many people were hurt in the *mêlée*, of whom five in all died, either trampled to death on the spot, or from the effects of their cudgelling; the meeting was scattered, and some hundreds of prisoners cast into gaol. A similar meeting had been treated in the same way a few days before at a place called Manchester,* which has now disappeared. Thus the "lesson" began. The whole country was thrown into a ferment by this; meetings were held which attempted some rough organisation for the holding of another meeting to retort on the authorities. A huge crowd assembled in Trafalgar Square and the neighbourhood (then a place of crowded streets), and was too big for the bludgeon-armed police to cope with; there was a good deal of dry-blow fighting;* three or four of the people were killed, and half a score of policemen were crushed to death in the throng, and the rest got away as they could. This was a victory for the people as far as it went. The next day all London (remember what it was in those days) was in a state of turmoil. Many of the rich fled into the country; the executive got together soldiery, but did not dare to use them; and the police could not be massed in any one place, because riots or threats of riots were everywhere. But in Manchester, where the people were not so courageous or not so desperate as in London, several of the popular leaders were arrested. In London a convention of leaders was got together from the Federation of Combined Workmen, and sat under the old revolutionary name of the Committee of Public Safety;* but as they had no drilled and armed body of men to direct, they attempted no aggressive measures, but only placarded the walls with somewhat vague appeals to the workmen not to allow themselves to be trampled upon. However, they called a meeting in Trafalgar Square for the day fortnight of the last-mentioned skirmish.

'Meantime the town grew no quieter, and business came pretty much to an end. The newspapers—then, as always hitherto, almost entirely in the hands of the masters—clamoured to the Government for repressive measures; the rich citizens were enrolled as an extra body of police, and armed with bludgeons like them; many of these were strong, well-fed, full-blooded young men, and had plenty of stomach for fighting; but the Government did not dare to use them, and contented itself with getting full powers voted to it by the Parliament for suppressing any revolt, and bringing up more and more soldiers to London. Thus passed the week after the great meeting; almost as large a one was held on the Sunday, which went off peaceably on the whole, as no opposition to it was offered, and again the people cried "victory." But on the Monday the people woke up to find that they were hungry. During the last few days there had been groups of men parading the streets asking (or, if you please, demanding) money to buy food; and what for goodwill, what for fear, the richer people gave them a good deal. The authorities of the parishes also (I haven't time to explain that phrase at present) gave willy-nilly what provisions they could to wandering people; and the Government, by means of its feeble national workshops, also fed a good number of half-starved folk. But in addition to this, several bakers' shops and other provision stores had been emptied without a great deal of disturbance. So far, so good. But on the Monday in question the Committee of Public Safety, on the one hand afraid of general unorganised pillage, and on the other emboldened by the wavering conduct of the authorities, sent a deputation provided with carts and all necessary gear to clear out two or three big provision stores in the centre of the town, leaving papers with the shop managers promising to pay the price of them: and also in the part of the town where they were strongest they took possession of several bakers' shops and set men at work in them for the benefit of the people;—all of which was done with little or no disturbance, the police assisting in keeping order at the sack of the stores, as they would have done at a big fire.

'But at this last stroke the reactionaries were so alarmed, that they were determined to force the executive into action. The newspapers next day all blazed into the fury of frightened people, and threatened the people, the Government, and everybody they could think of, unless "order were at once restored." A deputation of leading commercial people waited on the Government and told them that if they did not at once arrest the Committee of Public Safety, they themselves would gather a body of men, arm them, and fall on "the incendiaries" as they called them.

'They, together with a number of the newspaper editors, had a long interview with the heads of the Government and two or three military men, the deftest in their art that the country could furnish. The deputation came away from that interview, says a contemporary eye-witness, smiling and satisfied, and said no more about raising an anti-popular army, but that afternoon left London with their families for their country seats or elsewhere.

'The next morning the Government proclaimed a state of siege in London,—a thing common enough amongst the absolutist governments on the Continent, but unheard-of in England in those days. They appointed the youngest and cleverest of their generals* to command the proclaimed district; a man who had won a certain sort of reputation in the disgraceful wars in which the country had been long engaged from time to time. The newspapers were in ecstasies, and all the most fervent of the reactionaries now came to the front; men who in ordinary times were forced to keep their opinions to themselves or their immediate circle, but who began to look forward to crushing once for all the Socialist, and even democratic tendencies, which, said they, had been treated with such foolish indulgence for the last sixty years.*

'But the clever general took no visible action; and yet only a few of the minor newspapers abused him; thoughtful men gathered from this that a plot was hatching. As for the Committee of Public Safety, whatever they thought of their position, they had now gone too far to draw back; and many of them, it seems, thought that the Government would not act. They went on quietly organising their food supply, which was a miserable driblet when all is said; and also as a retort to the state of siege, they armed as many men as they could in the quarter where they were strongest, but did not attempt to drill or organise them, thinking, perhaps, that they could not at the best turn them into trained soldiers till they had some breathing space. The clever general, his soldiers, and the police did not meddle with all this in the least in the world; and things were quieter in London that week-end; though there were riots in many places of the provinces, which were quelled by the authorities without much trouble. The most serious of these were at Glasgow and Bristol.

'Well, the Sunday of the meeting came, and great crowds came to Trafalgar Square in procession, the greater part of the Committee amongst them, surrounded by their band of men armed somehow or other. The streets were quite peaceful and quiet, though there were many spectators to see the procession pass. Trafalgar Square had no body of police in it; the people took quiet possession of it, and the meeting began. The armed men stood round the principal platform, and there were a few others armed amidst the general crowd; but by far the greater part were unarmed.

'Most people thought the meeting would go off peaceably; but the members of the Committee had heard from various quarters that something would be attempted against them; but these rumours were vague, and they had no idea of what threatened. They soon found out.

'For before the streets about the Square were filled, a body of soldiers poured into it from the north-west corner and took up their places by the houses that stood on the west side. The people growled at the sight of the red-coats; the armed men of the Committee stood undecided, not knowing what to do; and indeed this new influx so jammed the crowd together that, unorganised as they were, they had little chance of working through it. They had scarcely grasped the fact of their enemies being there, when another column of soldiers, pouring out of the streets which led into the great southern road going down to the Parliament House (still existing, and called the Dung Market), and also from the embankment by the side of the Thames,* marched up, pushing the crowd into a denser and denser mass, and formed along the south side of the Square. Then any of those who could see what was going on, knew at once that they were in a trap, and could only wonder what would be done with them.

'The closely-packed crowd would not or could not budge, except under the influence of the height of terror, which was soon to be supplied to them. A few of the armed men struggled to the front, or climbed up to the base of the monument which then stood there,* that they might face the wall of hidden fire before them; and to most men (there were many women amongst them) it seemed as if the end of the world had come, and to-day seemed strangely different from yesterday. No sooner were the soldiers drawn up aforesaid than, says an eye-witness, "a glittering officer on horseback came prancing out from the ranks on the south, and read something from a paper which he held in his hand; which something, very few heard; but I was told afterwards that it was an order for us to disperse, and a warning that he had legal right to fire on the crowd else, and that he would do so. The crowd took it as a challenge of some sort, and a hoarse threatening roar went up from them; and after that there was comparative silence for a little, till the officer had got back into the ranks. I was near the edge of the crowd, towards the soldiers," says this eye-witness, "and I saw three little machines being wheeled out in front of the ranks, which I knew for mechanical guns. I cried out, 'Throw yourselves down! they are going to fire!' But no one scarcely could throw himself down, so tight as the crowds were packed. I heard a sharp order given, and wondered where I should be the next minute; and then—It was as if the earth had opened, and hell had come up bodily amidst us. It is no use trying to describe the scene that followed. Deep lanes were mowed amidst the thick crowd; the dead and dying covered the ground, and the shrieks and wails and cries of horror filled all the air, till it seemed as if there was nothing else in the world but murder and death. Those of our armed men who were still unhurt cheered wildly and opened a scattering fire on the soldiers. One or two soldiers fell; and I saw the officers going up and down the ranks urging the men to fire again; but they received the orders in sullen silence, and let the butts of their guns fall. Only one sergeant ran to a machine-gun and began to set it going; but a tall young man, an officer too, ran out of the ranks and dragged him back by the collar; and the soldiers stood there motionless while the horror-stricken crowd, nearly wholly unarmed (for most of the armed men had fallen in that first discharge), drifted out of the Square. I was told afterwards that the soldiers on the west side had fired also, and done their part of the slaughter. How I got out of the Square I scarcely know: I went, not feeling the ground under me, what with rage and terror and despair."

'So says our eye-witness. The number of the slain on the side of the people in that shooting during a minute was prodigious; but it was not easy to come at the truth about it; it was probably between one and two thousand. Of the soldiers, six were killed outright, and a dozen wounded.'

I listened, trembling with excitement. The old man's eyes glittered and his face flushed as he spoke, and told the tale of what I had often thought might happen. Yet I wondered that he should have got so elated about a mere massacre, and I said:

'How fearful! And I suppose that this massacre put an end to the whole revolution for that time?'

'No, no,' cried old Hammond; 'it began it!'

He filled his glass and mine, and stood up and cried out, 'Drink this glass to the memory of those who died there, for indeed it would be a long tale to tell how much we owe them.'

I drank, and he sat down again and went on.

'That massacre of Trafalgar Square began the civil war, though, like all such events, it gathered head slowly, and people scarcely knew what a crisis they were acting in.

'Terrible as the massacre was, and hideous and overpowering as the first terror had been, when the people had time to think about it, their feeling was one of anger rather than fear; although the military organisation of the state of siege was now carried out without shrinking by the clever young general. For though the ruling-classes when the news spread next morning felt one gasp of horror and even dread, yet the Government and their immediate backers felt that now the wine was drawn and must be drunk. However, even the most reactionary of the capitalist papers, with two exceptions, stunned by the tremendous news, simply gave an account of what had taken place, without making any comment upon it. The exceptions were one, a so-called "liberal" paper* (the Government of the day was of that complexion), which, after a preamble in which it declared its undeviating sympathy with the cause of labour, proceeded to point out that in times of revolutionary disturbance it behoved the government to be just but firm, and that by far the most merciful way of dealing with the poor madmen who were attacking the very foundations of society (which had made them mad and poor) was to shoot them at once, so as to stop others from drifting into a position in which they would run a chance of being shot. In short, it praised the determined action of the Government as the *acmé* of human wisdom and mercy, and exulted in the inauguration of an epoch of reasonable democracy free from the tyrannical fads of Socialism.

'The other exception was a paper* thought to be one of the most violent opponents of democracy, and so it was; but the editor of it found his manhood, and spoke for himself and not for his paper. In a few simple, indignant words he asked people to consider what a society was worth which had to be defended by the massacre of unarmed citizens, and called on the Government to withdraw their state of siege and put the general and his officers who fired on the people on their trial for murder. He went further, and declared that whatever his opinion might be as to the doctrines of the Socialists, he for one should throw in his lot with the people, until the Government atoned for their atrocity by showing that they were prepared to listen to the demands of men who knew what they wanted, and whom the decrepitude of society forced into pushing their demands in some way or other.

'Of course, this editor was immediately arrested by the military power; but his bold words were already in the hands of the public, and produced a great effect: so great an effect that the Government, after some vacillation, withdrew the state of siege; though at the same time it strengthened the military organisation and made it more stringent. Three of the Committee for Public Safety had been slain in Trafalgar Square: of the rest, the greater part went back to their old place of meeting, and there awaited the event calmly. They were arrested there on the Monday morning, and would have been shot at once by the general, who was a mere military machine, if the Government had not shrunk before the responsibility of killing men without any trial. There was at first a talk of trying them by a special commission of judges, as it was called—*i.e.*, before a set of men bound to find them guilty, and whose business it was to do so. But with the Government the cold fit had succeeded to the hot one; and the prisoners were brought before a jury at the assizes. There a fresh blow awaited the Government; for in spite of the judge's charge, which distinctly instructed the jury to find the prisoners guilty, they were acquitted, and the jury added to their verdict a presentment, in which they condemned the action of the soldiery, in the queer phraseology of the day, as "rash, unfortunate, and unnecessary." The Committee of Public Safety renewed its sittings, and from thenceforth was a popular rallying-point in opposition to the Parliament. The Government now gave way on all sides, and made a show of yielding to the demands of the people, though there was a widespread plot for effecting a *coup d'état* set on foot between the leaders of the two so-called opposing parties in the parliamentary faction fight. The well-meaning part of the public was overjoyed, and thought that all danger of a civil war was over. The victory of the people was celebrated by huge meetings held in the parks and elsewhere, in memory of the victims of the great massacre.

'But the measures passed for the relief of the workers, though to the upper classes they seemed ruinously revolutionary, were not thorough enough to give the people food and a decent life, and they had to be supplemented by unwritten enactments without legality to back them. Although the Government and Parliament had the law-courts, the army, and "society" at their backs, the Committee of Public Safety began to be a force in the country, and really represented the producing classes. It began to improve immensely in the days which followed on the acquittal of its members. Its old members had little administrative capacity, though with the exception of a few self-seekers and traitors, they were honest, courageous men, and many of them were endowed with considerable talent of other kinds. But now that the times called for immediate action, came forward the men capable of setting it on foot; and a new network of workmen's associations grew up very speedily, whose avowed single object was the tiding over of the ship of the community into a simple condition of Communism; and as they practically undertook also the management of the ordinary labour-war, they soon became the mouthpiece and intermediary of the whole of the working classes; and the manufacturing profit-grinders now found themselves powerless before this combination; unless *their* committee, Parliament, plucked up courage to begin the civil war again, and to shoot right and left, they were bound to yield to the demands of the men whom they employed, and pay higher and higher wages for shorter and shorter day's work. Yet one ally they had, and that was the rapidly approaching breakdown of the whole system founded on the World-Market and its supply; which now became so clear to all people, that the middle classes, shocked for the moment into condemnation of the Government for the great massacre, turned round nearly in a mass, and called on the Government to look to matters, and put an end to the tyranny of the Socialist leaders.

'Thus stimulated, the reactionist plot exploded probably before it was ripe; but this time the people and their leaders were forewarned, and, before the reactionaries could get under way, had taken the steps they thought necessary.

'The Liberal Government (clearly by collusion) was beaten by the Conservatives, though the latter were nominally much in the minority. The popular representatives in the House understood pretty well what this meant, and after an attempt to fight the matter out by divisions in the House of Commons, they made a protest, left the House, and came in a body to the Committee of Public Safety: and the civil war began again in good earnest.

'Yet its first act was not one of mere fighting. The new Tory Government determined to act, yet durst not re-enact the state of siege, but it sent a body of soldiers and police to arrest the Committee of Public Safety in the lump. They made no resistance, though they might have done so, as they had now a considerable body of men who were quite prepared for extremities. But they were determined to try first a weapon which they thought stronger than street fighting.

'The members of the Committee went off quietly to prison; but they had left their soul and their organisation behind them. For they depended not on a carefully arranged centre with all kinds of checks and counter-checks about it, but on a huge mass of people in thorough sympathy with the movement, bound together by a great number of links of small centres with very simple instructions. These instructions were now carried out.

'The next morning, when the leaders of the reaction were chuckling at the effect which the report in the newspapers of their stroke would have upon the public—no newspapers appeared; and it was only towards noon that a few straggling sheets, about the size of the gazettes of the seventeenth century, worked by policemen, soldiers, managers, and press-writers, were dribbled through the streets. They were greedily seized on and read; but by this time the serious part of their news was stale, and people did not need to be told that the GENERAL STRIKE had begun. The railways did not run, the telegraph-wires were unserved; flesh, fish, and green stuff brought to market was allowed to lie there still packed and perishing; the thousands of middle-class families, who were utterly dependent for the next meal on the workers, made frantic efforts through their more energetic members to cater for the needs of the day, and amongst those of them who could throw off the fear of what was to follow, there was, I am told, a certain enjoyment of this unexpected picnic—a forecast of the days to come, in which all labour grew pleasant.

'So passed the first day, and towards evening the Government grew quite distracted. They had but one resource for putting down any popular movement—to wit, mere brute-force; but there was nothing for them against which to use their army and police: no armed bodies appeared in the streets; the offices of the Federated Workmen were now, in appearance, at least, turned into places for the relief of people thrown out of work, and under the circumstances, they durst not arrest the men engaged in such business, all the more, as even that night many quite respectable people applied at these offices for relief, and swallowed down the charity of the revolutionists along with their supper. So the Government massed soldiers and police here and there—and sat still for that night, fully expecting on the morrow some manifesto from "the rebels," as they now began to be called, which would give them an opportunity of acting in some way or another. They were disappointed. The ordinary newspapers gave up the struggle that morning, and only one very violent reactionary paper (called the *Daily Telegraph*)* attempted an appearance, and rated "the rebels" in good set terms for their folly and ingratitude in tearing out the bowels of their "common mother," the English Nation, for the benefit of a few greedy paid agitators, and the fools whom they were deluding. On the other hand, the Socialist papers (of which three only, representing somewhat different schools, were published in London)* came out full to the throat of well-printed matter. They were greedily bought by the whole public, who, of course, like the Government, expected a manifesto in them. But they found no word of reference to the great subject. It seemed as if their editors had ransacked their drawers for articles which would have been in place forty years before,* under the technical name of educational articles. Most of these were admirable and straightforward expositions of the doctrines and practice of Socialism, free from haste and spite and hard words, and came upon the public with a kind of May-day freshness, amidst the worry and terror of the moment; and though the knowing well understood that the meaning of this move in the game was mere defiance, and a token of irreconcilable hostility to the then rulers of society, and though, also, they were meant for nothing else by "the rebels," yet they really had their effect as "educational articles." However, "education" of another kind was acting upon the public with irresistible power, and probably cleared their heads a little.

'As to the Government, they were absolutely terrified by this act of "boycotting"* (the slang word then current for such acts of abstention). Their counsels became wild and vacillating to the last degree: one hour they were for giving way for the present till they could hatch another plot; the next they all but sent an order for the arrest in the lump of all the workmen's committees; the next they were on the point of ordering their brisk young general to take any excuse that offered for another massacre. But when they called to mind that the soldiery in that "Battle" of Trafalgar Square were so daunted by the slaughter which they had made, that they could not be got to fire a second volley, they shrank back again from the dreadful courage necessary for carrying out another massacre. Meantime the prisoners, brought the second time before the magistrates under a strong escort of soldiers, were the second time remanded.

'The strike went on this day also. The workmen's committees were extended, and gave relief to great numbers of people, for they had organised a considerable amount of production of food by men whom they could depend upon. Quite a number of well-to-do people were now compelled to seek relief of them. But another curious thing happened: a band of young men of the upper classes armed themselves, and coolly went marauding in the streets, taking what suited them of such eatables and portables that they came across in the shops which had ventured to open. This operation they carried out in Oxford Street, then a great street of shops of all kinds. The Government, being at that hour in one of their yielding moods, thought this a fine opportunity for showing their impartiality in the maintenance of "order," and sent to arrest these hungry rich youths; who, however, surprised the police by a valiant resistance, so that all but three escaped. The Government did not gain the reputation for impartiality which they expected from this move; for they forgot that there were no evening papers; and the account of the skirmish spread wide indeed, but in a distorted form; for it was mostly told simply as an exploit of the starving people from the East-end; and everybody thought it was but natural for the Government to put them down when and where they could.

'That evening the rebel prisoners were visited in their cells by *very* polite and sympathetic persons, who pointed out to them what a suicidal course they were following, and how dangerous these extreme courses were for the popular cause. Says one of the prisoners: "It was great sport comparing notes when we came out anent* the attempt of the Government to 'get at' us separately in prison, and how we answered the blandishments of the highly 'intelligent and refined' persons set on to pump us. One laughed; another told extravagant long-bow stories* to the envoy; a third held a sulky silence; a fourth damned the polite spy and bade him hold his jaw—and that was all they got out of us."

'So passed the second day of the great strike. It was clear to all thinking people that the third day would bring on the crisis; for the present suspense and ill-concealed terror was unendurable. The ruling classes, and the middle-class non-politicians who had been their real strength and support, were as sheep lacking a shepherd; they literally did not know what to do.

'One thing they found they had to do: try to get the "rebels" to do something. So the next morning, the morning of the third day of the strike, when the members of the Committee for Public Safety appeared again before the magistrate, they found themselves treated with the greatest possible courtesy—in fact, rather as envoys and ambassadors than prisoners. In short, the magistrate had received his orders; and with no more to do than might come of a long stupid speech, which might have been written by Dickens in mockery, he discharged the prisoners, who went back to their meeting-place and at once began a due sitting. It was high time. For this third day the mass was fermenting indeed. There was, of course, a vast number of working people who were not organised in the least in the world; men who had been used to act as their masters drove them, or rather as the system drove, of which their masters were a part. That system was now falling to pieces, and the old pressure of the master having been taken off these poor men, it seemed likely that nothing but the mere animal necessities and passions of men would have any hold on them, and that mere general overturn would be the result. Doubtless this would have happened if it had not been that the huge mass had been leavened by Socialist opinion in the first place, and in the second by actual contact with declared Socialists, many or indeed most of whom were members of those bodies of workmen above said.

'If anything of this kind had happened some years before, when the masters of labour were still looked upon as the natural rulers of the people, and even the poorest and most ignorant man leaned upon them for support, while they submitted to their fleecing, the entire break-up of all society would have followed. But the long series of years during which the workmen had learned to despise their rulers, had done away with their dependence upon them, and they were now beginning to trust (somewhat dangerously, as events proved) in the non-legal leaders whom events had thrust forward; and though most of these were now become mere figure-heads, their names and reputations were useful in this crisis as a stop-gap.

'The effect of the news, therefore, of the release of the Committee gave the Government some breathing time: for it was received with the greatest joy by the workers, and even the well-to-do saw in it a respite from the mere destruction which they had begun to dread, and the fear of which most of them attributed to the weakness of the Government. As far as the passing hour went, perhaps they were right in this.'

'How do you mean?' said I. 'What could the Government have done? I often used to think that they would be helpless in such a crisis.'

Said old Hammond: 'Of course I don't doubt that in the long run matters would have come about as they did. But if the Government could have treated their army as a real army, and used them strategically as a general would have done, looking on the people as a mere open enemy to be shot at and dispersed wherever they turned up, they would probably have gained a victory at the time.'

'But would the soldiers have acted against the people in this way?' said I.

Said he: 'I think from all I have heard that they would have done so if they had met bodies of men armed however badly, and however badly they had been organised. It seems also as if before the Trafalgar Square massacre they might as a whole have been depended upon to fire upon an unarmed crowd, though they were much honeycombed by Socialism. The reason for this was that they dreaded the use by apparently unarmed men of an explosive called dynamite,* of which many loud boasts were made by the workers on the eve of these events; although it turned out to be of little use as a material for war in the way that was expected. Of course the officers of the soldiery fanned this fear to the utmost, so that the rank and file probably thought on that occasion that they were being led into a desperate battle with the men who were really armed, and whose weapon was the more dreadful, because it was concealed. After that massacre, however, it was at all times doubtful if the regular soldiers would fire upon an unarmed or half-armed crowd.'

Said I: 'The regular soldiers? Then there were other combatants against the people?'

'Yes,' said he, 'we shall come to that presently.'

'Certainly,' I said, 'you had better go on straight with your story. I see that time is wearing.'

Said Hammond: 'The Government lost no time in coming to terms with the Committee of Public Safety; for indeed they could think of nothing else than the danger of the moment. They sent a duly accredited envoy to treat with these men, who somehow had obtained dominion over people's minds, while the formal rulers had no hold except over their bodies. There is no need at present to go into the details of the truce (for such it was) between these high contracting parties, the Government of the empire of Great Britain and a handful of working-men (as they were called in scorn in those days), amongst whom, indeed, were some very capable and "square-headed" persons, though, as aforesaid, the abler men were not then the recognised leaders. The upshot of it was that all the definite claims of the people had to be granted. We can now see that most of these claims were of themselves not worth either demanding or resisting; but they were looked on at that time as most important, and they were at least tokens of revolt against the miserable system of life which was then beginning to tumble to pieces. One claim, however, was of the utmost immediate importance, and this the Government tried hard to evade; but as they were not dealing with fools, they had to yield at last. This was the claim of recognition and formal status for the Committee of Public Safety, and all the associations which it fostered under its wing. This it is clear meant two things: first, amnesty for "the rebels," great and small, who, without a distinct act of civil war, could no longer be attacked; and next, a continuance of the organised revolution. Only one point the Government could gain, and that was a name. The dreadful revolutionary title was dropped, and the body, with its branches, acted under the respectable name of the "Board of Conciliation and its local offices." Carrying this name, it became the leader of the people in the civil war which soon followed.'

'O,' said I, somewhat startled, 'so the civil war went on, in spite of all that had happened?'

'So it was,' said he. 'In fact, it was this very legal recognition which made the civil war possible in the ordinary sense of war; it took the struggle out of the element of mere massacres on one side, and endurance plus strikes on the other.'

'And can you tell me in what kind of way the war was carried on?' said I.

'Yes,' he said; 'we have records and to spare of all that; and the essence of them I can give you in a few words. As I told you, the rank and file of the army was not to be trusted by the reactionists; but the officers generally were prepared for anything, for they were mostly the very stupidest men in the country. Whatever the Government might do, a great part of the upper and middle classes were determined to set on foot a counter revolution; for the Communism which now loomed ahead seemed quite unendurable to them. Bands of young men, like the marauders in the great strike of whom I told you just now, armed themselves and drilled, and began on any opportunity or pretence to skirmish with the people in the streets. The Government neither helped them nor put them down, but stood by, hoping that something might come of it. These "Friends of Order,"* as they were called, had some successes at first, and grew bolder; they got many officers of the regular army to help them, and by their means laid hold of munitions of war of all kinds. One part of their tactics consisted in their guarding and even garrisoning the big factories of the period: they held at one time, for instance, the whole of that place called Manchester which I spoke of just now. A sort of irregular war was carried on with varied success all over the country; and at last the Government, which at first pretended to ignore the struggle, or treat it as mere rioting, definitely declared for "the Friends of Order," and joined to their bands whatsoever of the regular army they could get together, and made a desperate effort to overwhelm "the rebels," as they were now once more called, and as indeed they called themselves.

'It was too late. All ideas of peace on a basis of compromise had disappeared on either side. The end, it was seen clearly, must be either absolute slavery for all but the privileged, or a system of life founded on equality and Communism. The sloth, the hopelessness, and, if I may say so, the cowardice of the last century, had given place to the eager, restless heroism of a declared revolutionary period. I will not say that the people of that time foresaw the life we are leading now, but there was a general instinct amongst them towards the essential part of that life, and many men saw clearly beyond the desperate struggle of the day into the peace which it was to bring about. The men of that day who were on the side of freedom were not unhappy, I think, though they were harassed by hopes and fears, and sometimes torn by doubts, and the conflict of duties hard to reconcile.'

'But how did the people, the revolutionists, carry on the war? What were the elements of success on their side?'

I put this question, because I wanted to bring the old man back to the definite history, and take him out of the musing mood so natural to an old man.

He answered: 'Well, they did not lack organisers; for the very conflict itself, in days when, as I told you, men of any strength of mind cast away all consideration for the ordinary business of life, developed the necessary talent amongst them. Indeed, from all I have read and heard, I much doubt whether, without this seemingly dreadful civil war, the due talent for administration would have been developed amongst the working men. Anyhow, it was there, and they soon got leaders far more than equal to the best men amongst the reactionaries. For the rest, they had no difficulty about the material of their army; for that revolutionary instinct so acted on the ordinary soldier in the ranks that the greater part, certainly the best part, of the soldiers joined the side of the people. But the main element of their success was this, that wherever the working people were not coerced, they worked, not for the reactionists, but for "the rebels." The reactionists could get no work done for them outside the districts where they were all-powerful: and even in those districts they were harassed by continual risings; and in all cases and everywhere got nothing done without obstruction and black looks and sulkiness; so that not only were their armies quite worn out with the difficulties which they had to meet, but the non-combatants who were on their side were so worried and beset with hatred and a thousand little troubles and annoyances that life became almost unendurable to them on those terms. Not a few of them actually died of the worry; many committed suicide. Of course, a vast number of them joined actively in the cause of reaction, and found some solace to their misery in the eagerness of conflict. Lastly, many thousands gave way and submitted to "the rebels"; and as the numbers of these latter increased, it at last became clear to all men that the cause which was once hopeless, was now triumphant, and that the hopeless cause was that of slavery and privilege.'

CHAPTER XVIII

THE BEGINNING OF THE NEW LIFE

'Well,' said I, 'so you got clear out of all your trouble. Were people satisfied with the new order of things when it came?'

'People?' he said. 'Well, surely all must have been glad of peace when it came; especially when they found, as they must have found, that after all, they—even the once rich—were not living very badly. As to those who had been poor, all through the war, which lasted about two years, their condition had been bettering, in spite of the struggle; and when peace came at last, in a very short time they made great strides towards a decent life. The great difficulty was that the once-poor had such a feeble conception of the real pleasure of life: so to say, they did not ask enough, did not know how to ask enough, from the new state of things. It was perhaps rather a good than an evil thing that the necessity for restoring the wealth destroyed during the war forced them into working at first almost as hard as they had been used to before the Revolution. For all historians are agreed that there never was a war in which there was so much destruction of wares, and instruments for making them as in this civil war.'

'I am rather surprised at that,' said I.

'Are you? I don't see why,' said Hammond.

'Why,' I said, 'because the party of order would surely look upon the wealth as their own property, no share of which, if they could help it, should go to their slaves, supposing they conquered. And on the other hand, it was just for the possession of that wealth that "the rebels" were fighting, and I should have thought, especially when they saw that they were winning, that they would have been careful to destroy as little as possible of what was so soon to be their own.'

'It was as I have told you, however,' said he. 'The party of order, when they recovered from their first cowardice of surprise—or, if you please, when they fairly saw that, whatever happened, they would be ruined, fought with great bitterness, and cared little what they did, so long as they injured the enemies who had destroyed the sweets of life for them. As to "the rebels," I have told you that the outbreak of actual war made them careless of trying to save the wretched scraps of wealth that they had. It was a common saying amongst them, Let the country be cleared of everything except valiant living men, rather than that we fall into slavery again!'

He sat silently thinking a little while, and then said:

'When the conflict was once really begun, it was seen how little of any value there was in the old world of slavery and inequality. Don't you see what it means? In the times which you are thinking of, and of which you seem to know so much, there was no hope; nothing but the dull jog of the mill-horse under compulsion of collar and whip; but in that fighting-time that followed, all was hope: "the rebels" at least felt themselves strong enough to build up the world again from its dry bones,—and they did it, too!' said the old man, his eyes glittering under his beetling brows. He went on: 'And their opponents at least and at last learned something about the reality of life, and its sorrows, which they—their class, I mean—had once known nothing of. In short, the two combatants, the workman and the gentleman, between them—'

'Between them,' said I, quickly, 'they destroyed commercialism!'

'Yes, yes, YES,' said he; 'that is it. Nor could it have been destroyed otherwise; except, perhaps, by the whole of society gradually falling into lower depths, till it should at last reach a condition as rude as barbarism, but lacking both the hope and the pleasures of barbarism. Surely the sharper, shorter remedy was the happiest.'

'Most surely,' said I.

'Yes,' said the old man, 'the world was being brought to its second birth; how could that take place without a tragedy? Moreover, think of it. The spirit of the new days, of our days, was to be delight in the life of the world; intense and overweening love of the very skin and surface of the earth on which man dwells, such as a lover has in the fair flesh of the woman he loves; this, I say, was to be the new spirit of the time. All other moods save this had been exhausted: the unceasing criticism, the boundless curiosity in the ways and thoughts of man, which was the mood of the ancient Greek, to whom these things were not so much a means, as an end, was gone past recovery; nor had there been really any shadow of it in the so-called science of the nineteenth century, which, as you must know, was in the main an appendage to the commercial system; nay, not seldom an appendage to the police of that system. In spite of appearances, it was limited and cowardly, because it did not really believe in itself. It was the outcome, as it was the sole relief, of the unhappiness of the period which made life so bitter even to the rich, and which, as you may see with your bodily eyes, the great change has swept away. More akin to our way of looking at life was the spirit of the Middle Ages, to whom heaven and the life of the next world was such a reality, that it became to them a part of the life upon the earth; which accordingly they loved and adorned, in spite of the ascetic doctrines of their formal creed, which bade them contemn it.

'But that also, with its assured belief in heaven and hell as two countries in which to live, has gone, and now we do, both in word and in deed, believe in the continuous life of the world of men, and as it were, add every day of that common life to the little stock of days which our own mere individual experience wins for us: and consequently we are happy. Do you wonder at it? In times past, indeed, men were told to love their kind, to believe in the religion of humanity, and so forth. But look you, just in the degree that a man had elevation of mind and refinement enough to be able to value this idea, was he repelled by the obvious aspect of the individuals composing the mass which he was to worship; and he could only evade that repulsion by making a conventional abstraction of mankind that had little actual or historical relation to the race; which to his eyes was divided into blind tyrants on the one hand and apathetic degraded slaves on the other. But now, where is the difficulty in accepting the religion of humanity, when the men and women who go to make up humanity are free, happy, and energetic at least, and most commonly beautiful of body also, and surrounded by beautiful things of their own fashioning, and a nature bettered and not worsened by contact with mankind? This is what this age of the world has reserved for us.'

'It seems true,' said I, 'or ought to be, if what my eyes have seen is a token of the general life you lead. Can you now tell me anything of your progress after the years of the struggle?'

Said he: 'I could easily tell you more than you have time to listen to; but I can at least hint at one of the chief difficulties which had to be met: and that was, that when men began to settle down after the war, and their labour had pretty much filled up the gap in wealth caused by the destruction of that war, a kind of disappointment seemed coming over us, and the prophecies of some of the reactionists of past times seemed as if they would come true, and a dull level of utilitarian comfort be the end for a while of our aspirations and success. The loss of the competitive spur to exertion had not, indeed, done anything to interfere with the necessary production of the community, but how if it should make men dull by giving them too much time for thought or idle musing? But, after all, this dull thunder-cloud only threatened us, and then passed over. Probably, from what I have told you before, you will have a guess at the remedy for such a disaster; remembering always that many of the things which used to be produced—slave-wares for the poor and mere wealth-wasting wares for the rich—ceased to be made. That remedy was, in short, the production of what used to be called art, but which has no name amongst us now, because it has become a necessary part of the labour of every man who produces.'

Said I: 'What! had men any time or opportunity for cultivating the fine arts amidst the desperate struggle for life and freedom that you have told me of?'

Said Hammond: 'You must not suppose that the new form of art was founded chiefly on the memory of the art of the past; although, strange to say, the civil war was much less destructive of art than of other things, and though what of art existed under the old forms, revived in a wonderful way during the latter part of the struggle, especially as regards music and poetry. The art or work-pleasure, as one ought to call it, of which I am now speaking, sprung up almost spontaneously, it seems, from a kind of instinct amongst people, no longer driven desperately to painful and terrible over-work, to do the best they could with the work in hand—to make it excellent of its kind; and when that had gone on for a little, a craving for beauty seemed to awaken in men's minds, and they began rudely and awkwardly to ornament the wares which they made; and when they had once set to work at that, it soon began to grow. All this was much helped by the abolition of the squalor which our immediate ancestors put up with so coolly; and by the leisurely, but not stupid, country-life which now grew (as I told you before) to be common amongst us. Thus at last and by slow degrees we got pleasure into our work; then we became conscious of that pleasure, and cultivated it, and took care that we had our fill of it; and then all was gained, and we were happy. So may it be for ages and ages!'

The old man fell into a reverie, not altogether without melancholy I thought; but I would not break it. Suddenly he started, and said:

'Well, dear guest, here are come Dick and Clara to fetch you away, and there is an end of my talk; which I daresay you will not be sorry for; the long day is coming to an end, and you will have a pleasant ride back to Hammersmith.'

CHAPTER XIX
THE DRIVE BACK TO HAMMERSMITH

I said nothing, for I was not inclined for mere politeness to him after such very serious talk; but in fact I should liked to have gone on talking with the older man, who could understand something at least of my wonted ways of looking at life, whereas, with the younger people, in spite of all their kindness, I really was a being from another planet. However, I made the best of it, and smiled as amiably as I could on the young couple; and Dick returned the smile by saying, 'Well, guest, I am glad to have you again, and to find that you and my kinsman have not quite talked yourselves into another world; I was half suspecting as I was listening to the Welshmen yonder that you would presently be vanishing away from us, and began to picture my kinsman sitting in the hall staring at nothing and finding that he had been talking a while past to nobody.'

I felt rather uncomfortable at this speech, for suddenly the picture of the sordid squabble, the dirty and miserable tragedy of the life I had left for a while, came before my eyes; and I had, as it were, a vision of all my longings for rest and peace in the past, and I loathed the idea of going back to it again. But the old man chuckled and said:

'Don't be afraid, Dick. In any case, I have not been talking to thin air; nor, indeed to this new friend of ours only. Who knows but I may not have been talking to many people? For perhaps our guest may some day go back to the people he has come from, and may take a message from us which may bear fruit for them, and consequently for us.'

Dick looked puzzled, and said: 'Well, gaffer, I do not quite understand what you mean. All I can say is, that I hope he will not leave us: for don't you see, he is another kind of man to what we are used to, and somehow he makes us think of all kind of things; and already I feel as if I could understand Dickens the better for having talked with him.'

'Yes,' said Clara, 'and I think in a few months we shall make him look younger; and I should like to see what he was like with the wrinkles smoothed out of his face. Don't you think he will look younger after a little time with us?'

The old man shook his head, and looked earnestly at me, but did not answer her, and for a moment or two we were all silent. Then Clara broke out:

'Kinsman, I don't like this: something or another troubles me, and I feel as if something untoward were going to happen. You have been talking of past miseries to the guest, and have been living in past unhappy times, and it is in the air all round us, and makes us feel as if we were longing for something we cannot have.'

The old man smiled on her kindly, and said: 'Well, my child, if that be so, go and live in the present, and you will soon shake it off.' Then he turned to me, and said: 'Do you remember anything like that, guest, in the country from which you come?'

The lovers had turned aside now, and were talking together softly, and not heeding us; so I said, but in a low voice: 'Yes, when I was a happy child on a sunny holiday, and had everything that I could think of.'

'So it is,' said he. 'You remember just now you twitted me with living in the second childhood of the world. You will find it a happy world to live in; you will be happy there—for a while.'

Again I did not like his scarcely veiled threat, and was beginning to trouble myself with trying to remember how I had got amongst this curious people, when the old man called out in a cheery voice: 'Now, my children, take your guest away, and make much of him; for it is your business to make him sleek of skin and peaceful of mind: he has by no means been as lucky as you have. Farewell, guest!' and he grasped my hand warmly.

'Good-bye,' said I, 'and thank you very much for all that you have told me. I will come and see you as soon as I come back to London. May I?'

'Yes,' he said, 'come by all means—if you can.'

'It won't be for some time yet,' quoth Dick, in his cheery voice; 'for when the hay is in up the river, I shall be for taking him a round through the country between hay and wheat harvest, to see how our friends live in the north country. Then in the wheat harvest we shall do a good stroke of work, I should hope,—in Wiltshire by preference; for he will be getting a little hard with all the open-air living, and I shall be as tough as nails.'

'But you will take me along, won't you, Dick?' said Clara, laying her pretty hand on his shoulder.

'Will I not?' said Dick, somewhat boisterously. 'And we will manage to send you to bed pretty tired every night; and you will look so beautiful with your neck all brown, and your hands too, and you under your gown as white as privet, that you will get some of those strange discontented whims out of your head, my dear. However, our week's haymaking will do all that for you.'

The girl reddened very prettily, and not for shame but for pleasure; and the old man laughed, and said:

'Guest, I see that you will be as comfortable as need be; for you need not fear that those two will be too officious with you: they will be so busy with each other, that they will leave you a good deal to yourself, I am sure, and that is a real kindness to a guest, after all. O, you need not be afraid of being one too many, either: it is just what these birds in a nest like, to have a good convenient friend to turn to, so that they may relieve the ecstasies of love with the solid commonplace of friendship. Besides, Dick, and much more Clara, likes a little talking at times; and you know lovers do not talk unless they get into trouble, they only prattle. Good-bye, guest; may you be happy!'

Clara went up to old Hammond, threw her arms about his neck and kissed him heartily, and said: 'You are a dear old man, and may have your jest about me as much as you please; and it won't be long before we see you again; and you may be sure we shall make our guest happy; though, mind you, there is some truth in what you say.'

Then I shook hands again, and we went out of the hall and into the cloisters, and so in the street found Greylocks in the shafts waiting for us. He was well looked after; for a little lad of about seven years old had his hand on the rein and was solemnly looking up into his face; on his back, withal, was a girl of fourteen, holding a three-year-old sister on before her; while another girl, about a year older than the boy, hung on behind. The three were occupied partly with eating cherries, partly with patting and punching Greylocks, who took all their caresses in good part, but pricked up his ears when Dick made his appearance. The girls got off quietly, and going up to

Clara, made much of her and snuggled up to her. And then we got into the carriage, Dick shook the reins, and we got under way at once, Greylocks trotting soberly between the lovely trees of the London streets, that were sending floods of fragrance into the cool evening air; for it was now getting toward sunset.

We could hardly go but fair and softly all the way, as there were a great many people abroad in that cool hour. Seeing so many people made me notice their looks the more; and I must say, my taste, cultivated in the sombre greyness, or rather brownness, of the nineteenth century, was rather apt to condemn the gaiety and brightness of the raiment; and I even ventured to say as much to Clara. She seemed rather surprised, and even slightly indignant, and said: 'Well, well, what's the matter? They are not about any dirty work; they are only amusing themselves in the fine evening; there is nothing to foul their clothes. Come, doesn't it all look very pretty? It isn't gaudy, you know.'

Indeed that was true; for many of the people were clad in colours that were sober enough, though beautiful, and the harmony of the colours was perfect and most delightful.

I said, 'Yes, that is so; but how can everybody afford such costly garments? Look! there goes a middle-aged man in a sober grey dress; but I can see from here that it is made of very fine woollen stuff, and is covered with silk embroidery.'

Said Clara: 'He could wear shabby clothes if he pleased,—that is, if he didn't think he would hurt people's feelings by doing so.'

'But please tell me,' said I, 'how can they afford it?'

As soon as I had spoken I perceived that I had got back to my old blunder; for I saw Dick's shoulders shaking with laughter; but he wouldn't say a word, but handed me over to the tender mercies of Clara, who said—

'Why, I don't know what you mean. Of course we can afford it, or else we shouldn't do it. It would be easy enough for us to say, we will only spend our labour on making our clothes comfortable: but we don't choose to stop there. Why do you find fault with us? Does it seem to you as if we starved ourselves of food in order to make ourselves fine clothes? or do you think there is anything wrong in liking to see the coverings of our bodies beautiful like our bodies are?—just as a deer's or an otter's skin has been made beautiful from the first? Come, what is wrong with you?'

I bowed before the storm, and mumbled out some excuse or other. I must say, I might have known that people who were so fond of architecture generally, would not be backward in ornamenting themselves; all the more as the shape of their raiment, apart from its colour, was both beautiful and reasonable—veiling the form, without either muffling or caricaturing it.

Clara was soon mollified; and as we drove along toward the wood before mentioned, she said to Dick—

'I tell you what, Dick: now that kinsman Hammond the Elder has seen our guest in his queer clothes, I think we ought to find him something decent to put on for our journey to-morrow: especially since, if we do not, we shall have to answer all sorts of questions as to his clothes and where they came from. Besides,' she said slily, 'when he is clad in handsome garments he will not be so quick to blame us for our childishness in wasting our time in making ourselves look pleasant to each other.'

'All right, Clara,' said Dick; 'he shall have everything that you—that he wants to have. I will look something out for him before he gets up to-morrow.'

CHAPTER XX

THE HAMMERSMITH GUEST-HOUSE AGAIN

Amidst such talk, driving quietly through the balmy evening, we came to Hammersmith, and were well received by our friends there. Boffin, in a fresh suit of clothes, welcomed me back with stately courtesy; the weaver wanted to button-hole me and get out of me what old Hammond had said, but was very friendly and cheerful when Dick warned him off; Annie shook hands with me, and hoped I had had a pleasant day—so kindly, that I felt a slight pang as our hands parted; for to say the truth, I liked her better than Clara, who seemed to be always a little on the defensive, whereas Annie was as frank as could be, and seemed to get honest pleasure from everything and everybody about her without the least effort.

We had quite a little feast that evening, partly in my honour, and partly, I suspect, though nothing was said about it, in honour of Dick and Clara coming together again. The wine was of the best; the hall was redolent of rich summer flowers; and after supper we not only had music (Annie, to my mind, surpassing all the others for sweetness and clearness of voice, as well as for feeling and meaning), but at last we even got to telling stories, and sat there listening, with no other light but that of the summer moon streaming through the beautiful traceries of the windows, as if we had belonged to time long passed, when books were scarce and the art of reading somewhat rare. Indeed, I may say here, that, though, as you will have noted, my friends had mostly something to say about books, yet they were not great readers, considering the refinement of their manners and the great amount of leisure which they obviously had. In fact, when Dick, especially, mentioned a book, he did so with an air of a man who has accomplished an achievement; as much as to say, 'There, you see, I have actually read that!'

The evening passed all too quickly for me; since that day, for the first time in my life, I was having my fill of the pleasure of the eyes without any of that sense of incongruity, that dread of approaching ruin, which had always beset me hitherto when I had been amongst the beautiful works of art of the past, mingled with the lovely nature of the present; both of them, in fact, the result of the long centuries of tradition, which had compelled men to produce the art, and compelled nature to run into the mould of the ages. Here I could enjoy everything without an afterthought of the injustice and miserable toil which made my leisure; the ignorance and dulness of life which went to make my keen appreciation of history; the tyranny and the struggle full of fear and mishap which went to make my romance. The only weight I had upon my heart was a vague fear as it drew toward bed-time concerning the place wherein I should wake on the morrow: but I choked that down, and went to bed happy, and in a very few moments was in a dreamless sleep.

CHAPTER XXI
GOING UP THE RIVER

When I did wake, to a beautiful sunny morning, I leapt out of bed with my over-night apprehension still clinging to me, which vanished delightfully however in a moment as I looked around my little sleeping chamber and saw the pale but pure-coloured figures painted on the plaster of the wall, with verses written underneath them which I knew somewhat over well.* I dressed speedily, in a suit of blue laid ready for me, so handsome that I quite blushed when I had got into it, feeling as I did so that excited pleasure of anticipation of a holiday, which, well remembered as it was, I had not felt since I was a boy, new come home for the summer holidays.

It seemed quite early in the morning, and I expected to have the hall to myself when I came into it out of the corridor wherein was my sleeping chamber; but I met Annie at once, who let fall her broom and gave me a kiss, quite meaningless I fear, except as betokening friendship, though she reddened as she did it, not from shyness, but from friendly pleasure, and then stood and picked up her broom again, and went on with her sweeping, nodding to me as if to bid me stand out of the way and look on; which, to say the truth, I thought amusing enough, as there were five other girls helping her, and their graceful figures engaged in the leisurely work were worth going a long way to see, and their merry talk and laughing as they swept in quite a scientific manner was worth going a long way to hear. But Annie presently threw me back a word or two as she went on to the other end of the hall: 'Guest,' she said, 'I am glad that you are up early, though we wouldn't disturb you; for our Thames is a lovely river at half-past six on a June morning: and as it would be a pity for you to lose it, I am told just to give you a cup of milk and a bit of bread outside there, and put you into the boat: for Dick and Clara are all ready now. Wait half a minute till I have swept down this row.'

So presently she let her broom drop again, and came and took me by the hand and led me out on to the terrace above the river, to a little table under the boughs, where my bread and milk took the form of as dainty a breakfast as any one could desire, and then sat by me as

I ate. And in a minute or two Dick and Clara came to me, the latter looking most fresh and beautiful in a light silk embroidered gown, which to my unused eyes was extravagantly gay and bright; while Dick was also handsomely dressed in white flannel prettily embroidered. Clara raised her gown in her hands as she gave me the morning greeting, and said laughingly: 'Look, guest! you see we are at least as fine as any of the people you felt inclined to scold last night; you see we are not going to make the bright day and the flowers feel ashamed of themselves. Now scold me!'

Quoth I: 'No, indeed; the pair of you seem as if you were born out of the summer day itself; and I will scold you when I scold it.'

'Well, you know,' said Dick, 'this is a special day—all these days are, I mean. The hay-harvest is in some ways better than corn-harvest because of the beautiful weather; and really, unless you had worked in the hay-field in fine weather, you couldn't tell what pleasant work it is. The women look so pretty at it, too,' he said, shyly; 'so all things considered, I think we are right to adorn it in a simple manner.'

'Do the women work at it in silk dresses?' said I, smiling.

Dick was going to answer me soberly; but Clara put her hand over his mouth, and said, 'No, no, Dick; not too much information for him, or I shall think that you are your old kinsman again. Let him find out for himself: he will not have long to wait.'

'Yes,' quoth Annie, 'don't make your description of the picture too fine, or else he will be disappointed when the curtain is drawn. I don't want him to be disappointed. But now it's time for you to be gone, if you are to have the best of the tide, and also of the sunny morning. Good-bye, guest.'

She kissed me in her frank friendly way, and almost took away from me my desire for the expedition thereby; but I had to get over that, as it was clear that so delightful a woman would hardly be without a due lover of her own age. We went down the steps of the landing-stage, and got into a pretty boat, not too light to hold us and our belongings comfortably, and handsomely ornamented; and just as we got in, down came Boffin and the weaver to see us off. The former had now veiled his splendour in a due suit of working clothes, crowned with a fantail hat, which he took off, however, to wave us farewell with his grave old-Spanish-like courtesy. Then Dick pushed off into the stream, and bent vigorously to his sculls, and

Hammersmith, with its noble trees and beautiful water-side houses, began to slip away from us.*

As we went, I could not help putting beside his promised picture of the hayfield as it was then the picture of it as I remembered it, and especially the images of the women engaged in the work rose up before me: the row of gaunt figures, lean, flat-breasted, ugly, without a grace of form or face about them; dressed in wretched skimpy print gowns, and hideous flapping sun-bonnets, moving their rakes in a listless mechanical way. How often had that marred the loveliness of the June day to me; how often had I longed to see the hayfields peopled with men and women worthy of the sweet abundance of midsummer, of its endless wealth of beautiful sights, and delicious sounds and scents. And now, the world had grown old and wiser, and I was to see my hope realised at last!

CHAPTER XXII

HAMPTON COURT AND A PRAISER OF PAST TIMES

So on we went, Dick rowing in an easy tireless way, and Clara sitting by my side admiring his manly beauty and heartily good-natured face, and thinking, I fancy, of nothing else. As we went higher up the river, there was less difference between the Thames of that day and the Thames as I remembered it; for setting aside the hideous vulgarity of the cockney villas* of the well-to-do, stockbrokers and other such, which in older time marred the beauty of the bough-hung banks, even this beginning of the country Thames was always beautiful; and as we slipped between the lovely summer greenery, I almost felt my youth come back to me, and as if I were on one of those water excursions which I used to enjoy so much in days when I was too happy to think that there could be much amiss anywhere.

At last we came to a reach of the river where on the left hand a very pretty little village with some old houses in it came down to the edge of the water, over which was a ferry;* and beyond these houses the elm-beset meadows ended in a fringe of tall willows, while on the right hand went the tow-path and a clear space before a row of trees, which rose up behind huge and ancient, the ornaments of a great park: but these drew back still further from the river at the end of the reach to make way for a little town of quaint and pretty houses, some new, some old, dominated by the long walls and sharp gables of a great red-brick pile of building, partly of the latest Gothic, partly of the court-style of Dutch William,* but so blended together by the bright sun and beautiful surroundings, including the bright blue river, which it looked down upon, that even amidst the beautiful buildings of that new happy time it had a strange charm about it. A great wave of fragrance, amidst which the lime-tree blossom was clearly to be distinguished, came down to us from its unseen gardens, as Clara sat up in her place, and said:

'O Dick, dear, couldn't we stop at Hampton Court for to-day, and take the guest about the park a little, and show him those sweet old buildings? Somehow, I suppose because you have lived so near it, you have seldom taken me to Hampton Court.'

Dick rested on his oars a little, and said: 'Well, well, Clara, you are lazy to-day. I didn't feel like stopping short of Shepperton* for the night; suppose we just go and have our dinner at the Court, and go on again about five o'clock?'

'Well,' she said, 'so be it; but I should like the guest to have spent an hour or two in the Park.'

'The Park!' said Dick; 'why, the whole Thames-side is a park this time of the year; and for my part, I had rather lie under an elm-tree on the borders of a wheat-field, with the bees humming about me and the corn-crake crying from furrow to furrow, than in any park in England. Besides—'

'Besides,' said she, 'you want to get on to your dearly-loved upper Thames, and show your prowess down the heavy swathes of the mowing grass.'

She looked at him fondly, and I could tell that she was seeing him in her mind's eye showing his splendid form at its best amidst the rhymed strokes of the scythes; and she looked down at her own pretty feet with a half sigh, as though she were contrasting her slight woman's beauty with his man's beauty; as women will when they are really in love, and are not spoiled with conventional sentiment.

As for Dick, he looked at her admiringly a while, and then said at last: 'Well, Clara, I do wish we were there! But, hilloa! we are getting back way.' And he set to work sculling again, and in two minutes we were all standing on the gravelly strand below the bridge, which, as you may imagine, was no longer the old hideous iron abortion, but a handsome piece of very solid oak framing.

We went into the Court and straight into the great hall, so well remembered, where there were tables spread for dinner, and everything arranged much as in Hammersmith Guest-Hall. Dinner over, we sauntered through the ancient rooms, where the pictures and tapestry were still preserved, and nothing was much changed, except that the people whom we met there had an indefinable kind of look of being at home and at ease, which communicated itself to me, so that I felt that the beautiful old place was mine in the best sense of the word; and my pleasure of past days seemed to add itself to that of to-day, and filled my whole soul with content.

Dick (who, in spite of Clara's gibe, knew the place very well) told me that the beautiful old Tudor rooms, which I remembered had been the dwellings of the lesser fry of Court flunkies, were now much used by people coming and going; for, beautiful as architecture had now become, and although the whole face of the country had quite recovered its beauty, there was still a sort of tradition of pleasure and beauty which clung to that group of buildings, and people thought going to Hampton Court a necessary summer outing, as they did in the days when London was so grimy and miserable. We went into some of the rooms looking into the old garden, and were well received by the people in them, who got speedily into talk with us, and looked with politely half-concealed wonder at my strange face. Besides these birds of passage, and a few regular dwellers in the place, we saw out in the meadows near the garden, down 'the Long Water,'* as it used to be called, many gay tents with men, women, and children round about them. As it seemed, this pleasure-loving people were fond of tent-life, with all its inconveniences, which, indeed, they turned into pleasure also.

We left this old friend by the time appointed, and I made some feeble show of taking the sculls; but Dick repulsed me, not much to my grief, I must say, as I found I had quite enough to do between the enjoyment of the beautiful time and my own lazily blended thoughts.

As to Dick, it was quite right to let him pull, for he was as strong as a horse, and had the greatest delight in bodily exercise, whatever it was. We really had some difficulty in getting him to stop when it was getting rather more than dusk, and the moon was brightening just as we were off Runnymede.* We landed there, and were looking about for a place whereon to pitch our tents (for we had brought two with us), when an old man came up to us, bade us good evening, and asked if we were housed for that night; and finding that we were not, bade us home to his house. Nothing loth, we went with him, and Clara took his hand in a coaxing way which I noticed she used with old men; and as we went on our way, made some commonplace remark about the beauty of the day. The old man stopped short, and looked at her and said: 'You really like it then?'

'Yes,' she said, looking very much astonished, 'don't you?'

'Well,' said he, 'perhaps I do. I did, at any rate, when I was younger; but now I think I should like it cooler.'

She said nothing, and went on, the night growing about as dark as it would be; till just at the rise of the hill we came to a hedge with a gate in it, which the old man unlatched and led us into a garden, at the end of which we could see a little house, one of whose little windows was already yellow with candle-light. We could see even under the doubtful light of the moon and the last of the western glow that the garden was stuffed full of flowers; and the fragrance it gave out in the gathering coolness was so wonderfully sweet, that it seemed the very heart of the delight of the June dusk; so that we three stopped instinctively, and Clara gave forth a little sweet 'O,' like a bird beginning to sing.

'What's the matter?' said the old man, a little testily, and pulling at her hand. 'There's no dog; or have you trodden on a thorn and hurt your foot?'

'No, no, neighbour,' she said; 'but how sweet, how sweet it is!'

'Of course it is,' said he, 'but do you care so much for that?'

She laughed out musically, and we followed suit in our gruffer voices; and then she said: 'Of course I do, neighbour; don't you!'

'Well, I don't know,' quoth the old fellow; then he added, as if somewhat ashamed of himself: 'Besides, you know, when the waters are out and all Runnymede is flooded, it's none so pleasant.'

'*I* should like it,' quoth Dick. 'What a jolly sail one would get about here on the floods on a bright frosty January morning!'

'*Would* you like it?' said our host. 'Well, I won't argue with you, neighbour; it isn't worth while. Come in and have some supper.'

We went up a paved path between the roses, and straight into a very pretty room, panelled and carved, and as clean as a new pin; but the chief ornament of which was a young woman, light-haired and grey-eyed, but with her face and hands and bare feet tanned quite brown with the sun. Though she was very lightly clad, that was clearly from choice, not from poverty, though these were the first cottage-dwellers I had come across; for her gown was of silk, and on her wrists were bracelets that seemed to me of great value. She was lying on a sheep-skin near the window, but jumped up as soon as we entered, and when she saw the guests behind the old man, she clapped her hands and cried out with pleasure, and when she got us into the middle of the room, fairly danced round us in delight of our company.

'What!' said the old man, 'you are pleased, are you, Ellen?'

The girl danced up to him and threw her arms round him, and said: 'Yes I am, and so ought you to be grandfather.'

'Well, well, I am,' said he, 'as much as I can be pleased. Guests, please be seated.'

This seemed rather strange to us; stranger, I suspect, to my friends than to me; but Dick took the opportunity of both the host and his grand-daughter being out of the room to say to me, softly: 'A grumbler: there are a few of them still. Once upon a time, I am told, they were quite a nuisance.'

The old man came in as he spoke and sat down beside us with a sigh, which, indeed, seemed fetched up as if he wanted us to take notice of it; but just then the girl came in with the victuals, and the carle missed his mark, what between our hunger generally and that I was pretty busy watching the grand-daughter moving about as beautiful as a picture.

Everything to eat and drink, though it was somewhat different to what we had had in London, was better than good, but the old man eyed rather sulkily the chief dish on the table, on which lay a leash of fine perch, and said:

'H'm, perch! I am sorry we can't do better for you, guests. The time was when we might have had a good piece of salmon up from London for you; but the times have grown mean and petty.'

'Yes, but you might have had it now,' said the girl, giggling, 'if you had known that they were coming.'

'It's our fault for not bringing it with us, neighbours,' said Dick, good-humouredly. 'But if the times have grown petty, at any rate the perch haven't; that fellow in the middle there must have weighed a good two pounds when he was showing his dark stripes and red fins to the minnows yonder. And as to the salmon, why, neighbour, my friend here, who comes from the outlands, was quite surprised yesterday morning when I told him we had plenty of salmon at Hammersmith. I am sure I have heard nothing of the times worsening.'

He looked a little uncomfortable. And the old man, turning to me, said very courteously:

'Well, sir, I am happy to see a man from over the water; but I really must appeal to you to say whether on the whole you are not better off in your country; where I suppose, from what our guest says, you are brisker and more alive, because you have not wholly got rid of competition. You see, I have read not a few books of the past days, and certainly *they* are much more alive than those which are written now; and good sound unlimited competition was the condition under which they were written,—if we didn't know that from the record of history, we should know it from the books themselves. There is a spirit of adventure in them, and signs of a capacity to extract good out of evil which our literature quite lacks now; and I cannot help thinking that our moralists and historians exaggerate hugely the unhappiness of the past days, in which such splendid works of imagination and intellect were produced.'

Clara listened to him with restless eyes, as if she were excited and pleased; Dick knitted his brow and looked still more uncomfortable, but said nothing. Indeed, the old man gradually, as he warmed to his subject, dropped his sneering manner, and both spoke and looked very seriously. But the girl broke out before I could deliver myself of the answer I was framing:

'Books, books! always books, grandfather! When will you understand that after all it is the world we live in which interests us; the world of which we are a part, and which we can never love too much? Look!' she said, throwing open the casement wider and showing us the white light sparkling between the black shadows of the moonlit garden, through which ran a little shiver of the summer night-wind, 'look! these are our books in these days!—and these,' she said, stepping lightly up to the two lovers and laying a hand on each of their shoulders; 'and the guest there, with his over-sea knowledge and experience;—yes, and even you, grandfather' (a smile ran over her face as she spoke), 'with all your grumbling and wishing yourself back again in the good old days,—in which, as far as I can make out, a harmless and lazy old man like you would either have pretty nearly starved, or have had to pay soldiers and people to take the folk's victuals and clothes and houses away from them by force. Yes, these are our books; and if we want more, can we not find work to do in the beautiful buildings that we raise up all over the country (and I know there was nothing like them in past times), wherein a man can put forth whatever is in him, and make his hands set forth his mind and his soul.'

She paused a little, and I for my part could not help staring at her, and thinking that if she were a book, the pictures in it were most lovely. The colour mantled in her delicate sunburnt cheeks; her grey eyes, light amidst the tan of her face, kindly looked on us all as she spoke. She paused, and said again:

'As for your books, they were well enough for times when intelligent people had but little else in which they could take pleasure, and when they must needs supplement the sordid miseries of their own lives with imaginations of the lives of other people. But I say flatly that in spite of all their cleverness and vigour, and capacity for story-telling, there is something loathsome about them. Some of them, indeed, do here and there show some feeling for those whom the history-books call "poor," and of the misery of whose lives we have some inkling; but presently they give it up, and towards the end of the story we must be contented to see the hero and heroine living happily in an island of bliss on other people's troubles; and that after a long series of sham troubles (or mostly sham) of their own making, illustrated by dreary introspective nonsense about their feelings and aspirations, and all the rest of it; while the world must even then have gone on its way, and dug and sewed and baked and built and carpentered round about these useless—animals.'

'There!' said the old man, reverting to his dry sulky manner again. 'There's eloquence! I suppose you like it?'

'Yes,' said I, very emphatically.

'Well,' said he, 'now the storm of eloquence has lulled for a little, suppose you answer my question?—that is, if you like, you know,' quoth he, with a sudden access of courtesy.

'What question?' said I. For I must confess that Ellen's strange and almost wild beauty had put it out of my head.

Said he: 'First of all (excuse my catechising), is there competition in life, after the old kind, in the country whence you come?'

'Yes,' said I, 'it is the rule there.' And I wondered as I spoke what fresh complications I should get into as a result of this answer.

'Question two,' said the carle: 'Are you not on the whole much freer, more energetic—in a word, healthier and happier—for it?'

I smiled. 'You wouldn't talk so if you had any idea of our life. To me you seem here as if you were living in heaven compared with us of the country from which I came.'

'Heaven?' said he: 'you like heaven, do you?'

'Yes,' said I—snappishly, I am afraid; for I was beginning rather to resent his formula.

'Well, I am far from sure that I do,' quoth he. 'I think one may do more with one's life than sitting on a damp cloud and singing hymns.'

I was rather nettled by this inconsequence, and said: 'Well, neighbour, to be short, and without using metaphors, in the land whence I come, where the competition which produced those literary works which you admire so much is still the rule, most people are thoroughly unhappy; here, to me at least, most people seem thoroughly happy.'

'No offence, guest—no offence,' said he; 'but let me ask you; you like that, do you?'

His formula, put with such obstinate persistence, made us all laugh heartily; and even the old man joined in the laughter on the sly. However, he was by no means beaten, and said presently:

'From all I can hear, I should judge that a young woman so beautiful as my dear Ellen yonder would have been a lady, as they called it in the old time, and wouldn't have had to wear a few rags of silk as she does now, or to have browned herself in the sun as she has to do now. What do you say to that, eh?'

Here Clara, who had been pretty much silent hitherto, struck in, and said: 'Well, really, I don't think that you would have mended matters, or that they want mending. Don't you see that she is dressed deliciously for this beautiful weather? And as for the sun-burning of your hayfields, why, I hope to pick up some of that for myself when we get a little higher up the river. Look if I don't need a little sun on my pasty white skin!'

And she stripped up the sleeve from her arm and laid it beside Ellen's who was now sitting next her. To say the truth, it was rather amusing to me to see Clara putting herself forward as a town-bred fine lady, for she was as well-knit and clean-skinned a girl as might be met with anywhere at the best. Dick stroked the beautiful arm rather shyly, and pulled down the sleeve again, while she blushed at his touch; and the old man said laughingly: 'Well, I suppose you *do* like that; don't you?'

Ellen kissed her new friend, and we all sat silent for a little, till she broke out into a sweet shrill song, and held us all entranced with the wonder of her clear voice; and the old grumbler sat looking at her lovingly. The other young people sang also in due time; and then Ellen showed us to our beds in small cottage chambers, fragrant and clean as the ideal of the old pastoral poets; and the pleasure of the evening quite extinguished my fear of the last night, that I should wake up in the old miserable world of worn-out pleasures, and hopes that were half fears.

CHAPTER XXIII

AN EARLY MORNING BY RUNNYMEDE

Though there were no rough noises to wake me, I could not lie long abed the next morning, where the world seemed so well awake, and, despite the old grumbler, so happy; so I got up, and found that, early as it was, someone had been stirring, since all was trim and in its place in the little parlour, and the table laid for the morning meal. Nobody was afoot in the house as then, however, so I went out a-doors, and after a turn or two round the superabundant garden, I wandered down over the meadow to the river-side, where lay our boat, looking quite familiar and friendly to me. I walked up stream a little, watching the light mist curling up from the river till the sun gained power to draw it all away; saw the bleak* speckling the water under the willow boughs, whence the tiny flies they fed on were falling in myriads; heard the great chub splashing here and there at some belated moth or other, and felt almost back again in my boyhood. Then I went back again to the boat, and loitered there a minute or two, and then walked slowly up the meadow towards the little house. I noted now that there were four more houses of about the same size on the slope away from the river. The meadow in which I was going was not up for hay; but a row of flake-hurdles* ran up the slope not far from me on each side, and in the field so parted off from ours on the left they were making hay busily by now, in the simple fashion of the days when I was a boy. My feet turned that way instinctively, as I wanted to see how haymakers looked in these new and better times, and also I rather expected to see Ellen there. I came to the hurdles and stood looking over into the hayfield, and was close to the end of the long line of haymakers who were spreading the low ridges to dry off the night dew. The majority of these were young women clad much like Ellen last night, though not mostly in silk, but in light woollen most gaily embroidered; the men being all clad in white flannel embroidered in bright colours. The meadow looked like a gigantic tulip-bed because of them. All hands were working deliberately but well and steadily, though they were as noisy with merry talk as a grove of autumn starlings. Half a dozen of them, men and women, came up to me and shook hands, gave me the sele of the morning,* and asked a few questions as to whence and whither, and wishing me good luck, went back to their work. Ellen, to my disappointment, was not amongst them, but presently I saw a light figure come out of the hayfield higher up the slope, and make for our house; and that was Ellen, holding a basket in her hand. But before she had come to the garden gate, out came Dick and Clara, who, after a minute's pause, came down to meet me, leaving Ellen in the garden; then we three went down to the boat, talking mere morning prattle. We stayed there a little, Dick arranging some of the matters in her, for we had only taken up to the house such things as we thought the dew might damage; and then we went toward the house again; but when we came near the garden, Dick stopped us by laying a hand on my arm and said—

'Just look a moment.'

I looked, and over the low hedge saw Ellen, shading her eyes against the sun as she looked toward the hayfield, a light wind stirring in her tawny hair, her eyes like light jewels amidst her sunburnt face, which looked as if the warmth of the sun were yet in it.

'Look, guest,' said Dick; 'doesn't it all look like one of those very stories out of Grimm that we were talking about up in Bloomsbury? Here are we two lovers wandering about in the world, and we have come to a fairy garden, and there is the very fairy herself amidst of it: I wonder what she will do for us.'

Said Clara demurely, but not stiffly: 'Is she a good fairy, Dick?'

'O, yes,' said he; 'and according to the card,* she would do better, if it were not for the gnome or wood-spirit, our grumbling friend of last night.'

We laughed at this; and I said, 'I hope you see that you have left me out of the tale.'

'Well,' said he, 'that's true. You had better consider that you have got the cap of darkness, and are seeing everything, yourself invisible.'

That touched me on my weak side of not feeling sure of my position in this beautiful new country; so in order not to make matters worse, I held my tongue, and we all went into the garden and up to the house together. I noticed by the way that Clara must really rather have felt the contrast between herself as a town madam and this piece of the summer country that we all admired so, for she had rather dressed after Ellen that morning as to thinness and scantiness, and went barefoot also, except for light sandals.

The old man greeted us kindly in the parlour, and said: 'Well, guests, so you have been looking about to search into the nakedness of the land: I suppose your illusions of last night have given way a bit before the morning light? Do you still like it, eh?'

'Very much,' said I, doggedly; 'it is one of the prettiest places on the lower Thames.'

'Oho!' said he; 'so you know the Thames, do you?'

I reddened, for I saw Dick and Clara looking at me, and scarcely knew what to say. However, since I had said in our early intercourse with my Hammersmith friends that I had known Epping Forest, I thought a hasty generalisation might be better in avoiding complications than a downright lie; so I said—

'I have been in this country before; and I have been on the Thames in those days.'

'O,' said the old man, eagerly, 'so you have been in this country before. Now really, don't you *find* it (apart from all theory, you know) much changed for the worse?'

'No, not at all,' said I; 'I find it much changed for the better.'

'Ah,' quoth he, 'I fear that you have been prejudiced by some theory or another. However, of course the time when you were here before must have been so near our own days that the deterioration might not be very great: as then we were, of course, still living under the same customs as we are now. I was thinking of earlier days than that.'

'In short,' said Clara, 'you have *theories* about the change which has taken place.'

'I have facts as well,' said he. 'Look here! from this hill you can see just four little houses, including this one. Well, I know for certain that in old times, even in the summer, when the leaves were thickest, you could see from the same place six quite big and fine houses; and higher up the water, garden joined garden right up to Windsor; and there were big houses in all the gardens. Ah! England was an important place in those days.'

I was getting nettled, and said: 'What you mean is that you de-cockneyised the place, and sent the damned flunkies packing, and that everybody can live comfortably and happily, and not a few damned thieves only, who were centres of vulgarity and corruption wherever they were, and who, as to this lovely river, destroyed its beauty morally, and had almost destroyed it physically, when they were thrown out of it.'

There was silence after this outburst, which for the life of me I could not help, remembering how I had suffered from cockneyism and its cause on those same waters of old time. But at last the old man said, quite coolly:

'My dear guest, I really don't know what you mean by either cockneys, or flunkies, or thieves, or damned; or how only a few people could live happily and comfortably in a wealthy country. All I can see is that you are angry, and I fear with me: so if you like we will change the subject.'

I thought this kind and hospitable in him, considering his obstinacy about his theory; and hastened to say that I did not mean to be angry, only emphatic. He bowed gravely, and I thought the storm was over, when suddenly Ellen broke in:

'Grandfather, our guest is reticent from courtesy; but really what he has in mind to say to you ought to be said; so as I know pretty well what it is, I will say it for him: for as you know, I have been taught these things by people who—'

'Yes,' said the old man, 'by the sage of Bloomsbury, and others.'

'O,' said Dick, 'so you know my old kinsman Hammond?'

'Yes,' said she, 'and other people too, as my grandfather says, and they have taught me things: and this is the upshot of it. We live in a little house now, not because we have nothing grander to do than working in the fields, but because we please; for if we liked, we could go and live in a big house amongst pleasant companions.'

Grumbled the old man: 'Just so! As if I would live amongst those conceited fellows; all of them looking down upon me!'

She smiled on him kindly, but went on as if he had not spoken. 'In the past times, when those big houses of which grandfather speaks were so plenty, we *must* have lived in a cottage whether we liked it or not; and the said cottage, instead of having in it everything we want, would have been bare and empty. We should not have got enough to eat; our clothes would have been ugly to look at, dirty and frowsy. You, grandfather, have done no hard work for years now, but wander about and read your books and have nothing to worry you; and as for me, I work hard when I like it, because I like it, and think it does me good, and knits up my muscles, and makes me prettier to look at, and healthier and happier. But in those past days you, grandfather, would have had to work hard after you were old; and would have been always afraid of having to be shut up in a kind of prison along with other old men, half-starved and without amusement. And as for me, I am twenty years old. In those days my middle age would be beginning now, and in a few years I should be pinched, thin, and haggard, beset with troubles and miseries, so that no one could have guessed that I was once a beautiful girl.'

'Is this what you have had in your mind, guest?' said she, the tears in her eyes at thought of the past miseries of people like herself.

'Yes,' said I, much moved; 'that and more. Often—in my country I have seen that wretched change you have spoken of, from the fresh handsome country lass to the poor draggle-tailed country woman.'

The old man sat silent for a little, but presently recovered himself and took comfort in his old phrase of 'Well, you like it so, do you?'

'Yes,' said Ellen, 'I love life better than death.'

'O, you do, do you?' said he. 'Well, for my part I like reading a good old book with plenty of fun in it, like Thackeray's "Vanity Fair."* Why don't you write books like that now? Ask that question of your Bloomsbury sage.'

Seeing Dick's cheeks reddening a little at this sally, and noting that silence followed, I thought I had better do something. So I said: 'I am only the guest, friends; but I know you want to show me your river at its best, so don't you think we had better be moving presently, as it is certainly going to be a hot day?'

CHAPTER XXIV
UP THE THAMES: THE SECOND DAY

They were not slow to take my hint; and indeed, as to the mere time of day, it was best for us to be off, as it was past seven o'clock, and the day promised to be very hot. So we got up and went down to our boat—Ellen thoughtful and abstracted; the old man very kind and courteous, as if to make up for his crabbedness of opinion. Clara was cheerful and natural, but a little subdued, I thought; and she at least was not sorry to be gone, and often looked shyly and timidly at Ellen and her strange wild beauty. So we got into the boat, Dick saying as he took his place, 'Well, it *is* a fine day!' and the old man answering 'What! you like that, do you?' once more; and presently Dick was sending the bows swiftly through the slow weed-checked stream. I turned round as we got into mid-stream, and waving my hand to our hosts, saw Ellen leaning on the old man's shoulder, and caressing his healthy apple-red cheek, and quite a keen pang smote me as I thought how I should never see the beautiful girl again. Presently I insisted on taking the sculls, and I rowed a good deal that day; which no doubt accounts for the fact that we got very late to the place which Dick had aimed at. Clara was particularly affectionate to Dick, as I noticed from the rowing thwart; but as for him, he was as frankly kind and merry as ever; and I was glad to see it, as a man of his temperament could not have taken her caresses cheerfully and without embarrassment if he had been at all entangled by the fairy of our last night's abode.

I need say little about the lovely reaches of the river here. I duly noted that absence of cockney villas which the old man had lamented; and I saw with pleasure that my old enemies the 'Gothic' cast-iron bridges had been replaced by handsome oak and stone ones. Also the banks of the forest that we passed through had lost their courtly game-keeperish trimness, and were as wild and beautiful as need be, though the trees were clearly well seen to. I thought it best, in order to get the most direct information, to play the innocent about Eton and Windsor; but Dick volunteered his knowledge to me as we lay in Datchet lock* about the first. Quoth he:

'Up yonder are some beautiful old buildings, which were built for a great college or teaching-place by one of the mediæval kings—Edward the Sixth, I think' (I smiled to myself at his rather natural blunder).* 'He meant poor people's sons to be taught there what knowledge was going in his days; but it was a matter of course that in the times of which you seem to know so much they spoilt whatever good there was in the founder's intentions. My old kinsman says that they treated them in a very simple way, and instead of teaching poor men's sons to know something, they taught rich men's sons to know nothing. It seems from what he says that it was a place for the "aristocracy" (if you know what that means; I have been told its meaning) to get rid of the company of their male children for a great part of the year. I daresay old Hammond would give you plenty of information in detail about it.'

'What is it used for now?' said I.

'Well,' said he, 'the buildings were a good deal spoilt by the last few generations of aristocrats, who seem to have had a great hatred against beautiful old buildings, and indeed all records of past history; but it is still a delightful place. Of course, we cannot use it quite as the founder intended, since our ideas about teaching young people are so changed from the ideas of his time; so it is used now as a dwelling for people engaged in learning; and folk from round about come and get taught things that they want to learn; and there is a great library there of the best books. So that I don't think that the old dead king would be much hurt if he were to come to life and see what we are doing there.'

'Well,' said Clara, laughing, 'I think he would miss the boys.'

'Not always, my dear,' said Dick, 'for there are often plenty of boys there, who come to get taught; and also,' said he, smiling, 'to learn boating and swimming. I wish we could stop there: but perhaps we had better do that coming down the water.'

The lock-gates opened as he spoke, and out we went, and on. And as for Windsor, he said nothing till I lay on my oars (for I was sculling then) in Clewer reach, and looking up, said, 'What is all that building up there?'

Said he: 'There, I thought I would wait till you asked, yourself. That is Windsor Castle:* that also I thought I would keep for you till we come down the water. It looks fine from here, doesn't it? But a great deal of it has been built or skinned in the time of the Degradation, and we wouldn't pull the buildings down, since they were there; just as with the buildings of the Dung-Market. You know, of course, that it was the palace of our old mediæval kings, and was used later on for the same purpose by the parliamentary commercial sham-kings, as my old kinsman calls them.'

'Yes,' said I, 'I know all that. What is it used for now?'

'A great many people live there,' said he, 'as, with all drawbacks, it is a pleasant place; there is also a well-arranged store of antiquities of various kinds that have seemed worth keeping—a museum, it would have been called in the times you understand so well.'

I drew my sculls through the water at that last word, and pulled as if I were fleeing from those times which I understood so well; and we were soon going up the once sorely be-cockneyed reaches of the river about Maidenhead,* which now looked as pleasant and enjoyable as the up-river reaches.

The morning was now getting on, the morning of a jewel of a summer day; one of those days which, if they were commoner in these islands, would make our climate the best of all climates, without dispute. A light wind blew from the west; the little clouds that had arisen at about our breakfast time had seemed to get higher and higher in the heavens; and in spite of the burning sun we no more longed for rain than we feared it. Burning as the sun was, there was a fresh feeling in the air that almost set us a-longing for the rest of the hot afternoon, and the stretch of blossoming wheat seen from the shadow of the boughs. No one unburdened with very heavy anxieties could have felt otherwise than happy that morning: and it must be said that whatever anxieties might lie beneath the surface of things, we didn't seem to come across any of them.

We passed by several fields where haymaking was going on, but Dick, and especially Clara, were so jealous of our up-river festival that they would not allow me to have much to say to them. I could only notice that the people in the fields looked strong and handsome, both men and women, and that so far from there being any appearance of sordidness about their attire, they seemed to be dressed specially for the occasion,—lightly, of course, but gaily and with plenty of adornment.

Both on this day as well as yesterday we had, as you may think, met and passed and been passed by many craft of one kind and another. The most part of these were being rowed like ourselves, or were sailing, in the sort of way that sailing is managed on the upper reaches of the river; but every now and then we came on barges, laden with hay or other country produce, or carrying bricks, lime, timber, and the like, and these were going on their way without any means of propulsion visible to me—just a man at the tiller, with often a friend or two laughing and talking with him. Dick, seeing on one occasion this day that I was looking rather hard on one of these, said: 'That is one of our force-barges; it is quite as easy to work vehicles by force by water as by land.'

I understood pretty well that these 'force vehicles'* had taken the place of our old steam-power carrying; but I took good care not to ask any questions about them, as I knew well enough both that I should never be able to understand how they were worked, and that in attempting to do so I should betray myself, or get into some complication impossible to explain; so I merely said, 'Yes, of course, I understand.'

We went ashore at Bisham, where the remains of the old Abbey and the Elizabethan house* that had been added to them yet remained, none the worse for many years of careful and appreciative habitation. The folk of the place, however, were mostly in the fields that day, both men and women; so we met only two old men there, and a younger one who had stayed at home to get on with some literary work, which I imagine we considerably interrupted. Yet I also think that the hard-working man who received us was not very sorry for the interruption. Anyhow, he kept on pressing us to stay over and over again, till at last we did not get away till the cool of the evening.

However, that mattered little to us; the nights were light, for the moon was shining in her third quarter, and it was all one to Dick whether he sculled or sat quiet in the boat: so we went away a great pace. The evening sun shone bright on the remains of the old buildings at Medmenham;* close beside which arose an irregular pile of building which Dick told us was a very pleasant house; and there were plenty of houses visible on the wide meadows opposite, under the hill; for, as it seems that the beauty of Hurley* had compelled people to build and live there a good deal. The sun very low down showed us Henley* little altered in outward aspect from what I remembered it. Actual daylight failed us as we passed through the lovely reaches of Wargrave and Shiplake;* but the moon rose behind us presently. I should like to have seen with my eyes what success the new order of things had had in getting rid of the sprawling mess with which commercialism had littered the banks of the wide stream about Reading and Caversham:* certainly everything smelt too deliciously in the early night for there to be any of the old careless sordidness of so-called manufacture; and in answer to my question as to what sort of a place Reading was, Dick answered:

'O, a nice town enough in its way; mostly rebuilt within the last hundred years; and there are a good many houses, as you can see by the lights just down under the hills yonder. In fact, it is one of the most populous places on the Thames round about here. Keep up your spirits, guest! we are close to our journey's end for the night. I ought to ask your pardon for not stopping at one of the houses here or higher up; but a friend who is living in a very pleasant house in the Maple-Durham meads,* particularly wanted me and Clara to come and see him on our way up the Thames; and I thought you wouldn't mind this bit of night travelling.'

He need not have adjured me to keep up my spirits, which were as high as possible; though the strangeness and excitement of the happy and quiet life which I saw everywhere around me was, it is true, a little wearing off, yet a deep content, as different as possible from languid acquiescence, was taking its place, and I was, as it were, really new-born.

We landed presently just where I remembered the river making an elbow to the north towards the ancient house of the Blunts;* with the wide meadows spreading on the right-hand side, and on the left the long line of beautiful old trees overhanging the water. As we got out of the boat, I said to Dick—

'Is it the old house we are going to?'

'No,' he said, 'though that is standing still in green old age, and is well inhabited. I see, by the way, that you know your Thames well. But my friend Walter Allen, who asked me to stop here, lives in a house, not very big, which has been built here lately, because these meadows are so much liked, especially in summer, that there was getting to be rather too much of tenting on the open field; so the parishes here about, who rather objected to that, built three houses between this and Caversham, and quite a large one at Basildon,* a little higher up. Look, yonder are the lights of Walter Allen's house!'

So we walked over the grass of the meadows under a flood of moonlight, and soon came to the house, which was low and built round a quadrangle big enough to get plenty of sunshine in it. Walter Allen, Dick's friend, was leaning against the jamb of the doorway waiting for us, and took us into the hall without overplus* of words. There were not many people in it, as some of the dwellers there were away at the haymaking in the neighbourhood, and some, as Walter told us, were wandering about the meadow enjoying the beautiful moonlit night. Dick's friend looked to be a man of about forty; tall, black-haired, very kind-looking and thoughtful; but rather to my surprise there was a shade of melancholy on his face, and he seemed a little abstracted and inattentive to our chat, in spite of obvious efforts to listen.

Dick looked on him from time to time, and seemed troubled; and at last he said: 'I say, old fellow, if there is anything the matter which we didn't know of when you wrote to me, don't you think you had better tell us about it at once? or else we shall think we have come here at an unlucky time, and are not quite wanted.'

Walter turned red, and seemed to have some difficulty in restraining his tears, but said at last: 'Of course everybody here is very glad to see you, Dick, and your friends; but it is true that we are not at our best, in spite of the fine weather and the glorious hay-crop. We have had a death here.'

Said Dick: 'Well, you should get over that, neighbour: such things must be.'

'Yes,' Walter said, 'but this was a death by violence, and it seems likely to lead to at least one more: and somehow it makes us feel rather shy of one another; and to say the truth, that is one reason why there are so few of us present to-night.'

'Tell us the story, Walter,' said Dick; 'perhaps telling it will help you to shake off your sadness.'

Said Walter: 'Well, I will; and I will make it short enough, though I daresay it might be spun out into a long one, as used to be done with such subjects in the old novels. There is a very charming girl here whom we all like, and whom some of us do more than like; and she very naturally liked one of us better than anybody else. And another of us (I won't name him) got fairly bitten with love-madness, and used to go about making himself as unpleasant as he could—not of malice prepense, of course; so that the girl, who liked him well enough at first, though she didn't love him, began fairly to dislike him. Of course, those of us who knew him best—myself amongst others—advised him to go away, as he was making matters worse and worse for himself every day. Well, he wouldn't take our advice (that also, I suppose, was a matter of course), so we had to tell him that he *must* go, or the inevitable sending to Coventry would follow; for his individual trouble had so overmastered him that we felt that *we* must go if he did not.

'He took that better than we expected, when something or other—an interview with the girl, I think, and some hot words with the successful lover following close upon it, threw him quite off his balance; and he got hold of an axe and fell upon his rival when there was no one by; and in the struggle that followed the man attacked, hit him an unlucky blow and killed him. And now the slayer in his turn is so upset that he is like to kill himself; and if he does, the girl will do as much, I fear. And all this we could no more help than the earthquake of the year before last.'

'It is very unhappy,' said Dick; 'but since the man is dead, and cannot be brought to life again, and since the slayer had no malice in him, I cannot for the life of me see why he shouldn't get over it before long. Besides, it was the right man that was killed and not the wrong. Why should a man brood over a mere accident for ever? And the girl?'

'As to her,' said Walter, 'the whole thing seems to have inspired her with terror rather than grief. What you say about the man is true, or it should be; but then, you see, the excitement and jealousy that was the prelude to this tragedy had made an evil and feverish element round about him, from which he does not seem to be able to escape. However, we have advised him to go away—in fact, to cross the seas; but he is in such a state that I do not think that he *can* go unless someone *takes* him, and I think it will fall to my lot to do so; which is scarcely a cheerful outlook for me.'

'O, you will find a certain kind of interest in it,' said Dick. 'And of course he *must* soon look upon the affair from a reasonable point of view sooner or later.'

'Well, at any rate,' quoth Walter, 'now that I have eased my mind by making you uncomfortable, let us have an end of the subject for the present. Are you going to take your guest to Oxford?'

'Why, of course we must pass through it,' said Dick, smiling, 'as we are going into the upper waters: but I thought that we wouldn't stop there, or we shall be belated as to the haymaking up our way. So

Oxford and my learned lecture on it, all got at second-hand from my old kinsman, must wait till we come down the water a fortnight hence.'

I listened to this story with much surprise, and could not help wondering at first that the man who had slain the other had not been put in custody till it could be proved that he killed his rival in self-defence only. However, the more I thought of it, the plainer it grew to me that no amount of examination of witnesses, who had witnessed nothing but the ill-blood between the two rivals, would have done anything to clear up the case. I could not help thinking, also, that the remorse of this homicide gave point to what old Hammond had said to me about the way in which this strange people dealt with what I had been used to hear called crimes. Truly, the remorse was exaggerated; but it was quite clear that the slayer took the whole consequences of the act upon himself, and did not expect society to whitewash him by punishing him. I had no fear any longer that 'the sacredness of human life' was likely to suffer amongst my friends from the absence of gallows and prison.

CHAPTER XXV

THE THIRD DAY ON THE THAMES*

As we went down to the boat next morning, Walter could not keep off the subject of last night, though he was more hopeful than he had been then, and seemed to think that if the unlucky homicide could not be got to go over-sea, he might at any rate go and live somewhere in the neighbourhood pretty much by himself; at any rate, that was what he himself had proposed. To Dick, and I must say to me also, this seemed a strange remedy; and Dick said as much. Quoth he:

'Friend Walter, don't set the man brooding on the tragedy by letting him live alone. That will only strengthen his idea that he has committed a crime, and you will have him killing himself in good earnest.'

Said Clara: 'I don't know. If I may say what I think of it, it is that he had better have his fill of gloom now, and, so to say, wake up presently to see how little need there has been for it; and then he will live happily afterwards. As for his killing himself, you need not be afraid of that; for, from all you tell me, he is really very much in love with the woman; and to speak plainly, until his love is satisfied, he will not only stick to life as tightly as he can, but will also make the most of every event of his life—will, so to say, hug himself up in it; and I think that this is the real explanation of his taking the whole matter with such an excess of tragedy.'

Walter looked thoughtful, and said: 'Well, you may be right; and perhaps we should have treated it all more lightly: but you see, guest' (turning to me), 'such things happen so seldom, that when they do happen, we cannot help being much taken up with it. For the rest, we are all inclined to excuse our poor friend for making us so unhappy, on the ground that he does it out of an exaggerated respect for human life and its happiness. Well, I will say no more about it; only this: will you give me a cast upstream, as I want to look after a lonely habitation for the poor fellow, since he will have it so, and I hear that there is one which would suit us very well on the downs beyond Streatley; so if you will put me ashore there I will walk up the hill and look to it.'

'Is the house in question empty?' said I.

'No,' said Walter, 'but the man who lives there will go out of it, of course, when he hears that we want it. You see, we think that the fresh air of the downs and the very emptiness of the landscape will do our friend good.'

'Yes,' said Clara, smiling, 'and he will not be so far from his beloved that they cannot easily meet if they have a mind to—as they certainly will.'

This talk had brought us down to the boat, and we were presently afloat on the beautiful broad stream, Dick driving the prow swiftly through the windless water of the early summer morning, for it was not yet six o'clock. We were at the lock in a very little time; and as we lay rising and rising on the in-coming water, I could not help wondering that my old friend the pound-lock,* and that of the very simplest and most rural kind, should hold its place there; so I said:

'I have been wondering, as we passed lock after lock, that you people, so prosperous as you are, and especially since you are so anxious for pleasant work to do, have not invented something which would get rid of this clumsy business of going up-stairs by means of these rude contrivances.'

Dick laughed. 'My dear friend,' said he, 'as long as water has the clumsy habit of running downhill, I fear we must humour it by going up-stairs when we have our faces turned from the sea. And really I don't see why you should fall foul of Maple-Durham lock, which I think a very pretty place.'

There was no doubt about the latter assertion, I thought, as I looked up at the overhanging boughs of the great trees, with the sun coming glittering through the leaves, and listened to the song of the summer blackbirds as it mingled with the sound of the backwater near us. So not being able to say why I wanted the locks away—which, indeed, I didn't do at all—I held my peace. But Walter said—

'You see, guest, this is not an age of inventions. The last epoch did all that for us, and we are now content to use such of its inventions as we find handy, and leaving those alone which we don't want. I believe, as a matter of fact, that some time ago (I can't give you a date) some elaborate machinery was used for the locks, though people did not go so far as try to make the water run up hill. However, it was troublesome, I suppose, and the simple hatches, and the gates, with a big counterpoising beam, were found to answer every purpose, and were easily mended when wanted with material always to hand: so here they are, as you see.'

'Besides,' said Dick, 'this kind of lock is pretty, as you can see; and I can't help thinking that your machine-lock, winding up like a watch, would have been ugly and would have spoiled the look of the river: and that is surely reason enough for keeping such locks as these. Good-bye, old fellow!' said he to the lock, as he pushed us out through the now open gates by a vigorous stroke of the boat-hook. 'May you live long, and have your green old age renewed for ever!'

On we went; and the water had the familiar aspect to me of the days before Pangbourne* had been thoroughly cockneyfied, as I have seen it. It (Pangbourne) was distinctly a village still—*i.e.*, a definite group of houses, and as pretty as might be. The beech-woods still covered the hill that rose above Basildon; but the flat fields beneath them were much more populous than I remembered them, as there were five large houses in sight, very carefully designed so as not to hurt the character of the country. Down on the green lip of the river, just where the water turns toward the Goring and Streatley* reaches, were half a dozen girls playing about on the grass. They hailed us as we were about passing them, as they noted that we were travellers, and we stopped a minute to talk with them. They had been bathing, and were light clad and bare-footed, and were bound for the meadows on the Berkshire side, where the haymaking had begun, and were passing the time merrily enough till the Berkshire folk came in their punt to fetch them. At first nothing would content them but we must go with them into the hayfield, and breakfast with them; but Dick put forward his theory of beginning the hay-harvest higher up the water, and not spoiling my pleasure therein by giving me a taste of it elsewhere, and they gave way, though unwillingly. In revenge they asked me a great many questions about the country I came from and the manners of life there, which I found rather puzzling to answer; and doubtless what answers I did give were puzzling enough to them. I noticed both with these pretty girls and with everybody else we met, that in default of serious news, such as we had heard at Maple-Durham, they were eager to discuss all the little details of life: the weather, the hay-crop, the last new house, the plenty or lack of such and such birds, and so on; and they talked of these things not in a fatuous and conventional way, but as taking, I say, real interest in them. Moreover, I found that the women knew as much about all these things as the men: could name a flower, and knew its qualities; could tell you the habitat of such and such birds and fish, and the like.

It is almost strange what a difference this intelligence made in my estimate of the country life of that day; for it used to be said in past times, and on the whole truly, that outside their daily work country people knew little of the country, and at least could tell you nothing about it; while here were these people as eager about all the goings on in the fields and woods and downs as if they had been Cockneys* newly escaped from the tyranny of bricks and mortar.

I may mention as a detail worth noticing that not only did there seem to be a great many more birds about of the non-predatory kinds, but their enemies the birds of prey were also commoner. A kite hung over our heads as we passed Medmenham yesterday; magpies were quite common in the hedgerows; I saw several sparrow-hawks, and I think a merlin; and now just as we were passing the pretty bridge which had taken the place of Basildon railway-bridge,* a couple of ravens croaked above our boat, as they sailed off to the higher ground of the downs. I concluded from all this that the days of the gamekeeper were over, and did not even need to ask Dick a question about it.

CHAPTER XXVI
THE OBSTINATE REFUSERS*

Before we parted from these girls we saw two sturdy young men and a woman putting off from the Berkshire shore, and then Dick bethought him of a little banter of the girls, and asked them how it was that there was nobody of the male kind to go with them across the water, and where their boats were gone to. Said one, the youngest of the party: 'O, they have got the big punt to lead stone from up the water.'

'Who do you mean by "they," dear child?' said Dick.

Said an older girl, laughing: 'You had better go and see them. Look there,' and she pointed north-west, 'don't you see building going on there?'

'Yes,' said Dick, 'and I am rather surprised at this time of the year; why are they not haymaking with you?'

The girls all laughed at this, and before their laugh was over, the Berkshire boat had run on to the grass and the girls stepped in lightly, still sniggering, while the newcomers gave us the sele of the day. But before they were under way again, the tall girl said: 'Excuse us for laughing, dear neighbours, but we have had some friendly bickering with the builders up yonder, and as we have no time to tell you the story, you had better go and ask them: they will be glad to see you—if you don't hinder their work.'

They all laughed again at that, and waved us a pretty farewell as the punters set them over toward the other shore, and left us standing on the bank beside the boat.

'Let us go and see them,' said Clara; 'that is, if you are not in a hurry to get to Streatley, Walter?'

'O no,' said Walter, 'I shall be glad of the excuse to have a little more of your company.'

So we left the boat moored there, and went on up the slow slope of the hill; but I said to Dick on the way, being somewhat mystified: 'What was all that laughing about? What was the joke!'

'I can guess pretty well,' said Dick; 'some of them up there have got a piece of work which interests them, and they won't go to the haymaking, which doesn't matter at all, because there are plenty of people to do such easy-hard work as that; only, since haymaking is a regular festival, the neighbours find it amusing to jeer good-humouredly at them.'

'I see,' said I, 'much as if in Dickens's time some young people were so wrapped up in their work that they wouldn't keep Christmas.'

'Just so,' said Dick, 'only these people need not be young either.'

'But what did you mean by easy-hard work?' said I.

Quoth Dick: 'Did I say that? I mean work that tries the muscles and hardens them and sends you pleasantly weary to bed, but which isn't trying in other ways: doesn't harass you in short. Such work is always pleasant if you don't overdo it. Only, mind you, good mowing requires some little skill. I'm a pretty good mower.'

This talk brought us up to the house that was a-building, not a large one, which stood at the end of a beautiful orchard surrounded by an old stone wall. 'O yes, I see,' said Dick; 'I remember, a beautiful place for a house: but a starveling of a nineteenth-century house* stood there: I am glad they are rebuilding: it's all stone, too, though it need not have been in this part of the country: my word, though, they are making a neat job of it: but I wouldn't have made it all ashlar.'

Walter and Clara were already talking to a tall man clad in his mason's blouse, who looked about forty, but was I daresay, older, who had his mallet and chisel in hand; there were at work in the shed and on the scaffold about half a dozen men and two women, blouse-clad like the carles, while a very pretty woman who was not in the work but was dressed in an elegant suit of blue linen came sauntering up to us with her knitting in her hand. She welcomed us and said, smiling: 'So you are come up from the water to see the Obstinate Refusers: where are you going haymaking, neighbours?'

'O, right up above Oxford,' said Dick; 'it is rather a late country. But what share have you got with the Refusers, pretty neighbour?'

Said she, with a laugh: 'O, I am the lucky one who doesn't want to work; though sometimes I get it, for I serve as model to Mistress

Philippa there when she wants one: she is our head carver; come and see her.'

She led us up to the door of the unfinished house, where a rather little woman was working with mallet and chisel on the wall near by. She seemed very intent on what she was doing, and did not turn round when we came up; but a taller woman, quite a girl she seemed, who was at work near by, had already knocked off, and was standing looking from Clara to Dick with delighted eyes. None of the others paid much heed to us.

The blue-clad girl laid her hand on the carver's shoulder and said: 'Now, Philippa, if you gobble up your work like that, you will soon have none to do; and what will become of you then?'

The carver turned round hurriedly and showed us the face of a woman of forty (or so she seemed), and said rather pettishly, but in a sweet voice:

'Don't talk nonsense, Kate, and don't interrupt me if you can help it.' She stopped short when she saw us, then went on with the kind smile of welcome which never failed us. 'Thank you for coming to see us, neighbours; but I am sure that you won't think me unkind if I go on with my work, especially when I tell you that I was ill and unable to do anything all through April and May; and this open-air and the sun and the work together, and my feeling well again too, make a mere delight of every hour to me; and excuse me, I must go on.'

She fell to work accordingly on a carving in low relief of flowers and figures, but talked on amidst her mallet strokes: 'You see, we all think this the prettiest place for a house up and down these reaches; and the site has been so long encumbered with an unworthy one, that we masons were determined to pay off fate and destiny for once, and build the prettiest house we could compass here—and so—and so—'

Here she lapsed into mere carving, but the tall foreman came up and said: 'Yes, neighbours, that is it: so it is going to be all ashlar because we want to carve a kind of wreath of flowers and figures all round it; and we have been much hindered by one thing or other—Philippa's illness amongst others,—and though we could have managed our wreath without her—'

'Could you, though?' grumbled the last-named from the face of the wall.

'Well, at any rate, she is our best carver, and it would not have been kind to begin the carving without her. So you see,' said he, looking at Dick and me, 'we really couldn't go haymaking, could we, neighbours? But you see, we are getting on so fast now with this splendid weather, that I think we may well spare a week or ten days at wheat-harvest; and won't we go at *that* work then! Come down then to the acres that lie north and by west at our backs and you shall see good harvesters, neighbours.'

'Hurrah, for a good brag!' called a voice from the scaffold above us; 'our foreman thinks that an easier job than putting one stone on another!'

There was a general laugh at this sally, in which the tall foreman joined; and with that we saw a lad bringing out a little table into the shadow of the stone-shed, which he set down there, and then going back, came out again with the inevitable big wickered flask and tall glasses, whereon the foreman led us up to due seats on blocks of stone, and said:

'Well, neighbours, drink to my brag coming true, or I shall think you don't believe me! Up there!' said he, hailing the scaffold, 'are you coming down for a glass?' Three of the workmen came running down the ladder as men with good 'building legs' will do; but the others didn't answer, except the joker (if he must so be called), who called out without turning round: 'Excuse me, neighbours, for not getting down. I must get on: my work is not superintending, like the gaffer's yonder; but, you fellows, send us up a glass to drink the haymakers' health.' Of course, Philippa would not turn away from her beloved work; but the other woman carver came; she turned out to be Philippa's daughter, but was a tall strong girl, black-haired and gipsey-like of face and curiously solemn of manner. The rest gathered round us and clinked glasses, and the men on the scaffold turned about and drank to our healths; but the busy little woman by the door would have none of it all, but only shrugged her shoulders when her daughter came up to her and touched her.

So we shook hands and turned our backs on the Obstinate Refusers, went down the slope to our boat, and before we had gone many steps heard the full tune of tinkling trowels mingle with the humming of the bees and the singing of the larks above the little plain of Basildon.

CHAPTER XXVII
THE UPPER WATERS*

We set Walter ashore on the Berkshire side, amidst all the beauties of Streatley, and so went our ways into what once would have been the deeper country under the foot-hills of the White Horse;* and though the contrast between half-cocknified and wholly unsophisticated country existed no longer, a feeling of exultation rose within me (as it used to do) at sight of the familiar and still unchanged hills of the Berkshire range.

We stopped at Wallingford* for our mid-day meal; of course, all signs of squalor and poverty had disappeared from the streets of the ancient town, and many ugly houses had been taken down and many pretty new ones built, but I thought it curious, that the town still looked like the old place I remembered so well; for indeed it looked like that ought to have looked.

At dinner we fell in with an old, but very bright and intelligent man, who seemed in a country way to be another edition of old Hammond. He had an extraordinary detailed knowledge of the ancient history of the countryside from the time of Alfred* to the days of the Parliamentary Wars,* many events of which, as you may know, were enacted round about Wallingford. But, what was more interesting to us, he had detailed record of the period of the change to the present state of things, and told us a great deal about it, and especially of that exodus of the people from the town to the country, and the gradual recovery by the town-bred people on one side, and the country-bred people on the other, of those arts of life which they had each lost; which loss, as he told us, had at one time gone so far that not only was it impossible to find a carpenter or a smith in a village or a small country town, but that people in such places had even forgotten how to bake bread, and that at Wallingford, for instance, the bread came down with the newspapers by an early train from London, worked in some way, the explanation of which I could not understand. He told us also that the townspeople who came into the country used to pick up the agricultural arts by carefully watching the way in which the machines worked, gathering an idea of handicraft from machinery; because at that time almost everything in and about the fields was done by elaborate machines used quite unintelligently by the labourers. On the other hand, the old men amongst the labourers managed to teach the younger ones gradually a little artizanship, such as the use of the saw and the plane, the work of the smithy, and so forth; for once more, by that time it was as much as—or rather, more than—a man could do to fix an ash pole to a rake by handiwork; so that it would take a machine worth a thousand pounds, a group of workmen, and a half a day's travelling, to do five shillings' worth of work. He showed us, among other things, an account of a certain village council who were working hard at all this business; and the record of their intense earnestness in getting to the bottom of some matter which in time past would have been thought quite trivial, as, for example, the due proportions of alkali and oil for soap-making for the village wash, or the exact heat of the water into which a leg of mutton should be plunged for boiling—all this joined to the utter absence of anything like party feeling, which even in a village assembly would certainly have made its appearance in an earlier epoch, was very amusing, and at the same time instructive.

This old man, whose name was Henry Morsom, took us, after our meal and a rest, into a biggish hall which contained a large collection of articles of manufacture and art from the last days of the machine period to that day; and he went over them with us, and explained them with great care. They also were very interesting, showing the transition from the makeshift work of the machines (which was at about its worst a little after the Civil War before told of) into the first years of the new handicraft period. Of course, there was much overlapping of the periods: and at first the new handwork came in very slowly.

'You must remember,' said the old antiquary, 'that the handicraft was not the result of what used to be called material necessity: on the contrary, by that time the machines had been so much improved that almost all necessary work might have been by them: and indeed many people at that time, and before it, used to think that machinery would entirely supersede handicraft; which certainly, on the face of it, seemed more than likely. But there was another opinion, far less logical, prevalent amongst the rich people before the days of freedom, which did not die out at once after that epoch had begun. This opinion, which from all I can learn seemed as natural then, as it seems absurd now, was, that while the ordinary daily work of the world would be done entirely by automatic machinery, the energies of the more intelligent part of mankind would be set free to follow the higher forms of the arts, as well as science and the study of history. It was strange, was it not, that they should thus ignore that aspiration after complete equality which we now recognise as the bond of all happy human society?'

I did not answer, but thought the more. Dick looked thoughtful, and said:

'Strange, neighbour? Well, I don't know. I have often heard my old kinsman say the one aim of all people before our time was to avoid work, or at least they thought it was; so of course the work which their daily life *forced* them to do, seemed more like work than that which they *seemed* to choose for themselves.'

'True enough,' said Morsom. 'Anyhow, they soon began to find out their mistake, and that only slaves and slaveholders could live solely by setting machines going.'

Clara broke in here, flushing a little as she spoke: 'Was not their mistake once more bred of the life of slavery that they had been living?—a life which was always looking upon everything, except mankind, animate and inanimate —"nature," as people used to call it—as one thing, and mankind as another. It was natural to people thinking in this way, that they should try to make "nature" their slave, since they thought "nature" was something outside them.'

'Surely,' said Morsom; 'and they were puzzled as to what to do, till they found the feeling against a mechanical life, which had begun before the Great Change amongst people who had leisure to think of such things, was spreading insensibly; till at last under the guise of pleasure that was not supposed to be work, work that was pleasure began to push out the mechanical toil, which they had once hoped at the best to reduce to narrow limits indeed, but never to get rid of; and which, moreover, they found they could not limit as they had hoped to do.'

'When did this new revolution gather head?' said I.

'In the half-century that followed the Great Change,' said Morsom, 'it began to be noteworthy; machine after machine was quietly dropped under the excuse that machines could not produce works of art, and that works of art were more and more called for. Look here,' he said, 'here are some of the works of that time—rough and unskilful in handiwork, but solid and showing some sense of pleasure in the making.'

'They are very curious,' said I, taking up a piece of pottery from amongst the specimens which the antiquary was showing us; 'not a bit like the work of either savages or barbarians, and yet with what would once have been called a hatred of civilisation impressed upon them.'

'Yes,' said Morsom, 'you must not look for delicacy there: in that period you could only have got that from a man who was practically a slave. But now, you see,' said he, leading me on a little, 'we have learned the trick of handicraft, and have added the utmost refinement of workmanship to the freedom of fancy and imagination.'

I looked, and wondered indeed at the deftness and abundance of beauty of the work of men who had at last learned to accept life itself as a pleasure, and the satisfaction of the common needs of mankind and the preparation for them, as work fit for the best of the race. I mused silently; but at last I said—

'What is to come after this?'

The old man laughed. 'I don't know,' said he; 'we will meet it when it comes.'

'Meanwhile,' quoth Dick, 'we have got to meet the rest of our day's journey; so out into the street and down to the strand! Will you come a turn with us, neighbour? Our friend is greedy of your stories.'

'I will go as far as Oxford with you,' said he; 'I want a book or two out of the Bodleian Library.* I suppose you will sleep in the old city?'

'No,' said Dick, 'we are going higher up; the hay is waiting us there, you know.'

Morsom nodded, and we all went into the street together, and got into the boat a little above the town bridge. But just as Dick was getting the sculls into the rowlocks, the bows of another boat came thrusting through the low arch. Even at first sight it was a gay little craft indeed—bright green, and painted over with elegantly drawn flowers. As it cleared the arch, a figure as bright and gay-clad as the boat rose up in it; a slim girl dressed in light blue silk that fluttered in the draughty wind of the bridge. I thought I knew the figure, and sure enough, as she turned her head to us, and showed her beautiful face, I saw with joy that it was none other than the fairy godmother from the abundant garden on Runnymede—Ellen, to wit.

We all stopped to receive her. Dick rose in the boat and cried out a genial good morrow; I tried to be as genial as Dick, but failed; Clara waved a delicate hand to her; and Morsom nodded and looked on with interest. As to Ellen, the beautiful brown of her face was deepened by a flush, as she brought the gunwale of her boat alongside ours, and said:

'You see, neighbours, I had some doubt if you would all three come back past Runnymede, or if you did, whether you would stop there; and besides, I am not sure whether we—my father and I*—shall not be away in a week or two, for he wants to see a brother of his in the north country, and I should not like him to go without me. So I thought I might never see you again, and that seemed uncomfortable to me, and—and so I came after you.'

'Well,' said Dick, 'I am sure we are all very glad of that; although you may be sure that as for Clara and me, we should have made a point of coming to see you, and of coming the second time, if we had found you away the first. But, dear neighbour, there you are alone in the boat, and you have been sculling pretty hard, I should think, and might find a little quiet sitting pleasant; so we had better part our company into two.'

'Yes,' said Ellen, 'I thought you would do that, so I have brought a rudder for my boat: will you help me to ship it, please?'

And she went aft in her boat and pushed along our side till she had brought the stern close to Dick's hand. He knelt down in our boat and she in hers, and the usual fumbling took place over hanging the rudder on its hooks; for, as you may imagine, no change had taken place in the arrangement of such an unimportant matter as the rudder of a pleasure-boat. As the two beautiful young faces bent over the rudder, they seemed to me to be very close together, and though it lasted only a moment, a sort of pang shot through me as I looked on. Clara sat in her place and did not look round, but presently she said, with just the least stiffness in her tone:

'How shall we divide? Won't you go into Ellen's boat, Dick, since, without offence to our guest, you are the better sculler?'

Dick stood up and laid his hand on her shoulder, and said: 'No, no; let Guest try what he can do—he ought to be getting into training now. Besides, we are in no hurry: we are not going far above Oxford; and even if we are benighted, we shall have the moon, which will give us nothing worse of a night than a greyer day.'

'Besides,' said I, 'I may manage to do a little more with my sculling than merely keeping the boat from drifting down stream.'

They all laughed at this, as if it had been a very good joke; and I thought that Ellen's laugh, even amongst the others, was one of the pleasantest sounds I had ever heard.

To be short, I got into the new-come boat, not a little elated, and taking the sculls, set to work to show off a little. For—must I say it?—I felt as if even that happy world were made the happier for my being so near this strange girl; although I must say that of all persons I had seen in that world renewed, she was the most unfamiliar to me, the most unlike what I could have thought of. Clara, for instance, beautiful and bright as she was, was not unlike a *very* pleasant and unaffected young lady; and the other girls also seemed nothing more than specimens of very much improved types which I had known in other times. But this girl was not only beautiful with a beauty quite different from that of 'a young lady,' but was in all ways so strangely interesting; so that I kept wondering what she would say or do next to surprise and please me. Not, indeed, that there was anything startling in what she actually said or did; but it was all done in a new way, and always with that indefinable interest and pleasure of life, which I had noticed more or less in everybody, but which in her was more marked and more charming than in anyone else that I had seen.

We were soon under way and going at a fair pace through the beautiful reaches of the river, between Bensington and Dorchester.* It was now about the middle of the afternoon, warm rather than hot, and quite windless; the clouds high up and light, pearly white, and gleaming, softened the sun's burning, but did not hide the pale blue in most places, though they seemed to give it height and consistency; the sky, in short, looked really like a vault, as poets have sometimes called it, and not like mere limitless air, but a vault so vast and full of light that it did not in any way oppress the spirits. It was the sort of afternoon that Tennyson must have been thinking about, when he said of the Lotos-Eaters' land that it was a land where it was always afternoon.*

Ellen leaned back in the stern and seemed to enjoy herself thoroughly. I could see that she was really looking at things and let nothing escape her, and as I watched her, an uncomfortable feeling that she had been a little touched by love of the deft, ready, and handsome Dick, and that she had been constrained to follow us because of it, faded out of my mind; since if it had been so, she surely could not have been so excitedly pleased, even with the beautiful scenes we were passing through. For some time she did not say much, but at last, as we had passed under Shillingford Bridge (new built, but somewhat on its old lines),* she bade me hold the boat while she had a good look at the landscape through the graceful arch. Then she turned about to me and said:

'I do not know whether to be sorry or glad that this is the first time that I have been in these reaches. It is true that it is a great pleasure to see all this for the first time; but if I had had a year or two of memory of it, how sweetly it would all have mingled with my life, waking or dreaming! I am so glad Dick has been pulling slowly, so as to linger out the time here. How do you feel about your first visit to these waters?'

I do not suppose she meant a trap for me, but anyhow I fell into it, and said: 'My first visit! It is not my first visit by many a time. I know these reaches well; indeed, I may say that I know every yard of the Thames from Hammersmith to Cricklade.'

I saw the complications that might follow, as her eyes fixed mine with a curious look in them, that I had seen before at Runnymede, when I had said something which made it difficult for others to understand my present position amongst these people. I reddened, and said, in order to cover my mistake: 'I wonder you have never been up so high as this, since you live on the Thames, and moreover row so well that it would be no great labour to you. Let alone,' quoth I, insinuatingly, 'that anybody would be glad to row you.'

She laughed, clearly not at my compliment (as I am sure she need not have done, since it was a very commonplace fact), but at something which was stirring in her mind; and she still looked at me kindly, but with the above-said keen look in her eyes, and then she said:

'Well, perhaps it is strange, though I have a good deal to do at home, what with looking after my father, and dealing with two or three young men who have taken a special liking to me, and all of whom I cannot please at once. But you, dear neighbour; it seems to me stranger that you should know the upper river, than that I should not know it; for, as I understand, you have only been in England a few days. But perhaps you mean that you have read about it in books, and seen pictures of it?—though that does not come to much, either,'

'Truly,' said I. 'Besides, I have not read any books about the Thames: it was one of the minor stupidities of our time that no one thought fit to write a decent book about what may fairly be called our only English river.'

The words were no sooner out of my mouth than I saw that I had made another mistake; and I felt really annoyed with myself, as I did not want to go into a long explanation just then, or begin another series of Odyssean lies.* Somehow, Ellen seemed to see this, and she took no advantage of my slip; her piercing look changed into one of mere frank kindness, and she said:

'Well, anyhow I am glad that I am travelling these waters with you, since you know our river so well, and I know little of it past Pangbourne, for you can tell me all I want to know about it.' She paused a minute, and then said: 'Yet you must understand that the part I do know, I know as thoroughly as you do. I should be sorry for you to think that I am careless of a thing so beautiful and interesting as the Thames.'

She said this quite earnestly, and with an air of affectionate appeal to me which pleased me very much; but I could see that she was only keeping her doubts about me for another time.

Presently we came to Day's Lock,* where Dick and his two sitters had waited for us. He would have me go ashore, as if to show me something which I had never seen before; and nothing loth I followed him, Ellen by my side, to the well-remembered Dykes, and the long church beyond them, which was still used for various purposes by the good folk of Dorchester: where, by the way, the village guest-house still had the sign of the Fleur-de-luce* which it used to bear in the days when hospitality had to be bought and sold. This time, however, I made no sign of all this being familiar to me: though as we sat for a while on the mound of the Dykes looking up at Sinodun and its clear-cut trench, and its sister *mamelon* of Whittenham,* I felt somewhat uncomfortable under Ellen's serious attentive look, which almost drew from me the cry, 'How little anything is changed here!'

We stopped again at Abingdon,* which, like Wallingford, was in a way both old and new to me, since it had been lifted out of its nineteenth-century degradation, and otherwise was as little altered as might be.

Sunset was in the sky as we skirted Oxford by Oseney; we stopped a minute or two hard by the ancient castle* to put Henry Morsom ashore. It was a matter of course that so far as they could be seen from the river, I missed none of the towers and spires of that once don-beridden city; but the meadows all round, which, when I had last passed through them, were getting daily more and more squalid, more and more impressed with the seal of the 'stir and intellectual life of the nineteenth century,' were no longer intellectual, but had once again become as beautiful as they should be, and the little hill of Hinksey,* with two or three very pretty stone houses new-grown on it (I use the word advisedly, for they seemed to belong to it) looked down happily on the full streams and waving grass, grey now, but for the sunset, with its fast-ripening seeds.

The railway having disappeared, and therewith the various level bridges over the streams of the Thames, we were soon through Medley Lock and in the wide water that washes Port Meadow,* with its numerous population of geese nowise diminished; and I thought with interest how its name and use had survived from the older imperfect communal period, through the time of the confused struggle and tyranny of the rights of property, into the present rest and happiness of complete Communism.

I was taken ashore again at Godstow, to see the remains of the old nunnery,* pretty nearly in the same condition as I had remembered them; and from the high bridge over the cut close by, I could see, even in the twilight, how beautiful the little village with its grey stone houses had become; for we had now come into the stone-country, in which every house must be either built, walls and roof, of grey stone or be a blot on the landscape.

We still rowed on after this. Ellen taking the sculls in my boat; we passed a weir* a little higher up, and about three miles beyond it came by moonlight again to a little town,* where we slept at a house thinly inhabited, as its folk were mostly tented in the hay-fields.

CHAPTER XXVIII

THE LITTLE RIVER

We started before six o'clock the next morning, as we were still twenty-five miles from our resting place, and Dick wanted to be there before dusk. The journey was pleasant, though to those who do not know the upper Thames, there is little to say about it. Ellen and I were once more together in her boat, though Dick, for fairness' sake, was for having me in his, and letting the two women scull the green toy. Ellen, however, would not allow this, but claimed me as the interesting person of the company. 'After having come so far,' said she, 'I will not be put off with a companion who will always be thinking of somebody else than me: the guest is the only person who can amuse me properly. I mean that really,' said she, turning to me, 'and have not said it merely as a pretty saying.'

Clara blushed and looked very happy at all this; for I think up to this time she had been rather frightened of Ellen. As for me I felt young again, and strange hopes of my youth were mingling with the pleasure of the present; almost destroying it, and quickening it into something like pain.

As we passed through the short and winding reaches of the now quickly lessening stream, Ellen said: 'How pleasant this little river is to me, who am used to a great wide wash of water; it almost seems as if we shall have to stop at every reach-end. I expect before I get home this evening I shall have realised what a little country England is, since we can so soon get to the end of its biggest river.'

'It is not big,' said I, 'but it is pretty.'

'Yes,' she said, 'and don't you find it difficult to imagine the times when this little pretty country was treated by its folk as if it had been an ugly characterless waste, with no delicate beauty to be guarded, with no heed taken of the ever fresh pleasure of the recurring seasons, and changeful weather, and diverse quality of the soil, and so forth? How could people be so cruel to themselves?'

'And to each other,' said I. Then a sudden resolution took hold of me, and I said: 'Dear neighbour, I may as well tell you at once that I find it easier to imagine all that ugly past than you do, because I myself have been part of it. I see both that you have divined something of this in me; and also I think you will believe me when I tell you of it, so that I am going to hide nothing from you at all.'

She was silent a little, and then she said: 'My friend, you have guessed right about me; and to tell you the truth I have followed you up from Runnymede in order that I might ask you many questions, and because I saw that you were not one of us; and that interested and pleased me, and I wanted to make you as happy as you could be.

To say the truth, there was a risk in it,' said she, blushing—'I mean as to Dick and Clara; for I must tell you, since we are going to be such close friends, that even amongst us, where there are so many beautiful women, I have often troubled men's minds disastrously. That is one reason why I was living alone with my father in the cottage at Runnymede. But it did not answer on that score; for of course people came there, as the place is not a desert, and they seemed to find me all the more interesting for living alone like that, and fell to making stories of me to themselves—like I know you did, my friend. Well, let that pass. This evening, or to-morrow morning, I shall make a proposal to you to do something which would please me very much, and I think would not hurt you.'

I broke in eagerly, saying that I would do anything in the world for her; for indeed, in spite of my years and the too obvious signs of them (though that feeling of renewed youth was not a mere passing sensation, I think)—in spite of my years, I say, I felt altogether too happy in the company of this delightful girl, and was prepared to take her confidences for more than they meant perhaps.

She laughed now, but looked very kindly on me. 'Well,' she said, 'meantime for the present we will let it be; for I must look at this new country that we are passing through. See how the river has changed character again: it is broad now, and the reaches are long and very slow-running. And look, there is a ferry!'*

I told her the name of it, as I slowed off to put the ferry-chain over our heads; and on we went passing by a bank clad with oak trees on our left hand, till the stream narrowed again and deepened, and we rowed on between walls of tall reeds, whose population of reed sparrows and warblers were delightfully restless, twittering and chuckling as the wash of the boats stirred the reeds from the water upward in the still, hot morning.

She smiled with pleasure, and her lazy enjoyment of the new scene seemed to bring out her beauty doubly as she leaned back amidst the cushions, though she was far from languid; her idleness being the idleness of a person, strong and well-knit both in body and mind, deliberately resting.

'Look!' she said, springing up suddenly from her place without any obvious effort, and balancing herself with exquisite grace and ease; 'look at the beautiful old bridge ahead!'

'I need scarcely look at that,' said I, not turning my head away from her beauty. 'I know what it is; though' (with a smile) 'we used not to call it the Old Bridge time agone.'*

She looked down upon me kindly, and said, 'How well we get on now you are no longer on your guard against me!'

And she stood looking thoughtfully at me still, till she had to sit down as we passed under the middle one of the row of little pointed arches of the oldest bridge across the Thames.

'O the beautiful fields!' she said; 'I had no idea of the charm of a very small river like this. The smallness of the scale of everything, the short reaches, and the speedy change of the banks, give one a feeling of going somewhere, of coming to something strange, a feeling of adventure which I have not felt in bigger waters.'

I looked up at her delightedly; for her voice, saying the very thing which I was thinking, was like a caress to me. She caught my eye and her cheeks reddened under their tan, and she said simply:

'I must tell you, my friend, that when my father leaves the Thames this summer he will take me away to a place near the Roman wall in Cumberland;* so that this voyage of mine is farewell to the south; of course with my goodwill in a way; and yet I am sorry for it. I hadn't the heart to tell Dick yesterday that we were as good as gone from the Thames-side; but somehow to you I must needs tell it.'

She stopped and seemed very thoughtful for awhile, and then said smiling:

'I must say that I don't like moving about from one home to another; one gets so pleasantly used to all the detail of the life about one; it fits so harmoniously and happily into one's own life, that beginning again, even in a small way, is a kind of pain. But I daresay in the country which you come from, you would think this petty and unadventurous, and would think the worse of me for it.'

She smiled at me caressingly as she spoke, and I made haste to answer: 'O, no, indeed; again you echo my very thoughts. But I hardly expected to hear you speak so. I gathered from all I have heard that there was a great deal of changing of abode amongst you in this country.'

'Well,' she said, 'of course people are free to move about; but except for pleasure-parties, especially in harvest and hay-time, like this of ours, I don't think they do so much. I admit that I also have other moods than that of stay-at-home, as I hinted just now, and I should like to go with you all through the west country—thinking of nothing,' concluded she, smiling.

'I should have plenty to think of,' said I.

CHAPTER XXIX

A RESTING-PLACE ON THE UPPER THAMES

Presently at a place where the river flowed round a headland of the meadows, we stopped a while for rest and victuals, and settled ourselves on a beautiful bank which almost reached the dignity of a hill-side: the wide meadows spread before us, and already the scythe was busy amidst the hay. One change I noticed amidst the quiet beauty of the fields—to wit, that they were planted with trees here and there, often fruit-trees, and that there was none of the niggardly begrudging of space to a handsome tree which I remembered too well; and though the willows were often polled (or shrowded, as they call it in that country-side), this was done with some regard to beauty: I mean that there was no polling of rows on rows so as to destroy the pleasantness of half a mile of country, but a thoughtful sequence in the cutting, that prevented a sudden bareness anywhere. To be short, the fields were everywhere treated as a garden made for the pleasure as well as the livelihood of all, as old Hammond told me was the case.

On this bank or bent of the hill, then, we had our mid-day meal; somewhat early for dinner, if that mattered, but we had been stirring early: the slender stream of the Thames winding below us between the garden of a country I have been telling of; a furlong from us was a beautiful little islet begrown with graceful trees;* on the slopes westward of us was a wood of varied growth overhanging the narrow meadow on the south side of the river; while to the north was a wide stretch of mead rising very gradually from the river's edge. A delicate spire of an ancient building rose up from out of the trees in the middle distance, with a few grey houses clustered about it; while nearer to us, in fact not half a furlong from the water, was a quite modern stone house—a wide quadrangle of one story, the buildings that made it being quite low. There was no garden between it and the river, nothing but a row of pear-trees still quite young and slender;

and though there did not seem to be much ornament about it, it had a sort of natural elegance, like that of the trees themselves.

As we sat looking down on all this in the sweet June day, rather happy than merry, Ellen, who sat next me, her hand clasped about one knee, leaned sideways to me, and said in a low voice which Dick and Clara might have noted if they had not been busy in happy wordless love-making: 'Friend, in your country were the houses of your field-labourers anything like that?'

I said: 'Well, at any rate the houses of our rich men were not; they were mere blots upon the face of the land.'

'I find that hard to understand,' she said. 'I can see why the workmen, who were so oppressed, should not have been able to live in beautiful houses; for it takes time and leisure, and minds not over-burdened with care, to make beautiful dwellings; and I quite understand that these poor people were not allowed to live in such a way as to have these (to us) necessary good things. But why the rich men, who had the time and the leisure and the materials for building, as it would be in this case, should not have housed themselves well, I do not understand as yet. I know what you are meaning to say to me,' she said, looking me full in the eyes and blushing, 'to wit that their houses and all belonging to them were generally ugly and base, unless they chanced to be ancient like yonder remnant of our forefathers' work' (pointing to the spire); 'that they were—let me see; what is the word?'

'Vulgar,' said I. 'We used to say,' said I, 'that the ugliness and vulgarity of the rich men's dwellings was a necessary reflection from the sordidness and bareness of life which they forced upon the poor people.'

She knit her brows as in thought; then turned a brightened face on me, as if she had caught the idea, and said: 'Yes, friend, I see what you mean. We have sometimes—those of us who look into these things—talked this very matter over; because, to say the truth, we have plenty of record of the so-called arts of the time before Equality of Life; and there are not wanting people who say that the state of that society was not the cause of all that ugliness; that they were ugly in their life because they liked to be, and could have had beautiful things about them if they had chosen; just as a man or a body of men now may, if they please, make things more or less beautiful—Stop! I know what you are going to say.'

'Do you?' said I, smiling, yet with a beating heart.

'Yes,' she said; 'you are answering me, teaching me, in some way or another, although you have not spoken the words aloud. You were going to say that in times of inequality it was an essential condition of the life of these rich men that they should not themselves make what they wanted for the adornment of their lives, but should force those to make them whom they forced to live pinched and sordid lives; and that as a necessary consequence the sordidness and pinching, the ugly barrenness of those ruined lives, were worked up into the adornment of the lives of the rich, and art died out amongst men? Was that what you would say, my friend?'

'Yes, yes,' I said, looking at her eagerly; for she had risen and was standing on the edge of the bent, the light wind stirring her dainty raiment, one hand laid on her bosom, the other arm stretched downward and clenched in her earnestness.

'It is true,' she said, 'it is true! We have proved it true!'

I think amidst my—something more than interest in her, and admiration for her, I was beginning to wonder how it would all end. I had a glimmering of fear of what might follow; of anxiety as to the remedy which this new age might offer for the missing of something one might set one's heart on. But now Dick rose to his feet and cried out in his hearty manner: 'Neighbour Ellen, are you quarrelling with the guest, or are you worrying him to tell you things which he cannot properly explain to our ignorance?'

'Neither, dear neighbour,' she said. 'I was so far from quarrelling with him that I think I have been making him good friends both with himself and me. Is it so, dear guest?' she said, looking down at me with a delightful smile of confidence in being understood.

'Indeed it is,' said I.

'Well, moreover,' she said, 'I must say for him that he has explained himself to me very well indeed, so that I quite understand him.'

'All right,' quoth Dick. 'When I first set eyes on you at Runnymede I knew that there was something wonderful in your keenness of wits. I don't say that as a mere pretty speech to please you,' said he quickly, 'but because it is true; and it made me want to see more of you. But, come, we ought to be going; for we are not half way, and we ought to be in well before sunset.'

And therewith he took Clara's hand, and led her down the bent.

But Ellen stood thoughtfully looking down for a little, and as I took her hand to follow Dick, she turned round to me and said:

'You might tell me a great deal and make many things clear to me, if you would.'

'Yes,' said I, 'I am pretty well fit for that,—and for nothing else—an old man like me.'

She did not notice the bitterness which, whether I liked it or not, was in my voice as I spoke, but went on: 'It is not so much for myself; I should be quite content to dream about past times, and if I could not idealise them, yet at least idealise some of the people who lived in them. But I think sometimes people are too careless of the history of the past—too apt to leave it in the hands of old learned men like Hammond. Who knows? happy as we are, times may alter; we may be bitten with some impulse towards change, and many things may seem too wonderful for us to resist, too exciting not to catch at, if we do not know that they are but phases of what has been before; and withal ruinous, deceitful, and sordid.'

As we went slowly down toward the boats she said again: 'Not for myself alone, dear friend; I shall have children; perhaps before the end a good many;—I hope so. And though of course I cannot force any special kind of knowledge upon them, yet, my friend, I cannot help thinking that just as they might be like me in body, so I might impress upon them some part of my ways of thinking; that is, indeed, some of the essential part of myself; that part which was not mere moods, created by the matters and events round about me. What do you think?'

Of one thing I was sure, that her beauty and kindness and eagerness combined, forced me to think as she did, when she was not earnestly laying herself open to receive my thoughts. I said, what at the time was true, that I thought it most important; and presently stood entranced by the wonder of her grace as she stepped into the light boat, and held out her hand to me. And so on we went up the Thames still—or whither?

CHAPTER XXX
THE JOURNEY'S END

On we went. In spite of my new-born excitement about Ellen, and my gathering fear of where it would land me, I could not help taking abundant interest in the condition of the river and its banks; all the more as she never seemed weary of the changing picture, but looked at every yard of flowery bank and gurgling eddy with the same affectionate interest which I myself once had so fully, as I used to think, and perhaps had not altogether lost even in this strangely changed society with all its wonders. Ellen seemed delighted with my pleasure at this, that, or the other piece of carefulness in dealing with the river: the nursing of pretty corners; the ingenuity in dealing with difficulties of water-engineering so that the most obviously useful works looked beautiful and natural also. All this, I say, pleased me hugely, and she was pleased at my pleasure—but rather puzzled too.

'You seem astonished,' she said, just after we had passed a mill[1] which spanned all the stream save the water-way for traffic, but which was as beautiful in its way as a Gothic cathedral—'You seem astonished at this being so pleasant to look at.'

'Yes,' I said, 'in a way I am; though I don't see why it should not be.'

'Ah!' she said, looking at me admiringly, yet with a lurking smile in her face, 'you know all about the history of the past. Were they not always careful about this little stream which now adds so much pleasantness to the countryside? It would always be easy to manage this little river. Ah! I forgot, though,' she said, as her eye caught mine, 'in the days we are thinking of pleasure was wholly neglected in such matters. But how did they manage the river in the days that you—' Lived in she was going to say; but correcting herself, said—'in the days of which you have record?'

'They *mis*managed it,' quoth I. 'Up to the first half of the

[1] I should have said that all along the Thames there were abundance of mills used for various purposes; none of which were in any degree unsightly, and many strikingly beautiful; and the gardens about them marvels of loveliness.

nineteenth century, when it was still more or less of a highway for the country people, some care was taken of the river and its banks; and though I don't suppose anyone troubled himself about its aspect, yet it was trim and beautiful. But when the railways—of which no doubt you have heard—came into power, they would not allow the people of the country to use either the natural or artificial waterways, of which latter there were a great many. I suppose when we get higher up we shall see one of these; a very important one, which one of these railways entirely closed to the public,* so that they might force people to send their goods by their private road, and so tax them as heavily as they could.'

Ellen laughed heartily. 'Well,' she said, 'that is not stated clearly enough in our history-books, and it is worth knowing. But certainly the people of those days must have been a curiously lazy set. We are not either fidgety or quarrelsome now, but if any one tried such a piece of folly on us, we should use the said waterways, whoever gainsaid us: surely that would be simple enough. However, I remember other cases of this stupidity: when I was on the Rhine two years ago, I remember they showed us ruins of old castles, which, according to what we heard, must have been made for pretty much the same purpose as the railways were. But I am interrupting your history of the river: pray go on.'

'It is both short and stupid enough,' said I. 'The river having lost its practical or commercial value—that is, being of no use to make money of—'

She nodded. 'I understand what that queer phrase means,' said she. 'Go on!'

'Well, it was utterly neglected, till at last it became a nuisance—'

'Yes,' quoth Ellen, 'I understand: like the railways and the robber knights.* Yes?'

'So then they turned the makeshift business on to it, and handed it over to a body up in London, who from time to time, in order to show that they had something to do, did some damage here and there,—cut down trees, destroying the banks thereby; dredged the river (where it was not needed always), and threw the dredgings on the fields so as to spoil them; and so forth. But for the most part they practised 'masterly inactivity,' as it was then called—that is, they drew their salaries, and let things alone.'*

'Drew their salaries,' she said. 'I know that means that they were allowed to take an extra lot of other people's goods for doing nothing. And if that had been all, it really might have been worth while to let them do so, if you couldn't find any other way of keeping them quiet; but it seems to me that being so paid, they could not help doing something, and that something was bound to be mischief,—because,' said she, kindling with sudden anger, 'the whole business was founded on lies and false pretensions. I don't mean only these river-guardians, but all these master-people I have read of.'

'Yes,' said I, 'how happy you are to have got out of the parsimony of oppression!'

'Why do you sigh?' she said, kindly and somewhat anxiously. 'You seem to think that it will not last?'

'It will last for you,' quoth I.

'But why not for you?' said she. 'Surely it is for all the world; and if your country is somewhat backward, it will come into line before long. Or,' she said quickly, 'are you thinking that you must soon go back again? I will make my proposal which I told you of at once, and so perhaps put an end to your anxiety. I was going to propose that you should live with us where we are going. I feel quite old friends with you, and should be sorry to lose you.' Then she smiled on me, and said: 'Do you know, I begin to suspect you of wanting to nurse a sham sorrow, like the ridiculous characters in some of those queer old novels that I have come across now and then.'

I really had almost begun to suspect it myself, but I refused to admit so much; so I sighed no more, but fell to giving my delightful companion what little pieces of history I knew about the river and its borderlands; and the time passed pleasantly enough; and between the two of us (she was a better sculler than I was, and seemed quite tireless) we kept up fairly well with Dick, hot as the afternoon was, and swallowed up the way at a great rate. At last we passed under another ancient bridge;* and through meadows bordered at first with huge elm-trees mingled with sweet chestnut of younger but very elegant growth; and the meadows widened out so much that it seemed as if the trees must now be on the bents only, or about the houses, except for the growth of willows on the immediate banks; so that the wide stretch of grass was little broken here. Dick got very much excited now, and often stood up in the boat to cry out to us that this was such and such a field, and so forth; and we caught fire at his enthusiasm for the hayfield and its harvest, and pulled our best.

At last as we were passing through a reach of the river where on the side of the towing-path was a highish bank with a thick whispering bed of reeds before it, and on the other side a higher bank, clothed with willows that dipped into the stream and crowned by ancient elm-trees, we saw bright figures coming along close to the bank, as if they were looking for something; as, indeed, they were, and we—that is, Dick and his company—were what they were looking for. Dick lay on his oars, and we followed his example. He gave a joyous shout to the people on the bank, which was echoed back from it in many voices, deep and sweetly shrill; for there were above a dozen persons, both men, women, and children. A tall handsome woman, with black wavy hair and deep-set grey eyes, came forward on the bank and waved her hand gracefully to us, and said:

'Dick, my friend, we have almost had to wait for you! What excuse have you to make for your slavish punctuality? Why didn't you take us by surprise, and come yesterday?'

'O,' said Dick, with an almost imperceptible jerk of his head toward our boat, 'we didn't want to come too quickly up the water; there is so much to see for those who have not been up here before.'

'True, true,' said the stately lady, for stately is the word that must be used for her; 'and we want them to get to know the wet way from the east thoroughly well, since they must often use it now. But come ashore at once, Dick, and you, dear neighbours; there is a break in the reeds and a good landing-place just round the corner. We can carry up your things, or send some of the lads after them.'

'No, no,' said Dick; 'it is easier going by water, though it is but a step. Besides, I want to bring my friend here to the proper place. We will go on to the Ford; and you can talk to us from the bank as we paddle along.'

He pulled his sculls through the water, and on we went, turning a sharp angle and going north a little. Presently we saw before us a bank of elm-trees, which told us of a house amidst them, though I looked in vain for the grey walls that I expected to see there.* As we went, the folk on the bank talked indeed, mingling their kind voices with the cuckoo's song, the sweet strong whistle of the blackbirds, and the ceaseless note of the corn-crake as he crept through the long grass of the mowing-field; whence came waves of fragrance from the flowering clover amidst of the ripe grass.

In a few minutes we had passed through a deep eddying pool into the sharp stream that ran from the ford, and beached our craft on a tiny strand of limestone-gravel, and stepped ashore into the arms of our up-river friends, our journey done.

I disentangled myself from the merry throng, and mounting on the cart-road* that ran along the river some feet above the water, I looked round about me. The river came down through a wide meadow on my left, which was grey now with the ripened seeding grasses; the gleaming water was lost presently by a turn of the bank, but over the meadow I could see the mingled gables of a building where I knew the lock must be, and which now seemed to combine a mill with it. A low wooded ridge bounded the river-plain to the south and south-east, whence we had come, and a few low houses lay about its feet and up its slope. I turned a little to my right, and through the hawthorn sprays and long shoots of the wild roses could see the flat country spreading out far away under the sun of the calm evening, till something that might be called hills with a look of sheep-pastures about them bounded it with a soft blue line. Before me, the elm-boughs still hid most of what houses there might be in this river-side dwelling of men; but to the right of the cart-road a few grey buildings of the simplest kind showed here and there.

There I stood in a dreamy mood, and rubbed my eyes as if I were not wholly awake, and half expected to see the gay-clad company of beautiful men and women change to two or three spindle-legged back-bowed men and haggard, hollow-eyed, ill-favoured women, who once wore down the soil of this land with their heavy hopeless feet, from day to day, and season to season, and year to year. But no change came as yet, and my heart swelled with joy as I thought of all the beautiful grey villages, from the river to the plain and the plain to the uplands, which I could picture to myself so well, all peopled now with this happy and lovely folk, who had cast away riches and attained to wealth.

CHAPTER XXXI

AN OLD HOUSE AMONGST NEW FOLK

As I stood there Ellen detached herself from our happy friends who still stood on the little strand and came up to me. She took me by the hand, and said softly, 'Take me on to the house at once; we need not wait for the others: I had rather not.'

I had a mind to say that I did not know the way thither, and that the river-side dwellers should lead; but almost without my will my feet moved on along the road they knew. The raised way led us into a little field bounded by a backwater of the river on one side; on the right hand we could see a cluster of small houses and barns, new and old, and before us a grey stone barn and a wall partly overgrown with ivy, over which a few grey gables showed. The village road ended in the shallow of the aforesaid backwater. We crossed the road, and again almost without my will my hand raised the latch of a door in the wall, and we stood presently on a stone path which led up to the old house* to which fate in the shape of Dick had so strangely brought me in this new world of men. My companion gave a sigh of pleased surprise and enjoyment; nor did I wonder, for the garden between the wall and the house was redolent of the June flowers, and the roses were rolling over one another with that delicious superabundance of small well-tended gardens which at first sight takes away all thought from the beholder save that of beauty. The blackbirds were singing their loudest, the doves were cooing on the roof-ridge, the rooks in the high elm-trees beyond were garrulous among the young leaves, and the swifts wheeled whining about the gables. And the house itself was a fit guardian for all the beauty of this heart of summer.

Once again Ellen echoed my thoughts as she said: 'Yes, friend, this is what I came out for to see; this many-gabled old house built by the simple country-folk of the long-past times, regardless of all the turmoil that was going on in cities and courts, is lovely still amidst all the beauty which these latter days have created; and I do not wonder at our friends tending it carefully and making much of it. It seems to me as if it had waited for these happy days, and held in it the gathered crumbs of happiness of the confused and turbulent past.'

She led me up close to the house, and laid her shapely sun-browned hand and arm on the lichened wall as if to embrace it, and cried out, 'O me! O me! How I love the earth, and the seasons, and weather, and all things that deal with it, and all that grows out of it,—as this has done!'

I could not answer her, or say a word. Her exultation and pleasure were so keen and exquisite, and her beauty, so delicate, yet so interfused with energy, expressed it so fully, that any added word would have been commonplace and futile. I dreaded lest the others should come in suddenly and break the spell she had cast about me; but we stood there a while by the corner of the big gable of the house, and no one came. I heard the merry voices some way off presently, and knew that they were going along the river to the great meadow on the other side of the house and garden.

We drew back a little, and looked up at the house: the door and the windows were open to the fragrant sun-cured air; from the upper window-sills hung festoons of flowers in honour of the festival, as if the others shared in the love for the old house.

'Come in,' said Ellen. 'I hope nothing will spoil it inside; but I don't think it will. Come! we must go back presently to the others. They have gone on to the tents; for surely they must have tents pitched for the haymakers—the house would not hold a tithe of the folk, I am sure.'

She led me on to the door, murmuring little above her breath as she did so, 'The earth and the growth of it and the life of it! If I could but say or show how I love it!'

We went in, and found no soul in any room as we wandered from room to room,—from the rose-covered porch to the strange and quaint garrets amongst the great timbers of the roof, where of old time the tillers and herdsmen of the manor slept, but which a-nights seemed now, by the small size of the beds, and the litter of useless and disregarded matters—bunches of drying flowers, feathers of birds, shells of starling's eggs, caddis worms in mugs, and the like—seemed to be inhabited for the time by children.

Everywhere there was but little furniture, and that only the most necessary, and of the simplest forms. The extravagant love of ornament which I had noted in this people elsewhere seemed here to have given place to the feeling that the house itself and its associations was the ornament of the country life amidst which it had been left stranded from old times, and that to re-ornament it would but take away its use as a piece of natural beauty.

We sat down at last in a room over the wall which Ellen had caressed, and which was still hung with old tapestry, originally of no artistic value, but now faded into pleasant grey tones which harmonised thoroughly well with the quiet of the place,* and which would have been ill supplanted by brighter and more striking decoration.

I asked a few random questions of Ellen as we sat there, but scarcely listened to her answers, and presently became silent, and then scarce conscious of anything, but that I was there in that old room, the doves crooning from the roofs of the barn and dovecot beyond the window opposite to me.

My thought returned to me after what I think was but a minute or two, but which, as in a vivid dream, seemed as if it had lasted a long time, when I saw Ellen sitting, looking all the fuller of life and pleasure and desire from the contrast with the grey faded tapestry with its futile design, which was now only bearable because it had grown so faint and feeble.

She looked at me kindly, but as if she read me through and through. She said: 'You have begun again your never-ending contrast between the past and this present. Is it not so?'

'True,' said I. 'I was thinking of what you, with your capacity and intelligence, joined to your love of pleasure, and your impatience of unreasonable restraint—of what you would have been in that past. And even now, when all is won and has been for a long time, my heart is sickened with thinking of all the waste of life that has gone on for so many years!'

'So many centuries,' she said, 'so many ages!'

'True,' I said; 'too true,' and sat silent again.

She rose up and said: 'Come, I must not let you go off into a dream again so soon. If we must lose you, I want you to see all that you can see first before you go back again.'

'Lose me?' I said—'go back again? Am I not to go up to the North with you? What do you mean?'

She smiled somewhat sadly, and said: 'Not yet; we will not talk of that yet. Only, what were you thinking of just now?'

I said falteringly: 'I was saying to myself, The past, the present? Should she not have said the contrast of the present with the future: of blind despair with hope?'

'I knew it,' she said. Then she caught my hand and said excitedly, 'Come, while there is yet time! Come!' And she led me out of the room; and as we were going downstairs and out of the house into the garden by a little side door which opened out of a curious lobby,* she said in a calm voice, as if she wished me to forget her sudden nervousness: 'Come! we ought to join the others before they come here looking for us. And let me tell you, my friend, that I can see you are too apt to fall into mere dreamy musing: no doubt because you are not yet used to our life of repose amidst of energy; of work which is pleasure and pleasure which is work.'

She paused a little, and as we came out into the lovely garden again, she said: 'My friend, you were saying that you wondered what I should have been if I had lived in those past days of turmoil and oppression. Well, I think I have studied the history of them to know pretty well. I should have been one of the poor, for my father when he was working was a mere tiller of the soil. Well, I could not have borne that; therefore my beauty and cleverness and brightness' (she spoke with no blush or simper of false shame) 'would have been sold to rich men, and my life would have been wasted indeed; for I know enough of that to know that I should have had no choice, no power of will over my life; and that I should never have bought pleasure from the rich men, or even opportunity of action, whereby I might have won some true excitement. I should have wrecked and wasted in one way or another, either by penury or by luxury. Is it not so?'

'Indeed it is,' said I.

She was going to say something else, when a little gate in the fence, which led into a small elm-shaded field, was opened, and Dick came with hasty cheerfulness up the garden path, and was presently standing between us, a hand laid on the shoulder of each. He said: 'Well, neighbours, I thought you two would like to see the old house quietly without a crowd in it. Isn't it a jewel of a house after its kind? Well, come along, for it is getting towards dinner-time. Perhaps you, guest, would like a swim before we sit down to what I fancy will be a pretty long feast?'

'Yes,' I said, 'I should like that.'

'Well, good-bye for the present, neighbour Ellen,' said Dick. 'Here comes Clara to take care of you, as I fancy she is more at home amongst our friends here.'

Clara came out of the fields as he spoke; and with one look at Ellen

I turned and went with Dick, doubting, if I must say the truth, whether I should see her again.

CHAPTER XXXII

THE FEAST'S BEGINNING—THE END

Dick brought me at once into the little field which, as I had seen from the garden, was covered with gaily-coloured tents arranged in orderly lanes, about which were sitting and lying on the grass some fifty or sixty men, women, and children, all of them in the height of good temper and enjoyment—with their holiday mood on, so to say.

'You are thinking that we don't make a great show as to numbers,' said Dick; 'but you must remember that we shall have more to-morrow; because in this haymaking work there is room for a great many people who are not over-skilled in country matters: and there are many who lead sedentary lives, whom it would be unkind to deprive of their pleasure in the hayfield—scientific men and close students generally: so that the skilled workmen, outside those who are wanted as mowers, and foremen of the haymaking, stand aside, and take a little downright rest, which you know is good for them, whether they like it or not: or else they go to other countrysides, as I am doing here. You see, the scientific men and historians, and students generally, will not be wanted till we are fairly in the midst of the tedding,* which of course will not be till the day after to-morrow.' With that he brought me out of the little field on to a kind of causeway above the riverside meadow, and thence turning to the left on to a path through the mowing grass, which was thick and very tall, led on till we came to the river above the weir and its mill. There we had a delightful swim in the broad piece of water above the lock, where the river looked much bigger than its natural size from its being dammed up by the weir.*

'Now we are in a fit mood for dinner,' said Dick, when we had dressed and were going through the grass again; 'and certainly of all the cheerful meals in the year, this one of haysel* is the cheerfullest; not even excepting the corn-harvest feast; for then the year is beginning to fail, and one cannot help having a feeling behind all the gaiety, of the coming of the dark days, and the shorn fields and empty gardens; and the spring is almost too far off to look forward to. It is, then, in the autumn, when one almost believes in death.'

'How strangely you talk,' said I, 'of such a constantly recurring and consequently commonplace matter as the sequence of the seasons.' And indeed these people were like children about such things, and had what seemed to me a quite exaggerated interest in the weather, a fine day, a dark night, or a brilliant one, and the like.

'Strangely?' said he. 'Is it strange to sympathise with the year and its gains and losses?'

'At any rate,' said I, 'if you look upon the course of the year as a beautiful and interesting drama, which is what I think you do, you should be as much pleased and interested with the winter and its trouble and pain as with this wonderful summer luxury.'

'And am I not?' said Dick, rather warmly; 'only I can't look upon it as if I were sitting in a theatre seeing the play going on before me, myself taking no part of it. It is difficult,' said he, smiling good-humouredly, 'for a non-literary man like me to explain myself properly, like that dear girl Ellen would; but I mean that I am part of it all, and feel the pain as well as the pleasure in my own person. It is not done for me by somebody else, merely that I may eat and drink and sleep; but I myself do my share of it.'

In his way also, as Ellen in hers, I could see that Dick had that passionate love of the earth which was common to but few people at least, in the days I knew; in which the prevailing feeling amongst intellectual persons was a kind of sour distaste for the changing drama of the year, for the life of earth and its dealings with men. Indeed, in those days it was thought poetic and imaginative to look upon life as a thing to be borne, rather than enjoyed.

So I mused till Dick's laugh brought me back into the Oxfordshire hayfields. 'One thing seems strange to me,' said he—'that I must needs trouble myself about the winter and its scantiness, in the midst of the summer abundance. If it hadn't happened to me before, I should have thought it was your doing, guest; that you had thrown a kind of evil charm over me. Now, you know,' said he, suddenly, 'that's only a joke, so you mustn't take it to heart.'

'All right,' said I; 'I don't.' Yet I did feel somewhat uneasy at his words, after all.

We crossed the causeway this time, and did not turn back to the house, but went along a path beside a field of wheat now almost ready to blossom. I said: 'We do not dine in the house or garden, then?—as indeed I did not expect to do. Where do we meet, then? for I can see that the houses are mostly very small.'

'Yes,' said Dick, 'you are right, they are small in this country-side: there are so many good old houses left, that people dwell a good deal in such small detached houses. As to our dinner, we are going to have our feast in the church.* I wish, for your sake, it were as big and handsome as that of the old Roman town to the west, or the forest town to the north;[1] but, however, it will hold us all; and though it is a little thing, it is beautiful in its way.'

This was somewhat new to me, this dinner in a church, and I thought of the church-ales of the Middle Ages;* but I said nothing, and presently we came out into the road which ran through the village. Dick looked up and down it, and seeing only two straggling groups before us, said: 'It seems as if we must be somewhat late; they are all gone on; and they will be sure to make a point of waiting for you, as the guest of guests, since you come from so far.'

He hastened as he spoke, and I kept up with him, and presently we came to a little avenue of lime-trees which led us straight to the church porch, from whose open door came the sound of cheerful voices and laughter, and varied merriment.

'Yes,' said Dick, 'it's the coolest place for one thing, this hot evening. Come along; they will be glad to see you.'

Indeed, in spite of my bath, I felt the weather more sultry and oppressive than on any day of our journey yet.

We went into the church, which was a simple little building with one little aisle divided from the nave by three round arches, a chancel, and a rather roomy transept for so small a building, the windows mostly of the graceful Oxfordshire fourteenth century type. There was no modern architectural decoration in it; it looked, indeed, as if none had been attempted since the Puritans whitewashed the mediæval saints and histories on the wall.* It was, however, gaily dressed up for this latter-day festival, with festoons of flowers from arch to arch, and great pitchers of flowers standing about on the floor; while under the west window hung two cross scythes, their blades polished white, and gleaming from out of the flowers that

[1] Cirencester and Burford he must have meant.

wreathed them. But its best ornament was the crowd of handsome, happy-looking men and women that were set down to table, and who, with their bright faces and rich hair over their gay holiday raiment, looked, as the Persian poet puts it, like a bed of tulips in the sun.* Though the church was a small one, there was plenty of room; for a small church makes a biggish house; and on this evening there was no need to set cross tables along the transepts; though doubtless these would be wanted next day, when the learned men of whom Dick has been speaking should be come to take their more humble part in the haymaking.

I stood on the threshold with the expectant smile on my face of a man who is going to take part in a festivity which he is really prepared to enjoy. Dick, standing by me, was looking round the company with an air of proprietorship in them, I thought. Opposite me sat Clara and Ellen, with Dick's place open between them: they were smiling, but their beautiful faces were each turned towards the neighbours on either side, who were talking to them, and they did not seem to see me. I turned to Dick, expecting him to lead me forward, and he turned his face to me; but strange to say, though it was as smiling and cheerful as ever, it made no response to my glance—nay, he seemed to take no heed at all of my presence, and I noticed that none of the company looked at me. A pang shot through me, as of some disaster long expected and suddenly realised. Dick moved on a little without a word to me. I was not three yards from the two women who, though they had been my companions for such a short time, had really, as I thought, become my friends. Clara's face was turned full upon me now, but she also did not seem to see me, though I know I was trying to catch her eye with an appealing look. I turned to Ellen, and she *did* seem to recognise me for an instant; but her bright face turned sad directly, and she shook her head with a mournful look, and the next moment all consciousness of my presence had faded from her face.

I felt lonely and sick at heart past the power of words to describe. I hung about a minute longer, and then turned and went out of the porch again and through the lime-avenue into the road, while the blackbirds sang their strongest from the bushes about me in the hot June evening.

Once more without any conscious effort of will I set my face toward the old house by the ford, but as I turned round the corner which led to the remains of the village cross,* I came upon a figure strangely contrasting with the joyous, beautiful people I had left behind in the church. It was a man who looked old, but whom I knew from habit, now half-forgotten, was really not much more than fifty. His face was rugged, and grimed rather than dirty; his eyes dull and bleared; his body bent, his calves thin and spindly, his feet dragging and limping. His clothing was a mixture of dirt and rags long over-familiar to me. As I passed him he touched his hat with some real good-will and courtesy, and much servility.

Inexpressibly shocked, I hurried past him and hastened along the road that led to the river and the lower end of the village; but suddenly I saw as it were a black cloud rolling along to meet me, like a nightmare of my childish days; and for a while I was conscious of nothing else than being in the dark, and whether I was walking, or sitting, or lying down, I could not tell.

* * * * * *

I lay in my bed in my house at dingy Hammersmith thinking about it all; and trying to consider if I was overwhelmed with despair at finding I had been dreaming a dream; and strange to say, I found that I was not so despairing.

Or indeed *was* it a dream? If so, why was I so conscious all along that I was really seeing all that new life from the outside, still wrapped up in the prejudices, the anxieties, the distrust of this time of doubt and struggle?

All along, though those friends were so real to me, I had been feeling as if I had no business amongst them: as though the time would come when they would reject me, and say, as Ellen's last mournful look seemed to say, 'No, it will not do; you cannot be of us; you belong so entirely to the unhappiness of the past that our happiness even would weary you. Go back again, now you have seen us, and your outward eyes have learned that in spite of all the infallible maxims of your day there is yet a time of rest in store for the world, when mastery has changed into fellowship—but not before. Go back again, then, and while you live you will see all round you people engaged in making others live lives which are not their own, while they themselves care nothing for their own real lives—men who hate life though they fear death. Go back and be the happier for having seen us, for having added a little hope to your struggle. Go on living while you may, striving, with whatsoever pain and labour needs must be, to build up little by little the new day of fellowship, and rest, and happiness.'

Yes, surely! and if others can see it as I have seen it, then it may be called a vision rather than a dream.*

EXPLANATORY NOTES

3 *the League, says a friend*: the Socialist League was founded in December 1884, by Edward Aveling, Eleanor Marx Aveling, E. Belfort Bax, William Morris, and others, as a breakaway group from the Social Democratic Federation led by H. M. Hyndman. This somewhat clumsy method of narrating the story in the third person ('says a friend') is quickly dropped.

divergent Anarchist opinions: Morris's tone here is clearly humorous; however, the increasing influence of anarchists was the main cause of his resignation from the Socialist League in November 1890.

the underground railway: the Metropolitan line (the world's first underground passenger railway) opened in 1863, and was extended to Hammersmith the following year. The earliest underground lines (the Metropolitan, District, and Circle) used steam trains and were built using the technique of cutting and covering a trench (often following the line of roads). Electrification and the use of a tunnelling shield (enabling deeper tunnels) were first used on the City and South London Line (later part of the Northern Line) which opened in 1890.

lost his temper . . . well used to: one of many remarks (some less obvious than others) identifying Morris with the narrator. Morris's temper—brief rages which ended as abruptly as they started—was well known.

ugly suspension bridge: the ornate and colourful (green and gold) suspension bridge with iron piers was designed by Sir Joseph Bazelgette (1819–91). The 400-foot bridge, linking Hammersmith and Barnes, was opened in 1887. It reused the piers and abutments of another suspension bridge (the first in London) built some sixty years earlier on the same site.

4 *Chiswick Eyot*: an 'eyot', or 'ait', is a small island. In this case, a well-known landmark in the Thames just off Chiswick, a suburb two miles west of Hammersmith.

let himself in: the house is Morris's own London home: Kelmscott House, 26 Upper Mall. The five bay, three-storey house, originally called 'The Retreat', was built in 1780, with a bowed back addition in 1801. It is separated from the river by a narrow roadway. Previous occupants included Sir Francis Reynolds, the inventor of the electric telegraph, and the author George MacDonald. Morris rented the house from 1878, and died there on 3 October 1896. Kelmscott House was in Hammersmith, the 'western suburb' referred to earlier, on the north side of the Thames. In the nineteenth century, Hammersmith had grown from a rural appendage of Fulham (with a population of 6,000 in 1801) to a bustling London borough (with a population of 112,000 in 1901).

5 *saw that it was so*: Guest has woken up at a new house on the site of Kelmscott House.

Biffin's: W. H. Biffen & Sons were a well-known Hammersmith boat-building and boat-letting company. They had two boathouses (the Anchor and Metropolitan) both on the Lower Mall road.

6 *stemming the tide*: making headway against the tide.

Putney: Putney was then a suburb in south-west London, a little over a mile east of Hammersmith, on the south bank of the Thames (now in the London Borough of Wandsworth). It had expanded from a village into a suburb in the nineteenth century, and few signs of pre-Victorian Putney survived.

Barn Elms: Barn Elms was the manor house of Barnes, on the south bank of the Thames west of Putney, belonging to Sir Francis Walsingham until his death in 1590. The park-like grounds of the house ran from Barnes Common down to the river. It was demolished in 1954 following a fire (only an ornamental pond and the ice house remain).

7 *damascened*: damascened means either inlaid with an ornamental design or given a wavy pattern by repeated heating and hammering. In the context of a clasp on a belt the latter meaning is perhaps more likely.

Surrey bank: that is, the south bank of the Thames.

the Tay: the Tay is the longest river in Scotland, flowing some 118 miles from Ben Lui (on the Argyll and Bute border) to the North Sea below Dundee. Famous for its salmon.

Thorneycroft's: J. Thorneycroft & Sons, founded in 1866, were a marine and mechanical engineering company based in Chiswick. The firm grew into a large shipbuilding concern, with their headquarters in Southampton from 1904.

the Ponte Vecchio: the Ponte Vecchio is the 'Old Bridge' across the river Arno in Florence, based on a design by Neri di Fioravente and built in 1345. The bridge is lined with shops and above them a covered arcade (added in 1565) runs the length of the bridge. Morris had travelled to Florence in 1873—he found the city rather melancholy—and visited the jewellery shops on the bridge.

8 *in 2003*: in the *Commonweal* version of the text, the bridge was said to have been built, or at least opened, in 1971. This and other alterations of dates are usually thought to reflect Morris's waning optimism about the imminence of revolution.

9 *after-piece*: a tip, gratuity.

casts: lifts.

10 *Victoria*: Queen Victoria (1819–1901), the last of the Hanoverian sovereigns, had the longest reign (1837–1901) of any British sovereign. Morris was opposed to monarchy, and especially scathing about the 'Empress Brown' (a jibe at Victoria's imperial enthusiasms and her friendship with

the Scottish manservant John Brown). The Socialist League organized a campaign against the 'Jingo Jubilee' in 1887.

piece . . . so delicately worked: a 'piece' is a coin of a particular value. This design appears on a number of nobles and half-nobles introduced in 1344 and minted until the death of Edward III in 1377.

Colney Hatch: Colney Hatch was a district in North London, on the borders of Southgate and Friern Barnet, associated with a mental asylum. Colney Hatch Asylum was built between 1849 and 1851 to house 1,000 inmates (it contained what was reputed to be the longest corridor in Europe). By 1896, the asylum held some 2,500 individuals, kept, according to a contemporary guide, 'without shackle or even a strait-waistcoat'. It was renamed the Friern Hospital in 1937, and closed down completely in 1993.

12 *familiar with them*: the subjects of the relief are not obvious, but the suggestion may be that they portray socialist contemporaries of Morris, and perhaps even Morris himself. A contemporary 'gallery of portraits of foreign socialists' in the French paper *Le Socialiste* contained pictures of Marx, Engels, Lavrov, Perovskaya, Morris, Bax, Aveling, Basly, Bebel, and Liebknecht.

Crosby Hall: Crosby Hall was a fifteenth-century merchant's house in Bishopsgate (in the City of London), the residence of Sir John Crosby (died 1476). Built in 1466–75, it was subsequently owned by Sir Thomas More, and was later the residence of Sir Walter Raleigh. In 1890, the house was being used as a restaurant. It was demolished in 1908, although part of the building was subsequently rebuilt in Chelsea.

13 *eaten in Turin*: these thin pipe-stems of wheaten crust are the famous Grissini breadsticks (allegedly invented by a Turin baker to tempt a sick prince).

14 *High Table . . . college hall*: that is, the long table, often on a slightly raised dais, at one end of the dining hall of an Oxford college, at which dons, rather than students, traditionally eat.

Hammersmith Socialists: in the *Commonweal* version this reads, 'Hammersmith Branch of the Socialist League'. Morris had left the League in November 1890, and formed the Hammersmith Socialist Society. The building in question was the two-storey coach house which abutted the left side of Kelmscott House (looking from the river). Morris had it converted first into a tapestry room, and later into a meeting place for the Hammersmith Branch of the Socialist League (and subsequently the Hammersmith Socialist Society). Almost every leading socialist in London spoke here at some point during the 1880s and 1890s.

William: the name is one of many similarities between Morris and the narrator.

Epping Forest . . . Woodford: these are all haunts of Morris's childhood. Epping Forest is a large and ancient deciduous woodland that runs north-east out of London. In medieval times the forest covered the south-west corner of Essex and stretched as far south as Leytonstone and Wanstead. In 1895 Morris, writing to protest against the excessive clearing of trees, recalled his youthful memories: 'The special character of it was derived from the fact that by far the greater part was a wood of hornbeams, a tree not common save in Essex and Herts. It was certainly the biggest hornbeam wood in these islands, and I suppose in the world. The said hornbeams were all pollards, being shrouded every four or six years, and were interspersed in many places with holly thickets; and the result was a very curious and characteristic wood, such as can be seen nowhere else' (Letter to the Editor of the *Daily Chronicle*, 22 April 1895). Walthamstow is situated between Leyton and Chingford, some six miles north-east of the City. This part of the Essex countryside was already beginning to succumb to the expansion of London (it is now in the London Borough of Waltham Forest). Morris described Walthamstow as 'a suburban village on the edge of Epping Forest, and once a pleasant place enough, but now terribly cocknified and choked up by the jerry-builder' (from the sketch of his life appended to a letter to Andreas Scheu, 15 September 1883, in *The Collected Letters of William Morris*, ed. Norman Kelvin, 4 vols. (1984–96), ii/1. 227; cited subsequently as *Collected Letters*, ed. Kelvin). Woodford, Essex, was a village right next to Epping Forest (it is now in the London Borough of Redbridge). The Morris family had moved to Woodford Hall (a brick mansion with a fifty-acre park, and a hundred-acre farm, bordering Epping Forest) in 1840.

15 *balm*: it is not certain which of the many fragrant garden herbs known as balm Morris is referring to. Perhaps the most likely is *Melissa officinalis* (often called lemon balm), a herbaceous plant common in Victorian gardens and prized for both its culinary and medicinal properties.

Queen Elizabeth's Lodge: Queen Elizabeth's Lodge in Chingford was built in 1543 as a timber-framed, three-storey 'standing' (a viewing platform) for Henry VIII to watch hunts in the Royal Forest. It was restored and extended for Elizabeth I. In 1878, the Lodge was acquired by the Corporation of London, by which time the frame had been filled in and the Lodge made into a half-timbered house. Morris had visited Queen Elizabeth's Lodge as a child.

High Beech: High Beech was a well-known beauty spot in Epping Forest (two miles north-east of Chingford). A guide to the environs of London, published in 1876, describes High Beech as 'a great resort for holiday-makers and excursionists', its main attraction being a view of a broad sweep of the Forest.

the Corporation of London: the Corporation of London was the municipal corporation governing the City of London. It was granted control of 6,000 acres of forest in 1878, and established a committee for 'Epping Forest and Open Spaces'.

pursuit of utilitarian knowledge: it is not certain that Morris had a particular cobbler in mind. However, literary artisans of a similar character are not unusual in nineteenth-century fiction. See, for example, George Eliot's *Felix Holt, the Radical*.

16 *fifty-six*: that is, the same age as Morris in 1890.

17 *as Scott says*: Walter Scott (1771–1832), Scottish poet, playwright, editor, critic, and a prolific writer of historical novels. Morris was a great admirer of Scott's novels which 'I read and re-read for ever' (letter to Thomas Horsfall, 7 April 1881, in *Collected Letters*, ed. Kelvin, ii/1. 41). This allusion is possibly to a passage in *Redgauntlet*, a novel first published in 1824, in which Alan Fairford describes his first meeting with the beautiful young Greenmantle: 'The door was opened—out she went—walked along the pavement, turned down the close, and put the sun I believe into her pocket when she disappeared, so suddenly did dullness and darkness sink down on the square, when she was no longer visible.'

grinder: can mean both an under-labourer, that is a lesser craftsman, and a bookish person, that is one preoccupied with narrow academic learning. Both senses are relevant here.

18 *Ne quid nimis!*: 'Nothing to Excess'. From Terence's version of a Socratic injunction: 'id arbitror, adprime in vita esse utile, ne quid nimis' (this I consider in life to be especially advantageous, that one do nothing to excess)'.

James Allen's: the reference here is not certain, although the 1881 census reveals one James Allen, with the occupation of coachman, living on the Goldhawk Road.

19 *wherry*: a wherry is a large four-wheeled dray or cart with no sides.

Boffin . . . Dickens: Nicodemus (Noddy) Boffin, 'the Golden Dustman' is a character in *Our Mutual Friend* (first published in book form in 1865) by Charles Dickens. Morris was a keen reader of Dickens, noting that 'to my mind of the novelists of our generation Dickens is immeasurably ahead' (from list of favourite books enclosed with letter to *Pall Mall Gazette*, 2 February 1886).

20 *Wessex wagon*: a Wessex wagon is a regional variety of simple, low, panel-sided, English farm wagon.

King Street: King Street in Hammersmith is roughly parallel to Upper Mall and forms part of the great western road running towards the City.

the Creek: a guide to the environs of London, published in 1876, describes the Creek as 'a dirty little inlet of the Thames'. It divided the Upper and Lower Mall, and was crossed at that time by a wooden bridge ('the high bridge') built for Bishop Sherlock in 1751.

21 *the Broadway*: Hammersmith Broadway was, in Morris's day, already one of the busiest traffic junctions in London. King Street runs into it.

Gothic . . . Saracenic . . . Byzantine: Gothic, Saracenic, and Byzantine are three distinct architectural styles. Gothic was first developed in France, and was the dominant architectural style between the twelfth and sixteenth centuries in Europe. It is characterized by the use of pointed arches, variations of rib vaulting, and flying buttresses. These forms allowed more frequent breaks in walls, and, as a result, more stained-glass windows and lighter church interiors. Saracenic (or Islamic) architecture is characterized by use of horseshoe arches, tunnel vaults of stone and brick, and rich surface decoration using carved stone, mosaic, and painting. It is often associated with the characteristic features of mosque architecture (minarets, prayer domes, and courtyards, for example). Byzantine architecture developed in the eastern division of the Roman Empire, and is characterized by its use of the round arch, cross, circle, and dome. It is also associated with sumptuous interiors which make use of rich mosaic ornament, marble, and wall painting.

21 *Baptistry at Florence*: the Baptistry is one of the oldest buildings in Florence. It is an octagonal building, situated opposite the Cathedral, and famous for its bas-relief doors—by Andrea Pisano (*c.*1290–1348/9) and Lorenzo Ghiberti (c.1378–1455). Morris admired the narrative effect of Ghiberti's work, but considered that his doors lacked 'decorative feeling' (letter to George Bernard Shaw, 11 October 1894, in *Collected Letters*, ed. Kelvin, iv. 215).

Mote-House: 'mote' or 'moot' is an archaic term for an assembly. Hence, in the present context, meeting hall.

22 *cross between us and them*: the offspring of interbreeding between these two groups.

23 *Kensington Market*: Kensington (now in the London Borough of Kensington and Chelsea) had once been a rural parish, noted for its market gardens and nurseries. By the end of the nineteenth century, however, it had long been a densely populated metropolitan borough.

it goes . . . Lea marshes: this new Middlesex forest covers a large area of North London, spreading north and west from Kensington. It connects up two ancient forests (the long-gone medieval forest of Primrose Hill and the beleaguered Epping Forest) at the same time as wiping out recent industrial development (Clapton, for example, the site of a railway boom and much poor housing).

Kensington Gardens . . . I don't know: Kensington Gardens (now in the London Borough of Kensington and Chelsea) were originally the grounds of a small country house known as Nottingham House (after the 2nd Earl of Nottingham). The house was rebuilt as a royal palace (Kensington Palace) by William and Mary, and enlarged by George I.

24 *like Windsor . . . of Dean*: Windsor Forest is the small forest to the south of Windsor, a town in Berkshire, situated on the Thames opposite Eton College (see note to p. 138). The Forest of Dean is a heavily wooded area (once a royal hunting ground) in Gloucestershire. It is bordered by the River Severn and the River Wye.

25 *a system of education*: Morris once expressed his hope that education in a

socialist society would be 'both more liberal, and wiser for all, than it is to-day for a few; and that it will be its function to develop any gifts which children or older people may have towards science, literature, the handicrafts, or the higher arts, or anything which may be useful or desirable to the community' ('The Dull Level of Life', *Justice*, 26 April 1884).

26 *books . . . you know*: Morris produced a number of handwritten and decorated books for his friends. (See the Chronology for examples.)

wandering from my lambs: wool-gathering, distracted from the subject.

27 *Westminster Abbey!*: the historic abbey church at Westminster, in London. The present building was begun in 1245, but had many subsequent (and in Morris's view, deleterious) alterations, including the western towers, designed by Christopher Wren and modified by Nicholas Hawksmoor. 'I do not think that it is an exaggeration', wrote Morris, 'to say that at the beginning of the sixteenth century it was the most beautiful of Gothic buildings. Everything which has been either taken away from or added to since then has done more or less to destroy this beauty, until to-day the exterior no longer exists as a work of art' (Letter to the Editor of the *Daily News*, 30 January 1889).

beastly monuments . . . knaves: Morris had strong views on the subject of the monuments in Westminster Abbey. He insisted that the only way to appreciate the 'matchless interior' of the Abbey was to try to ignore the incongruous monuments, which he judged, for the most part, to be 'the most hideous specimens of false art that can be found in the whole world; mere Cockney nightmares and aberrations of the human spirit' (Letter to the Editor of the *Daily News*, 30 January 1889).

28 *Houses of Parliament . . . use them?*: anti-parliamentarism was a distinctive feature of Morris's socialism in the 1880s. He often discussed parliamentary affairs in his journalism but, in his own words, 'never with respect, and most commonly only to point out the moral of the corruption of these latter days of capitalism' ('Anti-Parliamentary', *Commonweal*, 7 June 1890).

queer antiquarian society . . . set up its pipe: the queer antiquarian society is the Society for the Protection of Ancient Buildings (the 'Anti-Scrape'), founded by Morris and others in 1877. To 'set up one's pipe' is to speak up, to clamour.

St Paul's: St Paul's is a baroque cathedral built on Ludgate Hill in London, between 1675 and 1710, to a design by Sir Christopher Wren. Morris (who was not a fan of Wren's churches) maintained that, 'grand as St. Paul's undoubtedly is, it is only one of a class of buildings common enough on the continent—imitations of St. Peter's, Rome. In fact, St. Paul's can scarcely be looked upon as an English design, but, rather, as an English rendering of the great Italian original' (letter to the Editor of *The Times*, 15 April 1878).

29 *Piccadilly*: Piccadilly is a street (now in the London Borough of

Westminster) which runs from Hyde Park Corner to Piccadilly Circus (where it meets Regent Street). It is one of two ancient roads leading westward out of London (the other being Oxford Street).

29 *duds*: coarse articles of clothing.

31 *Latakia*: an aromatic variety of Turkish tobacco produced near Latakia (the ancient Laodicea), a sea port on the coast of Syria. Its use here represents another connection between Morris and the narrator. Morris claimed to get tongue-tied without his pipe, and Latakia 'pure and simple' was his preferred 'baccy'.

33 *Rhine . . . Steinberg*: Steinberg is a famous estate at Hattenheim, in the Rhinegau district of Germany (near Mainz). At the end of the nineteenth century Rhinegau Rieslings were amongst the most expensive and respected wines in the world.

34 *Blue-devils . . . Mulleygrubs*: varieties of depression, associated with hypochondriac melancholy and a fit of the spleen respectively.

36 *ugly church . . . cupolaed building at my back*: the 'ugly church' is St Martin's-in-the-Fields. This church with its distinctive combination of steeple and portico (subsequently much copied, especially in America) was designed by James Gibbs (1682–1754), and built between 1722 and 1726 on an ancient site. The 'nondescript ugly cupolaed building' is the National Gallery, founded in 1824, and holding one of the major national collections of pictures. It was built between 1833 and 1837 to a design by William Wilkins (1778–1839), and has been extended several times since.

chilly November afternoon: the recollection is of 'Bloody Sunday', 13 November 1887, when police forcibly prevented a demonstration in Trafalgar Square. Two thousand police, reinforced by four squadrons of cavalry, and 400 foot soldiers (each with twenty rounds of ammunition) were deployed to stop the demonstration. The demonstrators (socialists, radicals, Irish nationalist groups, and others) were attacked by the police and dispersed. No weapons were fired but over two hundred demonstrators were treated in hospital, many more were injured, and three people sustained subsequently fatal injuries. Morris had joined with the Clerkenwell branch of the Socialist League who were attacked and routed by police as they entered St Martin's Lane, some quarter of a mile from the Square. 'I confess', wrote Morris, 'I was astounded at the rapidity of the thing and the ease with which military organisation got its victory' ('London in a State of Siege', *Commonweal*, 19 November 1887).

Trafalgar Square!: Trafalgar Square (now in the London Borough of Westminster) was built between 1829 and 1841. A well-known meeting place, the name commemorates the Battle of Trafalgar (1805) in which Lord Nelson won a famous victory but lost his life. The central monument is a statue of Nelson on a tall column (see note to p. 99).

James' Social Democratic History: Morris may have intended to allude to a contemporary book, but, if so, the reference is not clear.

ward-mote: meeting of the citizens of a ward or district.

38 *prisons were like*: the rationale for, and the conditions of, contemporary prisons formed a frequent subject of Morris's journalism. 'The prison system of this country', he wrote, 'is, and is meant to be, a system of torture applied by Society to those whom it considers its enemies; but this fact is kept in the dark as much as possible, lest ordinary good-natured people, who do not want to torture persons unless fear drives them to it, should be shocked, and the system should be swept away—or at least altered' ('Notes', *Commonweal*, 17 May 1890).

before the middle . . . twentieth century: in the *Commonweal* version it was built 'quite in the beginning of the twentieth century'.

40 *and pondered*: the road-mending episode that follows did not appear in the serialized *Commonweal* version.

at Oxford . . . have looked: there are perhaps echoes here of the road-building project undertaken in 1874 by Oxford undergraduates (including Arnold Toynbee and Oscar Wilde) under the sponsorship of John Ruskin (1819–1900). Ruskin's Hinksey diggings were parodied in *Punch*, and criticized in *The Times*. (There is also a passing reference to communal road-repairing in book II of More's *Utopia*.)

41 *Spell ho*: a 'spell' is a pause in work, so 'spell ho' is a call for workers to cease labouring for a period.

42 *Long Acre*: Long Acre is a street slightly north of, and parallel to, The Strand (now in the London Borough of Westminster). It was once a cultivated plot of land belonging to the monks of Westminster Abbey.

three-score . . . proverb-book: see Psalms 90: 10.

Endell Street: Endell Street runs north from Long Acre to Princes Circus, just south of the British Museum. From here, Oxford Street runs westwards, and Holborn lies to the east.

Bishop of Ely . . . Richard III: the Bishop of Ely's house is mentioned in *Richard III*, III. iv. 31–3 (Richard: 'My Lord of Ely, when I was last in Holborn | I saw good strawberries in your garden there'). In 1578, Sir Christopher Hatton was given permission to build a house and gardens in the grounds of the palace. He gave his name to the broad street—Hatton Garden—which developed on the same site. A commercial centre in the nineteenth century, Hatton Garden is now associated with the diamond trade.

43 *British Museum*: the British Museum is a national museum of antiquities, established by public subscription in 1753. The collection is housed in a monumental neoclassical building designed by Sir Robert Smirke (1780–1867) and built between 1823 and 1846. The famous Reading Room, designed by his brother Sidney Smirke (1798–1877) was added later. It is situated in Bloomsbury, an area in central London (largely in the London Borough of Camden), in which a series of once residential squares and terraces mix with the more public architecture of the University of

London. The area has long had literary, artistic, and educational associations.

45 *Norfolk jacket*: a loose jacket with waistband.

46 *said I to myself*: this is the first suggestion that Hammond may be related to Guest. A later remark suggests that Hammond may be Guest's grandson.

49 *the tale and the lay*: Hammond is quoting from the words of Alcinous at the end of book VIII of Homer's *Odyssey*. Morris had published his own translation of Homer in 1887, and his own rendition of this passage reads: 'But this thing the Gods have fashioned, and have spun the Deathful Day | For men, that for men hereafter it might be the tale and the lay.'

51 *bed of Procrustes*: an allusion to Procrustes, a robber in Greek mythology who would force strangers to lie down on one of his two beds, hammering or racking them out to fit the longer one, or lopping them off to fit the shorter one. He was finally dealt with, in the same manner as his own victims, by Theseus.

52 *some such title*: 'The Husband Who Was to Mind the House' appeared in *Popular Tales from the Norse* (Edinburgh, 1858) translated by George Webb Dasent (1817–96). The story is of a malcontented husband who swaps jobs with his wife for the day, with unfortunate and didactic consequences. (With the benefit of hindsight, not his least mistake was in tethering the cow on the roof by a rope attached, down the chimney, to his own leg.) Dasent was a Scandinavian scholar whose work Morris read with pleasure, and who is sometimes thought to have influenced the style of Morris's own translations.

dry gibe: a taunt, sharp teasing remark.

cook . . . said I: another connection between Guest and Morris, who prided himself on being a competent cook.

53 *upon the children*: see Exodus 20:5.

54 *Jutish*: that is, from the Jutes, a Germanic people, possibly from Jutland, that settled in southern Britain in the fifth century.

gathered left-handed: to gather in a questionable manner, that is, to misunderstand.

bouncing share: a large generous share.

56 *Phalangsteries*: Phalangsteries are Hammond's way of referring to the model community proposed by the French utopian socialist Charles Fourier (1772–1837) (see note to p. 79). In Fourier's own terminology, the Phalanstery was only the main building of the community. The community was properly called a Phalanx and consisted of between 1,600 and 1,800 members.

modern . . . ancient Babylon: a modern Babylon would be a modern version of the proverbially degenerate city of the Bible. However, Morris viewed surviving artefacts from ancient Babylon—a city in Mesopotamia noted for its luxury, fortifications, and 'hanging gardens'—as evidence that, despite oppression elsewhere, 'on many sides art was still free, and labour abundantly illuminated by fancy and invention' (lecture entitled 'Of the Origins of Ornamental Art' first delivered 19 May 1896 quoted from *The Unpublished Lectures of William Morris*, ed. Eugene D. LeMire (Detroit, 1969), 143).

57 *on May-day*: Morris supported May Day as a day of international solidarity and Socialist demonstrations. See, in this context, his late poems, 'May Day' and 'May Day 1894' originally written for *Justice*.

Hood's Song of the Shirt: 'The Song of the Shirt' was a popular poem by Thomas Hood (1799–1845). It was first published (anonymously) in *Punch* in 1843, following a court case which had drawn attention to the conditions of some London workers. It recounted the struggles of a seamstress to support her family ('It is not the linen you're wearing out | But human creatures' lives').

58 *Swindling Kens*: a ken was vagabonds' slang for a house where thieves or disreputable characters met or lodged.

Aldgate: Aldgate (in the City of London) was a street named after the eastern Roman gateway into the city (on the ancient road to Colchester).

river Lea . . . Isaak Walton: the Lea is the most navigable of the tributaries of the Thames. It rises in Bedfordshire, runs past Walthamstow, and joins the Thames downstream of Greenwich. Isaak Walton (1593–1683) was the author of *The Compleat Angler* (1653 and 1655), a work which mixes practical advice about fishing with folklore, quotations from famous authors, songs and ballads, and romantic pastoral sketches. It is organized as a dialogue during a five-day fishing expedition on the upper reaches of the River Lea.

Stratford . . . Old Ford: Stratford (now in the London Borough of Newham) was a centre of early industrialization in the late nineteenth century. It was the site of, amongst others, the main locomotive and rolling stock works of the Eastern Counties Railway. Old Ford (now in the London Borough of Tower Hamlets) is a district of East London. The Roman road out of Aldgate to Colchester crossed the Lea here. At the end of the nineteenth century it was an industrial suburb characterized by great poverty and poor housing.

59 *Shooters' Hill*: Shooters' Hill (now in the London Borough of Greenwich) was a leafy suburb in Morris's day. It had once been a densely wooded hill (reaching 132 metres), a haven for highwaymen, and housing a famous gallows. Despite its steepness, the ancient Watling Street runs directly across the hill.

Canning's Town . . . Silvertown: Canning Town (now in the London Borough of Newham) was in Morris's day a relatively new industrial and residential area—possibly named from Sir Samuel Canning (1823–1908) the industrialist. Silvertown (now in the London Borough of Newham, and best known to Londoners as the site of the Tate & Lyle sugar refinery) was an industrial and residential area next to the Thames. Probably named from S. W. Silver & Co., manufacturers of rubber goods. An area of great poverty and poor environmental conditions, it was the scene of a huge industrial accident ('the Silvertown explosion') in 1917.

59 *Hampstead*: Hampstead in north-west London (now in the Borough of Camden) was a leafy and exclusive residential suburb, with extensive open areas (including Hampstead Heath and Parliament Hill). A guide to the environs of London, published in 1876, noted its 'heath, pure air, and fine scenery'. Hampstead had expanded hugely in the nineteenth century (its population grew from 4,300 in 1801 to 80,000 in 1900) but remained a wealthy area.

prepense: premeditated.

60 *Oxford*: Morris was not always enthusiastic about contemporary Oxford. He maintained that the Colleges and University had allowed much of architectural and historical interest in the city to be ruined. He was also sceptical of the 'commercial' education that was provided, describing the University as 'a huge upper public school for fitting lads of the upper and middle class for their laborious future of living on other people's labour' (letter to the Editor of the *Daily News*, 20 November 1885).

Cambridge: Morris's view of Cambridge was not a generous one. 'As to Cambridge', he wrote in an early letter, 'it is rather a hole of a place, and can't compare for a moment with Oxford' (letter to Cormell Price, 6 July 1855, in *Collected Letters*, ed. Kelvin, i. 13).

62 *first half of the twentieth century*: the Kelmscott Press edition has 'first part of the age of freedom'.

63 *Hindhead in Surrey*: Hindhead was an isolated hill in Surrey which had already attracted the Victorians in their droves. A collection of shops was surrounded by a growing expanse of big comfortable houses, with huge gardens full of rhododendrons and conifers.

64 *your Middlesex and Essex forest*: that is, the new North London forest (running from Kensington north and east to the Lea marshes) and Epping Forest.

Cumberland and Westmoreland ones: Cumberland and Westmoreland were two rural counties in north-west England (now part of Cumbria). They contained the Lake District.

Ingleborough and Pen-y-gwent: Ingleborough and Pen-y-gwent (or Pen-y-Ghent) are two of the highest peaks in the Pennine hills in northern England (723 and 693 metres respectively). They are two of the famous 'Three Peaks' of the Yorkshire Dales.

65 *disquisition*: a long and complicated discourse.

70 *Thou shalt not steal*: see Exodus 20: 15.

72 *"Go and sin no more"*: see John 8: 11. Jesus had the penalty remitted by saying 'let him who is without sin cast the first stone'.

73 *Snakes in Iceland*: Niels Horrebow, *The Natural History of Iceland* (1758), chapter 72 'Concerning Snakes' famously consists of one sentence: 'No snakes of any kind are to be met with throughout the whole island.'

with foreign nations: this discussion of national and international relations, consisting of the first eight paragraphs of this chapter, was added to the original serialized version of the book.

79 *Fourier*: the French utopian socialist Charles Fourier (1772–1837) insisted that work was not inherently unattractive. Under the right conditions, labour could be transformed into a source of pleasure and self-realization, talents would multiply and productivity increase. His imaginative solution to the problem of dirty jobs utilized the enthusiasm of some children for getting dirty—a corps of suitable youngsters (the 'little hordes') would collect rubbish and clean slaughterhouses.

80 *grapes . . . thistles*: see Luke 6: 44.

81 *abortions of the market*: that is, ugly and makeshift products made for profit alone.

82 *Red-skins*: historical evidence that such a policy was carried out, or that (if it was executed) it was responsible for outbreaks of smallpox, is much contested. However, it is known that Baron Jeffrey Amherst (1717–97), commander of British military forces in North America, proposed that blankets and handkerchiefs from smallpox hospitals be distributed amongst native Americans.

Stanley: Henry Morton Stanley (1841–1904) was a famous explorer and journalist. He had led expeditions which helped establish the 'Congo Free State' under the suzerainty of Leopold II of Belgium, furthered British imperial aims in East Africa, and famously found the missionary Dr Livingstone near Lake Tanganyika in 1871. Morris endorsed the view that 'the Rifle-and-bible newspaper correspondent Stanley . . . has done no good; killed a great many people for nothing; rescued a man who was in no danger, and didn't want to be rescued; and the reason why we are so fond of him is that we hope and believe that he is helping us Britons (who are fond of keeping curates for the rough work) in the "scramble for Africa", which is disgracing the nations of Europe at present' ('Notes on News', *Commonweal*, 3 May 1890).

83 *a genuine artist . . . revolutionist*: a suggestion that Hammond is the grandson of Guest. In making his authoritative guide a descendant there is perhaps an echo of *Pearl* (Morris was certainly familiar with medieval dream-poetry).

86 *Seven Swans . . . as Jacob Grimm*: presumably 'Die sechs Schwäne' (The Six Swans), 'Der König vom goldenen Berg' (The King of the Golden Mountain), and 'Der Froschkönig oder der eiserne Heinrich' (The Frog-King, or Iron Henry). Jacob Grimm (1785–1863) and Wilhelm Grimm (1786–1859) had compiled a three-volume anthology of German fairy tales (1812–22). Morris described their *Teutonic Mythology* as 'crammed

with the material for imagination' (list of favourite books enclosed with letter to *Pall Mall Gazette*, 2 February 1886).

87 *the bight*: the bend of a stream.

club-haunter: a frequenter of gentlemen's clubs.

92 *great crash*: the *Commonweal* version of the text stops at this point. It omits the remainder of the present paragraph together with the next fifteen paragraphs (including the remarks about the year 1952). It resumes with 'On some comparatively trifling occasion' (which in the *Commonweal* version appears as 'On some trifling occasion').

93 *jobbery*: misuse of collective funds for private advantage.

95 *Gladstone, or Gledstein*: William Ewart Gladstone (1809–98), British liberal statesman and prime minister. Gladstone entered politics as a Tory, but became leader of the Liberal party in 1867. His ministries were notable for a number of social and political reforms, and for his campaign for home rule for Ireland (which led to the defection of Unionists from the Liberal party). After Morris's conversion to socialism, he became much more critical of Gladstone. The remark about Scandinavian descent is perhaps Morris's humorous revenge for the story that Gladstone had once mocked a leaflet of the Social Democratic Federation because it contained the name of a foreigner (Morris's friend Andreas Scheu).

96 *Manchester*: Manchester formed the centre of a huge industrial area, which epitomized many of the failings of nineteenth-century industrialism for Morris. He visited the city several times, noting 'I think Manchester gets nastier & shabbier every time I come here' (letter to Jenny Morris, 4 December 1888, in *Collected Letters*, ed. Kelvin, iii/2, 839).

dry-blow fighting: beating without drawing blood.

the Committee of Public Safety: the Committee of Public Safety was set up as an emergency body in April 1793 during the French Revolution as a response to growing threats of foreign invasion and domestic unrest. It became increasingly dominated by Robespierre (1758–94) and was responsible for initiating the Terror. It was dissolved by the Directory in 1795. (The name was periodically resurrected, for example, under the Paris Commune.)

98 *the youngest . . . of their generals*: possibly an allusion to Sir Charles Warren (1840–1927) who, after a distinguished military career, had been appointed commissioner of the London Metropolitan Police in 1886. Morris believed that Warren had been appointed with the clear remit of 'driving our [socialist] propaganda off the streets', a policy which he pursued enthusiastically ('The Abolition of Freedom of Speech', *Commonweal*, 21 August 1886). Warren was responsible for the much-criticized police operations on 'Bloody Sunday', and was removed the following year.

last sixty years: the original serialized version in *Commonweal* has 'last twenty years'.

99 *great southern road . . . side of the Thames*: the 'great southern road' is

Whitehall, which follows a medieval route between Westminster and Charing Cross. It is now dominated by government buildings. The 'embankment' is the Victoria Embankment which runs between Westminster Bridge and Blackfriar's Bridge. It was constructed between 1864 and 1870 by Sir Joseph Bazalgette, on land reclaimed from the river. (Now in the London Borough of Westminster.)

then stood there: Nelson's Column was erected between 1839 and 1842. An eighteen-foot statue of Admiral Lord Nelson (1758–1805) by Edward Hodges Baily (1788–1867) stands at the top of a 185-foot-high Corinthian column of Devon granite designed by William Railton (1801–77).

101 *so-called "liberal" paper*: possibly an allusion to the *Daily News*, the most influential Liberal newspaper in London at the time. Morris was not an admirer of the paper, writing of its response to 'Bloody Sunday' that 'the feeble twitterings of the *Daily News* will be received with jeers by the triumphant Tories' ('London in a State of Siege', *Commonweal*, 19 November 1887).

The other . . . paper: possibly an allusion to *The Times* which gave what Morris regarded as an accurate report of 'Bloody Sunday'. In the words of its reporter: 'The police, mounted and on foot, charged in among the people, striking indiscriminately in all directions and causing complete disorder in the ranks of the processionists. I witnessed several cases of injury to men who had been struck in the head and face by the police' (*The Times*, 14 November 1887).

105 *Daily Telegraph*: the *Daily Telegraph* was a London daily founded in 1855. It adopted a conservative political standpoint, and what Morris referred to as 'the ravings of the Telegraph' occasionally formed the subject of his journalism.

published in London: possibly an allusion to *Commonweal*, the weekly organ of the Socialist League; *Freedom*, the monthly journal of the anarchists; and *Justice*, the weekly paper of the Social Democratic Federation.

forty years before: this date is not changed between the *Commonweal* and revised book edition of the text.

boycotting: 'boycott' was a recent word in Morris's day, used to refer to a combination to withhold relations of any kind (commercial, social, etc.). Captain Boycott was an Irish landlord who notoriously incurred this treatment in 1880.

106 *anent*: in the face of.

long-bow stories: to 'draw the long bow' is to make drawn-out or exaggerated statements.

108 *dynamite*: dynamite had been invented in 1867 by Alfred Nobel (using nitroglycerine absorbed in Kieselguhr). It was a light and destructive explosive whose use was associated with anarchism (not least as a result of the Haymarket affair in Chicago). 'Dynamite scares' were frequent at the time, including a case recorded by Morris in which one Mlle Drouin

had been arrested for possessing what turned out to be modelling clay. Morris mockingly reassured the guardians of law and order that 'the only danger it is fraught with is that it may be worked up into futile and ugly images' ('Notes on the News', *Commonweal*, 27 August 1887).

110 *"Friends of Order"*: possibly an allusion to the 'party of order', the counter-revolutionary groups that Admiral Saisset (1810–79) tried to unite in opposition to the Paris Commune. The Paris Commune was the municipal government (15 March to 26 May 1871), containing socialists and revolutionaries, elected after the Franco-Prussian War and the collapse of the Second Empire. It was brutally suppressed by government troops from Versailles (over 20,000 were massacred). The Paris Commune formed the subject of Morris's poem *The Pilgrims of Hope*.

122 *somewhat over well*: the suggestion is presumably that these verses are Morris's own. The allusion here is perhaps to Chaucer's *Book of the Duchess* (lines 321 ff.) in which the narrator wakes to find his chamber decorated with pictures from the history of Troy and the text of *Romance of the Rose*.

124 *slip away from us*: in August 1880, Morris travelled by boat (the 'Ark') from Kelmscott House to Kelmscott Manor along the Thames. He travelled with Jane Morris, May Morris, Cormell Price, Richard Grosvenor, William De Morgan, and Elizabeth Macleod. A humorous log (held in the British Library) of the voyage of the 'Ark' was kept by Grosvenor, with additional notes by Morris, Jane, and Price. A year later, Morris made the same journey in the 'Ark'; this time the party included William De Morgan, Charles Faulkner, Elizabeth Macleod, and Lisa Stillman.

cockney villas: Morris typically uses the word 'cockney' in a distinctive way to indicate the vulgar and materialistic. He also described these villas as built by 'Podsnap' (letter to Emery Walker, 20 December 1891, in *Collected Letters*, ed. Kelvin, iii. 368), the complacent man of business in *Our Mutual Friend* (described by Dickens as 'a member of "society" and a pompous self-satisfied man').

little village . . . ferry: the pretty little village is possibly Thames Ditton, then a small village with a railway station. The ferry is possibly the Queen's Ferry. (Some thirteen miles from Hammersmith.)

125 *great . . . Dutch William*: Hampton Court is a royal palace on the north bank of the Thames (now in the London Borough of Richmond). The red-brick buildings are partly Tudor and partly seventeenth century. The palace was built for Cardinal Wolsey, and then presented to Henry VIII. In 1690, under William III, much of the palace was pulled down and rebuilt, partly under the direction of Christopher Wren. (Some fourteen miles from Hammersmith.)

Shepperton: Shepperton was then a small village some seven miles along the Thames from Hampton Court. (Some twenty-one miles from Hammersmith.)

126 *'the Long Water'*: the Great Canal or Long Water is three-quarters of a mile long, and is situated in the East Gardens of Hampton Court Palace. It was constructed in the 1660s for Charles II, and was originally bordered by an avenue of lime trees bought from Holland.

127 *Runnymede*: Runnymede is a long-level meadow on the south bank of the Thames near Windsor, famous as the place where the Magna Carta (a charter restricting the power of the king) was signed by King John in 1215. Some maintain that it was signed on a small eyot just north of Runnymede, now called Magna Carta Island. (Some twenty-eight miles from Hammersmith.)

132 *bleak*: small freshwater fish.

133 *flake-hurdles*: a flake hurdle is occasionally used as a generic name for any hurdle, typically a portable rectangular frame (constructed like a field gate) used to form temporary fences and pens. More often it is used to refer only to those hurdles whose horizontal bars have been interwoven or wattled with branches of hazel, willow, etc.

sele of the morning: 'sele' is from the Old English 'sæl' meaning 'happy'. To give someone the sele of the morning is to give them a friendly greeting, to wish them good day.

134 *according to the card*: by that token.

136 *Thackeray's "Vanity Fair"*: *Vanity Fair* is a historical novel, set at the time of the Battle of Waterloo, by William Thackeray (1811–63). A social satire of the English middle classes, peopled with hypocritical and unscrupulous characters, it provides a pessimistic portrait of a society riddled with corruption and idleness. It was published serially and completed in 1848.

137 *Datchet lock*: Datchet was then a small Buckinghamshire village, clustered around a green, about a mile from Eton. In an 1876 guidebook to the environs of London, it was described as a 'quiet genteel place of abode' in a 'beautiful and interesting neighbourhood'. It is now nearly engulfed by suburban development. The lock mentioned here is probably the Old Windsor lock rather than Romney Lock (which is nearly opposite Eton College). (Some thirty-one miles from Hammersmith.)

138 *a great college . . . blunder*: Eton College, the famous English public school, was founded in 1440 under the patronage of Henry VI. The original buildings were completed in 1523. (Some thirty-four miles from Hammersmith.)

Clewer reach . . . Windsor Castle: Clewer was a small village within view of Windsor Castle. Now swallowed up by Windsor. A 'reach' in this context is the stretch of river between two bends. Windsor Castle is a royal residence in Windsor, Berkshire, overlooking the Thames. It was founded by William the Conqueror but was extended by his successors, including Henry III, Edward IV, and Henry VII. (Some thirty-five miles from Hammersmith.)

139 *Maidenhead*: Maidenhead is a Berkshire town on the River Thames (with a population of some 8,000 in 1893). A stone bridge with thirteen arches connects it to the Buckinghamshire bank. In *Three Men in a Boat* (published in 1889), Jerome K. Jerome described Maidenhead as 'too snobby to be pleasant. It is the haunt of the river swell and his overdressed female companion.'

140 *'force vehicles'*: there is little material for serious speculation about the nature of the motive force that replaced steam. However, bemoaning the pollution generated by contemporary industry, Morris once remarked that 'it seems probable that the development of electricity as a motive power will make it easier to undo the evils brought upon us by capitalist tyranny when we regain our senses and determine to live like human beings' ('Why Not?', *Justice*, 12 April 1884).

Bisham . . . Elizabethan house: Bisham is a village in Berkshire. Bisham Abbey began as a preceptory of the Knights Templar, it was then used as an Augustinian priory, and finally became a Benedictine abbey in 1537. It lasted only three years, before being dissolved. The estate was granted to Sir Philip Hoby. The Elizabethan house has a complex architectural history, but is best known for being haunted. (Some forty-eight miles from Hammersmith.)

old buildings at Medmenham: Medmenham Abbey (Buckinghamshire) was founded in 1201 by Cistercians, but never prospered. The surviving buildings were rebuilt as a house in 1595, and again in the eighteenth century. The house was later used by the notorious Francis Dashwood and friends (the Hell-Fire Club).

Hurley: Hurley was a small village which contains extensive architectural remains from a Benedictine monastery (founded before 1087). Known as a meeting place of supporters of William of Orange. (Hurley is some fifty miles from Hammersmith.)

Henley: Henley-on-Thames, sometimes claimed as the oldest town in Oxfordshire. The town developed from the twelfth century as a river crossing, expanding rapidly after 1857 when the railway arrived. Seven miles from Reading, Henley holds a well-known rowing festival (Henley Royal Regatta) and has a reputation as being rather genteel. (Some fifty-six miles from Hammersmith.)

Wargrave and Shiplake: Wargrave (Berkshire) and Shiplake (Oxfordshire) were small villages on either side of the river, some three miles from Henley. Morris once described the area around Shiplake as 'one of the most beautiful parts of the Thames' (letter to Georgiana Burne-Jones, 19 August 1880, in *Collected Letters*, i. 582). (Some sixty miles from Hammersmith.)

141 *Reading . . . Caversham*: Reading is a large town in Berkshire. In the nineteenth century it had expanded greatly, and was the home of, amongst other manufacturers, Huntley and Palmer's biscuits. In *Three Men in a Boat* (published in 1889), Jerome K. Jerome described Reading

as doing its best 'to spoil and sully and make hideous as much of the river as it can reach'. Caversham was then a village on the outskirts of Reading. Now largely swallowed up by the town. (Some sixty-five miles from Hammersmith.)

Maple-Durham meads: that is, meadows by the small village of Mapledurham. (Some sixty-nine miles from Hammersmith.)

ancient house of the Blunts: Mapledurham House was built in 1588, some four miles outside Reading. One of the largest Elizabethan houses in Oxfordshire. It was the ancestral home of the Blounts, and, as such, became a sanctuary for Catholics (the ostensibly Anglican church has a 'closed aisle' which was used by the Catholic Blounts as a private chapel).

Basildon: Basildon was a small Berkshire village. Home of Basildon Park, a well-known Georgian mansion built in 1776. (Some seventy-four miles from Hammersmith.)

142 *overplus*: surplus.

144 *The Third Day on the Thames*: the chapter title in the *Commonweal* version was 'Still Up The Thames'.

145 *pound-lock*: a pound-lock consists of two gates enclosing a short stretch of water (forming a pound). They enable canals to deal with slopes, and rivers to remain navigable. Pound-locks first appeared on the Thames around 1638 (at Abingdon, Iffley, and Sandford). After a long period of neglect, there was a spate of lock building (following an Act of 1770) under the auspices of the Thames Commissioners in which flash weirs, essentially dams with removable parts, were replaced by pound locks. The last flash weir on the Thames, Medley Weir, was removed in 1937.

146 *Pangbourne*: Pangbourne was then a small Berkshire village. (Some seventy-two miles from Hammersmith.)

Goring and Streatley: Goring (Oxfordshire) and Streatley (Berkshire) are twin villages, either side of the Thames, some two miles from Basildon, joined by a long sequence of bridges and causeways. They share a weir, some Edwardian riverside developments, some gabled boathouses, and an increasing number of modern executive homes. Morris wrote of 'the over-rated half picturesque reach of Goring and Streatley' (letter to Georgiana Burne-Jones, 19 August 1880, in *Collected Letters*, ed. Kelvin, i. 583). (Some seventy-six miles from Hammersmith.)

147 *Cockneys*: a rare example of Morris using 'Cockney' in a more conventional sense to indicate an inhabitant of London.

railway-bridge: the Great Western Railway bridge crossed the Thames between Lower Basildon and Goring.

148 *The Obstinate Refusers*: this chapter was added to the original serialized version in *Commonweal*.

149 *nineteenth-century house*: the house appears to have been a real one, although I have not been able to locate it. On 11 August 1892, Sir Sydney

Cockerell recorded in his diary: 'Had breakfast at 6.30 and drove with W.M. to Lechlade for the 7.25 train. Came up with him to Paddington. He told me the names of all the interesting places and objects on the way, and pointed out the house that they were rebuilding in the twenty-sixth chapter of *News From Nowhere*.'

152 *Chapter . . . Upper Waters*: Chapters XXVII and XXVIII were originally one chapter (Chapter XXVI, entitled 'The Upper Waters') in the serialized *Commonweal* version.

the White Horse: a figure of a horse (some 360 foot long and 130 foot high) cut into a chalk hill at Uffington, Berkshire. The figure has been continuously maintained since the eighteenth century, but is considered by some to date back to the first century BCE. Morris estimated the white horse to be 1,100 years old, believing it to have been scored after the battle of Ashdown on the Berkshire downs, at which the Danes were defeated by the West Saxons led by Alfred the Great (*c.*8 January 871).

Wallingford: Wallingford is an ancient market town in Berkshire, on the River Thames. Wallingford bridge has seventeen arches, five of which span the river. Morris was not enamoured of 'stuffy, grubby, little Wallingford' when he stayed there overnight on his 1880 trip up the Thames (letter to Georgiana Burne-Jones, 19 August 1880, in *Collected Letters*, ed. Kelvin, i. 583). (Some eighty-two miles from Hammersmith.)

time of Alfred: Alfred (849–99), King of Wessex (871–99). Alfred led the military resistance that prevented the Vikings occupying south-west England, and gained a reputation as a reformer (who reorganized the military, introduced numerous legal and administrative changes, revived learning, and promoted the use of English).

Parliamentary Wars: Wallingford, like Oxford, was a royalist stronghold during the Civil War. The royalist forces at Wallingford Castle, led by Governor Colonel Blagge, held out against a parliamentary siege, led by Colonel Weldon, for sixteen weeks in 1645. The castle was subsequently demolished.

155 *the Bodleian Library*: the Bodleian is the main library of the University of Oxford. The original university library, established *c.*1320, had fallen into disrepair, and in 1598 Sir Thomas Bodley (1545–1613) retired from public life to refound it. The library formally reopened in 1602.

156 *my father and I*: presumably a slip. Up to this point, the 'praiser of past times' has been referred to as Ellen's grandfather. The same slip is repeated later.

157 *Bensington . . . Dorchester*: the village of Bensington, also known as Benson, is the site of a lock and a spectacular weir. In the eighteenth century, Benson was an important staging post for coaches between Oxford and Henley. (Some eighty-three miles from Hammersmith.) Dorchester is a small town (once a city) on the River Thame, near the confluence of the Thame and the Thames. Morris insisted that 'the whole country

hereabouts is full of interest, and, to a man who can use his eyes, of beauty also' (letter to Oscar Fay Adams, 12 June 1889). (The Thame joins the Thames some eighty-six miles from Hammersmith.)

Tennyson . . . always afternoon: Alfred Tennyson (1809–92) based his poem 'The Lotos-Eaters' (written in 1832) on the episode in Homer's Odyssey where Odysseus' sailors visit the land of the lotos-eaters in which, as a result of the opiate effect of their diet, 'it seemed always afternoon'.

158 *Shillingford . . . old lines*: Shillingford Bridge has three main stone arches, and is situated some two and a half miles above Wallingford. (Some eighty-four miles from Hammersmith.)

159 *Odyssean lies*: untruths having the character of the story of Odysseus, that is, in the present context, being both convoluted and involving foreign travel.

Day's Lock: Day's Lock is next to the village of Little Wittenham, and less than a mile from the confluence of the Thame and the Thames. (Some eighty-seven miles from Hammersmith.)

well-remembered Dykes . . . Fleur-de-luce: the 'well-remembered Dykes' are the Dyke Hills, a range of low mounds thought to be the remains of Saxon earthworks. The 'long church' is the abbey church of St Peter and St Paul in Dorchester, dating from *c.*1140. The church incorporates some Norman remains, although much of it was built in the late thirteenth century. It contains the tomb of St Birinus. Morris wrote of Dorchester's 'strange and beautiful Church known commonly for its very peculiar Jesse window in stone' (letter to Oscar Fay Adams, 12 June 1889, in *Collected Letters*, ed. Kelvin, iii. 74). The carved stone tracery of this window (the north window of the sanctuary) forms a 'tree' with five branches rising from the recumbent figure of Jesse, and showing the descent of Christ from Jesse (based on a reading of Isaiah 11:1). The 'village guest-house' is the Fleur-De-Lys Inn (*c.*1520) which is still a public house, situated on the High Street roughly opposite Dorchester Abbey.

Sinodun . . . Whittenham: Sinodun Hill near Little Wittenham. Remains of early fortifications are visible at the base of the hill. A mamelon is a small rounded hillock. The two mamelons were known locally as 'the Whittenham Clumps'.

Abingdon: Abingdon is the town (now in Oxfordshire), which grew up around Abingdon Abbey (founded in 675). It later prospered through the wool trade. (Some ninety-five miles from Hammersmith.)

Oseney . . . castle: Oseney, or Osney, Island is on the western side of Oxford. (Some 104 miles from Hammersmith.) The castle is Oxford Castle, built in the eleventh century alongside the most fordable part of the river. All that remains now is St George's Tower (1074) and the castle mound or motte.

160 *little hill of Hinksey*: Hinksey Hill lies to the south-west of Oxford, some three miles from the city centre.

Medley Lock . . . Port Meadow: Medley Lock is just south of Port Meadow. Port Meadow is a common which runs alongside north Oxford. It was a gift from William the Conqueror to the citizens of Oxford. Large parts of the common flood in most winters. (Some 106 miles from Hammersmith.)

Godstow . . . nunnery: the remains of the abbey and convent of Godstow are at the north end of Port Meadow. Godstow Abbey was a Benedictine nunnery founded in 1133. After the dissolution it was used as a house, and in 1645 it burnt down. A walled enclosure with the shell of a sixteenth-century chapel in the corner is all that remains of the abbey proper. Perhaps best known as the burial place of Rosamond Clifford (Fair Rosamond), the legendary mistress of Henry II. Morris described Godstow as 'less changed than any beautiful place I know, the very fields that stretch up to Wytham much the same as they always were with their wealth of poplar and willow trees, the most beautiful meadows to be seen anywhere' (letter to Georgiana Burne-Jones, summer 1882, in *Collected Letters*, ed. Kelvin, ii/1. 123). (Some 107 miles from Hammersmith.)

a weir: probably King's Weir, which had a roller slip. (Some 108 miles from Hammersmith.)

a little town: Eynsham is approximately this distance from King's Weir.

162 *there is a ferry!*: possibly the ferry at Bablock Hythe. Perhaps the best known of the Thames crossings, appearing, not least, as the place where the Scholar Gypsy of Matthew Arnold's eponymous poem crossed 'the stripling Thames'. The ferry no longer operates regularly. (Some 114 miles from Hammersmith.)

163 *Old Bridge time agone*: known to Morris as the New Bridge. Built in 1250 using stone which probably came from the Taynton quarries near Burford. It is often said to be the oldest bridge on the Thames (but see note to p. 170), and was the site of a Civil War skirmish. There are two long-established public houses either side of the bridge: The May Bush and Old Rose Revived (currently The Rose Revived). (Some 118 miles from Hammersmith.)

the Roman wall in Cumberland: that is, Hadrian's Wall, a defensive stone wall running some seventy miles from the Solway Firth to the Tyne estuary. Built *c.*122 on the instructions of the Emperor Hadrian (CE 76–138) to deter incursions by the Picts and Celts.

164 *with graceful trees*: the precise location of this 'bent' or grassy plain is not easily identified. The most probable spot lies just downstream of Rushy Lock (the site of the wooded islet). The spire of an ancient building visible to the north would be St Mary's church at Bampton (a stone-built market town on the edge of the Cotswolds). One of the largest churches in west Oxfordshire, this thirteenth- and early fourteenth-century

remodelling of a late Norman church underwent a destructive restoration in the nineteenth century. Morris described the thirteenth-century spire of Bampton church as having 'the same character (and perhaps built by the same hands)' as Christ Church Cathedral, Witney, and Broadwell churches ('Notes on the Churches of Inglesham and Kelmscott', 1889).

169 *entirely closed to the public*: in 1882 the Great Western Railway bought (indirectly) a majority stake in the Thames and Severn Canal (in part, to prevent a proposal to run a competing railway along its route). In the winter of 1885–86, they wound down the maintenance of the canal, dismissed several lock-keepers, and discontinued the carrying trade. (After much legal and political wrangling the canal was sold to the Thames and Severn Canal Trust in 1895.)

robber knights: profiteers.

body up in London . . . let things alone: the Thames Conservancy Board was established by Acts of Parliament in 1857 and 1866. Morris was often critical of their efforts, complaining variously about their rebuilding of lock-keepers' cottages, their cutting down of willows, and their failure to prevent pollution.

170 *another ancient bridge*: presumably Radcott Bridge, elsewhere described by Morris as the 'very pretty fifteenth-century bridge of three arches which carries the road from Bampton to Faringdon over the Thames at Radcott' ('Gossip about an Old House on the Upper Thames', 1894). Others have identified parts of the bridge as twelfth century, in which case it would pre-date 'the new Bridge' (see note to p. 163). (Some 128 miles from Hammersmith.)

171 *I expected to see there*: the house is Kelmscott Manor, Morris's home on the Upper Thames, near Lechlade. A beautiful informal stone house surrounded by barns and (in Morris's day) elm trees. It had been built *c.*1570, with late seventeenth-century additions. (Some 131 miles from Hammersmith.)

172 *cart-road*: just before the footbridge over the stream that runs past Kelmscott Manor, there is a broad track which runs up from the Thames to the village.

173 *led up to the old house*: this view from the path formed the basis for the frontispiece of the Kelmscott Press edition of *News From Nowhere*.

175 *old tapestry . . . of the place*: elsewhere Morris wrote: 'The walls of it are hung with tapestry of about 1600, representing the story of Samson; they were never great works of art, and now when all the bright colours are faded out, and nothing is left but the indigo blues, the greys and the warm yellowy browns, they look better, I think, than they were meant to look: at any rate they make the walls a very pleasant background for the living people who haunt the room . . . and, in spite of the designer, they give an air of romance to the room which nothing else would quite do'

('Gossip about an Old House on the Upper Thames', 1894). The subjects of the tapestry are 'Feast in Timnath', 'Samson and the Smitten Philistines', 'Delilah and Samson Blinded', and 'Samson and the Pillars of the House'.

176 *a little side door . . . curious lobby*: elsewhere Morris described this exit from the other direction: 'Going under an arched opening in the yew hedge which makes a little garth about a low door in the middle of the north wall, one comes into a curious passage or lobby, a part of which is screened into a kind of pantry by wooden mullions which have once been glazed, and offer something of a problem to the architect' ('Gossip about an Old House on the Upper Thames', 1894).

177 *tedding*: the spreading out of newly mown grass for drying.

by the weir: presumably the water above Harts Weir just past Kelmscott.

haysel: the festival of haymaking.

179 *in the church*: the church of St George at Kelmscott, a small rustic church built on a cruciform plan (unusual in a church of this size). The nave and chancel are usually dated *c.*1190.

church-ales of the Middle Ages: church ales were a medieval festival at which subscriptions in money or kind were collected and cakes and ale distributed. The drinking was often accompanied by games, music, and dancing.

on the wall: elsewhere Morris wrote: 'There are remains of paintings all over the church, the North transept having been painted with figure subjects of the life of Christ in trefoil head panels' ('Gossip about an Old House on the Upper Thames', 1894).

180 *the Persian poet . . . in the sun*: probably a reference to Abul Qasim Mansur Firdausi (*c.*935–1020), the Persian poet and author of the epic *Shahnama* or *Shanameh*, which recounts the legendary history of the ancient rulers of Persia. The poem was best known to nineteenth-century English readers as the source of the legend of 'Sohrab and Rustum' recounted by Matthew Arnold (1822–88). Morris had read the poem in the French translation by Julius Mohl, and began work on an English version (a manuscript fragment of which is held in the British Library) for his family. May Morris later recalled: 'His stories from the Persian Epic as we gathered round the evening fire are among my remembrances of the home life of those days' (*Collected Works of William Morris*, ed. May Morris, xvii (London, 1913), p. xxii). This particular reference is probably to the marriage of Kai Káús and the daughter of the King of Hámávarán, where the magnificent wedding party is described as looking as if 'the heaven hath planted tulips in the earth'.

181 *the village cross*: Morris thought that the cross was 'probably of the fifteenth century' ('Gossip about an Old House on the Upper Thames', 1894).

182 *than a dream*: the last lines of Keats's *Ode to a Nightingale* contrast a

'vision' with a 'waking dream'. However, there is also a more likely, and more appropriate, echo here of the last lines of More's *Utopia*, which contrast a 'wish for' with an 'expectation of' change along utopian lines.

A SELECTION OF **OXFORD WORLD'S CLASSICS**

JANE AUSTEN	**Emma** **Mansfield Park** **Persuasion** **Pride and Prejudice** **Sense and Sensibility**
MRS BEETON	**Book of Household Management**
LADY ELIZABETH BRADDON	**Lady Audley's Secret**
ANNE BRONTË	**The Tenant of Wildfell Hall**
CHARLOTTE BRONTË	**Jane Eyre** **Shirley** **Villette**
EMILY BRONTË	**Wuthering Heights**
SAMUEL TAYLOR COLERIDGE	**The Major Works**
WILKIE COLLINS	**The Moonstone** **No Name** **The Woman in White**
CHARLES DARWIN	**The Origin of Species**
CHARLES DICKENS	**The Adventures of Oliver Twist** **Bleak House** **David Copperfield** **Great Expectations** **Nicholas Nickleby** **The Old Curiosity Shop** **Our Mutual Friend** **The Pickwick Papers** **A Tale of Two Cities**
GEORGE DU MAURIER	**Trilby**
MARIA EDGEWORTH	**Castle Rackrent**

George Eliot	Daniel Deronda The Lifted Veil and Brother Jacob Middlemarch The Mill on the Floss Silas Marner
Susan Ferrier	Marriage
Elizabeth Gaskell	Cranford The Life of Charlotte Brontë Mary Barton North and South Wives and Daughters
George Gissing	New Grub Street The Odd Woman
Thomas Hardy	Far from the Madding Crowd Jude the Obscure The Mayor of Casterbridge The Return of the Native Tess of the d'Urbervilles The Woodlanders
William Hazlitt	Selected Writings
James Hogg	The Private Memoirs and Confessions of a Justified Sinner
John Keats	The Major Works Selected Letters
Charles Maturin	Melmoth the Wanderer
Walter Scott	The Antiquary Ivanhoe Rob Roy
Mary Shelley	Frankenstein The Last Man

A SELECTION OF **OXFORD WORLD'S CLASSICS**

Robert Louis Stevenson	**Kidnapped and Catriona** **The Strange Case of Dr Jekyll and Mr Hyde and Weir of Hermiston** **Treasure Island**
Bram Stoker	**Dracula**
William Makepeace Thackeray	**Vanity Fair**
Oscar Wilde	**Complete Shorter Fiction** **The Major Works** **The Picture of Dorian Gray**
Dorothy Wordsworth	**The Grasmere and Alfoxden Journals**
William Wordsworth	**The Major Works**

TROLLOPE IN OXFORD WORLD'S CLASSICS

ANTHONY TROLLOPE

An Autobiography
The American Senator
Barchester Towers
Can You Forgive Her?
The Claverings
Cousin Henry
Doctor Thorne
The Duke's Children
The Eustace Diamonds
Framley Parsonage
He Knew He Was Right
Lady Anna
The Last Chronicle of Barset
Orley Farm
Phineas Finn
Phineas Redux
The Prime Minister
Rachel Ray
The Small House at Allington
The Warden
The Way We Live Now

The Oxford World's Classics Website

www.worldsclassics.co.uk

- Information about new titles
- Explore the full range of Oxford World's Classics
- Links to other literary sites and the main OUP webpage
- Imaginative competitions, with bookish prizes
- Peruse the Oxford World's Classics Magazine
- Articles by editors
- Extracts from Introductions
- A forum for discussion and feedback on the series
- Special information for teachers and lecturers

www.worldsclassics.co.uk

MORE ABOUT **OXFORD WORLD'S CLASSICS**

American Literature

British and Irish Literature

Children's Literature

Classics and Ancient Literature

Colonial Literature

Eastern Literature

European Literature

History

Medieval Literature

Oxford English Drama

Poetry

Philosophy

Politics

Religion

The Oxford Shakespeare